About

Lena Diaz was born in Kentucky and has also lived in California, Louisiana and Florida, where she now resides with her husband and two children. Before becoming a romantic suspense author, she was a computer programmer. A Romance Writers of America Golden Heart Award finalist, she has also won the prestigious Daphne du Maurier Award for Excellence in Mystery/Suspense. To get the latest news about Lena, please visit her website, lenadiaz.com

Delores Fossen, a *USA Today* bestselling author, has written over 150 novels, with millions of copies of her books in print worldwide. She's received a Booksellers' Best Award and an RT Reviewers' Choice Best Book Award. She was also a finalist for a prestigious RITA Award. You can contact the author through her website at deloresfossen.com

The Sinful Sleuths Club

A DATE WITH DEATH:

The Sinful Sleuths Club

LENA DIAZ

DELORES FOSSEN

MILLS & BOON

First Published in Great Britain 2025
by Mills & Boon, an imprint of HarperCollins*Publishers* Ltd
1 London Bridge Street, London, SE1 9GF

www.harpercollins.co.uk

HarperCollins*Publishers*
Macken House, 39/40 Mayor Street Upper,
Dublin 1, D01 C9W8, Ireland

ISBN: 978-0-263-42081-4

AGENT UNDER SIEGE

LENA DIAZ

My prayers and condolences to all who have lost loved ones and friends during the horrendous, unimaginable pandemic that gripped our world in 2020. I hope that this story gives you a few hours of escape and that it puts a smile on your face. God bless.

Chapter One

Long before the shadow fell across the end of the dock and hovered over Bryson Anton's wheelchair, he knew the man was there. Motion sensors and security cameras had made Bryson's watch buzz against his wrist when the man parked his car in the driveway. More messages warned when the man crossed the back patio. And again, when he'd descended the gently sloping lawn that ended at the creek. Bryson didn't care who was now standing behind him, as long as he didn't have to engage in conversation.

"Nice place," the man's voice rang out. "Probably one of the highest views in the Tennessee side of the Smoky Mountains. I'll bet at night you can see nearly every light in downtown Gatlinburg from here."

Bryson sighed but didn't turn around. "My former boss took pity on me after I got myself hurt on the job. He gave me a boatload of money, and I was selfish enough to take it and buy this property. But that doesn't mean he can drop by any time he wants."

"I'm still your boss. I haven't accepted your resignation."

"That's not how it works, Mason. I resigned, whether you accept it or not. I'll never be a Justice Seeker again. I'm not going back to Camelot. You and your knights of the round table are better off without a washed-up former profiler jacking up your investigations."

"Is that why you're sitting out here drinking like a fish, because you think you jacked up everything?"

"Something like that." Bryson grabbed a can of beer from the cooler beside his wheelchair and popped the top. He took a deep long swallow, more to irritate his unwelcome visitor than because he wanted it.

Mason retrieved a beer and eyed the label, then tossed it back unopened. "Fish biting?"

"Do you see a fishing pole around here somewhere?" Bryson emptied his can in the water and dropped it on his lap before wheeling around. "Enjoy the view as long as you want. You paid for it." He rolled his chair up the flagstone walkway toward the house.

"Dalton and Hayley missed you at their wedding last week." Mason fell into step beside him.

"Yeah, well. I didn't have time to learn the latest dance steps." He stopped at the sliding glass doors and tossed the empty beer can in the recycle bin. When he reached for the door handle, Mason leaned past him and held it closed.

Bryson swore. "What do you want from me?"

"I want you to do your job. A new client came to Camelot yesterday. She specifically wants to hire *you*."

He scoffed. "You expect me to believe she asked for a washed-up former FBI agent to screw up her case so someone else will die? If she did, send her on over. I can accomplish that without lifting a finger."

Mason leaned back against the door. "That's a heck of a guilty conscience you're nursing. Or are you just feeling sorry for yourself?" He waved toward the wheelchair. "If you'd actually go to your physical therapy appointments instead of being a no-show half the time, you'd be out of that thing by now. Don't look so surprised. I pay your insurance premiums. I see what's billed. And there've been a surprising lack of medical invoices lately. You've given up, Bryson. The question is why?"

"Why?" he gritted out. "Let me remind you that when I was the FBI's golden boy, everyone treated my profiles like biblical text. So when I presented them with a profile for the Kentucky Ripper, they focused all their efforts on Avarice Lowe, the suspect at the top of my list. Meanwhile, Leviathan Finney—the real Ripper—was no longer under surveillance. To celebrate, he kidnapped and *gutted* another woman. Because of me, he was able to kill again."

"*Because of you*, the police were able to significantly narrow their list of suspects much faster than they could have otherwise. The choices they made after that weren't your fault. Hell, Bryson. If it wasn't for the work you did, it would have taken far longer to catch the Ripper and put him in prison."

"Tell that to the family of the last woman he killed."

Mason shook his head. "I hear someone anonymously sends money to the last victim's family every month. While I admire the generosity and kindness of the gesture, that person is making payments on a debt he doesn't owe. The only person responsible for that woman's death is the man who killed her—Leviathan Finney."

Bryson fisted his hands on the arms of the wheelchair. "Are we about done here? It's getting late."

"Big plans tonight?"

"I have to wash my hair."

Mason let out a deep sigh. "Just explain one thing, then I'll go. Why now? You left the FBI over three years ago and started working for me as one of the Justice Seekers. Why is the Ripper case bothering you again after all this time?"

Bryson stared at him incredulously. "Bothering me *again*? It never *stopped* bothering me. But I tried to make something good from the bad, atone for my sins by working investigations for you. And what did I do? I nearly got Hayley killed, got myself shot and here I sit with shrapnel they can't dig out of my hip without risking the loss of my leg. Do I sit here feeling sorry for myself? No. I don't deserve anyone's sympathy, least of all my own. The people who deserve sympathy are the ones I've hurt, those who nearly died because of me, and the one who *did*. Accept my resignation and leave me alone. I'm not going to risk hurting anyone else. I'm done."

Mason's jaw worked as he stared past him toward the creek. A full minute passed in silence before he finally met Bryson's gaze again. "Sounds like you've made up your mind."

Bryson arched a brow. "Sounds like you're finally listening."

"Oh, I've been listening. I just don't like what I'm hearing." He pulled a thick neon green folder covered with pink polka dots out from beneath his suit jacket and dropped it onto Bryson's lap. "Guess you won't be needing this."

He eyed the folder like he'd eye a coiled rattlesnake. "What is that hideous thing?"

"I was asked to give it to you. It's from the client I told you about, the one who requested that you work on her case. She put her pursuit of a master's degree in criminal justice on hold to perform research on an alleged serial killer. She believes that you're the only person who can convince the police that her conclusions are reasonable and help her catch him. She provided a summary of her research in that folder."

Bryson snorted and shook his head. "If she's convinced that a failed criminal profiler is the key to her theory, then she needs to go back to school. Her deductive reasoning is skewed."

"Personally, I found her work intriguing, her theories compelling. And I've already got my master's in criminal justice, not to mention a decade of experience as a chief of police and another seven years after that running The Justice Seekers." Mason straightened and tugged his suit jacket into place. "But I can see that I'm not going to change your mind. The funny thing is, I never took you for a quitter. Even after the FBI."

"Yeah, well. I never thought I'd be responsible for another innocent person almost being killed either. Guess we were both wrong."

Mason stared at him a long moment, then looked past him again toward the dock. "That really is a gorgeous view. Let me know when you decide to go fishing. I can bring a pole, throw out a line." He gave him a hard look. "*All* of your brothers and sisters at Camelot would love to toss you a line, including Hayley. You just have to ask." He shoved his hands in his pants pockets and strode away without waiting for a reply.

Bryson dropped his gaze to the ridiculous-looking pink-and-green folder in his lap. He stared at it long after he could no longer hear the sound of Mason's car driving away. Long after the sun began to set and the mosquitos started buzzing around his ears. Long after the twinkling lights of Gatlinburg reflected in the sliding glass door, studding the night sky like glitter on a black velvet canvas.

Then he tossed the folder in the trash.

Chapter Two

Teagan whistled as she stepped out of her car onto the brick-paved driveway. It was as if she was standing on top of the world, with the entire Smoky Mountains range spreading out around her in 360-degree views. There wasn't another house in sight, just the rambling one-story stone-and-brick mansion set so far back from the main road that she hadn't seen it until she'd almost passed it.

She wasn't sure what she'd expected of the home of a former FBI special agent, but it wasn't this. Either the FBI was paying way better than most people realized, or Bryson Anton's post-FBI career paid *extremely* well. He'd spent three years so far with The Justice Seekers, an agency of former law enforcement officers and ex-military whose professed goal was to obtain justice for people who couldn't get it via the traditional route. Having seen their quirky, state-of-the-art headquarters that they'd dubbed Camelot, she figured it was a safe assumption that's where Bryson had made his money.

When she reached the front porch, she was surprised that in addition to the broad front steps there was a ramp concealed behind the landscaping. No rocking chairs dotted the wide expanse. No flowers decorated the empty cedar window boxes, even though it was the middle of spring. If she had to describe the expensive, sprawling home in one word, it would be...*lonely*.

She was about to knock on the frosted glass double door when the left side jerked open. She blinked in slack-jawed admiration at the incredible work of art that greeted her wearing nothing but a frown and a white towel draped around his hips. His dark, shoulder-length hair was damp. Beads of water clung to the hair on his golden, sculpted chest. It almost killed her not to reach out and trace the trail of one very happy bead that ran toward his six-pack abs and disappeared below the top of his towel. On a scale of one to ten, she rated him sexy-as-hell.

"Hi." Of all the compelling, intelligent, well-formulated introductions that her summa cum laude education could have provided her, she came up with that one-word bit of brilliance. She cleared her throat so she could properly introduce herself.

"It's about time you got here," he practically growled. "I've been trying to work the cramps out of my hip all morning. If the muscles aren't loosened up soon, I'll end up in the wheelchair the rest of the day abusing an exqui-site bottle of scotch."

Leaning heavily on the cane in his right hand that she only just noticed, he limped across the expensive-looking shiny white floor before stopping beside one of the biggest black leather couches she'd ever seen. Except for the other couch in the room, which was just as big. The two of them formed an L with their backs to the bump-out of windows near the garage.

"Where do you want me?" he asked.

Was that a trick question? On a bed, on the kitchen counter, *anywhere*. Since he appeared to be waiting for an answer to his ridiculous query, she had to rewind the brief conversation in her head and remember what he'd said when he'd opened the door. Her previously absent brain clicked into gear, and she realized he was likely expecting either a massage therapist or a personal trainer. For his left hip, the one he was favoring as he leaned toward the cane on his right side. Apparently he wanted her to tell him where he should sit, or lie down, or whatever was required so that she could work out his muscle cramps.

Her ovaries screamed at her to say yes to anything he wanted. But it wouldn't be ethical to let this go on any longer when it was obviously a case of mistaken identity. All she had to do was tell him who she was and why she was there.

Now if she could just stop drooling long enough to remember her name.

He frowned. "What's wrong?" He glanced down at his towel. "I've got boxers on if you're worried that I'm naked under here."

"Oh, no, trust me. That wouldn't bother me *at all*." Drop the towel. And the boxers. *Please.* She cleared her throat. "What I meant to say is that—"

The doorbell rang, followed by a knock on the glass.

He swore. "Ever since my old boss came by yesterday, you'd think this was a Walmart on Black Friday. This makes the third person to come by in two days."

"Three visitors in two days. A veritable siege."

He gave her an odd look.

She smiled. It was either that or give in to the barbaric urge to grab his towel and toss it away. She curled her fingernails against her palms, trying her best to keep him safe.

His face was a study in pain as he limped to the door. She wondered at the source of that pain. His employer hadn't mentioned anything about an injury. Mason had only stated that Bryson was on temporary leave, but that he'd be more than happy to return to take her case. She had a feeling that Mason might have stretched the truth. A lot.

He opened the door with a bit of wariness this time, keeping his lower half hidden behind it.

Unable to make out what was being said, Teagan imagined it was far more clever than her conversation since they spoke longer than it took to say, "Hi." When he stepped back, a rather impressive woman entered. Bright, attention-getting red hair floated above baby-blue scrubs. She marched across the room with the authority of someone who had a legitimate reason to be there. Teagan was quite certain that the woman's muscular arms would have made a linebacker blush with envy. After snapping a white linen in the air and tucking it around the couch cushions, she ordered Bryson to lose the towel and lie down.

Teagan debated what to do. Should she go or should she stay?

"You." Bryson pointed at her. "Sit over there until I can stand again without wanting to drown myself in a bottle of tequila. Then we'll find out who you are and what you're doing here."

He dropped his towel and lay down on the couch, his left leg facing out toward the room. His thighs were just as muscular and beautiful as the rest of him. *Wowzah.*

The woman that Teagan mentally dubbed "Helga" placed a pad on the floor by the couch and propped her knees on top of it. Strong, man-size hands were stuffed into latex gloves. Then she shoved the side of Bryson's boxers up his leg and proceeded to squeeze and pummel his hip.

Personally, Teagan wouldn't have bothered with the gloves.

She tossed her purse onto the other couch and plopped down to enjoy the show. It was over far too soon. She almost groaned in disappointment when Bryson pushed to his feet, then pronounced his cramps gone and thanked the therapist. A few minutes later, Helga had left and Bryson returned from his bedroom in a pair of jeans and a black T-shirt.

Since the jeans caressed his muscular thighs and tight rear end and the T-shirt did nothing to hide the perfection of his pecs, Teagan decided that she didn't mind that he'd put on some clothes. It was a pleasure seeing the perfect male specimen in varying stages of undress. She just wished she could see him *completely* undressed for a fair comparison.

He limped to her couch, looking just as adorably grumpy as he had when he'd jerked open the front door and complained about her taking so long to get there. Well, complained that *Helga* had taken so long.

"Spill it," he said. "Mason sent you, didn't he?"

"I wouldn't put it that way."

"How would you put it?"

"I'd say that I went to Mr. Ford and asked if I could hire you. He said he was certain that you'd be interested, but that I'd have to ask you personally. He graciously provided your address and here I am. Technically, I sent myself." She remained seated on the ultra-plush couch and offered her hand. "Teagan Ray. Nice to meet you."

He didn't bother with a handshake. "Bryson Anton. I don't work for Mason Ford anymore. Get out of my house."

Chapter Three

"No."

Bryson stared at the defiant young woman sitting cross-legged on his couch. There was nothing about her sensible flat shoes, her conservative navy blue dress pants and short-sleeved white blouse that buttoned all the way to her neck to indicate that she was a radical militant bent on destroying the rest of his miserable morning. Even her black hair, which appeared to be curly based on the little wisps that framed her face, was mostly tamed in a tight braid that hung down the middle of her back. So why wasn't she cowed by his sour disposition and gruff commands? And why was she still sitting on his couch?

"Perhaps you didn't hear me correctly, Ms. Ray."

"Call me Teagan. I'll call you Bryson." She flashed a bright white smile that probably cost her parents a second mortgage.

"Ms. Ray, you may call me Mr. Anton, or the jerk who's throwing you out of his house. Because that's exactly what I'm doing. Tossing you out. I didn't invite you here so—"

"Actually, you did."

"Excuse me?"

She tapped her temple as if that would explain everything. "I have a photographic memory. I basically see words—"

"I know what a photographic memory is," he bit out.

"Excellent. It's good to use terminology we're both familiar with for the absolute best understanding, with no confusion. A common frame of reference will help us communicate better. Don't you think?"

"You lost me at *no confusion*."

She grinned. She seemed to do that a lot. "Let's go back to the part where you invited me here."

"I didn't invite you."

"When Mr. Ford told you about me, you told him, 'You expect me to believe she asked for a washed-up former FBI agent to screw up her case so someone else will die? If she did, send her on over.'" She spread her hands out beside her. "Here I am. Plus you invited me in at the front door. It's kind of like with vampires, once you let them in, that's it. You can't just throw them out."

"Watch me." He tossed his cane on the other couch, then scooped her up in his arms.

Her dark brown eyes got so wide he could see the beautiful little golden flecks around the irises.

He whirled around, then stumbled and had to steady his shin against the coffee table to keep from tipping over.

She boldly looped her tawny-brown arms around his neck and stared up at him with a look of concern. "I'm not sure you should be holding me like this without your cane. I don't want you to hurt yourself. Plus, even as gorgeous— with a capital *G*—as you are, I still think we should get to know each other better before we jump into each other's arms. Don't you?" She fluttered her impossibly long, thick eyelashes.

Actually *fluttered* them.

"Has anyone ever accused you of insanity?" he asked.

"All the time. It's one of my best qualities—the ability

to act crazy while I outmaneuver and outsmart everyone around me."

He scowled down at her.

She tightened her arms around his neck. "I could literally do this all day. We fit together perfectly. My soft curves, your hard muscles. Very comfy."

"Are you flirting with me, Ms. Ray?"

"I believe I am, Mr. Anton."

"Because you're trying to confuse and outmaneuver me so I'll let you stay?"

"Mostly. Is it working?"

"The jury's still out on that. But my hip's starting to hurt like the devil again, so I'm either going to drop you or set you down. I'm leaning toward dropping."

"I prefer setting."

"No sense of adventure." He let her legs slide down until she was standing. Then he gingerly let her go, trying not to move too fast and lose his precarious balance.

She grabbed his cane and handed it to him. "Is this one of those cool FBI things? Like if you twist the head it opens and becomes a rifle? Or maybe the tip has poison in it? You jab the bad guy and he dies a horrible death a few minutes later. Am I right?"

"It's a gun, of course. Poison is so beneath an FBI agent."

Her grin widened. "James Bond has nothing on you guys."

He rolled his eyes. It was all he could manage with the pain slicing through his muscles. When he thought he could shuffle across the room without falling to the floor in an embarrassing heap, he headed toward the kitchen. He eyed her morosely as she used her two perfectly healthy hips to hop onto one of the bar stools at the marble-topped island.

"Don't get too comfortable," he warned. "You haven't achieved victory. Once I liquor up enough to be able to haul you to the front door, I'll be throwing you out as promised."

"I consider myself forewarned." She motioned toward him. "Mind if I ask what's wrong with the leg? I noticed the ramp outside, and a wheelchair in the corner of the family room."

"You can *ask* all you want. And I can choose not to answer." Bypassing the scotch that he preferred for late-night drinking—alone—he grabbed a bottle of tequila along with a shot glass.

She motioned toward the cabinet. "Can you at least pretend that you have some manners and act like a host for a few minutes?"

"Are you even old enough to drink?"

She rolled her eyes. "I'm sure I don't look *that* young."

He sighed and reached for a second glass. After pouring two generous helpings, he set the bottle between them. "Ms. Ray. You seem like an intelligent young woman—"

She grimaced. "You say young as if you think I'm a child. I can't imagine that I'm more than ten, maybe eleven years younger than you."

He arched a brow. "Meaning that while you were in elementary school, I was losing my virginity to the homecoming queen at my high school."

She hesitated with a shot glass halfway to her mouth. "Can't top that. But I did have my first kiss quite early. Third grade. Behind the jungle gym. Ricky Southernton." She tossed her shot back with one gulp.

"On the lips?"

"On the cheek."

"Doesn't count. I was in *second* grade when I kissed Becky Louis. She bit my tongue."

"Maybe you shouldn't have shoved it down her throat."

He reluctantly smiled. "Maybe not." He tossed his own shot back and reveled at the smooth burn as it went down. A few more shots and he might be able to avoid the wheelchair until at least the dinner hour.

"Have you thought about getting prescription painkillers instead of drowning the pain with alcohol?"

He shot her a look that should have frozen her to the bar stool.

She held up her hands in a placating gesture. "Sorry. The filter between my brain and my mouth is defective. I shouldn't have asked."

The completely unrepentant look on her face, in direct opposition to her words, forced a laugh out of him. How long had it been since he'd laughed, or even smiled? He had no idea. But the novelty of both had him starting to relax, if only a little. "I was on pretty strong pain pills in the beginning, but it was like living in a brain-fog all the time. Had to wean myself off them. Drinking works better for me, and it's a heck of a lot more fun." He refilled his glass, then paused in question with the bottle poised over hers.

"Yes, please."

He topped off her shot, then drained his while watching her. If he hadn't been paying close attention, he wouldn't have noticed the tiny, involuntary shudder when she tossed it back.

"That's a waste of some pretty great tequila for someone who doesn't even like it."

She shoved the glass across the island for more. "What makes you think I don't like it?"

He poured more for himself, but not for her. "When you have ten or eleven more years of experience behind you, maybe you'll figure it out. Go home, Teagan. There's nothing for you here. I can't help you."

"You mean you *won't* help me?"

"The intent doesn't matter. The result is the same."

"Then I guess we're back to drinking. Shots with a hot guy before noon. I can think of worse ways to spend my morning." She grabbed the bottle.

He tugged it away from her. "If you're trying to win me over with the hot guy talk, you can stop right now. Like I said, I'm not going to help with your case. And I'm not buying this over-the-top happy, flirty personality you're presenting. Nobody's that cute. You're trying too hard."

"You think I'm cute?" She grinned and fluttered her long lashes again.

"I think you're nervous and overcompensating. It's time to drop the act."

Her smile dimmed and she seemed genuinely confused. "What do you mean?"

He rested his forearms on the island. "Profiler, remember? At least, I used to be one. It took me a few minutes to realize what was happening. Probably because I'm out of practice and I do my best to avoid people these days. But you don't have to keep pretending, trying to be something you're not. Maybe it's the tequila that I drank, maybe it's that I admire your spunk and the effort you've put into this. Whatever it is, you've earned a slight reprieve. I'll listen to your spiel so you can get it out of your system. *Then* I'll throw you out."

She stared at him, wide-eyed, then grabbed his full shot glass and tossed it back before he could stop her.

He silently cursed himself for not being more careful. Given her small stature and the strength of the tequila, her ability to safely drive herself home was now seriously in question.

"Better?" he asked dryly.

"Better. Although I'll admit that scotch I saw in your cabinet is more to my taste."

"Don't even think about it."

She grinned.

"This is where I warn you that I haven't read the information that Mason left me."

"I kind of figured, since the folder I gave him is hanging half-out of your garbage can on your back patio." She motioned toward the glass doors on the far side of the kitchen.

"Observant, I'll give you that. Then again, it's hard to miss a neon green folder with hideous pink polka dots."

"Not a polka-dot fan?"

"Not in the least."

"Pity."

He shifted his weight to help ease the tightness in his hip. "Maybe you can brief me on what's in the folder. Mason mentioned you think you're on the trail of a serial killer."

She nodded and ran her hands up and down her arms, looking slightly less eager now that the discussion was at hand. She reached for the tequila.

He swore and placed the bottle on the counter behind him. "Trust me. You're already going to have a heck of a hangover. No more alcohol. Now, for a common reference, so there's *no confusion*, what name are you dubbing your alleged killer?"

She drew a deep breath, then straightened her shoulders as if she was about to head into battle. "The Kentucky Ripper."

Chapter Four

Bryson froze, then slowly straightened. "That's not funny."

Teagan's eyes widened. "I'm not making a joke. I'm serious. The Ripper is the killer I've been researching."

"At least now I know why you asked Mason for me, specifically. Well, forget it. Rehashing past failures isn't my idea of fun."

She held up her hands. The overhead lights winked off several gold rings. "Just hear me out. I've been researching this for a long time. I'm not here to cast blame. I'm here for your insight. And I'm here to ask a very important question." She squeezed her hands together. "What if the guy they thought was the Ripper is actually a copycat and the real serial killer is still at large?"

He winced, then eyed his empty glass with longing. "If that's true, then I screwed up even worse than I thought."

"Not at all. *You* didn't make the mistakes during the Ripper investigation. The *police* did."

He tore his gaze from the shot glass. "Maybe I drank too much tequila too because that one went right over my head. I'm lost, in spite of our *common frame of reference*."

"Then I'll be happy to explain. First, profiles are tools, not biblical text."

He stared at her as his own words were thrown back at him. "Did Mason say that to you?"

She frowned. "No. Why?"

He shrugged. "Just wondering. Go on."

She crossed her arms on top of the island. "When your profile indicated that one of the two top suspects was the most likely killer, the police went after him with everything they had. Meanwhile, their other prime suspect was no longer under surveillance. He took advantage of their mistake to abduct and murder a woman. Instead of thinking of your profile as a divining rod, they should have stayed the course, kept their surveillance on both suspects until some evidence tipped the scales." She motioned in the air as if waving away her words. "Regardless, my point is that, based on my research, I think your profile was spot-on. The first guy *was* the real Ripper. The guy they put in prison is a copycat. The police got sidetracked by the last murder and pursued that killer to the exclusion of everyone else. So, while there's plenty of blame to go around for how everything turned out, none of it should have ever blown back on you."

He was going to filet Mason for giving this misguided, albeit beautiful woman his address. Her theories were bogus. Unfortunately, he could tell how vested she was in them and he didn't want to destroy her confidence before her law enforcement career was even off the ground.

Using his nonjudgmental teaching voice, the one he'd adopted while presenting guest lectures at Quantico, he explained, "For that theory to hold water, the first requirement would be that the Ripper is still active. But no other women have been tortured and brutalized per his specific signature since he was put away. Explain how your theory addresses that."

"No other women *that you know of.*"

"Fair enough. That I know of. But if new cases had popped up, I can't imagine the media not making a connection even if the police didn't. The Ripper case was bread and butter to them. It made for great ratings. If something that sensational happened again, they'd be all over it."

"The media in Kentucky, yes, absolutely. Other places, not necessarily. They don't know about the original cases and wouldn't realize there was a serial killer operating in the area."

"Maybe."

"Definitely," she countered.

He admired her confidence, even if she was dead wrong. "Why would the killer change locations?"

"Because he's smart. He knew he'd been given a tremendous opportunity, that a mentally disturbed fall guy had taken credit for his crimes and turned attention away from him. He knew that if he killed again in the same area, the police would know right away that they'd caught a crazy guy bent on enjoying the spotlight and confessing to crimes he didn't do. They'd be back on the trail of the real Ripper, reassemble the task force. But stopping, not killing anymore, isn't an option either. Our psychopath is driven by an urge to kill that he can't control. So in addition to changing locations, he also changes his MO, his modus operandi, the way he kills."

He could see why Mason had found her compelling. She spoke with authority, like someone who'd had real-life experience with this sort of thing rather than just book knowledge. He decided to press her some more, see whether she'd backtrack and second-guess herself, or hold firm and defend her theory. "Don't serial killers always keep the same MO?"

She gave him a wounded look that almost had him feeling guilty. "You're treating me like a student, testing me, aren't you? Pushing to see if I know what I'm talking about."

"Do you? Know what you're talking about?"

Her gaze dropped to the island. "Yes," she whispered. "I do."

Her ragged tone put him on alert, had him studying her body language. The best indicator of honesty and genuine emotion as opposed to lies and bravado was how a person moved, how they spoke, not the words they used. Her body language told him that something else was at play here, something she wasn't yet ready to say out loud, something that had dread curling in his chest. "You were talking about modus operandi."

She cleared her throat. "What I was saying is that serial killers don't always maintain the same MO, their method, *how* they kill. Modus operandi is a conscious choice. They can change it if necessary. Like if a killer starts out tying his victims with shoelaces. If one of them manages to break a shoelace and escapes, the next time he abducts someone he'll use handcuffs. Different MO, same killer."

"That's a good way to explain it," he allowed. "But I'd add that MO is more about what's necessary, or what the killer *feels* is necessary, in order to carry out his crime. Outside of forensics, with no fingerprints or even DNA, what would convince you that some murders were done by the same killer if the MO had changed?" Again, he watched her closely, trying to decipher the subtext, the meaning beneath her words.

"Signature. A serial killer, a true psychopath, is driven to kill. He can change parts of what he does, but the signature is an intrinsic part of his killing ritual. It's the part of his crimes that he *can't* change. Signature is a subconscious action, something he doesn't choose to do or not to do. It's something he's compelled to do." She clasped her hands on top of the island. "Like the Ripper carving an *X* across the abdomen of each of his victims after he abducts them. That's his way of branding them, of letting them know that he…he *owns* them."

She wasn't meeting his gaze anymore. Instead, she slowly traced the veining in the marble top of the island. Her stark words had his throat tightening as he carefully watched her, weighing every move, even the tone of her voice.

"Signature is often a reliable means for linking crimes," she continued. "But the police often confuse MO with signature, or assume something is the signature when it's just another thing the killer does each time, but isn't *compelled* to do. And even though it's been documented many times that serial killers can and sometimes do change their victimology, go outside their comfort zone and choose a victim that doesn't fit with their history, the police automatically think that means it's a different killer. It's not their fault. Most will never come across a serial killer case their entire career. They're not equipped to evaluate the complexities, dive deeper, weigh a killer's thirst to kill versus his desire not to get caught. They don't understand his willingness or ability to adapt."

"You've circled back to the Kentucky Ripper again." He kept his voice gentle, encouraging her to finish what she came here to say, what she so obviously *needed* to say. And all the while he cursed Mason for sending her, for *using* her to get to him. "His original victimology included Caucasian women in their mid-to late thirties, married, with children. They all lived within the same fifty-square-mile geographical region in Eastern Kentucky. None of them worked outside the home."

She nodded. "Yes, but I'm saying he could have changed all of that. He could have moved to another state, gone after someone who was younger, single, without children. Someone who worked outside the home, even if only to take temporary odd jobs to make ends meet. Even if the signature was the same, most people in law enforcement would think it was another copycat, a one-off, since the alleged real guy is in prison. They wouldn't realize what they're dealing with, or even that they have a serial killer operating in their midst."

What he'd started to suspect just moments ago had solidified into a cold hard knot of dread that had him clenching his teeth so hard they ached.

Holding on to the edge of the countertop to maintain his balance, he limped around the island until he was standing beside her. Then, keeping his voice as gentle as possible, he asked, "How old are you? Don't give me a flippant answer either. I'm serious."

His question didn't seem to surprise her. "Just turned twenty-six. My birthday was last month."

Younger than he'd thought. Her guesstimate of their age difference was off by several years. "You're not Caucasian."

Her perfectly shaped brows rose. "Gee, what gave that away?" Her sarcasm did little to hide the underlying pain in her tone.

"Mason didn't mention where you're from. I'm guessing it's not Kentucky."

"Never even been to Kentucky. My home is in northeast Florida, Jacksonville." Her bottom lip trembled.

He tightened his grip on the island. "Single?"

She nodded, her eyes over-bright, as if she was fighting back tears.

"No kids?"

She squeezed her eyes shut, then shook her head. "No kids."

"You take odd jobs to make ends meet while doing your investigation?"

She slowly nodded.

"Show me," he whispered, still praying that he was wrong, but just as certain that he wasn't.

Without hesitation, she gripped the hem of her blouse, then pulled it up to her chin.

Angry puckered welts marred her skin, forming a five-by-five-inch X on her abdomen. His hands shook as he gently pulled her blouse back down. "When?"

"Two years ago." Pain leached from every word. "I was halfway through my master's degree program. But I had to put it on hold until...until I recovered. But after that, I couldn't focus, couldn't even think about going back. The police had no leads, no suspects. They still don't." She shook her head. "That's when I put my education to the test, began my own investigation. That folder I gave you is a year and a half of my life. My conclusion is that the man in prison known as the Kentucky Ripper killed *one* person, even though he claimed responsibility for many more. The real Ripper changed locales and victimology."

She finally looked up, her tortured gaze meeting his. "I believe that I'm a victim from his second spree. There are probably others as well, cases no one has connected, including me. And more women will suffer and die if I don't stop him. I'm also worried that I'm a loose end for him, that he'll come back to finish what he started." Her gaze searched his, as if looking for answers. "Please, Bryson. Help me find him and send him to prison. I don't want to die." The tears she'd been holding back spilled over and streamed down her cheeks.

He swore and lifted her into his arms. Daring his hip to interfere, he cradled her against his chest and strode from the kitchen.

Chapter Five

Teagan rubbed her bleary eyes and rolled her head on the pillow. She was in Bryson Anton's bedroom. In his bed. But he wasn't there, and his side of the bed hadn't been disturbed. She didn't know whether to applaud his old-fashioned gentlemanly conduct or curse him for it. She sighed and threw the covers off her before shuffling to the open bedroom door.

Bryson glanced up from the couch behind the coffee table, a stack of papers in his hand and more spread out across the wooden surface.

She stretched her arms above her head as she padded across the family room in her dress socks. She had no idea where her shoes and purse were. "Not to bruise your ego, but after you took me to bed, I don't remember anything. Maybe we should have a redo so you can refresh my memory."

He gave her the side-eye. "Trust me. If I took you to bed, you'd remember."

She grinned. "I have a feeling you're right."

He rolled his eyes. "You passed out in my arms, and I generously allowed you to use my bedroom to sleep it off. You're a lightweight when it comes to alcohol."

"Won't argue that." She yawned and gestured toward the cup on the table beside him. "I don't suppose that's coffee?"

In reply, he held the cup out to her.

She took a huge gulp before handing it back to him. "I think I'm half in love with you."

"That's the tequila talking. You're still drunk."

"Can't be. Had to have slept it off by now. How long was I out?"

He glanced at his watch. "Seventeen minutes."

"Oh. Then I'm definitely still drunk. More please."

He handed her the mug without looking up.

She shifted around to see what he was doing, then sat beside him, her thigh pressed to his.

"Boundaries, Teagan." He glanced pointedly at their legs, plastered together.

She sighed and moved over, just enough so they weren't touching. "You're either married, have a girlfriend, or we play for the same team, because nothing I'm trying is working."

"Never married. My girlfriend dumped me months ago because hanging with a guy with a limp cramped her style. And, trust me, you and I are definitely not playing for the same team."

"What is it then? I haven't struck out this many times since high school softball."

"Maybe you're not my type."

"Pfft. Have you *seen* me? These legs go all the way up."

He arched a brow. "We need to work on this low self-esteem of yours."

She laughed and shuffled through some of the papers he'd spread out in front of him. When she realized what he was looking at, hope flared in her chest. "You're reading my file?"

He shrugged. "I was bored. I had seventeen minutes to kill."

"Does this mean you're going to help me?"

"My history of helping people isn't exactly stellar. I'm only committing to looking through your research to offer suggestions that you can take or leave. Maybe I can put a different spin on it so you can think in new directions. I wouldn't get excited, if I were you. Like I said, I don't have a great track record. This ruined hip is because I messed up a pit maneuver a rookie could have performed in his sleep. I managed to knock the killer's vehicle into a ditch, but knocked myself silly in the process. Before I could even scramble for my gun, I'd been shot, shoved out the door, and the killer was taking off in my car with a hostage. The only reason the hostage survived is because one of my coworkers was able to rescue her after I nearly got her killed."

"I have a feeling there's way more to it than that." She started to pat his leg, then jerked her hand back at his reproachful look. "Have I mentioned that I'm a touchy-feely sort of person? I'll try to behave." She bit her lip. "You're still going to help me, right?"

He blew out a breath. "I thought you were *acting* earlier, that you were overcompensating."

"Sorry to disappoint. This is the real me."

"I didn't say I was disappointed."

She stared at him, hoping he'd explain *that* comment. But instead, he turned back to the papers in front of him. After a few minutes, she said, "If you change your mind about you and me, and I miss a signal, just let me know, okay?"

He let out a deep sigh and pinned her with an exasperated look. "Teagan?"

"Yes, Bryson?"

"Shut up."

She grinned and scooted back on the couch to sit cross-legged while he reviewed her research. It was taking him far longer than she'd expected. The folder wasn't *that* thick. She'd brought the summary, not the detailed reports. But he kept thumbing through the pages, comparing things, rereading. She was dying to know what he thought. She was also dying for an entirely different reason.

She climbed off the couch. "Where's the nearest toilet in this monstrosity? I'm about to pee my pants." She hopped back and forth from one foot to the other. "Never mind, I'll figure it out." She ran into his master bedroom and chose door number one. "Found it!" she called back, before slamming it closed.

BRYSON STARED AT his bedroom doorway where Teagan the Tornado had just disappeared. He'd expected a different woman when she woke, figuring her earlier actions were a type of bravado, a coping mechanism because of what had happened to her. Then again, she hadn't slept long enough to sober up.

He took his cell phone from one of the piles of paper on the coffee table, idly rubbing his aching hip as he reluctantly pressed a programmed number that he should have deleted months ago. When the line clicked he said, "You're trying to kill me."

"Delightful, isn't she?" Mason chuckled.

"You mean she's always like this? There isn't a cure?"

"I'm not taking her back. If that's what you want, I'm hanging up."

He turned his head, looking through the glass doors at the back of the kitchen. The creek was too low to see from here unless he stood. But the pilings holding the dock in place reached like spindly fingers toward the bright blue sky overhead, a reminder of his last conversation with Mason. Had it been only yesterday?

"Bryson? You still there?"

"I'm here. You mentioned when I was ready, that you'd throw me a line. Looks like I'm going to at least dip my toes in, whether I want to or not."

"She's a hard person to say no to."

"Yes. She is."

"Whatever you need, it's yours. Just name it." Mason's tone was all business now.

"My files, all those boxes I foolishly—and against FBI policy—saved from the Ripper case with the Bureau. I asked you to store them along with other case files you archived for The Justice Seekers. Is it possible to get them sent here, when you have time?"

"You'll have them within the hour."

Teagan appeared in his bedroom doorway, looking slightly green and more than a little woozy as she gripped the doorframe. She really didn't know how to hold her liquor, which for some reason he found adorable. "Thanks, Mason."

"For the files?"

He tightened his hand on the phone. "We'll start with that, for now." He hung up. Then he grabbed his cane and laboriously climbed to his feet.

Teagan trudged toward him and stopped a few feet away, her hand clutching her stomach. Bryson had a feeling he was about to finally meet the real Teagan.

She looked up at him, misery drawing tight lines at the corners of her eyes. "Did I really tell you I had to pee?"

He smiled. Maybe he'd already met the real Teagan after all. "Come on. I'll make you some fresh coffee and my special hangover blaster."

Chapter Six

When Bryson had mentioned a hangover blaster, the name alone should have warned Teagan to just say no. But she had to admit, even sitting on his master bathroom floor with her head hanging over a toilet, that awful concoction had done the trick. Too bad that meant throwing up everything she'd eaten or drank for the past *week*.

She shuddered and sat back. At least she could be grateful that the man was a neat freak. Either that or he hired really great cleaning people. His bathroom floor was spotless. She winced. Or it had been, until she'd come along. With her tummy finally settling, she pushed herself to her feet and then wobbled to the sink.

After rinsing her mouth out with some mouthwash that she'd found in a cabinet and brushing her teeth with her finger and a dab of toothpaste, she felt almost human again. She washed her face, made sure her stubborn hair hadn't escaped its braid, then did a quick refresh of the bathroom. The sound of voices engaged in conversation had her hurrying through the master bedroom and opening the door.

The front double door was wide open. Bryson was in his wheelchair directing a man with a hand truck full of bankers boxes toward a hallway that ran across the back of the house. Careful not to get in the way, she plopped down cross-legged on a leather padded bench just outside the bedroom and waited.

By the time the man was finished and Bryson locked the door behind him, she'd counted over a dozen boxes.

He wheeled his chair up to her. "Feeling better?"

"Much. Although I'm not sure whether the cure is worse than the hangover." She motioned toward his chair. "I see you ran out of tequila and traded in the cane."

"My liver cried uncle for the day."

"If you strip, I'd be happy to play Helga and massage your hip for you." She rubbed her hands together in anticipation.

"Helga?"

"The masseuse from this morning. What I lack in professional training I'd more than make up for with enthusiasm."

He coughed as if to cover a laugh. "Yes, well. I appreciate the offer but another massage isn't going to do the trick at this point. The hip gives out once the muscles get overworked and won't support me anymore."

"Are you doing physical therapy?"

"Let me guess. You can help me with that too?"

"If I'd known I'd meet you one day, I would have changed majors in college so I could say yes."

This time he laughed out loud. "Let me worry about the therapy, or lack thereof." He waved toward the back hallway. "Go on. Ask me about the boxes. I can tell that your curiosity is eating you alive."

She frowned. "Your earlier theory about your girlfriend dumping you because of your limp probably isn't right. I think she left you because you're always profiling people and reading their minds. Okay, yes, the curiosity is driving me batty. What's in the boxes?"

"I don't read minds. Profiling, or more accurately,

Criminal Investigative Analysis, is science, not art. Although some might argue it's both. And the answer to your question is that the boxes contain my research on the Kentucky Ripper. I was fresh out of polka-dot folders."

"All you had to do was ask. I could have let you borrow some of mine." She waved toward the cased opening where he'd directed the man with the hand truck. "Did the FBI send over copies of their research on the case?"

"The FBI doesn't allow former agents access to their case files. Those are copies I made of everything that passed my desk back when I worked on the investigation. Well, more accurately, when I worked on the profile. Technically, I wasn't an investigator. But the case consumed me and left me with more questions than answers, even after the killer was convicted. I religiously copied as much as I could and snuck it home every chance I got. From start to finish, the case took two years. Those copies added up."

She put her hands on her hips. "I knew it. You don't think the right guy was put away or you wouldn't have risked your career taking that stuff home. Admit it. My theory holds water."

"I admit nothing. But I'm willing to take a fresh look, which is why I had this stuff brought out of storage." He motioned toward the doorway at the end of the room. "Come on. Might as well give you a tour of this *monstrosity* and show you where those boxes went."

"That monstrosity comment I made earlier was under duress. I didn't mean it."

"Yes, you did. And I don't take offense. It *is* a rather large house, too big for one person. But it met my requirements when I was house shopping."

"Let me guess. Requirement number one, no carpet, for easier mobility with the cane and wheelchair?"

"Anyone could have guessed that."

"Requirement number two," she said. "It's only one story. You're not ready to tackle stairs just yet."

"Again, too easy. What about the third requirement?"

She shook her head. "Stumped on that one."

"The isolated location so people wouldn't bother me." He arched a brow at her.

She winced. "Ah, well. Two out of three isn't bad. That's sixty-six percent, still a passing grade, in high school at least."

"Somehow I can't imagine you ever being satisfied with anything less than an A. You were valedictorian, weren't you?"

"Takes one to know one?"

He smiled. "Come on. You've already seen the kitchen, family room, and made yourself completely at home in my master bedroom and bathroom." He waved toward two more doors on the far right wall. "Closet and half bath."

"I was so close earlier. Didn't realize there was a half bath over there."

"At least you made it to a bathroom. Can't complain about that." He wheeled his chair toward the back of the room.

She fell in step beside him. "What is this floor made out of? I can't figure it out."

He leaned over the side of the chair as if noticing the floor for the first time. "Beats me. Came with the house. Come on, right turn, obviously, since the hall starts here."

Along the way, he pointed out the various rooms but didn't stop until they reached the far end.

He motioned toward the door in front of them. This leads—"

"Let me guess. Man cave?"

"Home office."

"Oh. Kind of anticlimactic after walking all this way."

"It wasn't *that* far."

She gave him a droll look. "Says the man who *rolled* all the way here. I've already gotten my ten thousand steps for the day. And that's just since I walked out of your bedroom."

"Do you want to see the coolest part of the house or not?"

"Coolest? Robert Downey Jr. in *Iron Man* cool or Keanu Reeves in *John Wick* kind of cool?"

"More like Bruce Willis in *anything* kind of cool."

She grinned and they fist-bumped. "Then my answer is most definitely yes."

He shoved the door open. Then he moved back and motioned her forward. "After you."

The excitement on his face had her expecting something amazing when she stepped inside the room.

She wasn't disappointed.

Chapter Seven

Bryson rolled into his office behind Teagan and did something he rarely did these days. He simply enjoyed the moment. He didn't worry about his aching hip or rehash the would haves, could haves, should haves of his life. Instead, he basked in the sheer joy on her face as she turned in slow circles, taking it all in.

There was a lot to take in.

The expansive room was a microcosm of the house itself, fully contained with a kitchenette in one corner, a bathroom, a bedroom intended for those all-nighters if he needed a quick nap before heading back into the main room to continue his work.

On the left side was the library. Floor-to-ceiling cherrywood bookshelves were filled with all kinds of law enforcement textbooks on topics like forensics, crime scene analysis, and profiling. Past the library, nearly every inch of wall space was adorned with matching cherrywood cabinets, drawers and open shelving. Storage would never be a problem here. The boxes that Mason had sent over were neatly stacked beside some of those storage cabinets. Something for him to tackle later, after everything was scanned electronically. That was the real beauty of this room—the technology.

A large round stone table in the middle of the room was

control central for the massive daisy-chained monitors that took up most of the opposite wall. From that table, he could bring up reports or photographs or even the internet and display the information on any individual monitor, or slide it across all of them to form one picture. It was a profiler's dream, to be able to have everything at his fingertips at one time so he could make comparisons and see the entire case at a glance.

Too bad he'd never actually used the darn thing on a case.

Teagan had made a full circuit of the room, opening doors and checking behind them, looking into the storage cabinets. But she surprised him by returning to the library, rather than the round table. She traced her hands almost reverently across the books, like a beautiful butterfly, flitting from tome to tome. When she finally turned around, she motioned toward the two leather wing chairs and circular rug that completed the library effect.

"This is amazing. You have books I've only dreamed of reading, rare ones that my college couldn't even get their hands on when I tried borrowing them through our library system. Two of the books have your name on them. I didn't know you'd authored any texts."

"Neither do most people," he said dryly. "My publisher lost a fortune on those."

"Then they don't deserve to be your publisher. They obviously don't know how to market your work or it would have sold a gazillion books."

"Are you one of the six people who bought a copy? Is that how you know they're amazing?"

She rolled her eyes. "I'm sure you're exaggerating."

"Not by much, unfortunately."

"Well, based on your reputation in the field, I'd love to become reader number seven, if you'll let me borrow them."

"You can *have* them. I've got plenty more. What about the rest of the room? You don't seem as impressed as I'd hoped. My ego's a bit deflated. I thought you'd run straight to the table and start salivating."

"I would have, if it wasn't for your library. I'm a book lover, through and through. But the entire room is incredible." She strode to the table and ran her fingers across it. "You must have enjoyed being a Justice Seeker more than you've let on. This is fit for the *knights of the round table*, just like the one that Mason told me that you all have in some super-secret hidden room at The Justice Seekers' home base."

"Almost. It's not quite as large as his since I don't have twelve Seekers, or so-called *knights*, to fill it up. But I admit I enjoyed his flair for the medieval and the fun of the whole Camelot concept, so I stole some of that for myself. I converted an existing study and two bedrooms into this office with the intention of using it to work from home while recuperating from being shot. But the recovery has been slower than I'd expected, and I ended up with way too much time to think about my failures. Resigning seemed like the reasonable thing to do."

"Wait. Are you saying that you've never used this office, or *great hall*, if you call it that like Mason does? Once it was finished, it just sat here unused?"

"I don't call it a great hall. It's got the stone floors, walls and table, but nothing else that resembles a castle like Mason's does. And, yes, you're absolutely right. I can't remember the last time I've traipsed across the house to this room. If it wasn't for the cleaning company that comes in once a week, there'd be cobwebs and dust all over the place."

"Wow. If I'd known that, I'd have snuck in through a back window and claimed squatters' rights long ago. I could happily live here for weeks and not come up for air." She lowered herself into one of the cushy leather chairs at the round table. "Ahhh. World class. You have great taste." She waved toward the monitors. "Feel free to feed your ego by giving me a demonstration. How big are those screens anyway? Six or seven feet tall?"

He rolled one of the other leather chairs out of the way and positioned his wheelchair beside her. "Each one is six feet by three feet. I wanted twelve, to keep with the Camelot theme. But it seemed like overkill and would have restricted the space too much, so I settled on nine. They work together as one monitor if I want, or I can load something different on each one. That's the real benefit, being able to put up information about different crimes on each screen and compare them. I can use a computer tablet at the table to select which screen I want and use a light pen to draw circles around different items or highlight them, edit them, whatever."

"Definitely cool. Can I drive?" She held out her hand. "Give me the reins. Let's do this."

Instead of popping up one of the computer tablets from a hidden compartment in the table, he adjusted his chair to face her and took her hands in his.

Her eyes widened and a slow grin spread across her face.

"Don't," he said. "Whatever sexy, funny, or smart-ass comment you're about to make about me holding your hands, just wait. I need to have a serious conversation with you. Can you focus for a few minutes without any wisecracks?"

A look of wariness crossed her face. "Why do I feel like I'm about to be sent to the principal's office?"

He sighed and let her go.

"Okay, okay." She grabbed his hands with both of hers. "No jokes, no tangents. I'm listening."

He arched a brow, not sure whether or not to believe her.

"Really," she said. "I can be serious when I need to. Go on. What is it?"

"I just want you to be sure that you know what you're getting into before we go any further. You've been like a whirlwind, blowing into my life. I met you, what, a few hours ago? And somehow you've managed to make me excited about working again. That's why I brought you to this room, to show you the tools we've got at our disposal so we can work together, if that's truly what you want to do."

"Are you kidding? It's all I've wanted since I first came across the Ripper case and saw your contributions to the investigation. I want to work with you to catch the Ripper before—"

"We're not going to work on the Ripper case."

She blinked. "My turn to be confused."

He gently entwined their fingers, trying to convey that he was there for her if she needed his support. "I'm going to hire a temp to scan in and catalog the data in those boxes. That will take several days, maybe even a week. In the meantime, the only case that I've had a chance to scan is yours. While you were recovering from your tequila binge, I used the scanner in my study to process your folder. That's what I want to bring up on these screens. But there's a world of difference between looking at something on an eight-by-ten sheet of paper, and seeing it on a six-foot-tall screen. A lot of this stuff is deeply personal. Are you sure you can handle it?"

"I don't understand your concerns. I put that folder together. I know what's in it. I want you to see it, to review it with me."

"Your descriptions of the most recent attack that you allege was made by the Ripper didn't mention you by name. That's quite telling. And there's far more detail to what happened to you than what you had in that folder. A lot more. We have to review all of the information, not just some of it, if we have a chance at solving this thing."

"Well of course there's more, all the detailed reports that support the summaries I wrote. I didn't bring those with me."

"That's not what I mean. There are other details, things you didn't reference even at a high level in your summaries."

"Like what?"

He squeezed her hands before letting go. Then he pushed down on top of the table in front of him and the section flipped over to reveal a computer tablet. He typed some commands into the control program, then pressed enter. Teagan looked up at the screens. Her eyes widened and she put a hand over her mouth before turning away.

"Where did you get those?" she whispered.

He tapped the tablet and the screens went dark. "I still have a few contacts in law enforcement."

She crossed her arms over her middle. "Well, they shouldn't have shared my hospital photos with you. They're—"

"Too personal? None of my business?"

She flinched and dropped her gaze.

He rolled back from the table. "Come on. It's okay. Forget all this. You're not ready."

"Wait. Just…give me a minute to catch my breath, okay? I can handle it. Really."

"Teagan. There's no reason for you to have to catch your breath, to handle it. You lived through the abduction, the torture, once already. You shouldn't have to do that again, reopen old wounds. Leave the investigation to me. Maybe because I admire your spunk, or maybe just because I'm ready to jump back in the game and didn't realize it until now. Regardless of the reason, I want to do this. But the only way I can is by going through every piece of data surrounding your abduction, everything that happened to you. *Everything.* It's the only way to make sure nothing was missed, that every possible clue has been considered. Meanwhile, you can go back to Florida, get on with your life. When I have something to report, I'll contact you." He wheeled to the door and held it open for her. "Come on. We're done here."

Chapter Eight

When Teagan crossed her arms and gave him a mutinous stare, Bryson sighed and let the office door close. She'd made no move toward the doorway. She wasn't backing down without a fight. But neither was he. "Teagan, we should—"

"You caught me off guard. That's all. I didn't expect to see…those pictures, okay? You should have warned me."

"If I'd warned you, I might not have received an honest reaction. You would have covered up your true emotions, or at least tried, with false bravado. Now I know the truth. This is all still too raw for you to be involved in the investigation. And there's nothing wrong with that. Victims don't typically work on their own cases, for good reason."

"I'm not a victim," she snapped. "I'm a survivor."

"Fair enough. That doesn't change anything that I said."

She waved toward the stacks of boxes. "Why can't we start with these? I already know the man who attacked me is the real Kentucky Ripper, not Leviathan Finney, the guy in prison. There's no reason to review every nitty-gritty detail about what happened to me. We're past that. We know who did it, that first guy you profiled back in Kentucky, the one the police let get away, Avarice Lowe."

"Did you tell the detectives on your case that you believed Lowe was the one who'd abducted you?"

"Yes. I did."

"And? Let me guess. They did a cursory look at him and either couldn't locate him at all or said he had an alibi. And they went no further than that."

"They couldn't find him. But they didn't try very hard."

"Why do you suppose that is?"

She threw her hands in the air. "I don't know. Probably because they're lazy and wanted to work on easier cases."

He wheeled over in front of her. "Can you think of another reason? Come on. Set aside emotion and use that valedictorian mind of yours."

She gave him another mutinous look. "They don't believe Lowe is the Ripper and had no evidence to tie him to my case. But that's because they refused to listen."

"Detectives, good ones at least, follow the evidence. The only reason you feel that the Ripper is the one who abducted you is because the man who hurt you carved that X on your abdomen. Everything else about your case is different, including the fact that you survived."

"Then let's go through your case files and find more similarities. That's why you brought them here."

He shook his head. "I brought them here to review *after* I review your case, and then, only if we decide the two cases are connected, or highly likely connected. What happens if we do it your way, spend all our time on the Ripper case, and discover that you're wrong? We've wasted weeks, or longer by that time going through all of the Ripper's cases. We'd be starting over at ground zero without having made any progress figuring out who attacked you. If you truly want my help in finding out who hurt you, I'm all in. But I have to do it my way. I follow the evidence. And that means, starting at the beginning, with what happened to you."

She stared at the stacks of boxes for a long moment.

When she finally met his gaze, naked pain radiated back at him. "I spent over a year and a half on this to find the man who hurt me. I don't want to start over. I can't."

Disappointment shot through him, but he forced a smile. "Then don't. Keep doing what you're doing. Follow the leads where you believe they'll take you."

"Without you."

He nodded. "Without me."

"Bryson's way or the highway, is that it?"

He hated the hurt in her voice. He especially hated that he was at least partly the cause. But it would be far worse if he gave in, if he went against everything he'd learned as a Justice Seeker in how to run investigations as well as his profiling experience with the FBI. She'd managed to awaken a hunger in him for justice again, a desire to right the wrongs of his past and prove he was better than the mistakes he'd made. Starting out by making another mistake wasn't how he'd atone for his sins.

Steeling himself against the censure and sense of betrayal in her beautiful brown eyes, he responded to her accusation. "Bryson's way was to enjoy his hermit-like existence and never talk to another human being again. I was perfectly happy here all by myself until you showed up. So don't act like I'm suddenly pushing you to do something that I want you to do. You came here for my help. I was willing to help you the only way I know how, by using my training and experience and following the right steps from beginning to end to build a profile. I would have gathered as much evidence along the way as I could. Then, I would have worked with the police to get them moving on it. None of that is sexy or flashy. It's a heck of a lot of work. But that's the way it's done. Period. And you said you can't do that, which means *we're* done. Follow your own path and I'll follow mine. There's a creek full of fish in my backyard. Maybe I'll get a pole and cast a line. There are worse ways to spend my time. Go home. I mean it. I wish you the best, I truly do. But when I come back inside, I want you gone."

He wheeled out of the room and a few minutes later he was on the dock, nursing a can of beer as if the twenty-four hours since Mason's visit had never happened. But as he listened to the creek splashing over the rocks and watched the cars far below that seemed like toys from this distance, he realized that everything had changed. There *was* no going back. Mason had started a quiet rumble inside him. Teagan had built that rumble into an earthquake that had rocked him from his complacency. She'd reminded him of the thrill of the chase, the satisfaction of solving a puzzle, and the reason he'd gone into his line of work to begin with—to help people. But just as he hadn't helped Hayley when he'd gotten shot, he hadn't helped Teagan.

He swore and crumpled the now-empty can in his hand. He'd been far too rough on her. Every word he'd said had been true, his truth at least. But she obviously wasn't ready for that kind of honesty. She wasn't one of his peers, a hardened or jaded agent who he could talk to without guarding his words. She was a victim, a survivor. She deserved nothing but respect and kindness as she struggled to come to terms with what had happened to her. If going after the Ripper was her way of coping, then who was he to stand in her way? He should have encouraged her. Instead, he'd lectured her on the "right" way to conduct an investigation.

The distant sound of her car starting up in his driveway had his shoulders slumping in disappointment. Not with her. With himself. She'd probably head back to her hotel room, or wherever she was staying, and continue her research like a hamster on a wheel never getting where they truly wanted to go. She needed guidance from someone willing to pursue the angle she wanted to pursue, not the angle that Bryson had insisted was the right place to start. So how could he help her?

It all boiled down to contacts.

He'd joked earlier that he still had a *few* contacts in law enforcement. In reality, he had far more than a few. After all, he'd only gone on hiatus as a Justice Seeker six months ago. Before that, with his combined years as a Seeker and an FBI special agent, he'd worked with hundreds, maybe thousands of peers in his field. Many of them had become close friends that he still had to this day. Maybe, just maybe, he could give Teagan what she wanted—someone to talk to who'd worked on the Ripper cases.

He pulled out his cell phone and placed a call to Special Agent Pierce Buchanan. There was the usual small talk, asking about Pierce, his wife, Madison, and their toddler, Nicole. That was followed by some groveling and apologizing for Bryson having refused the couple's many requests to let them visit him after the shooting. But they worked out an agreement. In exchange for Pierce contacting Teagan and offering her an insider's view of the Ripper murders, Bryson would fly to Pierce's home in Savannah for a long weekend later this summer. Bryson wasn't sure if he was the winner or loser in that negotiation. Three of Pierce's four brothers and his father were in law enforcement. They'd likely show up and grill him about every detail of the shooting and its aftermath.

After ending that call, he made one more.

To the airport.

Chapter Nine

Death and its close cousin, extreme violence, had walked this meandering path before. They'd held hands in the dark shadows beneath these towering live oaks. They'd carefully avoided the bulging tree roots that lifted and cracked the concrete, quietly stalking their prey. Here, in the near-darkness where thick branches and leaves blotted out the hot Florida sun overhead, they'd crouched in this ten-foot-wide space lined on both sides by six-foot-tall wooden fences. The fences were supposed to ensure the privacy of the homeowners whose properties backed onto the nature trail in The Woods subdivision while joggers and walkers enjoyed these paths. But two years ago, these same fences had protected and concealed evil.

This was where Teagan Ray had been attacked, brutalized and then abducted.

There were theories that extreme violence, whether or not it ended in death, left an indelible mark on a place. It tainted the soil, the trees, even the air with its negative energy and could be felt for years afterward. Standing here now with a sense of dread and oppressiveness weighing down on him, Bryson was more inclined to believe those theories than to dispel them. Because it wasn't the GPS coordinates that had made him stop when he'd reached this spot. It was an overwhelming feeling of doom.

He shook his head at those thoughts. It was more sci-
entific than that. He'd stopped here because he'd tried to
mentally place himself in the role of a man stalking prey.
This is where he'd have lain in wait for a potential victim. It
was a particularly dark spot, with thick overgrown bushes
providing the perfect cover. And over two years ago, unfortunately, Teagan was the one who'd happened through
here at just the wrong time. And she'd paid for that dearly.

After the initial attack, the belief was that she'd been
drugged. Still able to walk with assistance, but not coher-
ent enough to fight back or even understand what was happening to her, she was led by her abductor to wherever he'd
parked his vehicle. Or, at least, that was the theory. There
weren't any witnesses to fill in those details.

Her first lucid memories, after the attack on the path,
were that she was blindfolded and tied up in the shack
where he'd taken her. Two weeks later, when he'd left on
one of his so-called supply trips that he took every few
days, she'd miraculously escaped. But she'd gotten lost in
the wilds of the Florida backcountry for days. By the time
a hiker had found her, she was dehydrated and sunburned
and half out of her mind. Once she'd recovered enough
in the hospital to explain that she'd escaped a kidnapper,
over two days had passed. The police used scent dogs to
backtrack to the shack where she'd been held. Turns out
she'd been about an hour and a half from her hometown
of Jacksonville, deep in the woods outside of Live Oak,
near the Suwannee River. But the abductor wasn't there,
and he never came back after that.

The owner of the shack was cleared. Not because Teagan couldn't pick him out of a lineup. She couldn't pick
anyone out of a lineup. She'd been drugged, blindfolded,
deprived of water and food. Her abductor had kept the
shack mostly dark, with room-darkening drapes and few

sources of light. He'd told her from the beginning that he planned to kill her. But until then, he was super careful, obviously in case she somehow escaped, which she did.

Because of his extreme care to conceal his identity, she'd told the police she could probably pass him on the street and would never know it. That was likely one of the reasons she had put her education and the rest of her life on hold to try to find the man who'd attacked her. Knowing he was in prison and could never hurt her again would no doubt be the only way she could ever live without the fear of him finding her again, and finishing what he'd started.

Too bad her abductor hadn't been the owner of the shack. That would have made everything neat and tidy and it would all be over by now. But the owner lived in Canada, where he went to work every day and had plenty of people to vouch for that. The shack was where he stayed two or three times a year when he came down to work at clearing the land around it in preparation for building the retirement cabin he dreamed about.

Bryson made some notes on the police report, marking things on the map of the trail that he'd noticed today. Then he tucked the report into his jacket pocket and took one last look around. He intended to walk all of the paths in this community today if his hip could handle it, or use his wheelchair if he had to, which seemed likely by how badly his hip was already throbbing. He wanted to see whether there were other good ambush spots on other trails. If so, then maybe someone with homes backing up on those paths might have spotted a man walking the trails back then, choosing his ultimate hiding place. There could be some witnesses who didn't even realize they'd seen something important.

There were 4.1 miles of nature walks and trails in this community, according to its website. Other statistics that he'd gleaned about The Woods were that it had 811 homes and 18 man-made ponds. It boasted a so-called natural setting, thus the name. From his perspective, that meant there were a heck of a lot of trees and overgrown bushes, providing great hiding places for would-be attackers. But because the community was gated, the residents had been lulled into thinking they were safe.

Maybe that explained why Teagan had thought nothing of walking through this overgrown, dark, far less traveled section of the trails as the sun was going down. Her parents lived just a few streets away, and she'd been home from college on a visit. Having grown up here without any major crime incidents in an upper-middle-class area that was generally considered safe, she had felt there was nothing to worry about. In a perfect world, there shouldn't have been. But unfortunately, there were some very bad people sharing the same air as the rest of them, and Teagan had the misfortune of coming across one. Wrong place, wrong time.

Or did that really explain it? Could the attacker have been after her specifically?

That was one of the questions Bryson needed to answer. The assumption all along in the police reports, and by Teagan and her parents as well, had been that she was a randomly chosen victim. There wasn't any evidence to the contrary. But Bryson wasn't the type to assume anything.

A low growl had him turning around, leaning on his cane with one hand as he flipped back his jacket with the other to grab the pistol holstered on his hip. But he didn't pull his weapon. Instead, he let his jacket fall back into place and rested both of his hands on the cane to steady himself as he glanced from the impressive, still-growling German shepherd to the gorgeous young woman holding its leash.

Teagan.

The accusation that she might have somehow gotten Pierce to tell her where he was and then followed him to Jacksonville died on his lips unspoken. She hadn't expected to see him here. It was evident by her wide eyes and the way her left hand was pressed against her throat.

"What are you doing here?" he demanded. "I thought you'd be in Savannah by now." His accusatory tone did exactly what he'd intended. It gave her something to focus on instead of the fright from seeing a man standing in the shadows where she'd once been attacked.

She dropped her hand and gave the dog a command that had him sitting on his haunches. His tongue lolled out as if he hadn't been poised to rip out Bryson's throat seconds earlier.

"Why would I be in Savannah?" She sounded genuinely confused.

It was his turn to be surprised. "Didn't you get a call? From FBI special agent Pierce Buchanan?"

She shook her head. "No. But I haven't checked my messages since leaving your place yesterday. My phone number listed in the folder I gave you is a landline at my apartment. It's not one that I share with many people. And it's not registered under my name."

The truth sent a wave of anger and sympathy straight through him. "You carry a burner phone, don't you? You're worried that your attacker might trace you."

Her gaze was her answer, darting toward the fences on either side of the path and the thick trees and bushes blocking the view of anyone behind them. He wondered why the homeowners association hadn't voted to clear out these dangerous hiding places, especially after what had happened to Teagan. But mostly, he wondered why she was here.

He took a step forward, hesitating when her dog emitted another threatening growl.

"Zeus, stop." She shook the leash and the dog quieted, but his dark eyes followed Bryson's every move. "Why would an FBI agent be looking for me?" Her eyes widened again. "Have they found something? In Savannah? Oh no. Someone else wasn't attacked, were they?"

Ignoring the new round of growls from her dog, he limped toward her, stopping just out of lunging distance. "No. I'm not aware of any more attacks linked to the man who hurt you. Pierce is a good friend of mine who lives in Savannah. Because of his experience with serial killer cases, he ended up assisting on the task force in Kentucky. We worked the Ripper case together. After you left yesterday—"

"After you threw me out, you mean," she accused. "I thought you Justice Seekers were supposed to be honorable and help people in need."

He smiled, pleased to see a return of the sassy confident woman he'd met in Gatlinburg. "Yes, well. I was on hiatus from the Seekers at the time. So you weren't officially my client. But I did want to help you. So after I threw you out, I called Pierce and asked him to give you an insider's reading of the Ripper cases and to answer any questions that you had."

Her brows crinkled in confusion. "Why would you do that? You told me that looking into the Ripper case was the wrong approach."

He started to move closer, but Zeus stood up, his ears flattening. Shooting her dog to defend himself was the last thing he wanted to do, so he took a step back.

"I'm glad you have Zeus with you, for protection," he told her. "That's smart."

She winced and looked away.

Understanding had him filled with regret. "I wasn't trying to say that you shouldn't have been out here without him that first time." When she didn't answer, he leaned to the side, trying to get her to look at him. "Teagan?"

She sighed and met his gaze. "What?"

"It wasn't your fault." He waved his hands along the path. "None of this is your fault. A woman should be able to dance naked through the streets without worrying about some Neanderthal attacking her. It's *never* the victim's fault. The only person to blame is the monster who hurt you."

A reluctant smile tugged at the corners of her mouth. "You sound like my parents."

Now it was his turn to wince. "Ouch."

She laughed, then winked, looking more like her old self again. "Don't worry. There's exactly zero chance of me confusing Hot Guy with my parents."

"Good to know. I think. Assuming I'm Hot Guy?"

She grinned. "Definitely." Her smile dimmed, and some of her earlier uneasiness had her glancing around again. "I'm staying with my parents for a few days. And like I do every time I see them, I walk this trail. Not because I want to go…where it happened…some survivor's weird hang-up or something. But because it's the same routine I had before the attack. I've walked these trails almost daily since I was a little girl. And I refuse to change that because of…because of what happened. He took so much from me. It might seem silly, but letting him take away my joy of nature and long walks would be letting him win." She patted the dog beside her. "My only concession now is to bring my mom's dog Zeus and Annie along."

The dog seemed to be licking his lips in anticipation of sinking its teeth into his hide—if dogs had lips.

"Wait. Annie? Who's Annie?"

She slid her hand into the pocket of her jeans and pulled out a compact .22-caliber pistol. "Meet Annie."

"Let me guess. After Annie Oakley?"

Her gorgeous smile made another appearance. "Very good, Sherlock. Maybe you should be an FBI agent." She shoved it back into her pocket.

"Been there, done that." He gestured toward her pocket. "Should I ask for your concealed carry permit?"

"That depends. Did you become a police officer since the last time we met?"

"Touché. Don't worry. Your secret's safe with me. I won't call any of my JSO contacts to tell them about Annie."

"Is that how you got past the gates? Someone from the Jacksonville Sherriff's Office told the guard to let you through?"

"Actually, I got in the old-fashioned way."

"The old-fashioned way?"

"Ben Franklin. A bribe."

He'd expected a laugh. Instead, her face turned ashen.

"Teagan? Are you okay?" Risking the wrath of Zeus, he leaned toward her.

Predictably, the dog barked and pulled against the leash trying to reach him.

She frowned and yanked him back. "Zeus, enough. Friend. He's a friend." She motioned toward Bryson. "Hold your hand out for him to sniff, palm down."

"You're kidding, right?"

"No. I'm serious. Let him smell you." She slipped her hand under the back of the dog's collar. "Friend, Zeus. Friend."

Telling himself he was an idiot, he did as she'd asked, holding his hand out.

Zeus snuffled his hand for a good ten seconds, then his

tongue lolled out and he gave it a long sloppy lick before sitting back on his haunches.

Bryson made a face at the saliva on his hand, then looked up in time to see Teagan trying to hide a grin. He narrowed his eyes suspiciously. "You did that on purpose."

"Yeah, well. It's kind of funny, seeing you dressed up in a business suit with dog slobber all over your hand."

After a quick glance at Zeus, who seemed far more interested in a butterfly flitting around a nearby bush now that he'd supposedly accepted Bryson as a nonthreat, he reached out and wiped his hand on Teagan's shirt.

She gasped in dismay at the wet stain on her formerly white blouse. "I can't believe you did that."

"We're even now. Don't go planning your revenge."

"Hmm. We'll see about that." She glanced around again. "You said you bribed the guard at the gate to let you in? You didn't show him some kind of old FBI credentials or anything like that?"

Now he understood why she'd paled earlier. "You're surprised at how easy it was for someone who doesn't live here to get in. Is that it?"

She nodded. "Not that I should be surprised. After all, the police ruled out the suspect as living in the community. They supposedly researched every single resident. We knew he had to have come from outside somehow. I just didn't think it would be that easy to drive on in."

"Yeah, well. It's not like you have to be a former cop to be a security guard. Pretty much anyone can be one. And they aren't paid enough to make them above reproach, some of them anyway. I'm sure most are great people and genuinely try to do a good job."

She snorted. "Now you're pandering, trying to make me feel better. I preferred it when you were being brutally honest."

"Brutal? Ouch again."

"If the truth fits." She shrugged, then winked as if to soften her criticisms.

"This isn't going at all the way I'd planned when I flew down here late last night."

"You thought I was in Georgia. You didn't plan on running into me."

"No. I didn't. But now that I have, I'm wondering why I did. After being so intent on finding information on the Ripper, why would you come back to Jacksonville? Are you taking a break from the investigation? Returning to school to finish your master's?"

She straightened her shoulders. "No break. I'm digging in harder than before. And I'm taking your advice. I'm starting at the beginning. And this—" she waved her hand toward the trees and bushes around them "—is where it all began."

Chapter Ten

The look on Bryson's face had Teagan stiffening. "Why are you so surprised? I went to you for help and advice because I respected your experience and expertise. Did you think I'd completely ignore your suggestions?"

He nodded, surprising her with his honesty. "I assumed anyone stubborn enough to work past my annoyance over the mistaken identity thing and then pretend they liked tequila enough to make themselves sick would be far too one-track minded to give up over a year of research to essentially start over."

"Yeah, well. Maybe you shouldn't judge people so fast when you meet them."

His mouth quirked up in that sexy half-smile that had her practically drooling again just like the first time she'd seen him. Good grief he was dangerous, the kind of danger that had her wishing she'd worn shorts instead of jeans. She was actually sweating now, and it couldn't be more than eighty degrees. A mild spring day around here.

"Looks like my profiling skills are even dustier than I'd realized," he said. "My apologies for making assumptions." He shifted on his feet, and she didn't miss the telltale wince as he rested both hands on the top of his cane.

"Your hip is bothering you."

"Are you playing Watson to my Sherlock now?"

"Oh heck no. I'll never be the sidekick. If anything, I'm Wonder Woman and you're Steve Trevor."

"Doesn't he die in the end?"

"Everyone dies in the end."

His grin faded. "I didn't mean to bring up bad memories again."

She shook her head. "Trust me. You didn't. They're always there, in the back of my mind. That's why I'm doing this investigation. When I escaped that day, I got out of the shack. But I didn't escape him. He's still out there. Until he's put away for good, I'll never be able to move on. Not really."

He sighed heavily. "I was worried that might be a big part of this for you. What happens if you never find him?"

Zeus whined beside her and she realized she was unconsciously tugging his leash, transmitting her agitation to him. She forced her hand to relax and rubbed his head. "That's a problem for future Teagan to worry about. Right now, I'm on the case, determined to do everything I can to bring this guy to justice. The real question is, now that we're both committed to this endeavor, do we work on it together or go our separate ways again?"

He subtly shifted, resting his back against one of the live oaks lining the path. This was the longest that she'd seen him standing without giving in to his wheelchair, and he'd been out here before she'd arrived. He had to be about ready to collapse.

"How about we discuss it over dinner?" he asked.

She blinked. "Dinner? Did I miss a signal somewhere?"

He laughed. "It's just dinner. I'm hungry, and to be honest my hip is going to give out soon if I don't sit. Rather than fall down in an embarrassing heap on the concrete, I'm inclined to head to my car then off somewhere to eat before my next appointment which isn't for—" he glanced at his watch "—another two hours. What do you say? Want me to drive you home so you can put up Zeus and then go eat with me?"

"What appointment?"

"It was too much to hope you'd let that pass." He pushed away from the tree and leaned on the cane. "I'm interviewing the Brodericks tonight, a couple who used to own one of the homes that backs up to this spot on the path. They moved shortly after everything happened, to one of the homes in the back of the subdivision, on Beautyberry Circle. Tomorrow I'm interviewing some other people who live along this path to see if they've remembered anything in the years since your attack. But also to get more of a lay of the land, try to get more of a sense of what your abductor may have been thinking back then."

She stepped toward him, not stopping until she had to crane her head back to look him in the eyes. "Don't tease me, Bryson. You're mentioning these interviews because you're offering to let me participate. Is that right? You wouldn't be cruel enough to bring them up otherwise, would you?"

He smiled sadly and feathered a hand across her cheek. The touch was so unexpected, so soft and gentle that she'd swear her heart skipped a beat. Even more of a surprise, he leaned down and pressed an equally soft kiss against her forehead before straightening. But he didn't drop his hand. Instead, he left it there, cupping her cheek, his thumb gently stroking her skin as if he didn't want to break the connection between them.

"I'm not teasing," he said, his voice a strained whisper. "And I would never deliberately be cruel to you. I shouldn't have been so harsh, so short with you in Gatlinburg. I thought I was being noble, protecting you. But I had no idea that instead of influencing you to go off in an innocuous direction where you'd be safe, you'd come back here to start over on your own. If the man who hurt you is still around here, and he realizes you're back in town trying to find him, then you're putting yourself in danger."

She frowned, ready to argue. "But I can—"

"Let me finish. While I'm not trying to send any signals…" He dropped his hand, his face reddening slightly as if he just realized that he was still touching her. He cleared his throat. "I'll admit that there's something about you, something special, that has me thinking about you far more than I should in ways I really shouldn't be thinking, not when I'm working a case. It's hell on my focus."

She blinked up at him. "You think I'm special?"

His gaze dropped to her lips. "No question." He shuddered as if waging some kind of internal war with himself. Then he moved back a step. "The point I'm trying to make, and not doing very well, is that it would be really hard to work this case with you and to also stay objective the whole time and not get…sidetracked. But it would be even more impossible to work the case alone, knowing you were somewhere out there potentially putting yourself in danger with no one to watch your back. I'd worry about you the whole time and wouldn't get anything done. So, I guess you've won this particular battle. To be crystal clear, no misunderstandings, I'm inviting you to work with me on your case, starting with the homeowner interview this evening. But only if we agree to keep our relationship professional." His gaze dropped to her lips again. "At least until the case is over."

Her stomach jumped at his last statement. She couldn't stop smiling. But not just because she now realized he was as interested in her as she was in him. Far more important was that he was going to help her find and put away the monster who haunted her dreams at night, who cast a pall of fear over her every waking hour no matter how hard she tried to pretend that he didn't. Bryson was the answer to her prayers. And she was going to enjoy every single minute that they were together, because the man was hopelessly fun to tease. Keep their relationship strictly professional? Pfft. Not a chance. But, of course, she wasn't going to admit to that. He'd figure it out eventually and by then he'd be so hooked on her that he'd be helpless to do anything about it.

That was her hope at least.

"I'll be crystal clear in my response." She hooked her right arm around his left one as if to flirt, when really she could tell he was struggling to remain upright and was probably too proud to ask for help. "I would love to work with you, starting with dinner, and then conducting the interview tonight. But first, as you mentioned earlier, we need to drop Zeus off. Like I said, he's my mom's. I just borrow him when I visit."

They started down the path together, him leaning heavily on the cane, her holding on to his left arm to keep him from falling over, and Zeus happily sniffing and following along at the end of his leash.

When they reached his rental car, she was surprised and a little disappointed to see that he'd chosen a luxury BMW sedan. Its dark blue color and the four doors gave it a decidedly mature, boring appearance even though it was definitely a nice car. Bryson Anton was still a young guy, in spite of his teasing her for being several years younger. And he really was hot. He'd look much better sitting in a red, sporty convertible with the top down than a glorified grocery-getter. Or maybe even a jacked-up four-wheel-drive truck with a gun rack in the back, although that seemed a little too country for him. He was refined, but not upper-crust. Definitely the convertible sports-car type.

But after he insisted on holding the door open for her, then slid into the driver's seat, his deep sigh and the look of relief on his face explained why he'd chosen this car. He needed the plush seats and comfort of a vehicle that would smooth out a bumpy road because of his bad hip.

"Have you thought of getting a second opinion on your hip?" she asked. "I mean, there has to be a way to fix it so it doesn't hurt so much all the time."

"I've had second, third and fourth opinions. The bullet is lodged close to my spine and presses on a nerve that makes the hip ache. Surgery isn't an option. I'm told there's a fifty-fifty chance that it will loosen on its own one day and then be removable and I'll be good as new, or it will loosen on its own one day and nick my spinal cord, putting me permanently in a wheelchair."

She pressed a hand to her mouth. "Oh my gosh. I'm so sorry."

He shrugged. "I'm learning to live with it. Partly thanks to you. I admit to wallowing a bit in self-pity before you came along. Now, if the bullet shifts and I can't walk anymore, at least it will happen while I'm trying to do something good rather than sitting around my house all day drinking tequila." He put the car in drive but kept his foot on the brake. "Enough about me. Where to, Ms. Ray?"

"Do a U-turn, Mr. Anton."

With Zeus taking up the tiny space behind the seats and lolling half-across the console that separated them, Bryson followed her directions to her parents' home, at the end of a long pond on Birch Bark Court, and pulled into the driveway. Beautiful mature crape myrtles dotted the sides of the yard, their hot pink flowers waving in the warm spring breezes. And standing out front on the walkway between the garage and entry were both of her parents, currently in the process of planting a batch of white and pink periwinkles in one of the flower beds.

"Give me a minute to get your door," he said as he popped open the driver's door. "Please don't embarrass me by getting out first. My mother would never forgive my poor manners if you do."

She grinned and gave him a thumbs-up. Of course she didn't need him to get her door. But she didn't mind the show of chivalry and old-fashioned manners, especially since he thought that she was special and made it hard for him to focus. She couldn't help chuckling at that declaration as he leaned on his cane, obviously struggling not to limp very much as he rounded the car to her side. Behind him, her dad and mom were staring with unabashed curiosity at the gorgeous white guy who'd brought her home, no doubt wondering what was going on.

After she and Zeus got out and he closed the door behind her, she gathered the dog's leash to keep him from taking off and looped her arm around Bryson's left one again.

He arched a brow in question. "That's probably not a good idea. You might give your parents the wrong impression about our relationship." He kept his voice low even as he nodded in answer to her father's wave.

Instead of letting go, she tightened her hold. "Did I ever mention that my dad has a bad heart?"

His eyes widened as they started up the driveway toward her parents. "I'm sorry. I had no idea."

"Oh, it's under good control. But it would probably make his heart go into palpitations if he realized that I'm investigating the killer again."

He stopped beside her. "They don't know?"

"Nope. And I aim to keep it that way. To protect Daddy." She tugged his arm to get him going again.

"Then what are you going to tell them about why I'm here?" he whispered harshly before passing his cane to his left hand so he could do the expected handshake with her father. Her mother hung a few feet back, glancing curiously between the two of them.

"I'm Nick Ray, Teagan's father. That's her mom, Sylvie."

"Nice to meet you both. I'm—"

"Bryson Anton, from Gatlinburg." Teagan flashed her best smile at her parents before dropping a bombshell. "My boyfriend."

Chapter Eleven

"Your boyfriend?" Bryson hissed almost two hours later as he was finally driving Teagan away from her parents' house. "And after telling that zinger you left me at the mercy of your very curious mom and dad while you disappeared to take a shower. I haven't had to dance that loose with the truth or change the subject so many times to avoid being pushed into a corner in, well, ever."

"But you did it. You managed to get through the inquisition and dinner while spinning the truth like a practiced politician—minus the lies. I especially liked it when my dad asked how long it had been since we'd first met and you said it felt like only yesterday." She flashed her magazine-cover smile at him.

He swore beneath his breath. "Why did you do it, Teagan? Lying by omission, or by not correcting what someone else said, is still a lie. And why trap me there for dinner when we were supposed to be there just long enough to drop off Zeus?"

Her smile faded and she looked out the window as he wove through the maze of streets toward the back of the development where the newer houses were built, where the Brodericks now lived.

They didn't want to be reminded of what had happened any more than Teagan did. It had taken quite a bit of cajoling to get them to agree to talk to him tonight. Thankfully, when he'd stepped outside of the Rays' home to make a call to ask them whether it was okay to bring Teagan, they'd said it was. He didn't want to surprise them by showing up with her. And he hadn't wanted to disappoint her either, since she was so set on going.

"Teagan?" he pressed, when she didn't answer.

She finally sighed and turned in her seat to face him. "I'm not going to apologize for doing it. Because I'd do it again if given the choice. But I do regret that I didn't warn you, and that it was so difficult for you. Honestly, I was selfishly focused on myself. I love my parents and assumed you'd enjoy their company. And my mom is a terrific cook. I hoped you would love her zucchini lasagna as much as I do and have a fun couple of hours before we—" she waved her hand toward the road as he made the last turn "—dove back into…this. I needed that break, that moment with my parents to prepare for the interview."

The sound of dejection in her voice had him feeling like a jerk. He pulled to the curb a few houses short of their destination, but left the air conditioner running to beat back the heat. He didn't know how people lived here in the summer. The humidity in March made it feel like he was stepping into a sauna every time he went outside.

"I liked your parents very much. Or, I would have, if I wasn't working so hard not to tell a bunch of lies that I'd have to apologize for later. And your mom is a fabulous cook. We couldn't have bought something at any restaurant around here and had better. But that's not the point. I'm already getting over my anger. But I deserve the truth. Why tell them I'm your boyfriend when I could have just been a friend or a friend of a friend? Now, when they ask you about me later and you tell them we broke up—or whatever your cover is going to be when I don't come back around—it will be that much harder. And it will probably make me look like a heel, thank you very much."

She clutched her hands together in her lap, and he suddenly felt like the heel he'd just described. After everything she'd been through, and the upcoming interviews about her ordeal, here he was dumping on her. Regardless of the little drama that had just played out, it was nothing compared to what she'd endured.

He placed his hand over the top of hers. She glanced at him in surprise.

"I'm sorry, Teagan. I'm making it out to be far more important than it was. Let's just drop it and—"

She shook her head. "No. I owe you an explanation. And it was far more important than you realize. Yesterday, at your house, you mentioned that your girlfriend left after your injury. Well you're not the only one. Except it was my longtime high school sweetheart. It wasn't official yet, but we'd always assumed we'd get married after we both graduated from college and got our careers going. He couldn't...he couldn't handle knowing what happened to me. Or how messed up I was for so long afterward."

He took her hand in his and entwined their fingers together. "You don't have to do this. It's okay. I understand—"

"No. You don't. Look, I'm over him. Way over him. Anyone who can't stick around through the bad isn't the one you want with you during the good. It was a blessing that I found that out before vowing to spend the rest of my life with him. The breakup was just a few months after the attack. I barely even think about him anymore. But I've never...since then I haven't...well, it's been hard to—"

"You haven't dated since?"

She squeezed her eyes shut, then nodded.

He waited in silence until she looked at him again. He

tugged one hand free and gently smoothed back a recalcitrant curl that had escaped the long braid down her back. "Since someone as gorgeous and bubbly as you could have a date any time she wants, that's obviously a personal decision. But your parents don't understand your choice, do they? They worry about you because you haven't, in their eyes at least, moved on."

She blinked as if in surprise. "How did you figure all that out so fast?"

He glanced down at his shirt and frowned. "Where's my I'm a Profiler badge? I could have sworn I was wearing that today right along with my Eagle Scout badge."

She managed a weak laugh and it warmed him inside to see her smile again. "You, Bryson Anton, were never a Boy Scout."

He pressed his free hand against his chest. "You wound me to think I couldn't be a scout." He winked. "What gave me away?"

She shook her head, her smile more carefree. "You'd have been bored to tears doing all the things they make you do to earn a badge. Instead, you'd rather be out there in the thick of things, getting lost in the woods just to see if you could find your own way out. Or setting a fire to see if you could put it out. Not exactly good scouts material."

"Looks like I'm not the only profiler around here." He squeezed her hand before letting it go. "If using me helps to make your parents worry less about you because they think you have a boyfriend, then I suppose the subterfuge is okay. Just give me some warning before you throw me in a fire next time, okay?"

He barely had time to blink before she was straddling the console, one thigh plastered against him, her generous breasts flattened against his chest. All his logical, well-thought-out arguments about not getting involved with her, especially while working the case, were incinerated the second her lips touched his.

So much for warning him before throwing him into another fire.

His whole body was being scorched from the outside in, her tongue doing amazing things with his, her long nails raising goose bumps of pleasure across the back of his neck. But he wanted more, so much more. He groaned deep in his throat and wrapped his arms around her sensuous body. Then he half turned, pulling her the rest of the way onto his lap. He kissed her the way he'd wanted to since the moment she'd stood in his doorway looking so adorable as she breathed the word "Hi." If the pain from his hip hadn't stopped him that day, he'd probably have done something juvenile, like drool. Instead, he'd focused on the pain to keep from acting like a letch.

Teagan was unlike any woman he'd ever met. He never knew what to expect from her. Half of him was annoyed that he couldn't predict her reactions even with his years of training as a profiler. The other half of him was sliding his hands around to the front of her shorts, grasping her zipper. Realizing what he was about to do, he drew on deep reserves of strength and forced his hands to release her zipper. Instead, he gently grasped her shoulders and eased her back to straddling the console instead of him. His lungs labored in his chest as they blinked at each other from only a foot apart. And he couldn't help but be pleased that she seemed to be struggling for air just as much as him.

"Holy smokes," she whispered, her voice breaking. She cleared her throat, her hands shaking as she reached up to check her hair. "Lennie what's-his-face was junior high compared to you. Heck, elementary school. That was *amazing*. I can't even remember what he looks like anymore. And we were an item for over eight years."

He grinned, his ego ridiculously inflated by her compliment. "Wait. Lennie? Your old boyfriend's name was *Lennie*?"

"No judging. People don't choose their own names." Her tongue flicked out to wet her lips, making him groan. "Kiss me again, Bryson. Before I start remembering what what's-his-face looked like."

He grabbed her upper arms and gently but firmly pushed her back. "Hell, no. We need to talk about this… thing going on between us before it goes any further. Besides, another kiss like that and I won't be able to walk for a week." He grimaced and shifted in his seat. "As it is, I won't be able to walk for a few minutes, at least."

Her gaze flew to his lap and her eyes widened. "Oh, mercy. Lennie *really* had nothing on you."

He laughed and pushed her farther away. "I'm starting to feel sorry for this Lennie guy."

Her lips firmed. "Don't. Trust me. He doesn't deserve your sympathy." She settled back down on her side of the car and drew a ragged breath.

Seeing her mood change so quickly, as if swimming through a layer of dark memories, had an ice water effect on his traitorous body—which was a good thing right now. But it also had him wanting to punch her ex-boyfriend for the hurt he'd obviously caused her.

"I've got a few friends at the Jacksonville Sheriff's Office," he said. "Where's Lennie live? I bet I could rack him up enough speeding tickets so he'd be riding the bus to work for the next six months."

Her mouth quirked in a reluctant smile. "Mercedes-Lennie on the city bus. Now that might be fun to watch."

"Just say the word."

She laughed, then pointed to the digital clock on his

dash. "Didn't you say the interview was supposed to start about now?"

He noted the time and grimaced. "Hopefully a couple of minutes won't make them change their minds. You sure you want to do this? You can drop me off and pick me up when I call."

"I've never wanted something this hard in my life. I've been in limbo for years. If you can help me end that, put this monster in prison once and for all, it will make all the difference. I can handle it. I promise."

He wasn't nearly as optimistic as she seemed to be. But he wasn't going to argue with her. If she wanted to be a part of this, as far as he was concerned, she had every right to be. Because it was her life and all about making her feel safe again.

"It's that gray-blue stucco over there, two houses down. Close enough to walk but with my hip, I'm going to be lazy and drive the last fifty yards." Once they were parked in the driveway, he grabbed his briefcase from the floorboard behind her seat.

Unlike at her parents' home, she didn't wait for him to open the door. He silently cursed his hip for slowing him down. But there was no way he could go even one more step without his cane. He hefted it from the back seat and limped after her, pain his constant companion.

He'd pushed himself harder today than any day since he'd been shot. And it showed. His hip was so stiff and ached so much that he was running more on willpower than physical strength. And after that little stunt that he and Teagan had just pulled in his car, he was practically a cripple. But he'd grit his teeth and keep going, somehow. At least until this interview was over. And the moment he reached his hotel room he was going to collapse on his bed, down some painkillers and not move until morning.

At the door, he rang the doorbell then started when Teagan clutched his right arm.

"Teagan—"

"Don't fuss at me. I'm not flirting, Bryson. Just give me a second."

He noted the stress lines around her eyes, the ashen gray tint to her brown skin. He wanted to take her hand in his, offer his strength. But he didn't have any to spare. If he let go of his cane he was afraid he'd fall down. All those times he'd blown off a rehab appointment were really coming back to bite him.

"It's okay, you've got this." He offered a reassuring smile. "*We've* got this. We're a team, together. I'm here for you, all right? Trust me."

She blew out a shaky breath and nodded just as the door opened.

A woman stood there, looking even more stressed than Teagan, her face so pale it was shockingly white in the dimly lit foyer.

Bryson lamely nodded rather than hold out his right hand since it was currently clutching his cane so he could remain upright. "Mrs. Broderick, it's nice to meet you in person. I'm Bryson Anton. This is Teagan Ray. Is this still a good time to speak with you and your husband about Teagan's abduction two years ago?"

"Of course." Her gaze darted from one to the other, then behind them before she stepped back. "We've been expecting you. Please, come in." Without waiting, she turned and strode through the long, dimly lit foyer away from them.

Bryson hesitated. "It seems as if this impending interview is far more upsetting to Mrs. Broderick than I'd expected. Maybe you should wait in the car."

"No way. I don't want to blow my chance. If I can't handle the emotions of this first interview, you won't let me go to the ones tomorrow. I'll be okay. You'll make sure of it. We're a team. That's what you said. Right?"

He regretted agreeing to take her with him for so many reasons. But they couldn't stand here waiting and make the Brodericks think they'd changed their minds. He motioned for her to step inside. She gave him a tight smile, and they started down the foyer together.

Mr. Broderick's deep voice sounded from the family room that was just visible through the arched opening a few feet away.

Teagan gasped and stopped.

He turned to see what was wrong. Her eyes were opened wide, a hand pressed to her mouth. She looked absolutely terrified.

"Teagan? What's wrong?"

"That v-voice," she croaked, obviously struggling to push any sounds out. "*His* voice."

Bryson swore as understanding dawned. He dropped his cane and clawed for the pistol holstered at his waist as he struggled to turn around without falling. White, hot pain exploded in his head and his hip crumpled beneath him. Teagan's scream was the last thing he heard as everything went dark.

Chapter Twelve

Teagan stood frozen, the horror of what was happening—again—seeping into her bones like leaden concrete, anchoring her in place. Her pulse hammered in her ears, blocking out the sounds around her. It was as if her mind had separated from her body and all of this was happening to someone else.

Bryson. Sweet, wonderful Bryson lay dead at her feet, his dark hair matted with blood. She'd only caught a glimpse of his battered body before jerking her gaze up toward the man who'd hit him, fully expecting the next blow from the baseball bat to land on her. Even so, she couldn't raise her arms to defend herself. She. Couldn't. Move.

Instead of hitting her, he'd taken Bryson's pistol out of his holster, then shoved his hand in her pocket and yanked out her gun too, all before she could even blink. How had he known she had the gun when even she, in her moment of need, had forgotten it?

He'd been just inches from her but after taking the guns, he'd walked away. She watched helplessly, uselessly still as a statue, as the man—oh God, *that voice*—crossed the family room to the woman cowering in the corner. What was her name? Broderick. Mrs. Broderick. A trap. She'd led Bryson and Teagan into a trap. Why? Why would she do that?

The woman's lips moved. She was looking up at the man, hovering over her with the bloody baseball bat in his right hand. She was saying something, pleading? The words were lost in Teagan's fractured mind, unable to penetrate the sound of her own heartbeat rushing in her ears. *Thump. Thump. Thump.* Her heart pounded against her rib cage, white noise that masked everything around her. The tableau played out like a silent movie before her, a nightmare. Because surely none of this was real. It couldn't be.

Not again. Not again. She couldn't survive this again.

The man lifted the bat.

No. Teagan tried to yell, to get her legs to move. She had to help the lady. But her throat was so tight she couldn't make a sound. Her legs were shaking so hard she couldn't take a step.

He brought the bat down in a deadly arc.

Bam! Bam! Bam!

Oh dear God, please, no! The bat. The woman. Bile rose in Teagan's throat. A low-keening moan filled her ears, and the man jerked around to look at her. She realized that she was the one making that awful sound.

The room around her darkened, like a tunnel, narrowing down to one point where all she could see was the man across the room, watching her. Everything centered on what she'd never seen until this very moment. His face. She'd known that voice, the devil's voice. To this day, it haunted her dreams. But that face. How could such evil hide behind such an average, kind-looking face?

There was nothing remarkable about it. He was white, clean-shaven, his light brown hair streaked with blond that had no doubt cost a fortune at some expensive salon. Which meant this man had money, a job, likely a home, a car. A family? He was just like anyone else she'd pass on the street.

Except that he wasn't.

The eyes. The eyes gave him away. They were dark, almost black, completely devoid of warmth. An abyss of emptiness, a deep well of evil with no soul to warm them. They were the eyes of the monster who'd hurt her two years ago. The same monster who'd just brutally killed Mrs. Broderick. And the wonderful man lying at Teagan's feet.

She couldn't look down. Couldn't stomach seeing the damage the bat must have done. She didn't want that image burned into her retinas. Bryson. Smart, gorgeous, sweet Bryson Anton, who wouldn't even be here if it wasn't for her.

Forgive me, Bryson.

Evil stared back at her from twenty feet away. Blood dripped from the bat in his hand. She shuddered as a wave of nausea gripped her.

He smiled, as if pleased at her distress. Then he started toward her, still holding that awful bat. Slowly. Like a lion stalking the weakest member of the herd, separating it out, readying for the kill.

Her mind screamed at her. *Move. Run. Do something.*

But she couldn't. Why not? She'd run before. Two years ago, when her attacker injected drugs to put her to sleep, but missed the vein, she'd taken advantage of his mistake. She'd pretended to be asleep. And then, after hearing the sound of his car driving away, she'd forced one foot in front of the other. She'd gotten away.

There were neighbors close by. Some of them had to be home. Most of them had to be home. The workday was over for the nine-to-fivers. All she had to do was turn around and...no.

She couldn't leave Bryson.

She didn't deserve to survive yet again when he lay at her feet in his own blood. It was her fault. This, then, would be her penance. Face the monster. Pay the price for bringing Bryson here, for destroying a wonderful man.

Shoes echoed against the floor. Hardwood. Like her parents' house. He was coming closer. Relentlessly. Slowly. Savoring her fear.

She whimpered, and hated herself for it. She was about to die. She wanted to face him with dignity in her last moments. But the wounds of the past were too much to overcome. Her body wasn't her own anymore to command. She couldn't stop shaking. Maybe she was already dead.

Evil stopped three feet away.

She forced herself to meet his gaze, to memorize every line, every bump, every angle of his ridiculously ordinary face, refusing to look away as fate raised the bat once more. If she couldn't run, at least she could stand here and pretend courage she didn't possess. There would be no defensive wounds for her. But as she stared at him, a strange sense of déjà vu swept through her. She'd seen him before. Not at the shack. He'd always concealed his identity back then. So she had to have seen him somewhere else. But where? Who was he?

He raised the bat higher, watching her, as if waiting to see what she would do. As she remained motionless, his smile faded. She wasn't giving him the satisfaction of cowering. She was ruining his fun.

Hooray for her. Finally she'd beaten him. If only in a very small way. This time it was her turn to smile.

Hate glittered in his eyes as he slowly lowered the bat. He tossed it onto a nearby chair and reached behind him. Metal glittered in the overhead lights. A gun? No. Silver circles. A short chain connecting them. Handcuffs. He'd bound her last time, tied her with strips of cloth. But never handcuffs. She'd cut through the strips with her teeth after the drug had failed to knock her unconscious. Perhaps he'd changed his routine since then. He'd learned from his mistakes.

He moved with a swiftness that was terrifying. Too late, she tried to twist away. But the sound of one of the cuffs ratcheting onto her left wrist echoed in the foyer. He yanked her wrist down toward the floor. She fell to her knees, sliding in the sticky wet blood. Bryson's blood.

Dear, sweet Bryson. Lying on the floor, his face turned toward her. Eyes closed forever.

His murderer slapped the other handcuff onto Bryson's right wrist and ratcheted it closed, anchoring her to his body. She looked up in question. He'd retrieved the bat, but instead of slamming it down on her, ending this, he turned away. His shoes clomped across the floor as he headed down the hall to the left. Dress pants. He was wearing gray dress pants and a white shirt. A formerly white shirt. Had he just left work? What kind of person did this—entered someone's house and beat them to death after getting off work, like it was a normal part of their day?

A hysterical laugh bubbled up in her throat, but died before reaching her lips. The monster had opened a door and headed inside. A muffled sound echoed from the room. Was someone else there? The sickening unmistakable crunch of wood on bone had her gasping in horror. The other half of the couple who lived here, Mr. Broderick. He must have been in the room, probably tied up. A bribe so that his wife would do what the monster told her to do.

Bile rose again in her throat. She turned away from Bryson's body just in time to empty the contents of her stomach against the foyer wall. She shuddered and wiped her mouth.

"Dear Lord," she prayed, the whisper finally passing through her tight throat. "Please let me die quickly. And don't let me grovel or beg for my life. Give me strength. Please, God. Help me."

Something fluttered against her shoe.

She gasped and whirled around. The fingers of Bryson's right hand moved against her, tapped her toe. She shot him a look of shock, and met his pain-filled startling blue gaze.

"Bryson," she whispered. "You're alive. Oh my God. Bryson." She lifted her shaking right hand to his face and gently cupped it. "I'm so sorry. Please forgive me."

His eyes seemed unfocused. He coughed and blood dribbled out of his mouth to the floor.

"Shhh," she whispered. "Don't try to talk." She jerked her head up, realizing there weren't any sounds in the other room anymore. He'd be coming out soon. Coming for her and Bryson. "Close your eyes," she whispered. "Play dead. He thinks you're dead. Just, no matter what happens to me, just lay there. Don't move. Do you hear me? Play dead. It's your only chance."

His fingers tapped her again and his lips moved.

She glanced down the hall, then leaned down, trying to hear what he was saying.

"Run. Get. Away." His whisper was so low she could barely make it out. "Go."

Tears splashed onto his face and she realized she was crying. "Oh, Bryson. I'm sorry. I thought you were… I thought it was too late. And I couldn't make myself leave you. And now, I can't." She lifted her left hand, showing him the handcuffs that bound them together. "It's okay, though," she whispered, looking down the hall again. What was taking the monster so long? What was he doing in there? "It's okay," she repeated. "There's nothing I can do to save myself. I accept that. But he thinks you're already dead. Lie very still. No matter what. You'll make it. Just play dead."

His lips moved again, his eyes pleading with her to listen. "Cane. Get. Cane."

"You think you can stand?" A rush of hope flooded through her. "Here. I'll help you."

"Cane," his hoarse whisper was louder now. "Get the cane."

She stretched out their linked hands and scrambled over, reaching out her right hand as far as she could. It took some contorting, but she was finally able to grab it. "Got it."

"I'll take that." The monster jerked it out of her hand and backed up several feet. "Getting feisty, Teagan? Planning on trying to beat me over the head with this like I did your friend?" He chuckled and motioned toward Bryson. "Give me his cell phone. And yours. Hurry."

"Mine is in my purse." She motioned toward her purse where it had fallen to the foyer floor earlier.

"Prove it. Turn your shorts pockets inside out."

She did as he asked.

"Now his. Get his cell phone and toss it to me so I can verify that you don't do something stupid, like try to press 911 before you give it to me. If you do that, you're both dead. Understood?"

She drew a ragged breath and nodded, then dug in Bryson's suit jacket pockets until she found his phone. For the briefest second, she hesitated, desperately wanting to press the three precious keys that would call for help. But the monster was watching. And he'd shifted the aim of his gun toward Bryson's head as if in warning. She hurriedly stood as best she could with her arm cuffed to Bryson and tossed him the phone.

After checking the screen, he threw the phone on the couch, then motioned toward Bryson again. "Take that watch thing off his wrist and get rid of it. I don't know what it can do, whether you can make calls with it. I'm not taking chances."

She quickly took it off and tossed it down the foyer.

"Help him up. We'll bring him with us. I need to know how much he knows before I kill him."

She hesitated. "He's already dead. Just uncuff me and I'll go with you."

He made a clucking, disapproving sound with his mouth. "Now, Teagan. Don't lie to me. I doubt I hit him hard enough to kill him. But if you'd rather I take care of things right now, to make it easier for you so you don't have to help him walk, I can get the bat—"

"No!" She shook her head. "Please. Don't. Just…give me the cane. I'll help him. But I need the cane to get him on his feet, to help him walk."

He tossed the cane down beside her. "I'd help but I don't want to get his blood on my nice clean shirt."

She blinked and realized he was wearing a different shirt now, a light blue one tucked into navy blue dress pants. Even his shoes, which had been black earlier had been exchanged for gunmetal gray ones. He must have washed himself off and changed into some of Mr. Broderick's clothes. Right after killing the poor man.

Swallowing hard, she looked down. Bryson's eyes were open again. He was staring at her.

I'm so sorry, she mouthed, regret heavy in her heart that she'd wasted her chance to get help for him. Had she suspected he was still alive, she would have forced herself to turn around, to run to the nearest neighbor and call 911. Instead, she'd been frozen by fear and the belief that he'd been killed. She'd given up. And because of her cowardly actions, now he was still in horrible danger, when she might have been able to save him.

"Get him on his feet. Now. If you take too long, I'll shoot you both and be done with it."

She wanted to demand that he be done with it right now. But that was no longer an option. It wasn't just her life on the line now. She had to be brave, strong, and somehow figure out how to get Bryson out of this mess. She awkwardly straightened his legs, apologizing profusely every time she jostled him because of their hands being handcuffed together.

Finally she got him into a sitting position with his back pressed against the opposite wall of the foyer from where she'd been sick. White lines around his mouth clearly mirrored his pain. His hip had to be excruciating right now, on top of the awful bump on his head. She reached up to test it and he winced, ducking away from her hand.

"You're not bleeding anymore," she whispered. "That's a good sign."

"Hurry up," the monster ordered. "The daughter will be home soon."

Teagan and Bryson exchanged a look of horror. The idea of a daughter coming home to find her parents slaughtered by this man was beyond awful. But still being here when she got home would ensure that she too would be killed. As if coming to the same realization, Bryson began pushing against the wall, struggling to get to his feet.

She faced him, their hands clasped together as she helped him up the rest of the way. As soon as she was sure he wasn't about to fall, she got the cane and put it in his left hand. He normally held it in his right, to compensate for his bad left hip when he raised his right leg. But with his right hand cuffed to hers, that wasn't an option. It would be rough going. She hoped she had the strength to keep him from falling.

"Come on. Out the back." The monster was holding a

gun now. Bryson's gun. He motioned with it and stepped out of reach of the cane or a well-aimed kick, not that they could manage either one shackled together with Bryson hurt.

More from willpower than physical strength, the two of them managed to hobble out the open French door, across the patio, all while being directed by the gunman. He closed the door behind them, probably to throw off anyone trying to find the perpetrator who'd murdered the Brodericks. But where was he going? He stopped at the six-foot-tall wooden privacy fence that encircled the large backyard.

He motioned them forward with the gun. When they stopped a few feet away, he lifted one of the sections of fence back from the post it should have been nailed to. Perhaps this was the way he'd gotten into the Brodericks' home? He'd come from behind them, loosening the section of fence to act much like a gate.

Just the way he'd abducted Teagan years earlier? Until this very moment, she'd never remembered how he'd managed to get her off the path without anyone seeing her. It had always been a confusing image in her mind—a creaking sound that she'd attributed to the breezes in the branches overhead, but that she now realized must have been him opening a pre-loosened section of fence; her turning around just as the bite of a needle plunged into her neck and a hand clamped over her mouth. Darkness descending around the edges of her vision as he'd tossed her over his shoulder. That creaking sound again. He'd closed the fence behind them. That must have been what happened.

"Teagan?" Bryson whispered, between lips white with pain. "We have to move."

The gunman was pointing the pistol at her. He must

have told her to get going and was threatening to shoot her. She squeezed Bryson's hand, then struggled forward with him leaning heavily against her, their cuffed hands clutched tightly together.

The gunman waved them toward the back of the house whose yard they were now in while he secured the section of fence behind them. As they reached the screened-in porch, the cut screen on the door told the story that she had feared. She exchanged a look of misery with Bryson before helping him through the door that the killer had obviously gone through earlier.

But how had he known that she would be at the Brodericks'?

That question was eating at her. And she had no answers. She wanted to ask Bryson, but doubted he could think much beyond the pain that was clearly radiating through his whole body. It was taking everything he had to remain upright, as evidenced by how hard he was leaning on her and how often he stumbled. It didn't help that the house was carpeted. It was much harder for him to keep his balance, and he fell against the wall more than once.

"To the garage, that door over there." The gunman motioned ahead to the right, then ducked through an archway to their left into the kitchen.

"Where are we?" Bryson whispered as they hobbled toward the garage.

"Bentwater Place," she whispered back. "The subdivision directly behind The Woods. The entrance to this subdivision is about a mile, maybe more, from the Hodges Boulevard entrance to The Woods."

He nodded as they reached the door that led from the house into the garage. It was standing wide open, revealing a small package delivery truck inside. Any hope that Teagan had that he hadn't hurt the driver died when she saw the piles of packages taking up most of the space on the other side of the garage. No driver would have willingly allowed someone to dump the contents of his truck. How many people had to be hurt or die because of whatever sick fantasies this guy had?

"Find the button that opens the garage door," Bryson urged. "If someone's outside, we can try to get their attention."

"Do it and I'll shoot both of you," the killer said from behind them.

Teagan stiffened and looked over her shoulder. His dark, empty eyes bored into hers. The maw of the pistol was pointed directly at the back of Bryson's head.

"What do you want us to do now?" She steadied Bryson's shaking body against the garage wall beside the doorway. He was so pale she was afraid he was about to pass out.

"Get in the back of the truck." The sound of sirens filled the air, coming from somewhere behind them. The killer froze, cocking his head to listen. The sirens got louder. There could be no mistake. They were racing toward the Brodericks' house. The daughter must have gotten home and called 911. And the police had to have been close by to be responding this quickly. Any minute now, they'd be standing in the home that was separated from this one by about fifty feet of grass and a privacy fence.

If she screamed, would they hear her?

As if reading the intention in her expression, the killer shoved the gun's muzzle against the back of Bryson's head. "In the truck. Now. If you scream, if you do anything to alert the police, I'll shoot both of you, him first. Then I'll find another family a few houses down to kill and drive away in their car as the police try to figure out where the shots came from. You'll be dead, another family will be dead, but I'll be just fine. Is that what you want? Me to kill your boyfriend and another innocent family, all because you refuse to follow instructions?"

"We're going." She forced the words out between clenched teeth.

Bryson looked like he wanted to argue. But he was in no physical condition to do so. They hobbled to the end of the truck. The gunman twisted the handles and yanked open both of the doors. Just as expected, it was empty. No windows. No pass-through to the cab. Just a metal box, with no way out but the back doors. Which required getting past their armed escort.

It took some grunting and contorting because of how their hands were cuffed together to get both of them into the back. As soon as their feet cleared the doors, one of them slammed shut.

The gunman paused in the opening of the other door. "I'll take that cane for now. Don't want you trying to poke me with it when I open the door again." He yanked the cane away from Bryson and sealed them inside.

Chapter Thirteen

"He didn't blindfold us," Teagan said.

Bryson hated the fear in her tone. He knew exactly what she was afraid of, that because the man who'd abducted them hadn't blindfolded them, it meant he intended to kill them. He wasn't worried about witnesses, or that they could identify him later. But reassuring her right now was beyond Bryson's abilities. He was struggling just to stay conscious. That blow to his head had really done a number on him.

The darkness in the back of the truck was absolute, which was disorienting enough. But his aching hip and throbbing head were each trying to outdo the other in the pain department, which made his efforts to wrangle his scattered thoughts next to impossible.

"Bryson?" She moved her left hand against his right one and interlaced their fingers. "How bad does it hurt? Your head?"

He gently squeezed her fingers. "Don't worry about me. I'm fine."

"Maybe if you said that without pain making your voice so raspy I'd believe you." She clasped her right hand over their joined hands. "I'm so sorry. None of this would have happened if it wasn't for me involving you. I never should have gone to Gatlinburg and interfered with your life. That was beyond selfish. And now, we're both going to die—"

"Hey, hey. Stop that. You didn't do anything wrong. I'm the professional. I should have been on guard against this type of possibility. But what matters right now is that you don't give up. You hear me, Teagan Ray? Don't you dare give up." He waited, but when she didn't respond he said, "If you're nodding or shaking that beautiful head of yours, or making some kind of rude gesture, your effort's wasted. I completely forgot to pack my night-vision goggles this trip."

A brief laugh reassured him like nothing else could have. He needed her present, engaged, not frozen and helpless the way he'd seen her in the foyer after he'd finally managed to swim through the darkness that had threatened to drag him under. He wasn't sure how long he'd lain there after that awful slam of the bat against his head. He hadn't even seen the bat until later, when they were leaving, lying on one of the chairs. It had shocked him that he was still alive with the amount of blood covering the bat.

Then he'd seen Mrs. Broderick.

She'd been curled in a lifeless heap on the other side of the room. He knew then that not all of the blood on the bat was his. The poor woman had been brutally attacked. Even though it didn't feel like it, he was lucky to be alive. For now.

"Aren't you going to say I told you so?" she asked, interrupting his thoughts.

He had to draw several deep breaths to push back the hazy fog that kept trying to drag him into unconsciousness. What had she said? Something about I told you so. "What are you talking about?"

"Avarice Lowe. I'd pegged him all along as the man who'd abducted me. But I was wrong. It's this man. Whoever's driving this stupid truck. The thing is, Lowe never seemed to fit the image of the monster in my head. I know it sounds wonky. But I always thought I'd know my abductor if I ever saw him, by the way he was built, his profile, something. Nothing ever clicked for me when I saw Lowe's pictures. And, to be honest, nothing clicked when I saw this guy today. Not really. I mean, his voice, yes. Definitely. And yet, even though he seems familiar, he doesn't seem…right. It's still not clicking." He could feel her shoulders move against him as she shrugged. "Listen to me. I'm not even making sense."

"Always…trust your instincts." He swallowed hard against the bile rising in his throat. Obviously he had a concussion. All he wanted to do was lie down and sleep. Or throw up. Or both. He cleared his throat and tried again to follow the conversation. "Instincts. They're telling you something. What did you mean when you said he seemed familiar?"

"His face."

"His face?"

"It just seemed…familiar. He's the kind of guy you could pass on the street a bazillion times and you might think, okay, he's kind of good-looking. Clean-cut. But nothing amazing. Just a typical, white-collar kind of man, you know? And yet, I would swear that I've seen him before. Not just once. Several times."

He rubbed his left temple, desperately trying to beat back the throbbing pain and focus on what she was saying. There was something important here, more important than her thinking she'd seen him before. But he couldn't seem to grasp what was bothering him about what she'd just said. Finally he dropped his hand to his side, giving up for now. Whatever was bothering him would come to him, eventually.

"Maybe he lives in The Woods," he offered. "You've passed him on the street, on the sidewalk. Or saw him at that amenity center. Do you ever use the tennis courts, the pool?"

"The pool sometimes. But I haven't in a long time. Not since, well, I never was a fan of a one-piece bathing suit. Too grandma for me. But I don't think wearing a bikini is exactly a good idea now."

He wanted to reassure her, tell her that no one would notice the X that had been cut into her skin. But people could be cruel. Some probably would stare. Others might ask a question, innocently thinking she'd had that X carved there on purpose, like a tattoo. They might wonder at the symbolism and significance, without realizing they were bringing up a horrific memory that she'd rather forget.

He'd just started to doze off again when she asked, "What are we going to do?" Her voice was a low whisper, as if to keep the driver from hearing them. "Please tell me you have a plan."

He didn't have a clue. He tightened his hold on her hand. "We'll figure it out. Together. Two against one. We've got this."

The truck hit a bump in the road, knocking them against each other. He scooted back against the wall, trying to keep from slamming into her. But she had no such compulsion. She moved closer, her body plastered against his side. But unlike earlier, there was nothing suggestive about her actions. He could feel the slight shaking of her shoulders and realized she was silently crying. Carefully, so he wouldn't hit her face, he maneuvered their handcuffed hands so that he could put his arm around her, pulling their linked hands tight against her belly. She cradled her head against his neck.

He tried to pay attention to the changes in road noise,

traffic sounds, the turns the truck made. But everything was so muffled that he had no clue where they might be. Had it been an hour? Two? He had no idea. With his watch gone, and his mind a fog, time as he knew it didn't exist anymore. His every moment was measured by stabs of pain that shot through his body with every beat of his heart. His hip had long ago gone numb. But, if anything, the pain in his head was worse than before. He felt every shift of the truck's wheels on the pavement, every pothole, every slide of gravel.

Wait. Gravel?

"We're slowing down," she whispered.

He nodded, then remembered she couldn't see him. "Yes. We are. And we've turned onto a gravel road. Wherever he's taking us, we're close." He carefully pulled their linked arms over her head so they were side by side again, instead of nestled against each other.

The brakes squealed as the truck lurched to a halt.

Her fingers clenched his. "Now would be a good time to share your plan."

Right. If only he had one. His thoughts were so jumbled. "Stay alert. Be observant. As soon as that door opens, evaluate your options and react. If he's stupid enough to stand in striking distance, we tackle him. But I don't expect he'll do that."

"So we have no plan."

He sighed. "Pretty much. But that doesn't mean there's no hope. All it takes is one mistake on his part, one moment when his guard is down. Then we'll get the upper hand."

"Do you really believe that?"

"I have to. We both have to. I'm not operating on all pistons right now, and my vision was blurry at the Brodericks' house so I'm not expecting much better when he lets us out of here. I need you to fill in the gaps. Pay attention when he opens that door. Get a three-sixty view. We need to know what's around us. Where to run if we get a chance."

"Okay. I'll… I'll do my best."

The driver's door creaked open.

"Come on," he urged. "Let's scoot to the end in case we can surprise him, take him down."

Getting to his knees was beyond his capabilities at the moment. Instead, he had to scoot across the metal floor of the truck. Thankfully, it wasn't that large and they were soon positioned beside each other at the doors.

The sound of shoes crunching on gravel came from outside. He was heading toward the back.

Bryson could feel her shivering against him. He silently cursed the man with all the power right now, the man who'd hurt her more than most people endured in their entire lifetime.

He gritted his teeth and braced himself, hoping she was ready to dive with him to tackle the man. There was no other option since they were still handcuffed together.

The left door flew back. Bryson hadn't planned on near total darkness and hesitated for a moment. But Teagan was already hopping out of the truck. He hurriedly followed and together they rushed forward, hoping to wrap arms around their attacker. They both met empty air and stumbled against each other before falling back against the closed right door. It was the only reason Bryson managed to remain upright.

Laughter sounded off to the left. A powerful flashlight switched on, forcing them to squint and shield their eyes against the brightness.

"Good try." The man chuckled again. "But I assumed you'd pull a stunt like that so I stayed behind the door, out of reach." He lowered the light to point at the ground, directly in front of them. Dirt and gravel mixed with pine needles and other debris. Since the only sounds were insects buzzing close by, it was a safe bet that they were somewhere outside of town, an hour, two, maybe more from Jacksonville if his judgment on how much time had passed was accurate. But he couldn't be sure. Their captor may have driven in circles to disorient them and then drove to some rural part of town. Jacksonville was the largest city in the country by landmass, so they could easily still be in Duval County but nowhere near any homes or businesses.

Teagan's fingers curled around his. Perhaps she was beginning to realize how isolated they were, and wondering the same thing that he was—what happens next?

Without the flashlight in his eyes, he was able to make out more details now. The moon and stars provided enough light to see that they were surrounded by trees and Florida scrub, mostly small thin bushes and sharp palmettos ready to skewer anyone foolish enough to go for a walk in the woods.

The gunman stood about twenty feet away, out of reach, a dark silhouette with his arm extended, pistol gleaming in his grip. "Get moving." He motioned with the flashlight to their right, aiming it at what was apparently their destination, a tiny cabin.

"I need my cane," Bryson called out.

The flashlight swept back toward their captor. He aimed it up toward his own face, a slow smile spreading across his cheeks as he pulled something out of his pocket. "Let me guess. Because you wanted these?" He shook the two tiny keys on the end of a chain, making them click against each other. "Handcuff keys hidden in the cane's handle. I knew you were awfully insistent on wanting that stupid thing. Took me half the trip fiddling with it to figure it out."

He threw the keys into the trees, then leaned down and grabbed the cane, which had been lying at his feet. "Afraid you'll have to do without it. I'm not risking another trick in that thing that I haven't figured out yet." He tossed the cane into the woods behind him. "Now go on." He swept the flashlight in an arc toward the cabin again. "Teagan, stop standing there like a statue and help your boyfriend before he falls down." He chuckled.

Bryson looked at her. She hadn't moved since they'd tried tackling the gunman without success. Her fingers holding his were cold, stiff. Her body shook as she stared wide-eyed at the little house in the clearing. And then it dawned on him why. He'd seen it before, in crime scene photos.

The killer had brought them back in time, two years to be exact. He'd brought them to the infamous shack where he'd once held Teagan captive.

Chapter Fourteen

The world had disappeared for Teagan. Everything had faded away the moment she'd jumped out of the truck and the flashlight revealed what she should have expected, but hadn't allowed herself to believe. He'd taken her back to the dilapidated shack where she'd spent two weeks in a drug-induced stupor, drifting in a haze of pain from the torture that her captor had put her through.

She pressed a hand to her belly, remembering that first night, when he'd slowly carved the X in her flesh. The pain had been excruciating. With her arms and legs tied and him straddling her, there was nothing she could do to escape the slow awful burn of the blade. She'd screamed so loudly that something in her throat burst and she'd almost drowned in her own blood.

After escaping this hellhole, she'd charted a new path for her life. She'd focused her energies on becoming stronger, both physically and mentally. When the police seemed to be getting nowhere with the investigation, she'd taken it over herself, doing everything she could to try to discover the identity of the man who'd reduced her to the broken woman she'd become for those fourteen days. And she'd thought she had. She'd been so sure that Avarice Lowe was the real Ripper, the man who'd branded her like a steer. The fact that no one else believed her didn't dissuade her.

Instead, it made her angry, and even more determined to find someone who'd help her put Lowe away. She'd thought Bryson was that someone, the one person who would read her file and finally tell her that she was right.

But she wasn't right. Bryson was right, had been all along.

It was as if everything she'd done for the past twenty-four months and nineteen days was a sham, a waste, a farce. Here she was again, where it had all started. And she'd managed to condemn Bryson to share this hell with her. This time, both of them would die.

"Sweetheart, look at me," Bryson's whispered words seemed to come to her from the end of a long tunnel. "Come back to me. Don't give up. Don't let him win."

She couldn't see him, couldn't see anyone, or anything. Not the dark shapes of the trees, or the twinkling lights of the stars, or the moon, or even the gravel rocks at her feet. The devil himself, the one who'd brought them here, had faded too. All she saw was the little shack.

Hovel was more accurate.

Four walls covered in weathered gray wood that was splintered and warped. No electricity, which meant no air-conditioning, unless that had been changed. The inside consisted of a small bedroom and bathroom on the back left corner, a tiny main room and a kitchen up front. Although calling the cooking area a kitchen was being generous. It consisted of a handful of homemade-looking cabinets and drawers, a tiny refrigerator like those in hotel rooms and a compact gas stove fed by a propane tank outside. The bathroom, as she remembered it, was so filthy she'd had to close her eyes when he'd shoved her inside and stood guard at the open door, watching. Always watching. Or touching, hurting her in unspeakable ways.

Dear Lord, please, let me die. Strike me with lightning, something, just don't let him...touch me...not again. Please.

"Teagan, look at me. Open your eyes." Bryson's gentle but firm voice cut through her terror, snapped her out of her semi-stupor.

She openly stared up at him. The moon's light wasn't enough to see the blue of his eyes, but she remembered their beautiful color, and the kindness in them. She remembered how ruggedly handsome he was. He was so sweet and smart and...*and he was going to die.*

A low keening moan slipped out between her clenched teeth. Her hands shook as she started to lift them. But her left hand pulled up short because of the cuffs. He bent his arm to allow her more movement, frowning, apparently wondering what she was doing, but helping her. Always helping her. She lifted her arms again and this time she was able to cup his face.

"We have to kill him," she whispered. "Before he makes us go into that horrible shack. He won't shoot me, not right away. That would spoil his fun. We'll refuse to go inside and he'll have to come close. As long as you duck down in front of me, I can shield you—"

"The hell with that." His clipped tone brooked no argument. "I'm not using you as a human shield." He grabbed her left hand and pulled it down with his, their handcuffs rattling against each other. "I don't have a plan yet but putting you in the line of fire isn't at the top of my list. It's not even *on* the list. Forget it."

"Hey, you two. Get moving." *Bam!*

The warning shot kicked up dirt near their feet. Teagan threw herself against Bryson's chest, desperately trying to shield his body with hers.

He swore and shoved her as far from him as the cuffs would allow. His glare told her exactly what he thought of her attempt to protect him. But without her to lean on, he stumbled. She rushed forward and jammed her left shoulder beneath his right, bracing him again. The pained look on his face told her he hated that he needed her help. But he didn't push her away again.

"Next one goes in your head, FBI guy. Or Justice Seeker. Is that what you go by? Seems I heard that somewhere. You need to do what I say, when I say it. Or you can seek your justice six feet under."

Justice Seeker? Bryson probably mentioned that he was a former FBI profiler when he spoke to the Brodericks to lend him credibility so they'd agree to speak to him. But would he say anything about being a Justice Seeker? Not likely. It had taken her months of digging to track Bryson to the Seekers. How did this animal know about them?

"I need my cane." Bryson's voice was hoarse, a testament to the amount of pain he was in after their little dance in the dirt. "I can't walk without it. Unlock these handcuffs and send Teagan to retrieve it for me."

"So she can take off and escape? I don't think so. Good try though. But I'm tired of waiting." He aimed the gun at Bryson's leg.

Teagan rushed in front of him to his left side to better help him, their cuffed hands pulled awkwardly across his waist. He was really struggling, his left leg shaking as if it was about to collapse.

His look of regret confirmed that he realized the same thing. He gave her a curt nod of thanks, then lurched forward.

The thirty or so feet to the shack felt more like a mile trudging through wet cement. But finally they were at the two steps that led up to the tilted, rotting front porch. There was no railing, nothing for Bryson to cling to except her. But they made the climb together, pausing just outside the front door.

Instead of the dry-rotting wood she remembered, this door was shiny and new, its glass front encased in a black wrought-iron frame with a network of vertical bars just like she'd expect to see on a jail cell. And both of the small front windows, to the left and right of the door, were covered in the same black bars. He'd converted the shack into a jail.

There'd be no escape this time.

She pulled the door open and glanced up at Bryson. His eyes were glazing over, unfocused. He tried to say something, but couldn't seem to get the words out.

She practically dragged him inside as he teetered back and forth. Thankfully the couch was right where it had been the last time, four or five feet from the door. If turned sideways, it would probably scrape both walls, if it would even fit.

He fell from her grip onto the cushions, pulling her down with him. She managed to push off the back cushion so she didn't fall on top of him. Instead, she slid to the floor, her left arm raised to not jerk his right arm. Not that he would have felt it. His eyes were already closed. He'd passed out.

The sound of metal grating against metal had her jerking her head around to see what the gunman was doing. To her relief, he hadn't followed them inside. But to her horror, he'd just locked the door. He grinned as he pulled his key out of the round lock that required a key on both sides—not the kind where you could flip it from the inside.

He aimed the flashlight up, casting an eerie, sinister look across his face. "I'll give you two lovebirds some alone time," he teased, adding a wink that had her wanting to throw up again. "Make sure he's ready to answer my questions when I get back. I want to know what the cops know. If he can't talk, he's of no use to me."

She'd wondered why he'd gone to the trouble of taking both her and Bryson instead of killing him at the Brodericks'. Now she knew it was because he wanted to interrogate him.

"Today caught me off guard, I gotta admit," he continued. "I'm not really prepared. Don't have my...supplies handy. But don't you worry. I remember everything you like. I'll make sure I come back with just the right stuff." He leaned closer, pressing his face against the glass. "How's my mark on your belly looking?"

She automatically pressed her hand against her stomach, her entire body shaking as she stared at him. Hot tears coursed down her cheeks in spite of her efforts to hold them back.

His grin widened, his bright white teeth sparkling in the light. "Don't worry. I'll freshen it up a bit, make sure it hasn't...faded, since our last meeting." He chuckled and hopped off the porch, the flashlight's beam bouncing across the gravel as he headed toward the truck.

Chapter Fifteen

Bryson blinked in the near darkness, a fog of confusion roiling through his mind. Where was he? How did he get here? And why was he lying on a couch that, judging by the lumps and musty smell, clearly wasn't his?

He braced his hands on the cushions to push himself up but the tug of a cold chain against his right wrist had him stopping to look down. A small form lay curled up on the floor, her left arm propped against the couch. As his eyes adjusted to the dark and he was able to make out more details, he noticed the gleaming silver circle around both their wrists. They were handcuffed together. Still confused, he leaned down for a better look. Teagan. She was on the floor, without even a pillow for her head.

What was going on?

Her eyes were closed and she was asleep, albeit a fitful one, her elegant brows drawn into a frown. Having never seen her hair anything but perfect, he was surprised to see curls forming a halo around her face, escaping the tight braid that hung down her back. Even worse, there were dark splotches on her blouse. The color was lost to him in the darkness, but there was no mistaking the metallic smell.

Blood.

Memories slammed into him. Awful glimpses of the

reality that had happened, and where those dark splotches had come from. He softly touched one to make sure it wasn't wet, then pulled his hand back in relief. It wasn't her blood. It was his. Thank goodness she hadn't been hurt. But that would change the moment their captor returned.

Careful not to jostle their joined wrists, he managed to push himself to a sitting position so he could take stock of their situation. It didn't look good. The front iron-barred door was closed, no doubt locked, but the glass provided a moonlit view of the gravel road and clearing out front. They were empty, the delivery truck nowhere in sight.

He studied all four walls in the main room as best he could in the limited light. Both of the front windows were covered in bars. He imagined the one other window that he'd seen in police photos, the one in the tiny bedroom down a short hall, was also barred. The adjacent bathroom didn't have a window, unless that had been changed over the past two years.

The place was too small to be called a hunting cabin, which was what the owner had called it in the police reports. Had he been the one to install the bars and new door after what had happened here? Or had he sold the cabin, unknowingly, to the very killer who'd been using it all along as his own? Maybe the original owner was the killer, and the police had mistakenly cleared him.

Those were only some of the questions going through his mind. Along with the one that had been niggling him since the tragedy that had happened at the Brodericks': How had the killer known that Teagan would be there?

"Bryson, are you feeling better?" Her voice sounded groggy.

She was shoving to her knees, already reaching up to check on him. He grabbed her hands in his and kissed them before letting go.

"I hate that I slept at all. But I needed it. I'm thinking more clearly."

"What about the pain? Your head? Your hip? I could massage—"

He stopped her wandering hands and teased. "Boundaries, Teagan."

She smiled, somewhat reluctantly. "I sure never thought our first time sleeping together we'd actually be, well, sleeping."

"Maybe next time it will be different."

Her eyes widened like an owl's in the darkness. "If you really mean that, I'll bust out one of these walls to get us out of here. And I'll hold you to your word."

He laughed, amazed that he *could* in a situation like this. "Now there's the sassy, sexy, smart woman I remember. I think that sleep did both of us some good. But we can't sit around any longer. We have to get out of here before he comes back."

She moved her arm, frowning when the short chain between their wrists stopped her movement. "You had handcuff keys in your cane. Why didn't you tell me?"

"I wasn't even sure they were still there. It was a gag gift from Bishop, one of the Justice Seekers, after the shooting. He gave me a set of handcuffs and put the keys in the head of the cane, teasing that I could use them to keep my girlfriend at my side through my convalescence. That was after the nurses complained about how bad a patient I was in the hospital."

The corners of her mouth turned up in a small smile. "I can imagine that. I've seen how grumpy you are when your hip hurts."

"I never thought about those handcuff keys again until I was lying on the floor in the Brodericks' foyer and realized we were cuffed together. That's the main reason I kept asking for the cane. But he kept us under such close scrutiny that I never got the chance to get them out. You have to twist open the top and tilt the cane up in the air. Not something you can do on the sly. Once he put us in the back of the truck and kept the cane, I figured I'd lost my opportunity so there was no point in bringing it up."

"I don't suppose there was a gun in there too," she said. "I asked you in Gatlinburg if there was a gun hidden inside and you said there was."

"I was joking. Being a jerk, really."

"No. Never a jerk." She squeezed their joined hands.

"We need to get these handcuffs off. It's the only way we'll have a fighting chance if he comes back before we get out of this shack."

"You really think we have a chance?"

Her left hand clutched his right one so hard that his fingers started going numb. She was trying to put on a brave front. But inside, she was obviously terrified.

He leaned down and tilted her chin up, their eyes meeting with understanding, before he pressed a soft kiss against her lips. He'd only meant to distract her for a few seconds, to make sure she knew that he was here for her and would do whatever he could to protect her. But with both their emotions running high, touching her was like putting a match to gasoline.

Suddenly she was straddling him like she'd done in his rental car. And the temperature went up a thousand degrees as they tangled against each other like two horny college kids on spring break. It was only when she moaned into his mouth that he realized he'd slid his hands up her belly and was working on the front clasp of her bra. The logical part of his brain was yelling at him to stop this madness, that they were wasting valuable time. The rest of him, which seemed to be winning, was arguing that maybe this was exactly what he should be doing in case these were his last moments on earth. What better way to go out of this world than making love to the most amazing, interesting, adorably sassy woman he'd ever met?

"The back," she whispered against his mouth. "The clasp is in the back."

What few brain cells he had left registered what she'd said, that to take off her bra he had to slide his hands around to her back. But if that was the case, what was the hard part in the front of her bra he'd just felt?

Underwire.

He broke the kiss and stared down at her. Somewhere along the line, either she or he had discarded her shirt as best they could. It was hanging over his forearm caught in the handcuff chain. And in the dim light filtering in through the windows and front door, two perfect breasts sat in all their glory, exposed, freed from the cups of her bra that was still fastened beneath them. More than almost anything, he wanted to pull each nipple into his mouth, treasure those soft, warm, incredible curves. But, as impossible as it seemed, there was something else he wanted more.

Her underwire.

He slid his hands around her back and fumbled with the clasp. She sighed with pleasure as he pulled her bra off, but her eyes flew open in surprise when he sat back.

He held the bra up, felt where the underwire ended, then tore at the delicate fabric with his teeth.

She stared at him in confusion. "What…what are you doing? If you want to put your mouth on something, trust me, there are better places to put it." She motioned toward her breasts.

He grinned even with the fabric in his mouth. She was definitely the type of woman who knew what she wanted.

If he could go back in time and keep her at his house instead of turning her away, he'd probably still be in bed with her days later.

"Bryson?" She was frowning now, obviously getting annoyed.

He made one last tear and the wire hit his teeth. He sat back, working at it with his fingers now, pulling it out of the fabric.

She gasped in dismay. "That bra cost over a hundred dollars."

He hesitated. "You're kidding. You wear hundred-dollar bras?"

"It's my only hundred-dollar bra. I was saving it for a special occasion." She arched a brow. "Why do you think I took a shower at my parents' house? Who do you think I put that bra on for?" She waved her hand toward her shorts. "I have matching panties too."

Boy oh boy did he want to see those matching panties. But more than that, he wanted her to *live*. He glanced toward the door, and the blessedly empty gravel road out front. "I'll buy you another hundred-dollar bra, a dozen. And matching underwear. But right now, I need this." He finally yanked the wire free and held it up. "Handcuff key."

Her eyes widened in surprise.

"Hold up your wrist. I'll try your side first."

She did as he'd asked, and he ran his fingers along the flat side of the metal circle until he found the little slot for the key, just where the metal was locked into the hole. He slid the end of the underwire inside, then carefully worked it back and forth. The cuff backed out one slot with a loud click, giving her a little more wiggle room.

"It's working!" Her voice was full of awe.

"Long way to go. Give me a minute. I have to be careful or the wire will break." He ratcheted the metal back one slow click at a time.

"I'm guessing our captor took Annie from you at the Brodericks'," he said as he twisted the wire in the cuffs. "Otherwise you'd have shot him full of holes."

"Annie? Oh, my gun?" At his nod, she shook her head. "I don't understand it. I had so many opportunities to get away, to get help. But I just…froze. In that foyer. He took your gun and mine before I even thought about trying to use them. Or run out the front door to a neighbor's. I can't believe I just…stood there."

The handcuff loosened another click. "It's the trauma from before. If he'd been anyone else, I imagine that wouldn't have happened. But your brain shut down the moment you realized who he was. That's not your fault. It's not something you could control."

"Nice of you to say, but I'm not so sure that—"

Click. He pulled the handcuff off her.

She rubbed her wrist and grinned. "I'm free!"

"Not quite. That was step one. Step two is getting out of this shack. Step three is disappearing into the woods long before he gets back." He slipped her end of the handcuffs over his still-cuffed wrist and clicked them loosely into place.

"What are you doing!" she exclaimed. "Why did you do that?"

"To save time. I can do whatever I need to do with both cuffs on the same wrist. I'll worry about getting them off later." He waved toward her shirt, which had fallen to the floor. "I'm having enough trouble focusing with this concussion without your gorgeous breasts distracting me. Mind putting your shirt back on?"

Her smile beamed at him, full wattage. "You think my breasts are gorgeous? What a sweet thing to say." She winked and grabbed her shirt. "Let's get out of here, Bryson. I want you to buy me those matching underwear sets so you can take them right back off again."

He laughed and tried to shove himself to his feet, but his hip gave out and he collapsed against the cushions. His face heated with embarrassment as he cleared his throat. "Looks like I'll need a little help standing. I should be able to walk but getting up off this couch is beyond my current abilities. I always get stiff after lying down for a while."

"I sure hope you do."

He glanced at her in confusion, then realized what she meant when she winked.

He shook his head, grinning. "You've got a one-track mind. Help me up." He held his hand out to stop whatever she was about to say. "Without another sexual innuendo. We're running out of time."

Her smile faded and fear took its place. He regretted being so blunt, but even though her natural tendency to block out her fears and worries by flirting and teasing was adorable in most circumstances, they were a liability in this one. Especially since the blow to his head had him thinking far less clearly than usual.

She helped him up, and thankfully he was able to limp unaided to the door.

"What do we do now?" She settled her shirt into place. "Try to pull out the hinge pins?"

He was already sticking the underwire into the door lock when her innocent question had him glancing up in surprise. The hinges were on the inside. Because doors like these were intended to keep people out, not in.

Their abductor might have finally made a mistake.

Chapter Sixteen

"You, Teagan Ray, are brilliant," Bryson told her. "I'll try the lock first, but I was worried this metal will be too soft for this. The hinge pins will likely be our ticket out of here. But we have to find something to use to pop them out." He motioned toward the stove, which was only about three feet from the door, and beyond that to the handful of cabinets that formed the tiny kitchenette. "Look through this kitchen, in the bedroom, under the couch. We'll need something we can either wedge under the end of the pin to pull it or something to stick in the hinge on the bottom to push it."

"I'm on it."

She moved past him and started slamming open cabinets and drawers. He could follow her progress through the tiny shack by the sound of her cursing and the sounds of her either kicking or hitting walls.

He blocked all that out and focused on trying to pick the lock using the underwire.

After half a dozen attempts, he realized it wasn't going to happen. The metal was just too soft and kept bending. He tossed it aside as she ran to him holding up a long metal rod and a foot-long piece of wood.

"Will this work?" She was breathing heavily from exertion. "I figure you can stick the metal up the bottom of the hinge and use the wood like a hammer to push out the pin."

"Do I even want to know where you got the steel rod? And why it's wet?"

"Probably not."

"Were you in the bathroom?"

"Like I said. You don't want to know."

He grimaced. The rod looked like one of those old-fashioned toilet-tank float rods that controlled how the toilet flushed. As to the wood, it was either a piece of baseboard or a piece of the floor itself. Judging by the dilapidated shape of the building, neither would surprise him.

The steel rod was the perfect size and slid in place beneath the middle hinge pin with ease. Hope flared in his chest as he slammed the wood against it. He slammed it over and over and over, but the pin wasn't moving. He finally stopped and leaned in close, trying to see if there was something keeping it in place. Then he took a closer look at the hinges in the door frame and cursed.

"What is it?" she asked.

"Locking hinge pins."

"Never heard of them. But I don't like how that sounds."

He tossed the wood and rod on the floor and wiped his hands on his dress pants. "I thought our captor made a mistake with the hinges on the inside. But he didn't. There's an extra screw that prevents the pin from being backed out. We'd need an Allen wrench and a screwdriver to get it out. No homemade tools are going to back out that screw. It's drilled into the wrought-iron frame."

Her shoulders slumped. "That's why he didn't try to drug us, or tie us up. He knew there was no way to escape."

"Don't give up on me now. I haven't thrown in the towel just yet."

She nodded. But he could tell she was rapidly losing hope.

"Talk to me," he said. "Tell me how you escaped the last time while I see what else is in here."

"There's nothing. Just the couch and a few aluminum pots and pans. The utensils in the drawer are plastic or rubber. There's nothing we could use to stab or hit him."

"He's got a gun. Nothing much trumps that. We need to get out before he returns. We have to think outside the box." He limped past the front door and the stove, then yanked open one of the cabinet drawers in the kitchenette. "Tell me about the shack, and how you got out."

"It's basically the same. Well, the bars are new. And the iron front door. There isn't a back door. He tied me up when he left, with cloth. He didn't use handcuffs. Mostly he used drugs to keep me docile. He'd knock me out for hours, and I wouldn't wake up until he was back. I was in detox for weeks after I got away."

He pulled the hardware, tested the corners of the drawer boxes. "Go on. What else."

She sighed heavily. "I was blindfolded whenever it was light outside. And he wore a hooded mask most of the time. That always gave me hope, thinking he'd eventually let me go because he was keeping his identity secret. But I don't know that he ever would have. He was just extra cautious, in case something happened and I got away. He's not worried about us identifying him. He's going to kill us."

He'd just started into the bathroom but turned around when she said that. "Not if I kill him first. Do *not* give up on me."

Her eyes widened, but he didn't stand around talking. The sense of time passing was making him feel edgy and nervous. He couldn't imagine that whatever their captor was doing would keep him gone much longer.

The bathroom was a total bust. It was pitch dark, for one thing, but tiny without even a cabinet under the sink to hide anything. No bleach or cleaners that he could toss in the gunman's face. He didn't know how Teagan had managed to think about the toilet rod or even how she'd gotten it out of the back of the tank in the darkness. He had to give her a lot of credit for ingenuity.

The bedroom was much the same as the rest. Bars on the lone small window. An empty closet. No bed, just a mattress lying on the floor. It looked new, thankfully. Not the one that had been here two years ago.

He paused in the tiny hallway outside the bedroom. As run-down as the place was, maybe they could push through a wall like Teagan had teased about earlier. He doubted it, but he sent her off to look for weaknesses in the walls while he returned to the kitchen corner of the main room. With her distracted, he leaned down to study the two-burner gas stove.

It had caught his attention earlier as he'd considered what he could do given the lit pilot light and the fact that the gas line ran through the wall to a propane tank on the outside. Filling the cabin with gas and causing an explosion would likely burn the dry-rotted cabin like kindling. And the fire could be seen for miles around. It would get first responders out here for sure. But being blown apart in the explosion or burning alive were both wholly unappealing.

"What are you looking at?" she asked.

"Nothing helpful. I'm going to check the bedroom again. Did you find any weaknesses in the walls?"

She followed him as he limped into the bedroom.

"No. But I'm no expert at building construction. And it's still so dark in here that I might have missed something. Unless you want more baseboards."

He straightened from his study of the wood beneath the window where he'd been hoping moisture might have rotted out the frame. "Baseboards. That's what you handed me to use as a hammer. Where did you find it?"

She pointed toward the closet. "In there. The board was broken already so I was able to kick out that piece I gave you." She rubbed her hands up and down her arms. "He'll be back soon, won't he?"

The wobble in her voice had him longing to hold her, to try to comfort her. Instead, he dropped to his knees to study the baseboards, grimacing at the jolt of pain that sizzled through his hip.

"You didn't finish telling me how you got away." He felt along the bottom of the closet as she talked behind him, telling him how her captor had missed the vein the last time when he'd tried to drug her.

"He was going on one of his supply trips," she said. "The injection made me groggy but didn't knock me out like usual. I pretended to be unconscious. After he left I shoved the blindfold up and used my teeth to loosen my bindings and got myself untied. The old front door was mostly rotten so I kicked it until it split away from the frame. Then I took off. Nothing amazing. I just ran until I couldn't. Then I walked. Then I crawled. A hiker found me several days later. Not that any of that matters. Our situation is different. We're good and stuck here."

He tugged on the board he'd been testing, pulling as hard as he could. It broke in half with a loud crack.

She jumped beside him. "What was that?"

He glanced over his shoulder. "The walls might be solid. But the floor isn't. Those baseboards came out easily for you because the whole floor in this section has been eaten up with termites." He waved toward a foot-long, four-inch-wide hole he'd made in the floor. "That's dirt down there. The crawl space under the cabin. This is how we're going to get out."

She was shaking her head before he finished. "No, Bryson. That's not the sound I heard. There was something else, out front."

He lurched to his feet, then limped as fast as he could into the main room. She ran after him and they both stumbled to a halt when they saw the headlights bouncing crazily across the trees. A vehicle was coming up the gravel road toward the shack.

They were out of time.

Chapter Seventeen

Teagan watched the lights bouncing across the trees. The road faced those trees but ran perpendicular to the front of the shack. They wouldn't be able to see the truck until it made the last turn and pulled up. But there was no reason for anyone else to come down this road. The killer was back. And when he came inside and saw they were out of their handcuffs, he'd cuff them again. Then he'd make a circuit of the shack and find the small hole that Bryson had started. He'd decide Bryson was too big a liability to keep around. He'd kill him for sure.

And then he'd come for her.

"Kill me, Bryson." She grabbed his arm. "Please. I can't do this again. Choke me. Hit me over the head. Something. It will be a mercy killing. Please."

He shook her hand off his arm. "This isn't over. You hear me? Don't you dare give up." He pointed to the couch. "We have to block the door. As small as this room is, we should be able to jam one end against the wall and the other against the door. He won't be able to get inside."

She looked from the lights outside to the couch and back again. "We'd just be delaying the inevitable. What's the point? I have a better idea. I'll make him so angry he has to shoot me. Then at least I won't have to bear his touch again."

He yanked her around to face him as the sound of gravel crunching beneath tires echoed outside. "All we have to do is break three or four more boards in that closet and we're out of here. But we have to buy some time. Help me get this couch into place." He grabbed her arm and tugged her away from the door as the headlights turned toward the shack.

"Grab that other end," he yelled. "We'll have to slide it past the hallway to turn it. Hurry."

She ran to the other end and together they slid the couch across the floor.

"It's clear," he said. "Now, turn it, turn it. This end toward the door."

They slid the couch sideways, one end facing the door, the other the hallway.

"He's here! He's here," she yelled. The truck had parked in front of the cabin.

"Slide it back. We have to wedge it between the wall and the door. Hurry!"

She pushed her end but couldn't get it against the wall. "It's too long. It won't fit. He'll be able to push the door and the couch will slide down the hall."

The engine cut off outside. A loud creak sounded. The truck door opening?

She started to shake. "Oh, God. He's here."

Bryson leaped over the back of the couch, stumbling and nearly falling before catching himself. Then he limped to her end. He bent down and somehow lifted the couch in spite of his bad hip, his face turning red as he shoved the couch up in the air. Then he dropped it against the wall just past the hallway opening. It fell down, but stuck with another foot to go. She didn't see how it would hold. When the killer pushed the door, if he pushed hard enough, the couch would slide up the wall and he'd still be able to get inside.

Bryson must have thought the same thing because he climbed onto the end of the couch that was against the wall and hopped up and down, one-legged, favoring his hip. He jumped again, and again. The couch springs squeaked in protest. Then it dropped down into place, wedged tight.

Keys rattled outside. "Hey, what are you doing in there?"

Bryson grabbed her arm and tugged her toward the hallway. "Go, go, go."

"Open the door!" The gunman pounded against it, his voice thick with rage.

Once they were inside the bedroom, Bryson released her and limped into the closet. Jamming his bad hip against the wall to keep his balance, he slammed his right heel down on the boards beside the hole, over and over. Wood crunched beneath his boot, dropping below. But the hole wasn't large enough for them to get through. Not even close.

Bam! Bam! Bam!

Teagan jerked around as bullets burst through the wall from the front of the shack and plowed through the opposite wall, throwing splinters up in front of her face.

"Down, get down!" Bryson tackled her to the mattress on the floor behind her.

More shots exploded through the wall, right where she'd been standing. She buried her head against his neck as he covered her with his body.

The front door rattled, followed by furious cursing and shouting. Then, nothing. Silence fell over the shack like a heavy blanket, except for the sound of their breathing and the blood rushing in her ears.

"What's he doing now," she whispered. "Where is he?"

He lifted off her and held a finger against his lips, telling her to be quiet.

She nodded to let him know she understood.

A thump sounded outside. Bryson grabbed her, stumbling and limping as he pulled her into the corner away from the window. Moments later, a flashlight shone through the glass. They both scrunched up against the wall, watching the light as it moved around the room. Then it stopped, shining directly on the hole in the closet floor. The light flicked off.

"Oh, no," she whispered.

He swore softly. Then he pressed his fingers to his lips again, and edged to the window to peer out.

A thump sounded from somewhere beneath them.

She covered her mouth to keep from screaming.

He grabbed her, pushing her in front of him toward the door, motioning for her to be as quiet as possible. He was obviously struggling to keep up, his unbalanced gait evidence of just how badly his hip must be hurting. But they made it to the hall, then hurried into the main room.

He limped to the door and tugged the handle. It moved just enough to prove it wasn't locked. But there was no way to open it with the couch against it. He motioned for her to put her hand on the knob, then bent down next to her ear. "When I lift the couch, run like hell. Get out of here. Run to the woods and don't stop for anything."

"What about you? You can't run."

"Don't worry about me."

"Bryson, I can't leave you—"

The sound of wood splintering in the other room was followed by a guttural yell. "You're dead, you hear me? I'm going to kill both of you!"

Shots rang out. Glass shattered. He must have shot out the window.

"He'll be through that floor soon. I need you to run. I need to know you're safe. Then I'll run a different way and hide. Our best chance is to split up. Promise me you'll run and won't look back. Promise!"

More wood splintered in the other room.

"Promise me." He lightly shook her.

"Okay, okay. Promise."

Bracing his left side against the door, he grabbed the bottom of the couch and pulled and tugged, wrestling to get it to move after being wedged in so tight.

A shot rang out.

She ducked, then looked at Bryson, who'd frozen in place. "Are you okay?"

His mouth tight, he nodded. "Get ready. Remember what I said. Run as fast as you can. Don't stop for anything."

She nodded and tightened her hand on the doorknob.

He heaved again. The couch finally jerked free and seemed to practically fly upward and over on its side, out of the way. As soon as it cleared the door, she tugged it open and ran. She ran as if the hounds of hell were on her heels, because that's exactly what it felt like. She didn't stop until she reached the far end of the clearing. Even though she'd promised not to stop, she did. She had to make sure he was okay. Ducking behind a pine tree, she peered around it at the shack. The front door was hanging open and the headlights didn't reveal anyone inside. He'd made it. He'd gotten out.

She turned and ran.

AS SOON AS Teagan took off running, Bryson dropped to his knees, grimacing as he scooted himself back against the wall, tucked between the door and the stove. He hadn't lied to her, not at first anyway. He'd thought he could run, or at least limp really fast. With a head start, he would have had a chance. But then things had changed. He slid his hand inside his suit jacket. It came away sticky and wet. That last bullet had hit its mark. He wiped the blood on his pant leg and closed his eyes.

Another shout of rage sounded from the bedroom. The man sure had an anger problem. Bryson wondered what he did for a living, because it would be really hard to hide that type of a temper in a nine-to-five office job. Something or someone would be bound to set him off. Whatever he did, it would be a solo kind of job. He'd have the freedom to set his own hours so he wouldn't be missed for weeks at a time when he was on a sociopathic spree. He'd have made an interesting profile.

A series of loud thumps and cursing echoed from the back room. The gunman was finally breaking through the floor.

Bryson coughed and blood sprayed out of his mouth. Not a good sign. Darkness was closing in on the edges of his vision again. He shook his head to stay awake. He still had one more thing that he had to do. Step one had been to get out of the handcuffs. Step two was to get Teagan out of the shack to safety. Step three was still to come. He had to ensure that first responders came out here to help her so she wouldn't die in those woods. And at this point, there was only one way he knew to do that.

He slid his hand behind the stove beside him, then yanked hard on the gas line. Like most things in this shack, it was old and brittle and much easier to pull loose than he'd expected. Finally something was going his way.

"I'm coming for you now!" the killer yelled from the other room. Shoes stomped on the hardwood floor and a hulking dark shape appeared in the hallway. Dawn was finally breaking on the little glade in the woods. And the first rays of sunlight shone through the door, glinting on the pistol in the other man's hand.

He narrowed his eyes at Bryson, his face red with anger and exertion. He looked left and right, not that he needed to in such a small space. One glance could clearly show that they were alone.

"Where is she?" He lifted his gun, aiming it at Bryson. "Tell me right now or I'll shoot."

Bryson smiled and held up the gas line, which was hissing and spewing out foul-smelling propane. "She's gone. Go ahead and shoot me. The flare from the muzzle will take us both out. And Teagan will never have to be afraid of you ever again, you scum-sucking, piece of human excrement. You're not even fit to lick the bottom of her shoes, pervert."

The other man's gun started shaking. His face was so bright red it looked like he would have a stroke at any moment.

As gas continued to fill the room, Bryson piled on more insults, trying to prod the killer's temper so he'd shoot. He wanted him to shoot. Because Teagan would be safe. She could finally live the life she deserved, without fear. And the explosion would bring the help she'd need to make it back to civilization.

"You stupid cop."

"Is that the worst you can think to say? Really?" Bryson clucked his tongue. "You're dumber than I gave you credit."

He roared with rage, then strode across the room toward Bryson and shoved the gun against his temple. But when he glanced at the gas line, he swore. He tossed a few more curses Bryson's way, then yanked open the door and headed outside.

Bryson swore a few choice curses himself. He hadn't defeated the devil after all. But he'd get the help Teagan needed. Of that he was sure. As soon as the gunman was far enough from the cabin to feel safe, he'd shoot that propane tank. He was too mad not to. The explosion would be spectacular. Half the firefighters and cops in the county would be here in minutes.

"Bryson, what are you doing?"

His eyes flew open. Teagan was running toward him from the hallway. "What the hell? The place is full of gas and he's going to—"

"Shoot the propane tank, I'm guessing? Was that your stupid plan?" She put her hands beneath his shoulders and hauled upward. "Help me. Hurry."

He swore a blue streak and drew on reserves of strength he never knew he had to push to his feet.

"Go, go, go," she yelled, repeating his earlier words to her.

They hobbled into the bedroom and she hopped down into the hole. He winced as he tried to lower himself, then gave up and went headfirst. She was reaching back to help him, but he shoved her toward the patch of sunlight just a few feet away. She hurried forward and he half-scrambled, half-crawled after her.

Out front, the truck engine started up. Tires crunched and the engine roared as he drove away from the cabin.

They cleared the structure, him leaning heavily on her once again as they stumbled toward the tree line. Just past the first stand of trees, palmettos viciously scraped their flesh.

"Down," he yelled. "Over here!" He yanked her behind a fallen tree log and rolled on top of her.

A shot sounded. The shack exploded, turning the clearing into a fiery inferno.

Chapter Eighteen

Teagan restlessly paced the hospital conference room. From the exasperated looks on the faces of most of the men sitting at the table, she knew they were getting tired of her jumping out of her chair. But she was too nervous, too freaking scared about what was going on with Bryson that she couldn't sit still for more than a few minutes.

"Ms. Ray," one of the Jacksonville Sheriff's Office detectives called out to her.

Which one was he? Burns, Rodriquez, Bunting? The names of the other two sitting at the long table had been forgotten right after they'd introduced themselves. How many detectives did it take to question one lone abduction victim? How many did it take to change a stupid light bulb?

"Ms. Ray," he called out again.

Burns. That was his name.

He motioned toward the other side of the table. "Will you please sit and answer some more questions?"

Five against one. JSO on one side, her on the other. Not that they were enemies, exactly. But their lack of interest, or ability, to solve her abduction and torture two years ago didn't make her much of a fan now. The only reason she was talking to them was because Bryson was in surgery after being life-flighted from Live Oak to the trauma unit at UF Health Shands Hospital here in Jacksonville.

It had nearly killed her watching the helicopter disappear in the sky with him on board. And she'd hated being stuck with a Florida Highway Patrolman as her assigned bodyguard, wasting time making her get checked out at a local Live Oak emergency room. When the doctors there confirmed what she'd said all along—that she was fine—the patrolman had finally taken off down Interstate 10 to drive her to Jacksonville. They'd arrived two hours ago, and she still didn't have an update on Bryson's condition other than that he was in surgery.

"Ms. Ray—"

"Tell you what, Detective Burns." She flattened her palms against the table but didn't sit. "How about you get me a real update this time on Mr. Anton's condition. Something more detailed than a simple acknowledgment that he's still in surgery, and then, maybe I'll answer more of your endless questions."

He sighed heavily, then left the room, presumably to get the information that she'd requested.

Another detective motioned toward her seat. "There are three murders attributable to your abductor—Mr. and Mrs. Broderick and the driver of the delivery truck that he hijacked. We need to catch this guy before he hurts someone else."

"Don't you think I know that?" She shook her head at his seeming callousness. Her heart ached over the senseless, brutal murders her kidnapper had carried out while trying to get to her. She wanted him caught just as badly as anyone else, probably more so. Because even though she wasn't the one who'd hurt those people, she'd always wonder whether she could have done something differently to prevent their deaths.

"Ms. Ray," he began again. "I know this is nerve-rack-ing, especially when you're worried about your fiancé. But we really need your help."

A twinge of guilt shot through her over the fiancé lie. But she'd wanted to make sure that the hospital would share information with her on Bryson's condition. Not that it had served her well so far. She'd been stuck in this room, answering dozens, maybe hundreds of questions during this inquisition. There just wasn't anything else she could tell them. Maybe if they'd actually work on the investigation, using the information that she'd already given them, they'd figure out the killer's identity and arrest him.

She plopped down in her chair. "I honestly don't know what else you think I can tell you. We've been over the timeline again and again. I told you the guy looked familiar but I couldn't figure out why, still can't. I sat with your sketch artist and you've got his likeness now. Why don't you put an APB out based on that and try to find the guy?"

"They don't use the term APB anymore, Ms. Ray," a familiar voice spoke from the doorway. "It's called a BOLO—be on the lookout."

Relief had her slumping in her chair at the sight of Bryson's boss from The Justice Seekers, Mason Ford. "Mr. Ford, thank you so much for coming."

He stepped inside the room. "I'm just glad that I was already in the state working a case when you called."

"Who the heck are you?" one of the detectives demanded. Rodriquez, she believed.

"A friend of the family. If you don't mind, I need to speak to Ms. Ray." He opened the door wider when they didn't move. "Privately."

The detectives shot sour looks at both of them but finally got up. As they headed out the door, Rodriquez turned back to Teagan and slid a business card across the table. "When you're ready to cooperate, give me a call. We need to jump on this case fast. Please don't take too long." With that he headed out the door.

She threw her hands in the air. "When I'm ready to co-operate? I've done nothing but cooperate. They keep asking me the same questions over and over."

Ford shut the door behind him and gave her an apologetic look. "And I'm about to ask you to repeat everything you just told them. Sorry about that. But you did call. I'm here, and the full force of my company is at yours and Bryson's disposal. I'm pulling everyone off noncritical cases effective immediately. We'll do everything we can to catch this guy."

Some of the tension that had taken hold of her for the past twenty-four hours began to melt away at his words. "Thank you, Mr. Ford. I can't tell you how good it is to hear someone say that. Those detectives treated me as if I was a suspect, the jerks."

His mouth tilted up in what she assumed passed for a smile for him. Back at The Justice Seekers headquarters he'd never cracked even a shadow of a smile. But he'd been nothing but courteous and had jumped at the chance to help once she'd called him on the way from Live Oak to Jacksonville to tell him that Bryson was hurt.

He set a leather portfolio on the table and sat across from her. "First, please call me Mason. After all, you being Bryson's fiancée makes you family, more or less."

She felt her cheeks heat. "I'm sure you realize we aren't really engaged. I made that up so the hospital would share updates about his condition. Not that they've bothered."

"Since you only met a few days ago, I kind of figured that was a ruse. The offer to call me Mason still stands."

"A few days ago? It feels like I've known him forever."

"Not surprising, given the trauma and emotional turmoil you've weathered together. As to those detectives being jerks, I'm sorry it feels that way. They're under a lot of pressure to solve this thing and probably don't even realize how they come across. Not that it excuses poor manners. As for Bryson's condition, I can update you on that."

She straightened in her chair. "The hospital gave you information?"

"Let's just say that I got the information from the hospital and leave it at that. Sometimes the end justifies the means. Don't you think?"

She grinned. "I like how you work, Mason. Please tell me how he's doing. Is he...is he going to—"

"He's going to be fine."

She dropped her face in her hands, unexpected tears flowing down her cheeks.

He waited silently until she regained control of her emotions. A few minutes later, she drew a ragged breath and sat back. "That's very good to hear. Thank you."

"Of course. He's actually in recovery now and should be awake soon." He placed his cell phone on the table. "The second he's lucid, that's going to vibrate. I'll take you right to him."

"Thank you," she whispered, fighting to hold back more tears.

"The bullet nicked his spleen but no other organs," he continued. "It went through and through. He lost a lot of blood. That on top of the concussion pretty much shut him down. That's why he was unconscious after the blast. Luckily you were both behind a log when the tank exploded, which shielded you from the shock wave. Otherwise, your insides would have liquefied."

She winced.

He smiled apologetically. "Sorry. That was graphic. Bottom line, he's going to be okay, eventually. He was lucky. You both were. If the explosion and resulting fire hadn't alerted authorities so that help arrived quickly, he'd have bled out."

She wrapped her arms around her waist. "Once again, he saved me, in spite of how badly he was hurt. He saved both of us. He's an incredible man."

"Yes. Yes, he is. And I want to do everything I can to protect both of you. We need to catch this guy and get enough evidence to ensure he'll either be executed or locked up so he can't hurt anyone else ever again. I know you're weary of answering questions. But I'm coming in late on this. So I'd very much appreciate it if you'd start from the top, right after you left my office in Gatlinburg." He pulled a computer tablet from his portfolio and set it on top of the table. Then he took out a small electronic device and set it a foot away from her. "To save time briefing my team, and to make sure I don't miss anything, I'm going to record this as well as take notes. If you're okay with it?"

"Absolutely." Covering the same ground yet again didn't bother her since it was Mason who was asking the questions. She believed that he'd actually do something with the information. None of the detectives she'd spoken to earlier had inspired that kind of confidence. "Did the police give you a copy of the likeness their sketch artist came up with?"

"Not yet." He picked up his phone. His fingers practically flew across the screen as he typed out a text. He waited a few seconds, then the phone buzzed. He checked the screen, then set it down. "My team will have the sketch within minutes." He poised his hands over the virtual keyboard on the tablet. "You were going to tell me the timeline. Don't leave anything out."

Half an hour later, a knock sounded on the door. Mason was out of his chair, gun in hand but hidden behind him before the door opened.

The detective who'd gone for a status update stood in the opening, a look of surprise on his face when he saw Mason. He took a quick glance into the room. "Where is everyone?"

"Not here. What can I do for you?"

"I, ah, wanted to let Ms. Ray know that Mr. Anton is out of surgery."

"Thank you." Mason closed the door before the detective could say anything else. He holstered his gun, then sat down. "You were saying?"

She clenched her hands together beneath the table. "You drew your gun. You think he'll show up here? At the hospital?"

"It's possible. Don't worry. I had a guard stationed outside the surgery room. He'll stay with Bryson in recovery as well."

She blinked. "How do the police feel about that?"

"I'm always as accommodating as possible with law enforcement. But I'm not about to leave the security of an injured member of my team to their care. The hospital administrator was more than okay with it after I offered a substantial donation in Bryson's name." He winked. "Now, if you don't mind. Please continue."

"Yes, of course. I, um, I guess I was up to the point of where I ran like a coward for the trees."

"No. I think you were telling me that you did exactly what Bryson asked you to do, so you wouldn't put him in more danger by making him worry about having to protect you rather than make his own escape. But I'm puzzled. If you ran into the woods at the front of the clearing, how did you end up behind the shack when it exploded?"

Her face heated. "I didn't exactly follow Bryson's instructions. I know he wanted me to keep going, to run as far away as I could. But I hadn't seen him leave the shack, and I was worried that he might have been pretending to feel better than he did, just to get me out of danger. All throughout our ordeal, he kept telling me to have faith, that it was two against one, that we could beat the bad guy together. And there I was running away. I just couldn't do it."

He crossed his arms on top of the table. "So what did you do?"

She wrapped her arms around her middle, remembering. "I circled through the woods to the back of the shack."

"Where was the gunman?"

"I wasn't sure. The truck was still parked out front. I didn't see him anywhere."

He stared at her, waiting.

"I got down on my belly and tried to see beneath the shack, through the crawl space. When I didn't see anyone moving around under there, I was terrified that the gunman was inside with Bryson. So I ran to the shack and crawled up into the closet through the hole in the floor."

He still didn't say anything. But his eyes widened slightly.

"I heard the gunman shouting in the other room. And I smelled gas. It was filling up the cabin. A moment later, the front door creaked. I peeked around the corner and saw the gunman running for his truck." She swallowed hard. "And Bryson, he was just sitting there, his back to the wall, holding the gas line in his hand."

She swiped at the tears in her eyes. "For a split second, I thought he was dead. But then I saw his chest rise and realized he was still alive. I yelled at him to get out. We dropped through the hole in the closet floor and made it to the woods just before the explosion." She wiped her tears again. "Like you said earlier, if it wasn't for Bryson getting both of us behind that log when he did, we'd both be dead. He deserves a medal of honor. Not a bullet in the back."

He cleared his throat. "That's quite a story. I gather you sat with him until help arrived?"

"Of course. I know CPR. But that's about the limits of my nursing abilities. He was breathing, and his heart was beating. But he wouldn't open his eyes. I didn't know what to do. All I could think of was to apply pressure to the wounds, even though they didn't seem to be bleeding all that much. I had no idea he was bleeding internally."

She squeezed her eyes shut for a moment and let out a shuddering breath. "Thank goodness the fire department and police arrived so quickly. I heard the sirens and ran to the clearing. They were amazing, ran with me around back, no questions asked. They immediately started an IV and got him on a gurney. I think they flew him out in a helicopter within a couple of minutes. They saved his life."

He slowly shook his head. "No, Ms. Ray. I think that distinction belongs to you. If you hadn't been stubborn enough and brave enough to go back into that shack to check on him, he'd be dead right now." His voice sounded oddly hoarse, and he cleared his throat before continuing. "Thank you. On behalf of all the Justice Seekers, thank you for saving our dear friend and coworker."

She was about to argue that he wouldn't have even been in danger in the first place if it wasn't for her, but his phone vibrated against the table.

He picked it up, then stood.

She shoved out of her chair. "Bryson's awake?"

He shook his head. "Not yet. But I'll go check on him right now. Meanwhile, you have visitors."

"Visitors?" She frowned. "The police are back?"

He hesitated at the door. "When you called me to help Bryson, I took the liberty of calling someone to help you. But I asked them to give me time to interview you first. They've been very accommodating. But they're out in the hall now, demanding to see you." He smiled his first real smile. "You're an incredibly brave and smart young woman. Thank you again for everything you did." Without waiting for her reply, he left the room.

A moment later, two people rounded the corner and paused in the doorway.

She let out a shriek and ran around the table, tears flowing again.

Her mother and father gathered her to them in a bone-crushing hug.

Chapter Nineteen

Teagan sighed deeply and shifted positions in the plastic chair a few feet from Bryson's hospital bed as he slept the morning away. Three days. It had been three days since she'd cried all over him in the recovery room after he woke up from surgery, only to have him gruffly tell her that he needed his sleep. Since then, he'd hardly spoken a word to her. He was acting just like the surly bear she'd encountered the first time they'd met. But they'd moved beyond that. Far beyond it. So why was he acting like they were strangers and he was the grouchy hermit again?

She'd asked him that very thing.

His answers were many. He had a headache. He was feeling fuzzy from the concussion. The pain from his surgery had him feeling bad and he just needed to sleep. All of that was probably true. But he was a strong man, and had overcome far worse to save both their lives. And he'd been at his kindest in the past when he was in tremendous pain, because he'd risen above it to save them. So none of his actions now made sense.

Thankfully, his boss—Mason Ford—didn't seem worried about Bryson's less than friendly attitude that seemed to extend to anyone unfortunate enough to be in his vicinity. He simply ignored Bryson's gruff responses and went about his business. And he kept Teagan up to date on everything going on with the investigation.

Which, unfortunately, wasn't much.

Even with half the Justice Seekers working the case here in Jacksonville, none of them seemed to be making any more headway than JSO. No one had discovered the identity yet of the man who'd abducted them and killed three innocent people. But Mason assured her they were doing everything they could and weren't giving up. And he did something else—he gave her a company credit card to use for all of her and Bryson's needs. He told her the card had no limit and to use it for anything at all, no questions asked.

He'd also ordered Bryson to let her make all the arrangements to get him set up at a local hotel after being discharged so he could get strong enough for the trip back to Gatlinburg. Teagan decided that she liked Mason Ford very much, especially since he made no secret that he was rooting for her to win this little cold war between her and Bryson.

She crossed her arms and waited another half hour before the doctor's morning rounds finally brought him to Bryson's room to perform a final evaluation before giving him discharge papers. Miraculously, he woke up just as the doctor stepped into the room. Teagan snorted and looked out the window, pretending indifference, when she was fuming inside.

The hurt had long ago faded. Or, at least, it was buried down deep. No more crying in front of him. She had her pride after all. And no crying on her mama's shoulder either, given that her mother now thought—along with the hospital staff—that she and Bryson were engaged. That was going to be a huge disappointment for her parents once he went back to Gatlinburg and she told them the "engagement" was off. They'd half fallen in love with him when he'd had dinner at their home. They fell the rest of the way after hearing everything he'd done to protect their only child.

But they wouldn't be the only ones nursing a broken heart.

She kept her face averted, pretending interest in something out the window while she wiped the wetness from her eyes. How could she still have all these inconvenient feelings for a man who didn't return them? She took a few deep breaths and reached down for her anger again, wrapping it around her other emotions like a shield, to keep her safe.

"All in all, you're an incredibly lucky man," the doctor said behind her as he apparently finished his exam. "Any one of your injuries—the blow to the head, the gunshot, the half-dozen pieces of wood that the explosion drove into your back—could have killed you. You might not feel lucky right now, but once the pain fades and you're back on your feet, I think you'll begin to realize just how fortunate you are. Someone was looking out for you."

She turned around, but steadfastly looked at the floor while he thanked the doctor and discussed the discharge instructions. Her anger had evaporated beneath the shock of what she'd just heard. She hadn't known about the wood driven into his back. On top of everything else that he'd endured, he'd basically been stabbed, *six times*, as the remnants of the shack rained down on them. But not one of those pieces of lethally sharp wood had hit her—because he'd protected her. Again. She had no right to be angry with him. And he had every right to be angry with her. He'd be sitting on his dock enjoying a cold beer right now, listening to the rippling water of the stream behind his house if it wasn't for her. Healthy, content, his only worry the ache in his hip when the tequila and scotch weren't enough to dull the pain.

What a selfish immature idiot she'd been, thinking only of herself.

The squeak of metal had her glancing up to see him struggling to lower the railing. The doctor must have left while she was consumed with her own thoughts.

She rushed over to him. "Here, let me." She gently pushed his hands away and lowered the railing. "Just, please, don't try to get out of bed on your own. I know you don't want my help, so I'll get the nurse to help you get dressed."

"Teagan, I—"

"It's okay. I understand. I'll have the car brought up and will meet you and the nurse out front."

He frowned. "What do you think you understand?"

Without answering, she hurried from the room.

BRYSON EASED BACK against the pillows that Teagan had just stuffed behind him so he could sit up in the hotel bed. "Thank you." He motioned toward the impressive fifteen-hundred-square-feet, two-bedroom suite that she'd reserved for them at the Omni hotel. The accommodations were luxurious, but more important, it was close enough to the hospital that he hadn't had to endure the agony of a long car ride. And since she'd insisted on him taking more pain pills after reaching the hotel, he was feeling pretty good right now. Physically at least. "Thank you for everything, Teagan."

She seemed surprised by his words, acknowledging them with a quick nod. Then she turned to finish putting away his clothes that she'd had brought from the other hotel he'd originally been staying in, closer to The Woods subdivision. Her surprise that he'd actually thank her had him feeling like even more of a jerk than he had since the moment he'd woken up in the recovery room.

All the memories of what had happened had slammed into him, stealing his breath. He'd made so many mistakes that could have cost her life. The very first one was in agreeing to take her with him to that ill-fated interview at the Brodericks'. Everything had gone downhill from there.

The worst part was knowing what had driven him to include her, to give in to her request even though he was the one experienced in law enforcement and knew better, knew the dangers. What had driven him was pure selfishness, his ridiculous fixation on her and desire, no—*need*—to be around her as much as possible. His obsession had clouded his reason. And just as soon as he was able to manage on his own, he'd set her free, break this tenuous bond that had developed between them. He'd ensure that none of his bad decisions could ever risk her life again. Obviously he hadn't learned the lessons of his past—from his sloppy handling of the Kentucky Ripper case to his failure to save Hayley from the person who'd ended up shooting him in the hip all those months ago. He had no business thinking he could really protect Teagan.

She was much better off without him.

Finally she stopped running around the suite putting things away, and stood by his bed. "I guess it's good that you already had a wheelchair and had it at your other hotel," she said. "Saved me from having to rent one while you're here. Goodness knows you'll need it for a while until you're back on your feet." She motioned beside the bed where she'd stored it within easy reach. "There's a cane too, for when you're feeling good enough to try to walk. It's nothing fancy. I got it at the hospital gift shop. Your other one, unfortunately, is locked up in evidence. It practically took an act of Congress just to get my purse released after the police took it from the Brodericks' home. They wouldn't even discuss the cane, for some reason. Anyway, in case you've forgotten your discharge instructions, they're in writing in the top drawer of your bedside table. But part of it is that the doctor wants you to try to stand and take at least a few steps several times a day. If you're in bed the whole time you could get blood clots and—"

"Teagan."

"Do you need something? A glass of water? Soda? There's a bar over there but you really shouldn't have any alcohol with the pain meds you're—"

"No. Thank you. I don't need anything. I—"

"Okay, then. I'm going to explore my room, catch up on some sleep. I haven't slept well at the hospital and—"

"Teagan."

"—if you need something, just text me on your phone. I left it on the nightstand. The police have both our phones in evidence so that's a new one. I had Mason program your team's numbers in there, so that should help. My new number's in there too, obviously, so you can text me. I'll check on you in a couple of hours."

"I need to talk to you."

"No, right now you need to sleep. We both do."

"Wait, please. Just give me a minute to—"

She hurried into the other bedroom, shutting the door hard behind her. But she hadn't turned fast enough to hide the tears in her eyes.

He swore and punched a fist into the mattress beside him.

Chapter Twenty

After spending five grueling days and nights in a tension-filled hotel suite with Bryson, Teagan was more than ready to see the last of the place, no matter how amazingly luxurious it was. She could have had a home health-care nurse take care of him while he recuperated. But since part of the reason that Mason had suggested they stay there together was to ensure that both of them were out of sight in case the killer came looking for them, it just made sense for her to take care of him herself.

But it hadn't been easy.

They'd hardly said two words to each other after their arrival. And since it wasn't looking promising that the killer would be found any time soon, it was time for both of them to try to get on with their lives. Well, as much as possible anyway. The police would have someone watching her parents' home while she was here, not that anyone expected the killer to be brazen enough to try to hurt her again. He was long gone, on the run.

Now, as the rented limo pulled up at her parents' home to drop her off so Bryson could fly in Mason's private jet back to Gatlinburg, she was so antsy to get away from him that she was pulling open the door before the driver had even come to a complete stop on the street out front.

"Wait," Bryson called out. "Let me walk you to the door."

"I've got it. No need." She grabbed her one piece of luggage from the seat beside her and hopped out, not even giving the driver a chance to open the door. "Take care, Bryson."

She heard him swearing as she slammed the door shut. Tears were already running down her cheeks by the time she sprinted across the front lawn and threw open the front door. "Mom, Dad, I'm home. Don't get up," she yelled, hurrying toward her old bedroom on the right side of the house. "I'll put away my stuff and freshen up. Talk to you in a few."

"Teagan? Are you okay?" her mom called out from the kitchen where insanely amazing smells were coming from. She must be cooking dinner.

"I'm great. Need to use the restroom, that's all," she lied, hurrying to toss her bag on the bedroom floor then running into the bathroom before her mother could stop her.

She shut the door, then turned around and slid to the floor, finally letting the tears fall that had threatened all morning. She hated crying, especially since she'd probably cried more lately than most people cried an entire lifetime. But it seemed to be the only outlet for her tumultuous emotions. Admitting to her mom that she was more upset over the way the relationship between her and Bryson had ended than the fact that a killer was still out there wasn't something she was keen about. Especially since the so-called relationship had never really begun in the first place. It wasn't real, none of this. It couldn't be. They hadn't even dated. So how could she possibly be in love with him? It wasn't love. It was lust, and shared trauma. In a few weeks, or months, this ache deep in her soul would be gone and she'd forget all about Bryson Anton.

Now if only she could convince her heart of that brazen lie, she'd be just fine.

After crying for a ridiculously long time, she actually felt better. She blew out a shuddering breath, then climbed to her feet. The mirror above the sink was not her friend. Her eyes were puffy and red. Her hair was escaping her customary braid. And her makeup was a disaster.

Thankfully, her mom and dad wouldn't care about her makeup. But they would care if they realized she'd been sitting in here crying for the past ten minutes. She grabbed a washcloth from the cabinet under the sink and washed her face, scrubbing off all of the makeup she'd painstakingly applied in the hotel bathroom. Not that Bryson had noticed. Her throat tightened. *Good grief. Stop it, Teagan. He's not worth it.* She lifted her gaze to the mirror and shook her head. Maybe if she kept lying to herself, she'd eventually believe the lies.

Straightening her shoulders, she drew a bracing breath and headed off to find her parents. Her mom smiled at her from the archway into the kitchen.

"Teagan, baby. Finally you're home." Her mom tossed a dishcloth onto the countertop and wrapped her arms around her.

"It's so good to be here. I missed you and Daddy so much." After a good long hug, she let her mom go and glanced around the kitchen. "It smells amazing in here. Did you cook all my favorites?" She crossed to the stove and bent down to smell the tantalizing aroma rising from the huge pot. "Jambalaya. You're the best, Mom."

"There's apple pie baking in the oven. It'll be ready by the time we finish supper."

She turned around to hug her mom again, then froze. Bryson was leaning against the wall beside the table at the other end of the kitchen, looking like a model out of a magazine in his charcoal gray tailored suit.

He straightened away from the wall and smiled. "Hello, Teagan."

"What…what are you doing here?" she demanded. "You're supposed to be on your way to the airport."

"I wanted to pay my respects to your parents and they invited me to dinner. You don't mind, do you?"

"Well, of course I mind." She put her hands on her hips. "You need to leave."

"Teagan Ray," her mother chided her. "That's not how we treat our guests, especially your fiancé."

"He's not—"

"Teagan!" Her father had just stepped inside from the backyard, holding a pitcher of sun tea that her mom must have had steeping on the porch table. Behind him, Zeus lay on the grass, sunning himself. Her father's mouth widened in a broad smile. "Your mom said you were finally home. Come over here and give dear old dad a hug." He nodded at Bryson, apparently unsurprised to see him, and set the jug on the table.

She reluctantly stepped into his embrace, glaring at Bryson over her father's shoulder. This farce had to end now. No way was she going to sit through dinner pretending everything was okay. When he let her go, she moved back beside her mother.

"Mom, Dad, there's something I need to tell you."

"You can relax," Bryson said. "I already told them."

Her jaw dropped open. "You told them?" She glanced from her mom to her dad. "Neither of you look furious with me. What exactly did he tell you?"

Her mom pressed a kiss against her cheek. "The truth. That you were never engaged, that you weren't even boyfriend and girlfriend. He explained how you told the hospital you were his fiancée so you could be in on his care plan, which I think is really sweet. I was just teasing you a minute ago about being engaged. I shouldn't have done that."

She blinked at her mom, then shot Bryson a confused look. "What did he tell you about why I said that he was my boyfriend?"

"*He* is standing right here and can speak for himself," Bryson teased, sounding lighthearted, which had her even more confused after everything that had happened. "I explained that you didn't want them to worry about you because of the bad breakup with your ex. You wanted to protect them, to keep them from thinking you hadn't moved on in your life."

"You said that?" she whispered, her throat tight.

"It's the truth, isn't it?"

She slowly nodded. "I still don't understand why you're here. You should be on the plane."

He stepped toward her, his limp barely noticeable. Then, to her complete and utter shock, he took both her hands in his.

"I couldn't leave with things the way they are between us," he said. "I need to explain why I've been a complete and utter jerk since waking up in recovery."

Her chin wobbled, and to her horror she realized she still had tears left to shed. She furiously blinked them back and glanced at her parents, who were both avidly watching without making any pretense at not trying to listen. She leaned forward, lowering her voice, even though she was certain they could still hear. "You don't owe me any explanations."

"Yes. I do. We can talk now, in front of your parents. Or somewhere private. But I'm not leaving until I apologize and give you an honest explanation."

"Why are you being so nice all of a sudden?" She leaned

in so close she was almost touching him and whispered, "You don't owe me anything, Bryson."

He slowly shook his head. "I owe you my life."

"Damn it," she muttered, stepping back. "You're making me cry again."

"Teagan—" her mother began.

"I know, I know. Language. Sorry, Mom." She wondered if her mother would still treat her like a kid when she hit thirty. She swiped at her wet eyes. "We'll talk in the backyard, Bryson. Then you can go."

"After dinner," her mother said. "Whatever you two have to say can be settled later. Now go wash up. Henry, show Bryson to the other bathroom so he can wash up too."

Teagan's face heated with embarrassment at being ordered around in front of Bryson. But since he was currently following her father to the master suite to the second bathroom, at least she wasn't the only one being bossed around like a child.

"You can thank me later," her mother whispered. "Now go fix your face before that handsome man comes back."

She gasped in dismay, remembering that she'd washed off her makeup, and ran for the bathroom.

"You didn't need to put on any makeup, you know," Bryson said after dinner as they both rested their arms on the top of the picket fence and stared out over the backyard pond.

Her face heated yet again. "I'm amazed you even noticed."

He sighed heavily. "I owe you a tremendous apology. I've been an absolute beast since waking up after the explosion."

She hesitated, his words surprising her. "I didn't think of it that way, that when you woke up in recovery it was your first time being awake since the explosion. You must have been really confused. In your place, I think I would have been terrified. Not knowing what had happened."

He turned to face her, his left hand braced on top of the fence. "I was beyond terrified, about you."

"About me? But… I was right there in the recovery room. You saw that I was okay."

"By the grace of God, yes. Teagan, what were you thinking coming back inside that shack? Just a few seconds earlier and that madman would have still been there to kill you or take you with him. A few seconds later and you'd have been killed in the explosion. You shouldn't have risked your life like that, especially after promising me you'd run as fast as you could and wouldn't stop."

"Sort of like you promised me that you'd run out of the shack too? If you'd told me you'd been shot, I would have helped you instead of running off and leaving you. If you'd been killed, how do you think that would have made me feel? How could I live with that kind of guilt on my conscience? If you think I'm the kind of woman who thinks it's romantic for a guy to die for her, then you don't know me at all. I don't want you to die for me. I want you to live."

His jaw tightened, and he turned to face the pond again.

She did the same, counting silently until she could speak again without her voice shaking. "So that's it then?" she finally said. "You've been mad at me ever since then because I couldn't bear for you to die if there was anything I could do to prevent it? Is this your apology? Because as apologies go, it totally sucks."

He suddenly turned and grasped her forearms, pulling her close. "Don't you get it, Teagan? When you walked in my door in Gatlinburg, you changed everything for me, everything. You made me care when I didn't want to. You made me want…you. And instead of shutting myself away to protect someone else from being hurt by another one of my lousy decisions, I decided to give it another try. I thought maybe, just maybe, I could help you and not be a bringer of doom. But look at how that worked out? I'm a jinx. Bad luck. Whatever you want to call it. If it hadn't been for me, you wouldn't have been at the Brodericks'."

She shook her head. "What you're saying doesn't even make sense. Mason told me what happened with Hayley, when you were shot in the hip. You were the only person for miles around who saw her with the kidnapper. You rammed her truck with your car to try to save her, and paid for it by getting shot." He started to interrupt, but she pushed his hands away to stop him. "The only one who thinks you were a failure in that incident is you. From what Mason said, the delay you caused before the abductor took off with Hayley again was enough of a delay to save her life. It gave other Seekers the time they needed to catch up to them. She's alive because of you. Period."

His jaw tightened. "Are you done yet?"

"No. I'm not. I won't bother getting into the details about the Ripper case. I already told you my own investigation proved to me that you were the only one who had that right. And, hey, look at me, I was the one who was dead wrong on who abducted me. It certainly wasn't Lowe. But as far as me going with you to interview the Brodericks, give me a break. You know me well enough by now to realize that if you hadn't agreed to work with me after running into Zeus and me on that path, I would have continued my investigation on my own. So what do you think would have happened when I took the steps you did, set up an interview with the Brodericks, and others. Eventually I'd have stumbled onto the killer, like you and I both did. But I'd have done it alone. How do you think that would have turned out? Without you to save me, I'd have never figured out how to get out of handcuffs, or thought to make a hole in the floor to escape the shack. Without you, I'd be dead right now. Don't you see that?"

His gaze searched hers. "After everything that's happened, how can you have such faith in me?"

"You've never let me down, not once. Why wouldn't I believe in you?"

He lifted her hands and gently pressed a kiss on the back of each of them. "I've been angry at myself, angry at you, because I care so much about you. I don't want anything bad to happen to you."

She tugged her hands free and cupped his cheeks. "Then maybe instead of pushing me away, you should be pulling me close. Because there's no one I'd ever trust more than you to keep me safe."

He groaned before taking her in his arms and kissing her. The kiss was so sweet, so tender, that she was crying when it was over.

He frowned and gently wiped away her tears. "I'm sorry, sweetheart. What is it? What did I do?"

She laughed through her tears. "You did everything exactly right. These are happy tears, for once."

He pulled her against his chest. "I don't know that I deserve your trust. Or that I deserve you at all. But you make me want to." He pressed a kiss against the top of her head.

She reveled in the feel of him in her arms, finally. The sweetness of his hug, and the kiss they'd just shared, melted away the hurt of the past week. Finally, she was exactly where she wanted to be. And it felt far better than she'd ever imagined it would.

"I'm so glad I took Zeus for a walk that day," she said. "And that you were with me when the killer found me. You're an amazing man."

He grew still, then gently pushed her back. "That's it. The missing puzzle piece. The path where you were abducted the first time, and where we met while you were walking Zeus. That has to be it."

She stared up at him in confusion. "What are you talking about?"

He pulled out his cell phone. "It's always bothered me that the killer knew you'd be at the Brodericks'. And that he had enough lead time to have carjacked the delivery guy and hidden the truck in that garage. He also had time to loosen a section of fence, all in anticipation of us coming over. Who knew you'd be with me that night?"

She shook her head. "No one. No one but you and me. I didn't even tell my parents where we were going."

"Exactly. You and I didn't talk to anyone about our plans. And there's no reason to assume the Brodericks would have told anyone either, or that they'd just happen to mention it when the killer was nearby."

"Okay, then the killer would have had to hear you and me discussing it. Is that what you're saying?"

"Bingo." He pressed a speed-dial number on his phone. "Mason, yeah, it's Bryson at my new number. Listen, are any of the Seekers in The Woods subdivision right now, maybe interviewing witnesses?" He shook his head for her benefit. "Okay, right. That's fine. I can—" He listened for a few moments, nodding. "JSO. Of course. I forgot they were conducting extra patrols out here. I'll call them now. I'll catch you up later. It's just a hunch."

"Bryson, what's going on?"

"Just a minute, sweetheart. One more call." He pressed another speed-dial number. "Detective Burns? Bryson Anton. Yes. I have a favor to ask." He idly turned away, slowly walking down the length of the fence as he explained whatever hunch he had to the detective.

She leaned against a post, smiling as she noted how well he was walking, without using his cane. His limp was barely noticeable. The last several days of rest had done wonders. And thankfully his surgery had been laparoscopic, making the recovery much easier. Still, he hadn't had a miracle cure. If he pushed too hard he'd end up having to use the new cane she'd gotten him to replace the old one. Or, worse, end up in his wheelchair for the rest of the day. What he really needed was to go home, to get on that flight to Gatlinburg, and give his body more time to fully recover.

As he turned back toward her, still talking on the phone, she wondered what was going to happen next. Not with the case. She was content to let others handle it at this point. What she wanted to know was what would happen with them. After all, he'd kissed her, in full view of her parents who were no doubt watching them through the back sliding glass doors this very minute. And he'd called her sweetheart. Twice in as many minutes. That had to mean something serious, didn't it?

He stopped a few yards away and leaned against the fence looking out at the water, phone still to his ear. But he wasn't talking. He seemed to be waiting for something. He suddenly straightened and looked at her, a slow smile spreading across his face. He said something else to the detective, then shoved his phone in his pocket and closed the distance between them.

"What is it?" she asked. "Did they…did they catch him?"

"Not yet. But we've got a great lead. I asked JSO to look for some kind of camera tucked up in the trees that overlook the path, at the spot where we were that day I met you with Zeus."

"And where I was abducted."

"Yes. It dawned on me that the only reasonable way the killer could have known about you going to the Brodericks' was if he heard us talking about it. And the only place we spoke about it was—"

"On the path."

"Exactly. The camera was about twenty feet up in an oak tree, tucked into a juncture with two other branches, with a fake bird's nest concealing all but a small hole for the lens. And it has audio capabilities as well as visual. He was watching and listening. There may be other cameras along the path too. Now that JSO knows what to look for, they'll be able to find them, if they exist. More importantly, they'll be able to get an expert on this, figure out the camera's range and triangulate the area where someone would have to be in order to receive the transmission."

"Wouldn't he have to be close by?"

"Probably. Which means it's likely he lives or works in this subdivision, and I'm guessing he did two years ago, as well. I doubt he targeted you specifically, not the first time. You just happened along the trail and met whatever criteria he has for his preferred victims."

She pressed a hand to her throat. "I'm still stuck on the first part, about him living or working here. JSO cleared everyone back then, everyone in the whole development."

He cocked his head. "They didn't clear everyone in the one next door."

She gasped. "Bentwater Place. The house where he took us and put us in the truck. He might live there?"

He shrugged. "JSO's looking into it. I would have thought if he did, they'd have figured that out already as part of the Broderick murder investigation. But it's possible he lives in one of the homes next door and would have known the house was empty the night we were doing the interview. Then again, he may live here in your subdivision and the police cleared someone they shouldn't have when your case was being actively looked into. Like you,

I'm a bit skeptical since they missed that camera and it's remained there all this time. But from what the officer said who found it, he never would have seen it if I hadn't specifically told him to look for one."

"Wait. Are you saying it's been there for *years*? Not that it was put there recently?"

He clasped her hands in his. "Based on the condition of the outside casing, it was probably there back when you were abducted. My guess is when the police didn't find it, the killer didn't risk going back to get it. And when months passed without it being discovered, he kept it active and checked in on the video every now and then."

"Which is how he knew I was here in Jacksonville, and where we were going that night."

He squeezed her hands. "I believe so, yes."

She stared up at him. "I was bound and determined to walk that path all week for my planned visit with my parents. I naively assumed I'd be okay with Zeus and my gun. But the way I froze back at the shack, and at the Brodericks' house, we both know I wouldn't have drawn my gun in time to protect myself. And knowing what I do now, I don't think Zeus could have stopped him either. Thank God you were there that day."

He leaned down and pressed a quick kiss against her lips. "That camera will hopefully lead them to the killer. And the BOLO they have with the police artist's sketch will ensure he doesn't get very far. But I'm not taking any chances. Pack a bag, Teagan. You're going with me to Tennessee."

Chapter Twenty-One

If any other man had *informed* Teagan that she was going to do something, or go somewhere, without asking her, she'd have ripped right into him. But this was Bryson. She knew his authoritarian dictate wasn't his typical way of operating, that he wanted to keep her safe, which was incredibly sweet. Besides, flying on a private jet to his home for who knew how many days or weeks of seclusion with him wasn't exactly a hardship. Especially since they'd worked through the tensions and self-recriminations of this past week. She was looking forward to this time alone with him.

But as she watched him snoozing in the limo seat across from her on the last leg of the trip to his house, she couldn't help feeling a twinge of disappointment. Between the toll that his injuries had taken on him and the effects of the pain pills and antibiotics, he'd slept most of the way here. He needed the rest to get better. But she was so hungry for time with him, quality time. She wanted that *get to know you* phase of the relationship that they'd skipped during their life and death struggles. She was greedy to learn the little things.

Like his favorite color.

His favorite food.

Was he partial to country music as so many people around here were?

Would it shock him to know that she hated country music but loved classical?

Since he hadn't mentioned his family before, and none of them had called or visited him in the hospital, was that because he didn't have any family? Or was he just trying to keep them from worrying? Did his boss know that he wouldn't have wanted them told about what had happened?

She couldn't help feeling jealous if he had siblings. She'd always wanted brothers and sisters. Well, mostly sisters. Brothers could be so mean, at least from what her dad said about her uncles. But growing up an only child, she'd always longed for more. She wanted a house full of her own children one day. Did he want children too? Would he love and cherish them and protect them from a world that could be hateful and mean when people didn't fit into those neat little racial categories?

"Want to talk about it?"

She met his questioning gaze. "You're awake."

"I am."

"How's your pain level? Need some pills?"

"I need to know what's bothering you." He grimaced as he straightened in his seat, but shook his head when she reached for the bottle of pills in her purse. "Don't. A little twinge here and there is better than sleeping my life away. Those things knock me out." He glanced out the window. "Almost home. But we still have time for you to tell me what has you frowning as if you want to kill someone. Hopefully it's not me," he teased.

When she didn't answer, his smile faded. "Seriously. What's wrong?"

"Nothing. Random thoughts. Silly things."

"You can be outrageous and deliciously sassy. But

you're never silly. What are these random thoughts? If you have questions about the investigation—"

"What's your favorite color?" she blurted out, even though it was the least important question rolling around in her mind right now.

"Ah. Now I understand the frown. You're contemplating some of life's most vexing problems."

"How do you feel about interracial marriages, and children?"

His eyes widened. "Well, Okay. That was unexpected. The answer is gray, by the way."

"Gray?"

"My favorite color."

"Gray can't be your favorite color. Gray isn't a color. It's a…shade."

He shrugged, unconcerned with her assessment. "As to interracial marriages and children, I'm against children getting married regardless of their race."

She stared at him deadpan. "When did you develop a sense of humor?"

"Apparently never. You're not laughing."

She looked out the window. "How much farther to your home?"

In answer, he tapped on the glass partition. It lowered and the driver met his gaze in the rearview mirror. "Yes, Mr. Anton?"

"Take the long way to my house."

"But, sir. We're already—"

"Up and down the mountain, then. We have a few things to settle before we arrive."

"Of course sir. Just let me know when you're ready to get there."

The glass went back up, sealing them in privacy again. He moved from his seat to settle beside her, then took her right hand in his left. "I'm assuming this is a hypothetical question. Or is there something else you want to add, so that it's more specific?"

Her face grew warm. "Forget I asked. It was a ridiculous question and completely inappropriate."

"It's a serious question, a deep question, and it deserves a serious, respectful and honest answer. As to being inappropriate, I can't imagine how it could be, unless maybe it's not hypothetical after all and you're talking about you and me—and you're worried about how I would take it?"

It didn't seem possible for her face to get hotter, but it did. "Like I said, forget I asked. It was inappropriate, because it assumes all kinds of things, like that whatever this is between us could ever grow into something to where the answer to that question would matter."

"You're talking marriage, between you and me."

She crossed her arms. "You don't have to sound so stunned. It's a logical progression in relationships. Not that I'm saying we're in a relationship, exactly, or that it would become a logical step for us. I mean, if we ever even, you know, dated. Which we haven't, really—"

He covered her mouth with his and gave her a slow, lazy and incredibly thorough kiss. When he pulled back, all she could do was sigh, and melt against the buttery leather seats.

"Wow," she finally managed to say. "If I could bottle you up and sell you, I'd make a fortune."

He laughed, then grew serious. "I'm not going to pretend that I can see into the future and tell where you and I might end up. We've had a rocky couple of weeks, and that's the biggest understatement ever. But I can say with absolute certainty that we are definitely in a relationship."

She swallowed, and managed a shaky smile. "Good to know."

"As to your other questions, the first one is easy. In case you haven't figured it out, I think you're one of the smartest, funniest and hottest women I've ever met."

She blinked up at him. "You think I'm hot?"

"Oh. Yeah. And that's not *in spite* of your brown skin or any other feature that makes you different from me. It's *because* of those features, because of all the things that make you uniquely you. You're an amazing, sexy, wonderful woman, Teagan Ray. Whoever you end up marrying, if you decide to marry, that man would be incredibly lucky and should feel honored that you chose him. And if he doesn't feel that way, then he doesn't deserve you."

She settled against him, resting her head in the crook of his shoulder as he put his arm around her. "You're an amazing man, Bryson Anton."

"You're not so bad yourself. And, Teagan?"

"Yes, Bryson?"

He kissed her neck just below her ear, making her shiver. "I couldn't begin to understand the ugliness the world may have shown you, the prejudice you've likely faced in your life, or the fears you live with every day about things I would never encounter, simply because we were born looking different from each other. But I can tell you this. Hypothetically, if you and I, for example, were to marry and were fortunate enough to have children, I would do everything in my power to protect them in every way. Above all, I would love them, and make sure they knew they were loved, always, unconditionally. And that I've got their backs, no matter what." He kissed the top of her head. "Does that answer all your questions?"

She shook her head. "Not even close. I have dozens more."

"Dozens?"

"Scores, actually."

He laughed. "Then I guess we'll be riding around this mountain for a good long time." He settled back more comfortably, pulling her with him. "Go ahead. Ask your questions. But be prepared. I might have a few of my own."

Chapter Twenty-Two

Teagan had learned so much about Bryson during that conversation in the limo two days ago. It had been fun learning about his family, his rather *large* family of three younger brothers and two older sisters who were both married and had six kids between them.

His family was spread out across the country from coast to coast. While his parents split their time between Canada and traveling all over the US, fully enjoying their retirement, they popped in throughout the year to visit their children and grandchildren.

Bryson had explained that after seeing how difficult it was for his family when he'd been shot during his last Justice Keepers assignment, he'd made Mason promise not to tell them if he got hurt again. That was why they hadn't been at the hospital. While she couldn't fathom not keeping her family informed about something like that, she respected his decision.

But in spite of the many new details that she'd learned about him, she realized she'd already known everything that really mattered. He was smart, loyal, considerate, and a million other wonderful things rolled up in an incredibly mouthwatering package that she wanted to devour.

Except that she couldn't. Not yet.

It was torture not being able to move their relationship

forward the way she wanted to. But he couldn't stand the way the pain pills made it hard to focus and concentrate on the investigation, so he'd all but stopped taking them. And that meant he was hobbling around on an aching hip again in the mornings, stuck using the wheelchair most afternoons. Her heart ached for him as she watched him limping across the family room right now with the aid of his cane, smiling at her and pretending he wasn't in pain. But the small white lines around his mouth weren't something he could hide.

"Ready?" He paused by the front door where she'd been waiting for him.

"Ready." She took his cane so he could grab his suit jacket from the hall tree and shrug into it.

She picked up her purse and let him open the door. It seemed to matter to him to open doors for her, so she'd stopped trying to run ahead or open them herself. As they crossed the front porch, she asked, "You really think a brainstorming session with the Justice Seekers is going to crack the case open?"

"We have to try something new to shake things loose. Plus Bishop texted me that he's back from interviewing Leviathan Finney and wants to talk about what he found. He'll meet us at Camelot."

"First of all, I forget, who's Bishop? Second, he interviewed the Kentucky Ripper in prison?"

He stopped on the walkway at the end of the porch. "Gage Bishop. He's one of the Justice Seekers, the first one Mason hired when he created the company. Everything I know about him would fill about a third of a sheet of paper. He keeps to himself, doesn't socialize with the others outside of work. Mason's the only one who knows whatever traumatic event ended his law enforcement career before he started over as a Justice Seeker."

He limped down the path again, toward the driveway.

"I'm confused. Traumatic event? I thought you didn't know anything about him."

He stopped again, leaning heavily on his cane. "I assumed if Mason was impressed enough to give you carte blanche with a company credit card after I was discharged from the hospital that he would have confided in you. I thought you knew."

"Knew what? I'm lost."

"The Justice Seekers. The whole reason the company was formed was to give a second chance to people who'd had their law enforcement careers destroyed through no fault of their own. It's a second chance for all of us."

"I had no idea. But I guess it makes sense. You felt you'd failed as a special agent—"

"I did."

"No. You didn't. But I understand now why you became a Justice Seeker. After you quit the FBI, you felt you had something to prove. And Mason gave you that chance."

"Not that I've done much with that second chance. He probably regrets hiring me."

They'd started down the path again, but she moved in front of him, blocking his way. "Don't you dare talk like that. I'd have been killed half a dozen times by now if it wasn't for you. I'm not going to listen to any more self-recriminations. You're an amazing guy with fantastic instincts. It's time you gave yourself some credit."

His jaw tightened, telling her he didn't agree. But to his credit, he didn't argue.

She stepped aside and followed him toward the driveway where she'd backed his metallic-blue Ford pickup out of the garage in preparation for the drive into town. It was decked out, with all the options. It wasn't the red convertible she'd pictured him driving. But Hot Guy in a pickup revved her engines even more than she'd thought possible.

A luxury car, like the rental he'd had in Jacksonville, would have been much easier on his hip. But the car that he'd owned, a classic older car he'd planned on restoring, had been totaled that day he'd been shot trying to save Hayley from a kidnapper. So it was either take his truck or hire another rental. She wished he'd opt for the rental because she knew it would be easier for him to climb in and out, and the bumps in the road wouldn't hurt so much in a car. But she also knew he was a proud man and didn't want to look weak in front of the team. To him, renting a car to drive when he had a perfectly good truck in his garage would be a neon sign that he wasn't okay.

At least he was letting her drive. That was the one concession he'd made. She was pretty sure he was relieved when she'd asked, even though he pretended to debate her question. Her insistence that she loved trucks and wanted to drive this one, which was certainly true, wasn't completely accurate since her main reason to drive was to help him save face. It was obviously much more comfortable to be a passenger than to pump his foot on the pedals.

Twenty minutes later they were at The Justice Seekers' headquarters, an enormous two-story modern-day castle that fully lived up to its nickname of Camelot. Even though she'd been here once before when she'd met with Mason Ford about hiring Bryson, she was still in awe. Especially when Bryson took her into a secret passage to a room few clients ever got to see, a truly medieval looking meeting room with an enormous round table in the middle. It had been dubbed the Great Hall. It was a much bigger version of Bryson's so-called office at his house. And judging by the enormous monitors forming a semicircle a short distance from the table, this Great Hall had all the technological gadgets that Bryson's did, maybe more.

"Welcome to Camelot," he whispered in her ear as they stood off to one side, just past the secret passage they'd walked through. "What do you think of Mason's pride and joy?"

"Stunning. A bit overwhelming, really. But supercool." She waved toward the round table, where three other people were seated. "Are those Justice Seekers?" At his nod, she said, "I thought they were in Jacksonville."

"Five of them are. The rest were working cases here and couldn't leave right away. There's one more Seeker we're waiting on before we start. When fully staffed, there are twelve of us, plus Mason, our fearless leader."

"Fully staffed?"

"One of our Seekers was killed last year. Mason's just now looking for a replacement. But let's not dwell on that. Like I said, there are basically twelve of us, plus the boss."

"The knights of the round table. And King Arthur?"

He smiled. "Yes. But if you call Mason King Arthur he'll never forgive you. That's the one part of his little game he hasn't adopted. He thinks it's pretentious." He motioned toward the right side of the table where a man just as broad-shouldered and tall as Bryson was pulling up a chair. "That's Bishop over there. When we sit down, you'll see that everyone has an assigned seat with their name and their moniker engraved on the stone table in front of them."

"Moniker? Like, what, Hot Guy?"

He laughed. "Don't say that too loudly or I'll never hear the end of it. The monikers are based on their former occupations. Bishop is The Bodyguard."

"I thought you didn't know what he did before he became a Justice Seeker?"

"We know he protected people, but we don't know who he worked for. A good guess is one of the alphabet agencies—FBI, CIA, NCIS. But only Mason knows for sure. That extremely extroverted lady on the left who's waving at you is The Cop, Brielle Walker. She used to be a Gatlinburg police officer."

She smiled and returned Brielle's wave. "And the guy beside her?"

"Han Li, The Special Agent."

"You both have the same moniker? Special Agent?"

"No. He was a special agent with Homeland Security. And he started here first, so he got to choose The Special Agent for his title."

"Then what are you?"

His mouth tightened. "The Profiler. Not my choosing. Mason stuck me with that title."

She splayed her fingers against his chest. "You're an amazing profiler, Bryson. If I have to tell you that a hundred times until you believe it, I will."

He arched a brow. "A hundred times, huh? That implies you're planning on sticking around for a while."

"If you want me to stay, I'm sure I'd enjoy you trying to convince me." She gave him an outrageous wink.

He was about to say something but the door to the hidden passageway opened and another man, wearing a Stetson, stepped into the room. Bryson's grin faded and his answering nod in response to the other man's friendly "hello" was decidedly cool.

"Who's that?" she kept her voice low.

"The Cowboy, Dalton Lynch."

"Why don't you like him?"

He gave her a surprised look. "What makes you think I don't like him?"

"Oh, I don't know. Maybe because it felt like a polar

vortex descended on the room when you barely returned his greeting."

His jaw tightened. "I have no problem with Dalton. But I don't go out of my way to inflict my presence on him. His wife is Hayley, the woman who almost died because of me."

She blinked in surprise. At the table, Dalton's expression as he eyed Bryson seemed to be more of regret, maybe even frustration. But there was absolutely no animosity or reproach. When he caught her looking at him, he nodded, then turned toward the others.

"Bryson, I don't think he blames you for what happened to his wife any more than you should blame yourself."

He put his hand on her back. "You're sweet to worry about me. But the only thing that matters right now is figuring out the identity of the man who almost killed you. And putting him away for a very long time. Come on, they're waiting."

He introduced her to the others. Then they all got really serious, really fast. She sat in the chair beside him, in the seat for Zack Foster, The Tracker. He'd whispered that Zack was the one who'd died, which had her feeling like an interloper. But he insisted no one minded her sitting there and it seemed to be true. They were all very respectful and nice to her.

Each of them had a computer tablet in front of them, and what they brought up was displayed on one of the huge screens at the front of the room so they could see everything at the same time. As efficiency went, it was amazing. They shared reports, pictures, investigative notes, all at the touch of a button or the swipe of a finger across their tablets that were each-hardwired into the computer for security.

She was a bit overwhelmed hearing what they'd been

doing. Every one of them was working her case now. It was humbling that they were all so vested in helping her. But then again, they were doing it for Bryson too. He was their brother-in-arms. The man they were after had almost killed him. And it was obvious that none of them were going to let a stone go unturned in their quest to bring the killer to justice and avenge their friend and fellow Seeker.

The hours ticked by, with short breaks here and there so everyone could use the restroom or make phone calls.

Lunch was brought in by some efficient person who suddenly appeared from the secret passageway and quietly set the food and drinks down on a table against one wall, then quietly disappeared.

They seemed to have exhausted just about every lead and angle possible by midafternoon. But there was one person who hadn't presented his findings yet—Bishop. The others sat back and the room went quiet as his notes from the prison interview with Finney, the Kentucky Ripper, filled the screen.

Chapter Twenty-Three

"A few days ago," Bishop began, "Bryson requested that I look into Leviathan Finney in relation to this case. The reason is obvious. Ms. Ray was abducted two years ago by a man who carved an X on her stomach, just like the Kentucky Ripper did to his victims. But since that same man abducted her again, and Finney is in prison for the Ripper's crimes, the question is whether Finney is the real Ripper or a copycat. The reason that matters is that if he's a copycat, then it's possible that the man who abducted her is the Ripper. Knowing that provides a lot more data to use to find this man. But we don't want to send ourselves, or the police, down the wrong investigative path. So it was important to figure out whether we could rule in her abductor as the Ripper, or rule him out."

He typed a few buttons on his tablet, then a table of dates, names and comments appeared on the screen.

"Those are the Ripper's victims," Teagan said.

"They are," Bishop agreed. "Along with the dates of their abductions and murders. I created this table to keep track of what Finney was supposedly doing at the time of each abduction or murder. It's his alibi list, basically. Or it was supposed to be. When I checked through court transcripts, the alibi information was rather thin. His lawyer didn't present much of a defense. Regardless, I dug as deep as I could in the time that I had. And then I went to the psychiatric hospital where Finney was being held before being deemed fit enough to be placed in the general prison population. I spoke to his doctors and was able to convince them to share information to help with my victim/alibi matrix."

Teagan blinked and shot Bryson a look, but he didn't seem fazed by Bishop's last statement. As far as she knew, doctors, especially a psychiatrist, would never disclose that kind of information about a living patient without a warrant. She wondered what Bishop had done to "convince" them to talk.

"After that," Bishop continued, "I spoke to Finney, for hours." He highlighted a handful of rows in the table on the screen. "After piecing together witness statements from the investigations, court transcripts, what his doctor said, and then interviewing people to corroborate what Finney told me, these four rows are the only ones where I couldn't positively alibi him out. But even these I'm fifty-fifty on." He sat back and glanced around the table, apparently finished speaking.

Teagan looked at the others. Brielle was furiously typing on her laptop. Han was swiping through screen after screen on his, as if searching for something. And the guy in the Stetson, Dalton, had jumped up from the table and was standing off in a corner on, of all things, a wall phone. She hadn't seen one of those in years.

At her questioning look, Bryson asked, "The phone? Most of Camelot is a giant Faraday cage."

"Fair a what?"

"Faraday. Electronic signals can't get in or out. We have to use dedicated landlines. It's for security. Even the computer tablets are hard-wired through the table to the main computer."

She thought that seemed like total overkill, but didn't really care at the moment. What mattered was that she was completely lost. "Why does everyone else seem to understand whatever Bishop just said about Finney? I'm confused."

Bishop remained silent, apparently content to let someone else explain.

Bryson took her hand in his. "To sum it up, he was able to prove, maybe not court of law proof, but proof to us, that Finney couldn't have killed most of the victims that he's accused of killing. He had solid alibis that either weren't presented at trial or weren't known at trial. There are only a few that Bishop couldn't speak to. Which goes to say that you were right all along. Leviathan Finney very likely isn't the Ripper. But he's not a copycat either. He was set up. Framed."

"By the police?"

"Doubtful. Most likely the real killer, to take the heat off."

"An innocent man is in prison. That sucks."

"We'll contact one of the Innocence Project groups to look into his case."

"Already did," Bishop chimed in.

"Great," she said. "I guess. But what does all this mean as far as finding the guy who abducted us? Are you saying he's the real Ripper?"

"It's a definite possibility, highly likely actually. The police never linked your case with the others in spite of the signature X because the Ripper was already in prison. But now that we know the Ripper was never caught, all of the murders attributed to him have to be reexamined in relation to your abduction. This is a huge break. There's an FBI field office in Jacksonville. Once our team brings them up to speed on this development, they'll be back in the game, looking into your case and reopening the Ripper investigation. Obviously there are formalities, like convincing JSO to call them in to help. But Mason will get that done. Just a matter of time. The number of people working this case is about to quadruple, easily. With some of the brightest law enforcement minds around. They'll catch this guy in no time."

Dalton returned to his seat. The others turned their attention toward Bryson.

"What about you?" Dalton asked. "Any theories about who this guy might be?"

"A few," Bryson said. "It's been bothering me that he was able to abduct Teagan two years ago without anyone seeing him. She was apparently drugged. She thinks she remembers him injecting her right after he accosted her on the path. After that, her memory is blank until she woke up at the shack. But that path through her neighborhood is well-traveled. And the entrance to the path on both ends is in even busier sections of the neighborhood. It seems far-fetched that he could have led or carried a drugged woman from the path without anyone seeing her. Which is why I called Mason early this morning and asked him to have our Seekers in Jacksonville re-interview everyone who lives close to that part of the trail and ask very specific questions."

"Like what?" Dalton asked.

"Like whether he could have loosened a section of fence like he did behind the Brodericks' house and taken her through the opening to someone's backyard. From there, if he did the same trick he pulled with us, he could have gone through someone's home while they weren't home and into their garage where he had a car waiting. Then, all he had to do was drive out of the subdivision. There's a guard shack at each of the two entrances. But the cameras only record people coming in, not going out. If he came in via the subdivision behind The Woods, like he did recently, he wouldn't be on any of the guard gate's cameras."

Teagan raised her hand.

Bryson smiled. "You don't have to ask permission to speak."

She felt her face heat and lowered her hand. "You said earlier that you thought he might live in one of the houses in Bentwater Place, near the one we went through to that delivery truck. Did anything ever come of that?"

"The police ruled that out. He definitely isn't one of the homeowners on that street or the neighboring streets. But one of those homes was vacant because it's for sale. He could have seen that for sale sign and broke in to conduct quick surveillance on the house next door. Once he was sure the owners weren't home, he used that house as part of his plan to abduct you."

Dalton tapped on the table as if in deep thought. "How close is that path to the Bentwater subdivision?"

Bryson looked at Teagan in question. "What do you think? Half a mile? The Woods is huge. That path is in the center of the subdivision."

She nodded. "Maybe even a mile, or more really if you consider all the twists and turns you'd have to take because of all the streets in between."

"He didn't walk from Bentwater to the path," Bryson concluded. "It's too far. There would have been multiple reports in the interviews that the police conducted after your abduction, reports of different people seeing a man walking toward that trail. There weren't any reports. None."

"Then how did he get in?" she asked.

He sat back, considering the question. "Getting back to basics, we have two choices. He walked or drove. Since no mysterious strangers were seen on the cameras at the guard shack, driving is out. But since he wasn't seen walking through the subdivision by anyone interviewed after your abduction, walking is out too. Which leads to one conclusion. The time frame that the police covered when canvassing the neighborhood was inadequate."

A few chairs over from him, Dalton nodded. "That's the only explanation. He was already in place. He went into the subdivision before the time range that the police checked." He turned toward the former police officer. "Brielle, I think you had that report on the video from the guard shack. How far back did they check?"

She was already typing. Then she punched a button and a report popped up on one of the big screens. "One week. Our killer had to be in place prior to that." She turned her focus on Teagan. "I haven't been in that development. But from what I've read, there aren't any actual woods where someone could hide out that long and not be found, are there?"

Teagan shook her head. "No. I mean, there are plenty of areas with lots of trees and bushes. But it's all personal property, or it backs up behind a strip mall on one side. The community areas are too heavily traveled, like those walking paths, to allow someone to camp out and not be seen."

"I agree," Bryson said. "And it goes back to the sheer volume of witnesses in that area. Even if he camped out, someone would have seen him at some point and reported it. Nothing like that happened. Which means he was in one of the houses. We already know he's not one of the owners, based on the extensive reports the police did on every homeowner. If he was visiting someone who lives there, again, they would have mentioned it to the police. That leaves one last possibility. He was using someone's house when they were out of town. We need a list of everyone who was out of town over a week before the attack."

"On it." Brielle started typing on her computer again. "I've got all of those types of records already from our earlier canvassing but didn't put it together the way you just did. I just need to cross-reference a couple of spreadsheets and I'll have it."

A few minutes later, the dejection on her face told the story even before she spoke. "Sorry, guys and gals. As impossible as it seems in a place with that many houses, no one was on vacation in that time span. At least, no one who didn't have a house sitter or friend at their place while they were gone."

Bryson sat forward in his chair. "Then the house was empty. Whoever owned it didn't live there anymore. How many homes were vacant, either for rent or for sale during that time frame?"

The tension was palpable in the room as they waited for Brielle once again.

She popped up the latest search results. "Three. All for sale, all vacant."

"Bentwater Place, the house that was empty and for sale that the police thought our killer might have used as his home base with the Broderick murders," Bryson said. "Does anyone have any additional information on that house?"

"Like what?" Dalton asked.

"The realty company. Better yet, the Realtor who listed it."

Dalton smiled. "Of course. On it."

"I'm on it too, for the ones in The Woods," Brielle said.

A few moments later, Dalton sat back. "Pine Acres Realty."

"Dang, I almost beat you," Brielle said. "I'm calling it a tie. Two of mine are with Happy Meadows Properties." She rolled her eyes at the name. "My last one, which happens to back up directly onto the path where Ms. Ray was attacked, is Pine Acres Realty."

Teagan blinked in shock. "He's a Realtor?"

"It appears likely," Bryson said. "And he probably works for Pine Acres Realty. We need pictures."

Bishop, who'd been quietly working on his own computer all along, punched a button. The screens filled with pictures of the smiling men and women who worked for that realty company.

Bryson arched a brow. "Thanks, Bishop."

Bishop nodded.

"Bottom row." Teagan's voice was hoarse. "If the screen wasn't so huge, I wouldn't have even noticed. And now I know why no one in the neighborhood recognized the police sketch."

"Why?" Dalton asked.

Bryson reached for Teagan's hand beneath the table and she gratefully clung to it. "Because he looks completely different in that picture. Hair color, hair style, glasses. There's only one thing that's the same."

"What's that?" Dalton pressed.

"His eyes." Teagan's hand tightened on Bryson's. "Pure evil, dead inside. That's him. It's definitely him. I've probably seen him on real estate flyers in the neighborhood. But I never connected the dots. His name?" She paused to draw a choppy breath. "I need to hear his name."

"Chris Larsen," Brielle announced.

She shook her head. "So average. So…normal."

Brielle started typing again. "I'll get this information to Mason and the team in Jacksonville right away."

"I'll give him a call," Dalton added. "I'll answer any questions he has about our thought processes and how we arrived at this conclusion." He smiled. "How *Bryson* arrived at it. Good job, Profiler. And it's good to have you back."

Bryson seemed surprised by Dalton's statement, but he nodded his thanks. "Call me with Mason's update on the hunt for this guy?"

"You don't want to hang around? If our team's in on the takedown we might get a live feed."

"I would, but my hip's aching something awful." He pushed to his feet, leaning heavily on his cane, and motioned to Teagan. "I know you'd rather hang around, but I don't think I can drive right now. Do you mind?"

She was struggling to maintain her composure with all of this information crashing down on her. And here he was, pretending that he was the one who needed to leave. She gratefully went along with his ruse. "I can get the updates later. I don't mind."

Once they were in his truck, the stress and worry that had been eating at her seemed to magically fade away. He had that effect on her, made her feel safe, more in control. "I know your hip really does hurt. But I also know you'd never admit that in front of your team. You did that for me, because you saw how I was struggling to hold it together. Thank you."

"It was nothing. But you're welcome anyway. How are you holding up? I can drive if I have to."

"I know, but I'm fine. It was all so…intense back there, finding out who he was, and realizing he's just a person. You know? Not some mythical monster impossible to stop. Hearing he's a Realtor kind of takes the drama down a notch. Makes it somehow bearable, especially knowing it's only a matter of time now before this is over."

When they pulled into the driveway, his phone buzzed in his pocket. She parked while he spoke to Dalton. When she got out, he frowned, obviously wishing she'd wait so he could open her door. He'd just put his phone in his suit jacket pocket and grabbed his cane when she opened his door and offered her hand.

"There's no one here but us, Bry. You can suck up your pride for a minute and let me help you. It *is* okay for a woman to help a man sometimes, you know."

He avoided her hand and hopped out on his own.

She rolled her eyes and moved to his side. "What did Dalton have to say? Is JSO cooperating? Did they put out a new BOLO on the killer now that we know his identity?"

He smiled and unlocked the front door. As he pushed it open for her he said, "Yes, JSO is *cooperating*, although I'm sure they think it's the other way around. A new BOLO was put out, but they already contacted the realty company to see if they had a lead on his whereabouts. That's why Dalton called, to give us an update about the realty company." He shut and locked the door, before giving her his full attention.

"They got him, Teagan. He's on his way downtown right now in the back of a squad car. It's over."

She burst into tears.

BRYSON TOSSED HIS cane to the floor and lifted Teagan in his arms. He couldn't make it very far, but he managed to stumble to the couch without dropping her. He settled back with his precious burden and held her while she cried out the hurt and the fear and the anxiety she'd been suffering for years.

It was a long time later before he settled Sleeping Beauty in his master bedroom that he'd given up while she was here. She'd readily invited him to stay with her in his bed that first night. But he knew the dangers. It didn't matter how his head hurt, or the wounds on his back, or his hip, or where the bullet went through him, or, good grief, how sore his belly still was from the surgery. He was a mess, physically. But if he got horizontal next to her none of it would matter. There'd be no stopping either of them from taking full advantage of that situation. And then he'd probably end up in the hospital again. But oh how he wished it could be different.

He quietly shut the door. But he didn't head to the guest room where he was staying. He had another destination tonight. And this one was too far for him to make using his cane. He'd used up the last of his stamina carrying Teagan. It was time to admit defeat, for now, and get the wheelchair.

A few minutes later he reached his office. As he opened files on the computer and began moving bits of information onto the various screens, he reflected on what Dalton had said at Camelot. He'd referred to his old moniker, Profiler. That one word, spoken by a fellow Seeker, had started an avalanche of thoughts in his mind.

Even though he'd been trying to work this case as best he could with a lingering concussion and his other injuries, he hadn't tried to approach it as a profiler. He was too used to scorning his previous profession, thinking of his failures instead of focusing on his successes. But he didn't think of it the same way anymore. Teagan had done that for him, made him start to accept that maybe he wasn't the big failure he once thought himself to be. And Dalton, of course, welcoming him back. That had been a surprise. If Dalton didn't blame him for Hayley's near miss, maybe he needed to rethink that whole episode.

But mostly it was Teagan's faith in him that was giving him a new perspective. Like that maybe he should trust himself, listen to the warning bells going off in his head. They were telling him that something wasn't right.

They'd caught the man who'd abducted Teagan. They'd caught the man who'd killed the Brodericks. So why did he feel like there was something left unfinished? The niggling feeling wouldn't leave him alone. So he was going back to the beginning as he'd once told Teagan to do. He was reexamining everything. And once he did that, he'd do what he hadn't done in years, and had never thought he'd do again.

He was going to build a profile.

Chapter Twenty-Four

Teagan finished brushing her teeth just as the morning sun began to peek through the windows. After giving her braid one last adjustment, she left the master bedroom to find Bryson. Much to her frustration, even though he'd ensconced her in the master suite since she'd come here, he was sleeping in a guest room. She understood it was because sleeping together was too tempting. Neither of them would want to *sleep*. Which would just set his recovery back. But she was getting so frustrated wanting him to get better, and just plain *wanting* him.

Everything about him appealed to her. And the more she got to know him, the worse her obsession became. Whether he was in butt-hugging jeans and a T-shirt or one of those sexy tailored suits that showed off his broad shoulders, she wanted to peel off his clothes and explore *every inch*. As if his sexy exterior wasn't enough of a turn on, Hot Guy was also intelligent, with a kind soul and the heart of a steadfast, loyal, intensely protective warrior. It was becoming nearly impossible not to weep with longing and desire every time he entered a room.

She could definitely fall in love with him. She was more than halfway there already. But she had no clue whether he felt the same. Oh, he liked her, a lot. And he wanted her. There was no denying the hungry look in his eyes that he tried so hard to hide. Clearly he suffered from the same affliction that she did. If they ever *really* got together, they'd probably spontaneously combust. But did he care about her? *Really* care, as in I could love you forever kind of care? She just didn't know.

Shaking her head at her fruitless thoughts, she headed to his room just down the hall. He wasn't there. The bed didn't even look as if it had been slept in. Growing concerned, she checked the main rooms in this part of the house. She even looked out the back door at the dock, where he could be found most evenings. But he wasn't there. She was just passing the little alcove to the left of the TV when she realized it was empty. Each night he stored his wheelchair there and used the cane the next day until the pain forced him to use the chair once again. But the wheelchair wasn't there. Why? Had he suffered a setback to his recovery?

Increasingly anxious, she headed down the back hall and looked in every door that she passed until she reached the end, his office. Light shining under the door had her letting out a relieved breath. He must have come here last night for some reason, then ended up sleeping in the attached bedroom rather than head all the way to the front of the house.

She knocked on the door. No answer. She knocked again. When he still didn't answer, her overactive imagination conjured up all kinds of awful scenarios, like him lying on the floor in a pool of blood, his wounds ripped open. Just the thought of him in pain, needing her, had her opening the door.

He wasn't on the floor dying.

And he wasn't sleeping in the guest room.

He was in his wheelchair at the round table, oblivious to her entry as he spoke to someone on his cell phone. All nine of the giant monitors were filled with documents. But that wasn't what had her gasping in surprise.

It was the pictures.

He glanced over his shoulder, then punched a button on the control panel, clearing the screens. "Mason, I'll call you back in a few minutes. Send me that list of dates as soon as you have it, all right? Yeah, thanks. Bye." He set the phone on the table. "Sorry. I didn't realize you were there or I wouldn't have had those pictures up."

She fought against the nausea the graphic, violent images had awakened in her as she joined him at the table. So many women. So much…carnage.

"I heard you talking to Mason. Does he have you working on a new case already and you stayed up all night studying crime scene photos?"

He hesitated, clearly uncomfortable with her questions. "I'm not working a new case, not exactly. I'm…reexamining an old one."

"Why would you do that?"

Again, he paused.

She glanced at the blank screens, her mind's eye trying to reconstruct what she'd seen seconds earlier. But she'd been too broadsided by the unexpected tableau to recall many details, even with her photographic memory. "How old is this case you're looking into?"

He looked at his wrist as if to check the time. But he hadn't replaced the fancy computer watch yet that Larsen had taken from him. "Is it morning already? I can whip us up something to eat." He backed his chair away from the table. "How about omelets? I can't remember the last time I—"

She leaned past him and punched the same key that he had earlier. The pictures popped back onto the screens.

He swore and cleared them again, but not before she saw a bloody X carved on one of the women's bellies.

"The Kentucky Ripper," she accused. "You're looking at the Kentucky Ripper cases. Why? The FBI is covering that angle. You said so at Camelot yesterday. And don't try to change the subject by acting like you suddenly love to cook. We both know better. You forget we played twenty questions times ten in the limo on the way home from the airport. I know a lot of things about you now that I didn't before. Like that you hate to cook. So spill. Why have you been here all night looking at murders that happened years ago instead of celebrating that the man who tried to kill both of us is sitting in a Jacksonville jail cell?"

He sighed heavily. "I didn't want to wait for a report from the FBI. I needed some answers now, to quiet some doubts I had, and make sure we'd covered every angle."

"What doubts? What angles?"

"Little details that don't add up. With Finney possibly innocent, the FBI is focusing on Larsen as the real Ripper. And it makes sense, given the signature and other details about the crime scenes, plus things we're starting to learn about Larsen."

She pulled out the chair beside him and sat down. "If it all makes sense, then what's bothering you?"

He hesitated.

"I'm not dropping this. You might as well tell me now or we'll be here all day," she warned.

He grimaced. "All right. What's bothering me is the puzzle pieces that don't fit. It's like with the original Ripper investigation. There are things that never matched Finney. But there was enough so-called evidence that some other evidence was basically ignored. And once he was in prison, the murders stopped. Everyone was content to let it drop, to ignore the inconsistencies."

"Not you," she reminded him. "You kept looking at the case long after it was over. You stored all those copies of the case files. That's what you were going through just now, isn't it? I'm guessing that means you hired that temp you talked about when I first arrived, to key everything into the system."

"I had Brielle work with someone while I was in the hospital," he admitted. "I'd always wanted everything digitized to make examination of the evidence easier. With you having been abducted again, I wanted to have the previous case information handy when I got a chance to review it. The obvious conclusion at the time was that Larsen was likely the Ripper, even before Bishop spoke to Finney. I expected when I eventually got home and went through this stuff, that conclusion would be cemented in my mind."

"But it wasn't."

"No. Far from it."

She shivered and rubbed her hands up and down her arms. "The man who attacked me, who attacked us, is behind bars. It shouldn't matter whether he's the Ripper or not. So why do you look so serious? And why am I starting to feel concerned?"

He took her hands in his. "Whatever I've found, or think I've found, there's no reason for you to worry. You're safe here, with me. There are four fellow Seekers twenty minutes away if we need them, which we don't. And I've got a pistol in the nightstand in my bedroom."

"Then why have you been up all night looking at the case file?"

A flicker of unease crossed his face before his expression cleared. "I like being thorough. And, as I said, I don't like puzzle pieces that don't fit."

"Show me those pieces."

"Teagan—"

"We're in this together. And we'll still be in this together when Larsen is brought to trial and we're both called to testify. Don't shut me out now. Show me."

His reluctance was obvious, but he wheeled back in front of the computer tablet. "I can clear the pictures. There's no reason for you to look at those. I was using them to double-check details in reports." His fingers flew across the keyboard as he closed files and moved things around on the tablet in front of him without sharing them to the big screens. Then he punched one of the keys, and the various Ripper case files appeared on the large monitors. True to his word, there weren't any pictures.

He continued to move things around, mostly closing out various documents until he was left with only one screen of data. It was essentially a huge list with different headings with bullets of information beneath each one.

She read some of the headings out loud. "Race, sex, age, marital status, victimology, criminal psychopathy, location, signature…" She shot him a look of surprise. "A profile. You're working up a profile."

"More or less. I compiled the information from the Ripper murders along with what we know about Larsen's recent crimes." He scrolled to one of the sections labeled *Organized vs. Disorganized.* "I'm sure you remember a lot of this from your criminal justice classes. An organized killer is one who plans his crime ahead of time, brings his weapons with him. The disorganized killer grabs a knife out of a victim's kitchen drawer to stab her. He's more spontaneous, less controlled and tends to make a lot of mistakes. A disorganized killer is generally easier to find than the organized one because of those mistakes. Which one would you say Larsen is?"

"Easy. Organized. He planned everything down to the last detail, from the camera hidden in the tree over the path where I went walking to the section of fence he loosened behind the Brodericks' home. He had to have spent months getting that shack set up as his own personal prison, installing the bars on the windows and doors."

"You get an A plus. He's definitely an organized killer, which gives us insight into his mind and how he thinks. Mason confirmed that Larsen purchased that shack over a year ago. I don't know whether he planned to go after you again, or someone else. But he was definitely preparing it well ahead of time for another victim. Knowing he was an organized killer helps predict other things, like that he probably had a steady job."

"He worked for a realty company," she said. "Not exactly nine to five, but he would have had some kind of schedule, checked in now and then, attended meetings." She crossed her arms, remembering what she'd researched on the Kentucky Ripper's crimes. "But that doesn't fit what I know about the Ripper."

"Maybe. Maybe not." He punched a few buttons and a list of names and dates appeared on the screen to the left of the main one they'd been looking at. "You should recognize those."

"The ripper's victims. Six of them."

"What do they have in common?"

"Other than the obvious? The carved X's in their bellies, the fact that they were abducted for days or weeks before being killed? That all of them were stabbed, including the ones you haven't listed. Some were shot too."

"Other than all of that. What type of killer was responsible for the kinds of crime scenes we found in those examples?"

She thought about it, then shrugged. "You're going to say whoever killed them was organized. I remember those crime scenes were pristine. Very little forensic evidence was found. No weapons were left behind. I could go on, but I can't argue that point. Those particular crime scenes were indicative of an organized perpetrator. But there were eight more killings. And those were the opposite of organized. They were…sloppy."

"Yes. They were." He displayed another list of names on the monitor to the right of the main one, the eight victims she'd just mentioned. "All of these were similar because they seemed to be the work of a disorganized killer."

"Right," she agreed. "Given the mix of organized and disorganized crime scenes, the conclusion goes more to a mental disease, like Finney suffered from. He was, is, bipolar. The theory was that he killed some in his manic state—the disorganized killings—and some in his depressive state—the organized ones."

"It's a popular theory, one the police bought into back then." He motioned toward the first list. "Consider these victims again. Although they were brutally killed, the number of stab wounds is low. Only three for the first victim, six on another, and something in between for the rest." He waved toward the second list. "These, however, had anywhere from twelve to thirty-one stab wounds in addition to being beaten in two of the cases. One victim even suffered cigarette burns all over her back."

"I remember." That sick feeling was roiling in her stomach again.

"It's called overkill," he said. "The killer inflicted far more wounds than necessary to kill his victims. Normally, that might suggest that he knew them, had personal feelings of hate toward them. But it can happen with a disorganized killer as well, with or without a mental defect. He kills in the heat of the moment, because of some imagined slight or explosive anger over something seemingly inconsequential to you or me but that is blown all out of proportion in his mind."

Again, he motioned toward the screen on the list, the names of the six victims that he'd grouped together. "Here's another take on these. In each of these cases, there's evidence that the killer spent a lot of time in the victim's home during the stalking phase while the victim wasn't there. What does that indicate?"

"I'm not sure. Maybe I need a refresher course on my college classes."

He smiled. "I'm sure it will all come back to you when you go back to finish your master's degree. Familiarity is the missing link here. We spend time somewhere when we feel comfortable there, because the location isn't foreign or unknown to us."

She stared at him a long moment. "I'm trying to follow, but all that tells me is that the Ripper likely lived in Kentucky, close to the crime scenes. That was part of the original geographical profiling. That's why Finney was such a good fit."

"And Lowe. Don't forget him, the second potential Ripper on the original suspect list. He was from Kentucky too, born and raised in the same general area as Finney."

"Okay. Yes, I remember that. It's part of the reason that I thought Lowe might have been the one who abducted me."

He swiveled his wheelchair to face her. "Think about the other things we know about those crime scenes. In the first list of victims, the bodies were left where they'd be easily found, potentially indicating the killer had some religious background, that he wanted them to get a Christian burial, or whatever religion he followed."

"The bodies weren't hidden in the rest of the killings either. They're the same."

"I'm going to disagree on that," he said. "In the overkill

list, the victims were, well, slaughtered for lack of a better description. Discarded. There was no caring emotion behind that action. The bodies were easily found only because the killer couldn't be bothered to try to hide them. Not so with the organized killer list. Those bodies were treated, after death anyway, with a modicum of respect. Left clothed or covered, lying down, almost as if they were sleeping as opposed to being tossed out like garbage. It's subtle, but it's a difference. If you look at every kind of comparison that can be made, those two lists of victims each present evidence of a very different kind of killer. In fact, it's my opinion that it proves there wasn't one Kentucky Ripper. There were two."

She sucked in a breath. But it really shouldn't have been a surprise after everything he'd just shown her. She glanced from list to list, read the headings on the middle screen, the bullets beneath them. "But, if you're right, then your original profile was wrong."

He surprised her by smiling. "Don't look so worried. You're not dashing my newly found confidence. There's more to the original profile than appeared in any police reports."

"Okay. Now you've lost me."

He shifted in his chair, a quickly hidden grimace telling her how much his night of research had cost him physically. His hip was aching. He needed a hot soak in a tub and a long nap. But she didn't want to embarrass him by pointing out the obvious, so she remained silent.

"When I profiled the murders allegedly attributed to the Kentucky Ripper," he continued, "I presented the police with *two* profiles. Two different killers. When Finney was arrested, it was the profile I gave them that most closely matched his characteristics that they used. The other profile I gave them was ignored. That's why you never saw it in any of the official case files that you researched."

"I still have to wrap my head around this. You've turned the investigation I did upside down."

"No. I haven't. I've proved that your original conclusions were right all along."

She threw her hands up in the air. "Now I'm beyond lost."

"Sorry. I'm not explaining this very well. To try to put it succinctly, if I look at Larsen and everything we now know about him, including that he used to live in Kentucky, he fits that first list of victims to a T."

"Larsen is the Ripper."

He sat forward in his chair. "He's one of them. That's where your research comes into play. Everything about that second victim list—if we consider that Bishop is right and Finney was a mentally ill fall guy who didn't kill anyone—that second list fits the man you believed all along was the Kentucky Ripper."

She pressed a hand to her throat. "Avarice Lowe."

He nodded. "All I'm waiting on for confirmation is a list of dates and alibis for Larsen. Mason's working on that to see if Larsen was on vacation or sick or whatever on the dates when the first set of victims was abducted. I've already cross-referenced everything I had on Lowe."

She glanced up at the dates he'd mentioned, the ones beside the disorganized list. They all had check marks beside them. "Lowe doesn't have alibis for the second set?"

"No. He doesn't."

She sat back. "Two Kentucky Rippers, and a third guy in prison who had nothing to do with the murders."

"It's worse than that," he told her. "There's one more puzzle piece that you haven't seen." He typed on his computer tablet again.

"What could be worse than two killers?" she asked.

He hesitated with his finger poised over one of the function keys. "How about this?"

A picture displayed on the screen. She stared at it a moment, trying to figure out what was supposed to be significant about what she was seeing. There was a small crowd of people standing behind yellow crime scene tape. Behind them were homes and police cars parked up and down the street.

"One of the Ripper's crime scenes? A crowd shot?"

"That's exactly what it is. Standard operating procedure in a case like this. The police photographer hides out of sight and takes pictures of any people watching the activity, just in case the killer ends up being in the crowd."

"Because killers often come back to the scene of the crime," she said. "They get a thrill from watching the police."

"Now observe the cropped, close-up version I made of that same picture." He pressed another key and the screen changed. "What's worse than two different killers?"

She gasped in shock. "A tag team of killers, partnering together." She stared at the close up of Avarice Lowe and Chris Larsen standing in the crowd, side by side, watching with riveted interest as the police worked one of the Kentucky Ripper crime scenes.

"Congratulations, Teagan."

She tore her gaze from the screen. "For what?"

"You were right all along. Lowe was the Kentucky Ripper. But so was Larsen. None of us saw that coming."

"You did," she said. "You created two profiles."

"Yes, well. My mistake was in not following through and pursuing both after the police went after Finney. I assumed I'd messed up. Instead, I should have pushed for more investigating. Maybe then, Finney wouldn't be in prison. Lowe would be in prison, along with Larsen. And then you'd have never been hurt. I'm so sorry." His jaw tightened.

She shook her head. "No. Don't you dare go there. What happened to me was not your fault. It was Larsen's."

He swallowed. "Thank you for that. But it gets even worse. I'm not sure it's just Larsen's fault. It may be Lowe's too. Remember that you said, even after knowing Larsen had abducted you, that he didn't seem like the right man, that he didn't fit your memories except for his voice?"

It took a moment for his words to sink in. When they did, she pressed a shaking hand to her throat. "Oh my God. You think that I was abducted by…both of them?"

He gave her a short, clipped nod. "I don't have any real proof. Just theories. But I think we should tell the police and the FBI to consider that they may have been a tag team on some of the same crimes, including what was done to you." He took her hand in his again. "I'm sorry. I probably shouldn't have even told you that."

"No, no. I don't want any secrets between us. I want to be included in everything." She forced a smile. "Honestly, it's not as huge of a shock as you'd expect. I was wrestling with my own doubts because some things didn't seem to fit with Larsen. Now, well, it kind of all makes sense." She squeezed his hand. "I assume you already told Mason about this?"

He kissed the back of her hand before letting go. "I was discussing it with him when you walked in. He's corroborating some data, but as soon as he saw that picture of Lowe and Larsen together, he was convinced. He's pulling the Seekers onto this right now."

"I guess everything's in good hands, then."

"The best."

She pushed to her feet, still feeling a bit nauseated and

shaky after the latest revelations. "I need to push all of this ugliness out of my head for now. I'm going to go call my mom and let her know I'm still alive. She's gotten a bit paranoid after this last…episode. She made me promise to call her every day, but I fell asleep last night and never did. I'm surprised she's not already blowing up my phone this morning." Her face heated. "Sorry about falling asleep with you as my pillow. But thanks for putting me to bed. Next time maybe you can join me." She gave him an outrageous wink, desperately trying to lighten the mood.

He gently cupped her face and pressed a soft kiss against her lips. "One day, very soon, sweet Teagan. I'll do more than just join you in that big bed."

She sighed with longing, already feeling better. He always made her feel better, even in her darkest moments.

He put his phone in his pocket before turning off the equipment. Backing away from the table, he said, "Hop on. I'll give you a ride." He arched his brows in a suggestive manner.

She laughed and eased herself onto his lap so she wouldn't jar his incisions. When they reached the family room, she carefully got up. "I'll call Mom from the bedroom."

"And I'll make breakfast. Toast or an omelet? Those are the only two breakfast meals in my culinary arsenal."

"Omelet. Always."

"Good choice. My toast always comes out burned. Meat lover, veggie lover, or deluxe?" He wheeled toward the kitchen.

"Deluxe. With sour cream on top, if you have it."

"You got it," he called back.

She smiled and went into the bedroom. But after three tries on her cell phone without the call going through, she gave up and headed to the kitchen.

He'd left his wheelchair sitting by the island and was leaning on his cane as he pulled ingredients for the omelets out of the refrigerator. He glanced up in surprise when she started helping him. "That was a quick call."

"It wouldn't go through. I think there must be a problem with the cell tower or something."

He frowned as he set a carton of eggs on the counter. "Is your battery low?"

"No. But there weren't any bars. No connection. I tried three times. All I got was static."

"Static?"

She nodded.

He pulled out his phone and checked the screen. Then he punched a button and held it to his ear. He swore and tossed his phone on top of the island. "Run back to the office and lock yourself inside." He hobbled to his wheelchair and plopped down.

"Why? What's going on?"

He wheeled around the island. "Someone's jamming the cell signal. And there's only one person I can think of who would have a reason to do that."

The blood rushed from her face, leaving her cold and shaking as she hurried after him into the family room. "Avarice Lowe. You think he's on his way here?"

"No." He glanced up at her as he wheeled past the L formed by the two couches. "I think he's *already* here. Probably lurking outside, gathering his courage." He glanced at his wrist and swore. "I should have replaced my computer-watch the moment I got back. It would have warned me if someone was on the property. Go to the office, Teagan. Hurry. There aren't any windows in there. Lock the main door, then lock the doors that lead into the bathroom and bedroom. Wedge a chair beneath the door to the hallway. *Go.*"

Ignoring his dictate, she ran after him into the master bedroom. "I'm not leaving you. Come with me."

He wheeled to the nightstand. "I've got this. I'll take care of Lowe. But I have to know you're safe, out of harm's way. Go on."

He yanked open the top drawer.

"Okay, okay." She headed toward the door. "But I wish you'd let me help you instead of—"

He was suddenly beside her in his wheelchair, shoving her back into the room. She stumbled but caught herself in time to see him shut the door and lock it. His face was drawn and pale as he met her questioning gaze. "My pistol's not in the nightstand. *He's inside the house.*"

Chapter Twenty-Five

He's inside the house.

Those horrifying words ran through Teagan's mind over and over as she watched Bryson leaning against the master bathroom counter after ditching the wheelchair because it was in his way. He was using duct tape to secure the thick towels that he'd wrapped around her arms. She didn't ask why. She knew why. The disorganized killer, the one who'd murdered eight of the Kentucky Ripper's victims, was quite the fan of knives. Bryson was using the towels to protect her in case Lowe got past him and came after her next. As to why he had duct tape in his bathroom, that was a discussion for another day. *If they lived another day.*

The psychopath in the main room had already tried to get into the bedroom once. He'd scraped knives underneath the closed door, swiping at Bryson's feet. Then Lowe had used his body like a battering ram, screaming obscenities as he tried to crash through the door. It was only because Bryson had used his own strength against the door that Lowe had given up. But not for long. He was still out there. Planning his next assault. Even now she could hear his shoes thumping and squeaking across the floor as he paced back and forth mumbling incoherent words to himself.

Dear God. Please help us.

Bryson tossed the roll of duct tape onto the counter and reached under the sink. "This is a last resort." He handed her an aerosol can of deodorant. "I don't want you near enough to him to use this. God willing, when you climb out the bedroom window, he'll be so busy with me that he won't get a chance to go after you."

She sucked in a breath, fear for both of them making her flush hot and cold.

"But if he gets past me," he continued, "and he catches up to you, spray his eyes. He won't expect that. It will hurt like hell and he'll be temporarily blinded. Run past him and go for the truck." He dug the keys out of his pocket and shoved them into her jeans pocket. "Drive down the mountain like a bat out of hell. Don't stop. Go straight to the police station. You hear me? Do not stop at some neighbor's house or a little country store. If he ends up following you, he could go after you again. Go straight to the police. It's almost a straight shot once you reach the bottom of the mountain. You remember the directions I told you?"

He lightly shook her when she didn't answer.

"I do. I remember," she said. "But none of this makes sense. Why don't you put towels on your arms too? And climb out the window with me?"

He gave her an exasperated look. "I was up all night. My hip never had a chance to recuperate. I'm not running anywhere. And the towels would make it too hard for me to maneuver in a fight. This is the way it has to be. He's already cracked the doorjamb. The next time he tries to get through the door, he'll be inside the bedroom. While I keep him occupied, you're going to climb out that window and run for the truck."

"I don't want to run away like a coward and leave you. Don't ask me to do that again."

He grabbed a small pair of scissors from one of the

drawers and set them on top of the counter. Next he grabbed a folded sheet from beneath the cabinet and tucked it under his arm. "You have to leave me. It's the only way."

She frantically shook her head and set the can back on the counter. "No. It's not. Two against one, remember? You and me against the world. He can't kill both of us. If we attack him together, we'll defeat him."

"No, Teagan. You heard his roar of rage earlier. You saw the knives he was shoving under the door. Probably the only reason he didn't shoot his way through is that he doesn't want to end his fun that quickly. He's a cutter. He wants to enjoy himself first. But if he sees you running for the truck through the front windows, he'll use the gun. You can't outrun a bullet. I have to distract him, try to get the gun to give you a chance."

He shoved the can in her hand, grabbed the pair of scissors and pulled her out of the bathroom.

A shoe squeaked against the polished floor outside the bedroom door.

Bryson scowled and dropped the folded sheet on top of the bed. He limped to the window and quietly eased it up. Rather than risk the noise of loosening the screen's frame and dropping it outside, he used the scissors to cut an opening. He motioned for her to stand in front of the window.

"The truck will detect the key fob in your pocket," he whispered. "All you have to do is press the button under the door handle and it will open. The engine's a push-button start. You remember, right? You've got this." He framed her face with his hands. "All you have to do is run, sweetheart. Everything's going to be okay."

Tears spilled down her cheeks as she looked into his beautiful blue eyes. "Bryson, I—"

Another squeak sounded outside the room. Lowe was getting restless, working up his courage for another assault.

Then there was another sound, something scraping across the floor. Something heavy. What was that?

Bryson pressed a quick, hard kiss against her lips. "You can do this," he whispered next to her ear. "Don't let me down."

Her pulse was rushing in her ears so loudly that she almost couldn't hear him. She grasped the windowsill. It was awkward with the ridiculous towels wrapped around her arms. But she managed.

Grabbing the sheet off the bed, he shook it out, quickly rolling and twisting it, holding it in both hands like a length of rope. It shook her to her core when she realized what he was doing: planning to use the sheet to defend himself against the knives. Her heart slammed in her chest so hard she marveled that it didn't crack one of her ribs.

She hated this, hated the thought of abandoning him. And yet, if she stayed, she'd be a distraction that could get him killed. All she could do now was follow his instructions and pray he was able to defeat Lowe.

With a concussion.

A bum hip.

Stitches both inside him and outside. Bruises all over.

With nothing but a sheet to defend himself against a madman with butcher knives and a pistol likely in his pocket.

This was insane.

A thump sounded against the door.

Get ready, he mouthed.

She clutched the stupid can of deodorant and prayed that a better plan would come to her than leaving him here to his likely death. But what could she do? How could she help?

Something heavy crashed against the door. The already cracked frame exploded in a hail of wooden shards as a side table from the family room flew through the ruined opening. Bryson ducked, then lunged forward, arms outstretched with the sheet between them as he grappled with Lowe. Both men moved backward into the family room, a flurry of flashing knives and billowing cloth as Bryson ducked and weaved and wielded his sheet in an effort to avoid being diced into pieces.

"Now, Teagan," he yelled, furiously fighting Lowe's flailing arms. "Go!"

She let out a sob and jumped.

With Teagan safely away, Bryson focused his undivided attention on the psychopath trying to hack him to death with a knife in each hand. Bryson wrenched his left arm up, using the sheet to deflect yet another blow. This time he twisted the sheet, then wrenched it back. The butcher knife in Lowe's right hand flew across the family room, skittering onto the floor with a metallic twang.

Lowe dropped to the floor. Without his weight as a counterbalance, Bryson's hip gave out. He crashed down on top of Lowe. A sickening scrape sounded and white-hot pain lanced through his side. Lowe's mouth curved in a delighted smile as he grabbed the knife now embedded beneath Bryson's ribs and yanked it out.

Bryson gasped, fighting for air now as he twisted and rolled with Lowe, desperately trying to gain control of the knife. He grabbed Lowe's wrist, muscles burning and shaking as he slowly won the tug of war, turning the man's hand. Bryson swiped the blade across the man's neck. A thin red line immediately formed. But it was only superficial. Lowe didn't even blink. He kept straining against Bryson, trying to turn the knife the other way. Muscles bunched and cramped as Bryson fought back.

The floor turned slippery with sweat and blood. They

rolled like two alligators in a death roll, each struggling to get the upper hand. Lowe was strong, and big, but he still wouldn't have been that difficult for a man Bryson's size to defeat. Except that Bryson had begun this match in a much-weakened state. And Lowe's knife had done considerable damage. His lifeblood was seeping from his side. A cold numbness spread across his middle, making him shiver. If he didn't end this, soon, it would be lights out. For him.

He threw everything he had left into fighting back. But his muscles ached. Weakness crept relentlessly through his body. It was a struggle just to hold up his arms.

Lowe gave one of his guttural yells, this one of satisfaction and triumph. He was winning. It was almost over. And he knew it.

Taking advantage of Lowe's distraction, Bryson managed to twist and jerk the man's knife hand again. This time he sliced deep into Lowe's biceps on his right arm. But before Bryson could follow up with a killing blow, Lowe twisted and rolled on top of him. Bryson couldn't get traction on the slippery floor. Blood saturated the knife handle. Bryson lost his grip. Lowe plunged the knife deep into Bryson's side again, and twisted.

Bryson arched off the floor, an inferno of lava-like pain scorching him from the inside out. He dropped back down, gasping, struggling to catch his breath. The rest of his strength seemed to drain away, leaving him limp, muscles twitching in agony as he squinted and blinked, trying to focus.

Lowe was a dark blur, climbing to his feet, staggering and clutching himself as he lumbered out of Bryson's sight-line. He rolled his head to the side, trying to follow the other man's progress. Cold. He was so cold. His teeth chattered as he frantically pushed against the floor, like a fiddler crab, trying to slide away. But all he could manage was a few inches.

His nemesis stopped by one of the couches and leaned down. When he turned around, Bryson blinked, trying to see what was in the man's hand. A gun. Probably Bryson's own pistol.

He held it up, no doubt gloating with triumph. Bryson could no longer see well enough to make out the man's expression. Maybe that was a blessing.

"Chris said you'd put up a good fight and you did." He spoke for the first time since their fight had begun, his words choppy as he too struggled to catch his breath. "I was his one call from jail. Imagine that. He called me instead of a lawyer." He shook his head. "What a gift. And I'm here paying him back. This is for what you did to Chris." He held his gun arm out toward Bryson. "After you're dead, I'll enjoy that girlfriend of yours. I'll gut her like a fish."

Bryson swore and tried to push himself up. But it was as if his body was glued to the floor.

The sound of a roaring engine had both of them jerking their heads toward the front windows. Bryson's pickup crashed through the house, tossing one of the couches across the room like kindling, and slamming into Lowe so hard he flew across the room.

Someone hopped out, but all he saw was a blur.

"Bryson! Bryson, I'm coming. Hold on."

Teagan.

She crawled over the destruction she'd wrought on his house. He wanted to yell at her for risking her life yet again for him. But he was so glad to see her, alive, and safe, because she'd killed Lowe. He didn't yell. He was too proud of his little warrior to risk hurting the tender feelings that she tried to hide with her sassy quips. He despised himself that it took dying for him to realize just what she meant to him.

And that he loved her.

Her shoes squeaked and slid across the wet floor as she scrambled toward him. He tried to tell her that he loved her, that he was proud of her. But he wasn't sure if the words came out or not. He was so tired. And cold. At least the awful pain had faded. He barely felt anything anymore. He closed his eyes, at peace, knowing that she was safe. That she would be okay.

TEAGAN GRABBED THE discarded gun she'd spotted on the floor next to a smashed piece of electronics that she could only guess was whatever Lowe had used to jam the cell signals. But Lowe was no longer a threat. He was lying in a lifeless heap about ten feet away.

After a treacherous slippery slide across the blood-streaked floor, she dropped to her knees beside Bryson, gun still clutched in her left hand as she knelt over him. "Can you hear me? Speak to me," she ordered through a cascade of tears.

He blinked, then slowly opened his eyes. "Teagan?" Her name was slurred. He seemed confused as he struggled to focus on her face.

"I'm here, baby. I'm here." She set the pistol down and leaned over him, pressing her hands against the floor on each side of him to keep her balance. Something bumped against her arm. She pulled back in horror to see the handle of a knife sticking out from his left side, embedded all the way to the hilt. Blood pooled beneath him, forming macabre rivulets across the formerly polished white floor. "Oh, no. Oh, no, no, no."

"You…okay?" he whispered, his lips an odd, bluish tinge. "Where's… Lowe? The…gun?"

She motioned toward the body on the other side of the room as she tore at the duct tape holding the towels around her left arm. "I hit the piece of scum with your truck. I drove it right up the front steps. Your gun's right here." She patted the floor beside him. "Don't worry. He can't hurt you again."

He blinked. "Truck?" He rolled his head to the side, obviously trying to make sense of what she was saying.

She finally freed the towel and leaned across him, pressing it around the wound while trying to not move the knife and make it worse.

"Down!" he rasped.

She automatically ducked as the sound of a guttural yell sounded off to the side. Bryson swept the pistol up and fired over and over and over. Then his hand dropped to his side and the pistol skittered across the floor. It was as if he'd gathered all the strength he had left to protect her, once again, and was completely spent.

She looked over her shoulder. Lowe was impossibly close to them, just a few feet away. She'd thought she'd killed him. She must have only knocked him out. Or he'd pretended to be unconscious. Neither of which mattered now. Bryson's aim had been true. He'd shot him in the head.

A sob escaped her. "I can't believe it. After seeing him through the window, holding that pistol, I drove through a wall to save you. But once again, you saved me." She turned back toward him, smiling through her tears.

His eyes were closed.

His jaw was slack.

"Bryson?" She frantically bent over him. "Open your eyes. Bryson?"

"Move. Get out of the way."

She whirled around, shocked to see Gage Bishop kneeling beside her. Behind him, Brielle, Dalton and Han had just stepped in through the ruined wall and were sweeping their pistols back and forth, looking for threats.

"Move." Bishop none too gently shoved her out of the way. He pressed his fingers against the side of Bryson's neck.

"Come on." Brielle was beside her now. "Let's give him room. The police and an ambulance are on their way. Mason told us he'd tried to call Bryson back and couldn't get through. He called us, then 911."

Teagan pressed her fist to her mouth to keep from screaming.

Bishop was performing CPR.

Chapter Twenty-Six

Three months later

Long before the shadow fell across the end of the dock and hovered over Bryson Anton's wheelchair, he knew some-one was there. Motion sensors and security cameras had made Bryson's new watch buzz against his wrist when they parked their car in the driveway. More messages warned when they crossed the back patio. And again, when they'd descended the gently sloping lawn that ended at the creek. But he didn't turn around.

Not yet.

"It's been nearly three months since you sent me away yet again, Bryson. One minute I'm at the hospital, thanking God that Bishop was able to keep you alive long enough to even get you there. Then I'm on my knees thanking God that you survived yet another arduous surgery. Only to visit you in recovery to discover you're acting like a griz-zly bear, just like last time, proving you're the worst pa-tient ever in the history of the universe. And then, when you're finally in your hospital room and we're alone, I'm ready to pour my heart out to you, and what do you do? You tell me to get out! You order me back to Jacksonville to work on my master's degree. What the heck, Bryson?"

"The summer semester was about to start. I didn't want you to have to wait until fall to start back again."

She said several unsavory things. "No phone calls from you. When I tried calling, you didn't answer. I don't even count the pathetic, generic texts you occasionally sent me. Then I find out that you've been talking to my dad every few days, asking how I was doing. If you were worried, all you had to do was talk to *me*, Bryson. Not my family."

"I was busy."

"Really? What's her name?"

He turned the wheelchair around to face her. She was wearing hunter-green shorts and a lime-green tank top in deference to the warm weather. As always, her rich brown skin was flawless, her full high breasts a reminder of the incredible body beneath those clothes. But his favorite part of her was that gorgeous bright mind of hers. And her beautiful, sassy mouth. He never knew what outrageous thing she was going to say next.

"Helga," he said.

She frowned. "Excuse me?"

"You asked me her name. Her name is Helga. Or, well, I actually don't even know her real name. But that's what you called her when she was here that first day you showed up on my doorstep."

She put her hands on her hips. "Does this mean that you've been doing the rehab the doctor ordered?"

"It does. I have."

She crossed her arms, looking only slightly less aggravated than before. "Well, that's good. But I still don't see why you couldn't text me a real hello, with feeling, every once in a while. Or actually speak to me on the phone. What makes you think you could just text me last night to come back and everything would be fine?"

He smiled. "You're here aren't you?"

She narrowed her eyes, then whirled around.

He caught her arm just before she could get out of reach and yanked her backward.

She let out a little squeak and landed right where he wanted her. In his lap.

"Let me go, Bryson. I'm not kidding."

He gently turned her face so she'd meet his gaze. "Is that really want you want, Teag? You want me to let you go?" The flash of unshed tears in her eyes surprised him. "Sweetheart?"

"You already have. You wouldn't let me stay to help with your recovery. You sent me back home like some child—"

"While I could never mistake you for a child, not even close—" he gently stroked her arm, unable to resist touching her "—there's definitely an age difference between us. Something to think about. You're young, still working on officially starting your career, although I heard the FBI is interested in grooming you as a future candidate."

She smiled. Not full wattage, but enough for him to know that he was right, that the FBI opportunity was important to her.

"There might be a nibble there," she admitted. "They were impressed with the detailed investigation I conducted, and that I was right about Avarice Lowe being a serial killer. Apparently my notes on him have helped them narrow down facts that blow apart his alibis for some of the killings. He may not be around for a trial. But at least some of his victims' families will have true closure now."

He pressed a kiss against her cheek and settled her more comfortably against him. The fact that she didn't resist being snuggled close was encouraging. "You have the most beautiful mind I've ever had the pleasure of knowing. It's about time the rest of the world figured that out."

She gave him the side-eye before looking away. "I'd say thank you, but it sounds like you're building another excuse to justify why you wanted me to leave you."

"Not leave me. Go back to school. Huge difference."

She shrugged.

"Teag, you're young, energetic, just starting out in life. I'm more toward the middle of mine."

She snorted.

"Okay, maybe not quite the middle just yet. Hopefully."

"Is this going somewhere?"

He motioned toward the wheelchair. "I wouldn't want you to ever regret spending time with a cripple when you could be out with guys your own age doing whatever you want."

She rolled her eyes with a dramatic toss of her head. "I think you're confusing me with the self-centered stuck-up jerk who used to be your girlfriend. I'm a little more creative than her. I can figure out lots of fun things to do with you even if you can't twirl me around a dance floor."

"Does that mean you could be happy if I never walked again?"

Her mouth fell open and she cupped his face in her hands, all signs of teasing and anger gone as she stared into his eyes. "Oh, Bry. Is that what the doctor said? Are you...are you paralyzed?"

He gently pulled her hands down and kissed them before letting go. "No. I'm not paralyzed. I've been very lucky, actually, after being shot twice in my life. Then stabbed. Twice. I just wanted to make sure that if something like that did happen, maybe down the road—considering how dangerous my career can be—that you'd still be okay sticking around."

Her brows arched in confusion. "Love isn't based on how mobile you are or what you can do for someone else.

Love is when your happiness revolves around the other person's happiness. Once again, I think you're confusing me with the ex who shall not be named."

He grinned.

She frowned.

"Did you just say that you loved me, Teagan? In that unique sassy way of yours?"

She crossed her arms. "That depends."

"On?"

"On why you're asking me these stupid questions and why you texted me last night that you had first class tickets waiting for me so I could fly up here today. Thanks for the first class, by the way. That was cool."

"You're welcome. Thanks for coming."

She twisted her mouth as if trying to figure something out. "You're acting awfully strange. And my infinite patience is wearing thin. Out with it. What exactly do you want? Are you asking me to be your girlfriend and you're worried I'll dump you because of the chair?"

"Will you?"

"Be your girlfriend? Are you asking me to be your girlfriend?"

"No."

"We're done here. Have a nice life, Bryson." She hopped off his lap and started up the dock.

"I'm not asking you to be my girlfriend," he called after her.

She raised her hand in the air and made a rude gesture without looking back.

He grinned. "I'm asking you to be my fiancée. For real this time."

She stopped so fast that she wobbled and almost fell into the water. Once she regained her balance, she slowly turned around. "What...what did you just say?"

He leaned down and flipped the top back on the cooler beside his chair. Then he pulled out a red velvet box and held it up in front of him. "I love you Teagan Eleanor Ray."

She gasped in outrage. "Did my mother tell you my middle name? I hate it. It makes me sound like an eighty-year-old."

"Well, maybe that will help with the age gap between us." He winked.

She marched back to him and stopped a few feet from his chair, eyeing the velvet box in his hands. "Be honest, Bryson. Exactly how much older than me are you?"

"Old enough to teach you a few things that I know you'll really, really enjoy. And young enough to demonstrate them with an expertise that will make your toes curl."

Her gaze flew to his. She swallowed, then cleared her throat. "Toes curl?"

He nodded.

"All of them?" she squeaked.

"Oh yeah."

She fanned herself, then wiped her hands on her shorts. "Um. Wasn't there a question you asked me, a moment ago, when my back was turned?"

He nodded again.

She put her hands on her hips. "Don't you think you should ask again? Face-to-face?"

"No."

Her eyes widened. She started to turn away.

He stood.

She froze and stared in wonder as he dropped down on one knee on the dock.

"I think I should ask it down here, do this the right way, on bended knee." He opened the box and tilted it so the ring would catch the light.

She pressed a hand to her throat. "You stood on your own. No cane. And you're on one knee. I don't understand."

"By the grace of God, when Lowe stabbed me, it knocked the bullet loose instead of into my spine. The doctors were able to extract it. And I've been doing everything the therapists ordered me to do. I'm not pain-free yet. But there's a good chance I will be. Eventually."

Her expression turned sad. "Are you in pain right now, Bryson?"

He shook his head. "No. And it's not because of tequila."

"Scotch?"

"Pain pills. Like I said, I'm following doctor's orders this time. No self-medicating with alcohol. No more skipping rehab appointments. And even though I hate how the pills make me feel, I wanted to be able to do this without grimacing. So I'm all doped up and feeling good. Now, about that question I asked—"

"The ring is beautiful," she breathed, stepping closer and eyeing the box again. "But not half as beautiful as you, you frustrating, stubborn man."

He smiled as he pulled the ring out of its bed of velvet. "I wanted something special, something as unique as you."

She moved even closer, then pressed her hand against her chest. "Opals. And diamonds. And rubies. I love opals and rubies. How did you know?"

"All those calls to your mom and dad weren't for nothing."

"Sneaky."

"Necessary. I wanted to surprise you. You just confirmed that you love opals and rubies. Diamonds too I hope?"

She rolled her eyes. "Everyone loves diamonds. Or they

should. I couldn't ask for anything more beautiful. Thank you." She held out her left hand.

He poised the ring in front of her finger. But before sliding it on, he looked up, meeting her gaze. "It's selfish of me to even ask you to marry me, because I think you could do a lot better. But I can't imagine my life without you in it. I love you, Teagan Ray. I think I loved you the moment you knocked on my door and the only word you could get out was hi." He grinned. "Will you do me the honor of being my wife? Will you marry me?"

"Are you kidding? Put the ring on already."

He laughed and slid the ring onto her finger. Then he stood.

Tears glittered in her eyes as she put her hands on his shoulders. "I can't believe you're standing here like this. I'm so happy for you."

"No happier than me, that you said yes. I wasn't sure how this was going to go."

"That makes two of us. I had no idea why you wanted to see me. I believe you owe me a kiss, future husband." She lifted her lips toward his and waited for him to bend down.

"Hold that thought. I have something else for you." He turned back to the cooler and reached inside.

She groaned. "You're killing me, Bryson. I don't want anything else but you."

"Oh, I don't know. I'm pretty sure you want this. And I did make a promise after all." He handed her a pink bag with little pink ribbons tied all over it, and the name of a very exclusive store on the outside of the bag.

Her eyes widened. "You didn't."

"I did."

She opened the bag and peeked inside, then squealed with delight as she shoved her hand in and pulled out an aqua-colored lace bra and panty set. "They're gorgeous, perfect. And they're my size. Oh my gosh, please don't tell me you asked my mother my sizes." She gasped. "Or my dad!"

"Give me more credit than that. I asked your mother for your best friend's name. Then I asked your best friend."

She laughed with obvious relief and sorted through the contents. "Twelve. You bought me a dozen bras and matching panties. Bryson! This cost a fortune!"

"I can afford it. I'd pay ten times that to see your eyes light up and your glowing smile."

The tears that had been threatening spilled over and down her cheeks. "I'm so happy."

"Because we're going to get married?"

She shook her head. "Because you promised that when you replaced my hundred-dollar bra that you'd buy me more, and then you'd take them off me."

He threw his head back and laughed harder than he had in ages.

"Hurry, Bryson. I'm not waiting one more minute for you to keep your promise. I'll strip right here on your back lawn if I have to."

Still laughing, he scooped her up in his arms and ran with her to the house. But before going inside, he let her legs slide down him as he'd done so long ago. And this time, he did what he'd wanted to do since the first time he'd seen her. He kissed her. Really kissed her. Kissed her with all his pent-up emotions, love and longing and lust all rolled into one. And when he was done, he pulled back to soak in the haze of passion in her eyes and the love reflected back in them.

His hands were shaking as he cupped her face. "I don't know what I did to make you love me. But I'll thank God every night for the rest of my life that you showed up on my doorstep. You're a treasure, Teagan. A gift to my battered soul. I love you so much."

She shifted the bag of lingerie to her left hand and grabbed his right in hers. "I love you too, Bryson Anton. But you have one more promise to keep. You have to make my toes curl."

"Challenge accepted." He scooped her up in his arms and kissed her again as he strode through the house.

Her toes were curling before they even reached the bedroom.

* * * * *

HIS BRAND OF
JUSTICE

DELORES FOSSEN

Chapter One

The moment Marshal Jack Slater brought his truck to a stop in front of the small country house, he drew his gun, threw open the door and raced up the porch steps. He'd already glanced around the road and the sprawling yard to see if there was any immediate danger. If there was, he hadn't spotted anything.

That didn't mean, though, that there wasn't a threat.

And that was why Jack had gotten here as fast as he could, once he'd received the call from the live-in nurse, Lucille Booker. From the instant he'd heard Lucille say "Marshal Slater, there might be a problem" in a breathy voice, Jack had known there was no *might* to it. There was trouble. Lucille had been at this job for three months, and never once had he heard that kind of concern in her voice. No, not just concern.

Fear.

Jack didn't knock. Instead, he flipped up the top of what appeared to be an ordinary doorbell to reveal a panel for the security system beneath it. He punched in the code, which would alert the two women inside that it was him. Only when he heard the clicks that let him know the alarms and locks had been temporarily disarmed did he open the door.

Lucille was there in the foyer, and she had a gun in the white-knuckle grip of her right hand. A gun that Jack had issued to her after making sure that she knew how to use it.

There was no blood on her, thank God. No signs of any injury, and the room showed no indications of a struggle. Everything in the house was neat and tidy, as it usually was.

Lucille was what no one would call petite—another reason Jack had wanted her for this job. Her beefy build, no-fuss choppy brown hair and sharply angled face all gave her the appearance of a woman who knew how to take care of herself. And it was true. In addition to being a nurse with twenty years of experience, Lucille had been an instructor of self-defense classes for women.

"What happened?" Jack asked as he reset the security system. "Where's Caroline?"

An answer to that second question wasn't necessary, though, because he soon saw the blonde in the kitchen. Caroline Moser. Jack cursed, because she was standing there with a butcher knife.

Unlike Lucille, there was nothing beefy about Caroline. She was lean and tall, and the loose pale blue cotton dress she was wearing didn't disguise her willowy body. She had an angel's face, he'd always thought. Like some painting on a museum wall. Once, before things had gone to hell in a handbasket, there'd been a lot of toughness and street smarts beneath those soft, delicate features.

No toughness now, though.

She was way too pale, and she looked way too fragile.

"When Caroline and I were clearing up after lunch, I saw a man," Lucille explained. "A stranger. He was by the pond."

Not good. No one should have been within a quarter of a mile of this place, since it wasn't anywhere on the beaten path. Of course, Jack could say that about lots of properties in the county, which was mainly made up of ranches, farms and small towns. Like Longview Ridge, the place where Jack had been born and raised and where he still lived. This safe house was only about fifteen miles from there—and from him. But it was still far enough away that someone shouldn't have just strolled by here.

"You saw this man, too?" he asked Caroline.

"Just a glimpse." There was plenty of worry and fear in her voice, but there was something else in her jewel-green eyes.

Suspicion.

Jack knew that particular reaction was for him.

She didn't trust him, not completely, anyway, and he'd seen that look plenty of times over the past three months since he'd become her handler in WITSEC. Before that, when she had known who he was, there'd been other emotions…ones that he wished he couldn't remember, either.

Jack wasn't sure why the doubt was there now. Or all the other times he'd visited her here in this safe house over the past weeks. Her doctors had said it was because of the trauma from her injuries and her amnesia. It was hard for her to trust anyone, they'd said, when there were way too many blanks in her mind.

Still, it cut him to the bone.

Of course, there were plenty other things that he should be thinking about right now, things that didn't involve whether she trusted him or not, and Jack went to the kitchen window. That vantage point would give him a good view of not only the pond but also the small barn and pasture.

Other than the two horses that Jack had personally delivered to the place, nothing and no one was out there. However, since Lucille wasn't easily spooked, she must have seen someone.

"You didn't recognize the man?" Jack pressed, glancing back at Lucille.

The nurse shook her head. She put away her gun in the slide holster at the back of her scrubs. "But he had dark hair and was wearing jeans and a black T-shirt. He darted behind the big oak tree when he spotted me."

Darting definitely wasn't a good sign, but Jack was holding out hope that this was just someone who'd strayed onto the property, only to realize that he was trespassing. Too bad the twisting feeling in his gut let him know that wasn't the case.

"I called you right away, just as you told me to do," Lucille added. "And I made sure Caroline stayed away from the windows." Again, that was as Jack had instructed.

Jack made a sound of approval, and while continuing to volley his attention out the window, he reached out to take the knife from Caroline. Her hand went stiff when his fingers brushed over hers. Actually, every part of her seemed to stiffen as her gaze collided with his. Her intense stare held a few long moments before she finally let go of the knife.

"Sorry, Marshal Slater," she muttered. "I'm a little spooked."

Marshal Slater. It wasn't a surprise that she called him that. In fact, it was the only thing Caroline had called him since she'd turned up in Longview Ridge three months ago with that head injury and the amnesia. She said his name with the same edgy suspicion that was in her eyes.

Before the memory loss, she had called him Jack. And

there'd sure as hell been no suspicion then. Only the heat from the scalding hot fire that he no longer saw or felt in any part of her.

I love you, Jack.

Those were the last words Caroline had said to him before she was taken hostage, before this nightmare had begun. Words she'd said when they thought it would be an ordinary, short goodbye. When Jack had thought there'd be plenty of other times for him to say *I love you* right back—and that was why he hadn't said it to her then. Now he might never get the chance.

He was a stranger to her now. He was *Marshal Slater.*

Jack tried not to let that eat away at him, especially since Lucille had insisted on calling him by his title and surname, too. But in Lucille's case, it just sounded as if she'd wanted to remind herself that he was there to protect Caroline and her. Which he was.

"You think it was a false alarm?" Lucille asked, joining him at the window.

Jack lifted his shoulder. "The sensors weren't tripped."

If they had been, Jack would have gotten the alert on his phone. Of course, the guy would have had to get closer to the house for that to happen, since the sensors were arranged around the perimeter of the yard and on the dirt road that led to the house.

There were also some cameras, and Jack fired off a text to his partner, Marshal Teagan Randolph. He asked her to cull out the video feed from all the cameras for the past hour and send it to him ASAP.

"I'll wait around for a while and keep watch," he assured Lucille and Caroline when he was done with the text.

A while was going to mean staying for the night. Or

longer. He didn't intend to take any risks with Caroline, because somewhere in those lost memories in her head was a piece of information he needed as much as the next breath he took.

She knew who'd murdered his father.

The images came. They always did whenever he thought of his dad, Sheriff Buck Slater. Buck had been the law in Longview Ridge, but that had ended one night in a hail of bullets and blood when someone had gunned him down. Caroline was the only person alive who could tell him what'd happened.

Other than the killer, of course.

And Jack suspected he wouldn't be getting any answers from him or her on that. Especially since he had a mile-long suspect list that he hadn't managed to whittle down much since his father's murder a little over a year ago.

He was betting Caroline was eager to uncover those memories, too. Well, maybe she was. She had to want to know what'd happened not just to his father but also to her. She would want to know how she got that head injury. But the doctors had said the amnesia could be a way of protecting herself from a nightmare that was too traumatic for her to face. Still, Jack had to hold on to hope that one day she would push the trauma aside and help him catch a killer.

"I'll make a fresh pot of coffee," Lucille volunteered, and she got busy doing that after she gave Caroline the once-over.

It was the kind of quick exam a nurse would take of her patient, probably to make sure Caroline wasn't on the verge of a panic attack. Jack hadn't witnessed one of the attacks, but he'd heard from Lucille and then Caroline's doctors that she'd had several in the three months that she'd been in WITSEC. It was the reason the US Marshals—and Jack himself—had wanted a nurse to be with her. Normally, when someone was placed in WITSEC, that didn't happen. The person merely started a new life with a new identity and no past.

But nothing about this situation was normal.

Jack had also had to convince his agency that this wouldn't be a conflict of interest for him, that he could do his job as Caroline's handler despite their prior personal relationship. And that it would be all right for him to place her in the local area where he could keep a close eye on her. Maybe some of his fellow marshals did know of his personal interest in the case. But none had doubted that he would do whatever it took to make sure Caroline was not only safe but that she also made a full recovery. Emphasis on the *full*.

When Lucille had moved from the kitchen window, Caroline had came closer to him. But not too close. She always gave him a wide berth, making sure they didn't accidentally bump into each other. Maybe that's why his merely touching her hand earlier had caused every muscle in her body to turn to iron.

"You think that man by the pond came here to kill me?" she asked.

If he hadn't thought that was possible, she wouldn't need to be in WITSEC. But the truth was, he just didn't know. Maybe there was no killer after Caroline, but he wasn't willing to take that chance. Because if there was someone after her, it would likely be the same person who'd murdered his father. The person could want to silence her permanently so she could never reveal his or her identity.

"We don't know who we're dealing with," he settled for saying. He usually gave her a variation of that whenever the subject of her safety came up. Which was often. No need to alarm her and spur one of those panic attacks by spelling out worst-case scenarios. "Was there anything about this man you recognized?"

"No. Like I said, I only got a glimpse." Caroline didn't hesitate, but she did huff. "Has my location been compromised? Will I have to move to another safe house?"

Possibly, but Jack decided to put a softer spin on that. "Let's just wait and see. I'm not going to let anything happen to you." He looked at her as the last of those words were leaving his mouth, and for just a split second he saw something more than distrust on her face.

Anger, maybe?

But it was gone as quickly as it had come.

"I don't know who killed your father," she insisted. The riled expression might be gone, but there was a tinge of agitation in her voice.

Jack glanced at Lucille to see if she had an explanation for this change in Caroline's attitude, and the nurse's mouth tightened a little. "Caroline found some articles on the internet."

Well, hell. That definitely explained it. There were plenty of sites that had gobs of sordid details about his father's shooting. About Deputy Dusty Walters, who'd also died that night, too. And Caroline's name came up often on those sites. Not in a good way, either. The press had had a field day with her because she'd disappeared. There'd been plenty of speculation that had gone along with questions about where she was and what'd happened to her.

Not many people knew the answer to that.

WITSEC had taken care of shielding her identity so that now she lived and worked in this house. In fact, work was the reason she had a laptop in the first place. The Justice Department had created a job for her where she was reviewing witness testimony in cases where no charges had been filed. It was one step above busy work, but obviously it hadn't kept her busy enough.

"Yes, the filters are still on the computer," Lucille assured him.

"I figured out how to get around them," Caroline quickly confessed. "And no, it wasn't something I remembered how to do. I just kept plugging away until I found a web page that the filter didn't catch."

Jack added another "hell." He'd need to tell the doctors about this so they could deal with it during her weekly therapy session. A session that would, ironically, be done online, since Jack had wanted to limit Caroline's visits into San Antonio along with also limiting the number of people who knew the location of the safe house. And he'd managed to do that by limiting that info to his partner, Lucille and his three brothers, who were all lawmen. Jack had wanted them to know in case they needed to make a quick response.

However, even with all the precautions they'd taken, Jack knew that the safe house information could be breached. Their computer filters were more elaborate than the ones on the laptop here, but someone determined to find Caroline could still get around them. A killer definitely fell into the "someone determined" category.

Caroline groaned softly and pushed her shoulder-length blond hair from her face. "I used to have a life. I've read about it," she added in a grumble. "I came from almost nothing. My prostitute mother was killed by a drug dealer when I was eight, and I ended up in foster care." She looked ready to tack on more to that recap of her childhood, but then she stopped, paused. "I got through all of that to get a job working for one of the top criminal profiling experts."

Jack nodded. Yep, all of that was true. She'd had a life, all right, and even though she was alive, she might never get that life back. Would certainly never undo the fallout to her reputation because of the work she'd done with that top expert.

What Caroline hadn't just mentioned in the rundown of her life was her police record. A sealed juvie rap sheet that she wouldn't have been able to access without the prime hacking skills that she'd had before she lost her memory.

This woman with the angel face and almost fragile-looking body had been arrested when she was fifteen for hacking into multiple state records to find the dealer who'd killed her mother. Caroline had then stolen a car, tracked down the man and managed to bash him in the gut with a baseball bat before calling the cops to come and get him. The cops had gone easy on her because of the extenuating circumstances, but she'd still spent some time in juvie lockup.

"I saw a picture of Eric Lang," Caroline went on. She groaned again. "I suppose you know all there is to know about him." But she waved that off. "Of course, you do. You're a marshal. You're Sheriff Buck Slater's son."

Jack stayed quiet, but he knew Eric all right. Eric had been the research assistant for Caroline and her boss/friend Gemma Hanson at the college where the three of them had been working on a new computer program for profiling serial killers. The irony was that Eric himself had been a serial killer, and neither Gemma nor Caroline had picked up on it. Eric had hidden it from the women. From everyone. Then, Eric had nearly killed both Caroline and Gemma when he'd taken them hostage. That was what had sent Jack's father to an abandoned hotel, where he'd been killed.

Gemma had managed to escape that night. Caroline hadn't. Eric had taken her and disappeared into the darkness with her. No one, not even Caroline, was certain what had happened after that, but she'd shown up in Longview Ridge a year later. Because of her amnesia, though, she hadn't been able to tell them what'd happened to her.

"Eric is dead," Jack reminded her. "He was shot and killed three months ago, shortly after you came back to Longview Ridge."

Of course, he'd already told her that, and she had almost certainly read about it in those internet articles, but Jack wanted to spell it out for her that she didn't have to be afraid of Eric. He couldn't come after her again.

"Was I stupid?" she blurted out. Man, the anger had returned with a vengeance, not just in her tone but in her expression. "Was that why I couldn't see a serial killer was working right next to me?"

Jack hated to see her beating herself up like this. "You definitely weren't stupid. I met Eric, too, and I didn't make him for a killer. A lot of people didn't."

That didn't seem to appease her one bit. Her forehead still stayed bunched up, making the scar there even more obvious. A scar that she'd gotten during her captivity. Possibly from Eric, when he'd clubbed her on the head that night she was taken hostage. Of course, until Caroline got back her memory, she wouldn't be able to confirm if that was what had actually happened.

"And what about *us*?" Caroline threw out there.

Lucille's gaze fired to Caroline, then him. Jack didn't know what to make of the question, either. In the past three months, Caroline hadn't asked about them as a couple, but that was because Jack had never stayed around for an actual conversation. He visited twice a week, to check if Caroline's memory had returned. And once Lucille and Caroline assured him that it hadn't, he always left.

Just as Lucille did now.

The nurse must have thought they needed some privacy, because she mumbled something about needing to get something from her bedroom and walked out. Jack hadn't even been sure that Lucille knew Caroline and he had once been lovers.

Had been in love, he mentally corrected.

Jack hadn't talked about that with Lucille or anyone else, for that matter. Still, maybe Lucille had picked up on something or had been doing her own reading about Caroline. That would only be natural, he supposed, since Lucille and Caroline lived under the same roof, and Lucille was partly responsible for Caroline's safety.

"There was something about *us* in the articles you read?" Jack countered.

Best not to blurt out any details that Caroline didn't know or hadn't remembered. That was what the doctors had told him to do anyway. Keep the interaction between them to a minimum so there'd be no risk of planting memories in her head. That way, when she did recall something, it would be because it was a genuine memory. It was another reason he'd need to let her doctors know about this conversation.

When Caroline didn't answer, he looked at her. He saw maybe a flicker of recognition, or something, before she turned away. As she'd done earlier, she waved that off.

Jack would have pressed her for more info, pushing just a little, but his phone dinged, and he saw the file his partner, Teagan, had sent. Lucille must have heard the sound, too, because she hurried back into the kitchen.

"Any problem?" Lucille asked.

"Video from the security cameras." He motioned for her to come closer so she could take a look. When Caroline moved in, too, Jack had to consider which would upset her more: if she saw a would-be killer or if he kept her from seeing one.

He decided to let her watch.

It put them in close contact, with Lucille on one side of him and Caroline on the other. Caroline still didn't touch him, even though her arm was less than an inch from his.

Jack sped up the feed, going through minutes of what the cameras had recorded. Minutes of nothing.

And then there was something.

He slowed down the speed and then paused it when the man came into view. The guy was just as Lucille had described him—dark hair and jeans, and he was indeed by the pond. Too bad the guy was turned away from the camera so that only the side of his face was visible.

The man didn't have a drawn weapon, but Jack didn't like the way he was just standing there. If this was someone who'd just wandered onto the property, he should have been firing glances all around. Or leaving.

Jack touched the screen, moving it frame by frame until he finally got a shot he wanted. The guy turned to face the camera. Jack paused it again, enlarging it so he could run it through facial recognition software.

Caroline gasped. "Oh, God. Jack, I know him."

Shaking her head, she stepped back and pressed her fingers to her mouth. But only for a moment. Caroline's eyes widened when she saw that she'd gotten his complete attention. He could also see that she quickly tried to shut back down to that flat expression she'd worn for the past three months. But it was too late for that.

For that mask.

Because Jack had seen the recognition in her eyes. Better yet, he'd heard it in her voice.

Jack.

"You remembered something?" Lucille quickly asked, maybe not picking up on the sudden slash of tension between her patient and Jack. "Do you really know who that man is?"

Caroline didn't even look at the nurse. She kept her gaze fastened on Jack. Recognition, definitely. And some defiance. She hiked up her chin, and her mouth went into a flat line.

"Yes, I know that man," Caroline said, her stare drilling into Jack. "And I know *you*."

Chapter Two

Caroline's heart had gone to her knees at the exact moment she'd said Jack's name. Mercy, what had she done?

She wanted to take back the last handful of seconds, wanted to fix her expression so that Jack wouldn't see right through her. But she couldn't. The lid was off Pandora's box, and it wasn't going back on. And if that wasn't bad enough, now she had that face on the security video to worry about.

Caroline swallowed hard and looked at Lucille, who immediately took hold of her arm. "You need to sit down," Lucille instructed. "You look like you're about to pass out." She tried to lead Caroline back into the living room, but she held her ground. "Did your memory really come back?" Lucille asked.

"Yes," Caroline managed to say.

Lucille let out a huge breath of relief. Of course, the nurse didn't know how dangerous the man she'd recognized was. She also didn't know something Jack had already figured out.

That she'd regained her memory days ago.

As if celebrating and relieved by the progress, Lucille hugged her. "I'll need to call your doctor. Maybe we can drive out to see him?"

Even though Caroline liked her doctors and she'd had no trouble on the previous trips to San Antonio for her exams, she definitely didn't want a doctor right now.

"No. Could you give me a moment alone with Marshal Slater?" Caroline asked. It probably seemed petty or insulting to Jack that she'd call him by his surname now, but saying *Jack* seemed too, well, intimate.

Considering all the other intimate things they'd done, it would be so easy to slip back into that. After all, she had only told one man that she loved him, and it was the same man who was now glaring at her.

Lucille continued to give her a long, concerned look. "Should I get your meds?"

"No," Caroline repeated. "I'm not going to have a panic attack." She thought that was true, anyway, and even if it wasn't, she couldn't deal with the haze that the meds created in her mind. "I just need a moment with Marshal Slater. It's…personal."

"Oh." Lucille seemed relieved, which meant that maybe she knew or had guessed that Jack and Caroline had once been involved.

Jack knew it too, of course. There was nothing wrong with his memory. Or his glare. He stood there, all lanky and lean, looking more cop than cowboy now—though he was both. He'd come from a long line of Texas cowboys, and it fit him as well as his jeans and his ice-blue shirt.

No ice in his eyes, though. There was so much fire and heat in the depths of all that gray. The color of a dangerous storm cloud ready to shoot some lightning bolts her way. His hair was even darker than that. Midnight black. And right now his clothes, his expression and everything else about him made him seem more than a little dangerous.

Caroline waited until Lucille was out of the room before she said anything else. She turned to Jack, and she answered his question before he could even ask it. "Three days ago. That's when I regained my memory."

Muscles stirred in his jaw, and she doubted his eyes could narrow even more. "Why the hell didn't you tell me?" he asked through clenched teeth.

Oh, he was so not going to like this, and worse, she wasn't going to have time to smooth it over. No time to try to make him understand. "I don't know who killed your father. That's the truth."

"And I'm just to believe that after you've lied to me for three days, or longer?" Jack snarled.

Good point, and Caroline conceded that with a weary sound of agreement. It hadn't been longer, but she doubted she could convince him of that.

"The night Eric Lang kidnapped me, he did injure me," Caroline continued. "He bashed me on the head with his gun." She idly rubbed the scar on her forehead that she'd gotten from that attack. "And when that wasn't enough to render me unconscious, he pumped me full of drugs. Then he hid me and Gemma in one of the rooms of the abandoned hotel, Serenity Inn."

No need for her to get into too many specifics on the location. Jack had almost certainly searched every inch of that old hotel and gone over all the details of the investigation that followed. He knew that Eric had indeed managed to escape with her, and Jack had likely found her blood or some other evidence in that crumbling, smothering room that had once been part of a Victorian mansion.

"Eric didn't kill your father," she went on. "Eric was with me, holding a gun to my bleeding head when I heard the shots. And yes, I know it was the shots that killed your dad, because I also heard Gemma scream. I could hear the chaos that followed." She had to pause and gather her breath. With her breath, though, came the images.

Mercy, the images.

Caroline had to try to rein all of that in. If she had a panic attack, Lucille would force her into taking those meds, and that couldn't happen. She needed to finish what she had to say.

"Eric got away with me," Caroline went on several moments later while Jack stood there and drilled holes in her with his intense stare. "By then, I was barely conscious, but he talked to someone on the phone. A cop or some kind of lawman. And that person helped him escape. I know the caller was in law enforcement because there was a police radio in the background."

She didn't expect Jack to buy that, and even if he did, it still wouldn't justify her withholding the information that she'd regained her memory or the fact that she hadn't trusted him enough to tell him.

"Before I got my memory fully back, before I remembered *us*, I thought the person talking to Eric that night was you," she said. That didn't come out right, so she shook her head. "Or rather, someone you knew, because the other words I heard were 'Longview Ridge Sheriff's Office.' I heard dispatch codes. I thought it could be someone you wouldn't believe would help a serial killer, and that your disbelief would allow him to get to me or someone else."

Now he cursed, and those jaw muscles went to war with each other. "I'm not dirty, and I don't know any marshal or cop who is. I sure as hell wouldn't have helped Eric."

"Maybe not. But someone with a badge did. And I decided that if I wanted to stay alive, I couldn't trust you, the other marshals or anyone in your family."

He opened his mouth as if to blast her with verbal fire, but then he stopped, and it looked as if he'd done some reining in of his emotions, as well. "Yet you let me put you here. You let me come here to visit you."

She lifted her shoulder, tapped her head. "I didn't know, not when I came here. Three days ago, when the memories came, I decided I was safe as long as you and everyone connected to you thought I wasn't a threat. Or as long as you believed that I could eventually tell you who killed your father." Caroline took his phone. "But he's a threat. I don't have to guess about that."

Jack's glare got even worse, and she could tell the last thing he wanted to do was switch subjects. But he was also a lawman, and he'd seen the way she'd reacted to the man. Of course, maybe he thought she had faked that fear, too.

She hadn't.

"His name is Kingston Morris," she continued when Jack didn't say anything else. "And he was friends with Eric. The fact that he's here means he knows where I am and that he could have come here to kill me. Maybe to tidy up loose ends for his old friend."

"Kingston Morris," he repeated, not just once but several times as if testing to see if it rang any bells. "His name didn't come up in the investigation."

"It wouldn't have. I only remember Kingston coming in one time to the office where Eric and I worked."

"The office at the college." There was plenty of skepticism in his voice. "And yet you remembered him after just one meeting."

She shrugged. "He gave me the creeps."

That was an understatement. The guy had made her skin crawl, and because Kingston had seemed to worship Eric, that was the first time Caroline had started to look at Eric in a different light. That was the beginning of her seeing the monster crouched just below the facade he put on as a research assistant. Too bad she hadn't seen it a whole lot sooner. If she had, Jack's dad might be alive. Many others, too.

"If Eric and he were friends, Kingston's name should have come up," Jack concluded.

"Eric had erased all of his contacts. Or rather, he only left contacts and info that he didn't mind being discovered. He just used burner phones for getting in touch with anyone who was important to him."

"And this Kingston was important?" Jack asked while he typed something on his phone. She then heard the swooshes of outgoing texts. Maybe he was reaching out to his marshal friends to do a quick background check on Kingston. She hoped he hadn't mentioned that she'd regained her memory.

She nodded in reply to his question. "After Eric managed to get me away from the abandoned inn, it was Kingston who helped Eric get some money. I heard their phone conversation, too, and Kingston was like a groupie. He idolized Eric, would do anything for him."

This time Jack said a single word of profanity. "And you didn't think you should give this info to someone?" He didn't wait for her to answer. "Even if you didn't trust me, you could have told the cops."

"I didn't know if I could trust them, either." She had to pause again. "And I really did have amnesia until three days ago."

He made a sound that conveyed a whole boatload of doubt.

"I was in a hospital in Mexico," Caroline went on. "I'm not sure how I got there, but I think Eric took me across the border, and then I escaped. Or he could have left me for dead. Someone found me in a ditch and took me to the hospital. I had injuries other than just to my head. Broken bones, and I'd been beaten. There were lots of cuts and bruises on my face."

Jack couldn't dispute any of those injuries, because he had almost certainly seen the report of the medical exam that she'd been given after she returned to Longview Ridge three months ago.

"I didn't see Eric or Kingston after that, and even if I had, I might not have recognized them because of the amnesia," she admitted.

Which meant she'd be dead right now if Eric had seen her.

"After my condition improved in the Mexico hospital, they moved me to a convalescent home because I couldn't use my right hand," she explained. "Because of the head trauma, too. I stayed there until three months ago, when I started regaining pieces of my memory. I still didn't know who I was, but the name Longview Ridge kept repeating in my head."

So had Jack's name. And what she'd said to him kept playing again and again, too. Caroline doubted he would appreciate her mentioning that now, though.

I love you, Jack.

Yes, she'd indeed told him that. After a lazy Sunday morning of sex, he'd gotten the call to go into work, and instead of saying a simple goodbye, she'd said those words aloud. They had just slipped out—as easily as the kiss he had given her only seconds earlier. She'd seen the surprise in his eyes. Maybe the "run for the hills" look. Whichever it was, he hadn't said it back to her.

Everything that came after had happened so fast that Caroline hadn't had time to think about what had been said or unsaid. Unlike the last three days. Plenty of time to think then, and she hadn't liked the conclusion. She'd been wrong to tell him she loved him, even if it had been true.

"If you thought I was such a threat, why did you stay here?" he snapped. "Why didn't you run again as soon as you remembered what had gone on?"

"I stayed so I could try to find out the truth. Like I said, I once had a life, and I want it back. I want to find out what happened that night of your father's murder, and to do that, I have to stay alive."

"And you don't believe I want you alive." It sounded as if that disgusted him. Maybe it did. If he was clean, and she had to pray that he was, then an accusation like that would cut him to the core. But it wasn't Jack who was her biggest worry. It was any and all of the other cops and marshals who would get called into this investigation before this was over.

She opened her mouth just as something flashed through her head. Not a memory. But a really bad thought.

"Gemma," she blurted out. "Oh, God. Kingston could go after Gemma. You have to warn her."

"I already have. I sent Kellan a text to give him a heads-up that there might be a problem with Gemma's safety. *Might*," he emphasized.

Kellan was his brother, the sheriff of Longview Ridge, but he was also Gemma's fiancé. Kellan would protect her, but it twisted at Caroline's insides that she hadn't thought of contacting Gemma the moment she'd seen Kingston's face on the screen. To the best of her knowledge, Gemma hadn't actually met Kingston, but that didn't mean the man wouldn't try to go after her or anyone else who'd been connected to his now dead idol, Eric.

"Just please make sure that no one hurts her," she said.

"Funny that you'd show this much concern for Gemma now. She's your friend and your former boss, but you lied to her, too. Lying by omission is still a lie," he insisted. "Why didn't you tell Gemma that you had regained your memory and suspected that a dirty cop could be part of this?"

"Because I knew she'd tell Kellan," Caroline readily admitted.

"Damn straight Gemma would have, and it would have been the right thing to do."

"Maybe," Caroline muttered, not convinced that it would have indeed been the *right thing*. "But when I came back to town and saw her with Kellan, I knew they were in love. Once I had my memory back, I decided that Kellan must have been a good cop or Gemma wouldn't have those feelings for him. I couldn't take the chance, though, that Kellan would say something to someone whose feelings weren't so *loving*."

"Like me," he snapped.

"No." Frustrated and flustered, Caroline shook her head. "I just couldn't risk anyone knowing—not then, anyway. I can't protect myself. Heck, I can't even shoot straight." She held up her right hand. "Too much damage from the broken bones, and I lost what muscle strength I had." She paused, pushed her hair from her face. "Lucille's been giving me self-defense training. In another month or so, I would have been ready to tell you the truth."

He wouldn't understand the need she had to stay sheltered and protected until she could fend for herself. But then, Jack hadn't been held hostage by a serial killer.

Caroline watched the debate Jack was having with himself, and she wasn't sure if he would hold his ground and continue to stand here and press her for every detail of information in her head, or if he'd continue to be her protector.

The protector won out.

"Lucille," he called out. "Go ahead and get Caroline's and your things packed. Bring only some essentials, one bag each. I need to take you to a new location and will have someone come for the rest of your things later."

Caroline released the breath that she didn't even know she'd been holding. "Please don't bring your brothers in on this," she insisted. "Don't bring anyone else in on it. Not yet."

Jack certainly didn't agree to that, but he did head in the direction of the bedrooms. There were only two of them, hers and Lucille's, and Lucille was in Caroline's room, shoving meds and the laptop into a small duffel bag. Caroline jumped right in to help her.

Jack stood in the doorway, continuing to view the footage from the cameras. "Caroline, did you contact anyone when you did those internet searches?" he asked. Lucille left the room, probably realizing this was a good time for her to get her own things ready.

Caroline supposed that was a necessary question, but it sent a coil of anger through her. "No. I didn't have anyone I could completely trust to contact. Not even Gemma. Because, as I said, she would have told Kellan."

She left it at that, but Jack probably knew that some of those searches would have brought up pictures of Eric's victims. So many of them. Those images would haunt her, too.

"I couldn't access anything about the investigation into your father's murder." Caroline added a change of clothes to the duffel. She was about to ask him if he had any new leads, but his phone dinged before she could.

"Kingston Morris," he read aloud. Obviously, someone had run a background check for him. "Age twenty-four. Address in Dallas. No record. Trust fund baby. His folks own a successful export business." Jack held up Kingston's DMV photo for her to see.

"That's him," she verified. "But he's not in Dallas. He was by the pond about a half hour ago. Maybe you can put out an APB on him—"

"I've already done that." Jack's attention landed on her again. "Still believe I'm trying to kill you?"

"I never believed that," she snapped. "I just thought…" But she waved that off and zipped up the duffel with a hard jerk as if it'd been the cause for the fit of temper she was feeling.

And the frustration, doubt and fear.

"I hate being afraid," she said under her breath. She hadn't meant for Jack to hear that, but judging from the way he huffed and cursed, he had. Worse, he was probably analyzing her now as the shrinks had done after she'd tracked down her mother's killer.

"Then you need to trust me." He didn't say it as a request or plea. It was an order, and he tipped his head to indicate he wanted her on the move.

Jack also drew his gun.

Her pulse hadn't exactly been at a resting pace, but the sight of the weapon jacked it up even more, as it did the hit of adrenaline. It didn't mesh well with that knot already in her stomach.

With a small suitcase gripped in her hand, Lucille joined them in the hall. "How close are you parked to the house?" she asked.

"Close," Jack assured the nurse. "I'll go out first. When I motion for you to leave the house, move fast and get in the truck. Understand?"

The moment Lucille and Caroline nodded, Jack disengaged the security system and went out onto the porch. As he'd done at that kitchen window, he glanced around. So did Caroline, and she wished she had a gun or some other weapon that she could actually use with her still-weak hand. There was no chance of Jack giving her anything like that.

Because he didn't trust her.

She knew plenty about distrust and had spent every waking moment of the past year feeling the same thing. It'd been worse when she hadn't even known who she was. Well, in some ways it had been. Once she'd remembered, the distrust had collided with the fear that someone out there could still want her dead.

Not Jack.

She knew that now. But while she could trust him, she couldn't trust the others who were in his life. Part of her wanted to strike out on her own. But that would involve plenty of risks, too.

Still keeping watch, Jack went down the porch steps and started his truck. He motioned for them to move only after he threw open the passenger-side door.

"Now," he called out.

She and Lucille hurried off the porch, and even though it hadn't been Caroline's intention, she ended up in the middle of the seat, right next to Jack. Since she'd arrived at the safe house she had avoided touching him, but that was impossible now. They were shoulder to shoulder and hip to hip.

Jack immediately hit the accelerator, and while he continued glancing around them, he made a call using the control on his steering wheel. A few seconds later, a woman answered.

"Teagan," Jack said.

Caroline knew that was his partner, Marshal Teagan Randolph. She'd heard Jack give Lucille the marshal's contact info in case there was an emergency and she couldn't reach Jack. That meant he must trust the woman, but Caroline didn't want anyone else brought into this just yet. She was about to tell him that, too, but he cursed before Teagan or she could say anything.

"What's wrong?" Teagan immediately asked.

"We have a tail," Jack spat out. "I'm on the east farm road about twelve miles from Longview Ridge. I need backup right now."

Chapter Three

The moment Jack said someone was following them, Caroline jerked her body around to look out the back window of his truck. She groaned, no doubt seeing exactly what Jack had caught sight of.

A black four-door sedan with a heavily tinted windshield.

The fact that it was a car made it stand out in a place where most folks drove trucks. Maybe a crazed groupie/killer wannabe hadn't gotten the memo on that, and had failed to blend in.

Jack hadn't had a choice about requesting backup. He'd noticed the sedan pulling out of a ranch trail just moments after he had driven past it. Of course, it was possible this wasn't someone after Caroline, that it was just a driver in the wrong place at the wrong time, maybe even someone who'd gotten lost, but Jack couldn't risk not having an extra gun if something bad went down. Or rather, if something *worse* was going down.

The *bad* had already happened.

There was no scenario Jack could come up with that made Kingston Morris showing up just yards from the safe house a good thing. Which was why he should have called for backup even sooner. Unfortunately, Jack had let himself get distracted with Caroline's bombshell. Now that he'd remembered he was a lawman and not her former lover—or the son of a murdered sheriff—he would press her more on why she'd lied. Press her more, too, on the bits of so-called evidence from the night his dad had been killed. For now, Jack just kept an eye on the car behind them.

"Are Caroline and Lucille okay?" Teagan asked. "Are *you* okay?"

"So far." Jack wanted it to stay that way.

"Do you think it's that guy, Kingston Morris, who you asked me to run?" Teagan added.

"Possibly." But the more honest answer would be "Yes." It would be hard to believe it was a coincidence that an Eric groupie to appeared on a security camera and then someone else showed up on this remote stretch of the road.

"There's no immediate threat," Jack added to his partner, "but I want backup in place."

"Understood."

Jack opened his mouth to give Teagan some instructions as to what he needed her to do, but Caroline tugged on his arm to get his attention. At first he thought that was because she'd seen the person behind that dark windshield, but she merely stared at him. No one had ever accused him of having ESP or even being tuned in to nonverbal cues, but he got this one all right.

Caroline didn't want him to mention that she'd gotten her memory back. Since he couldn't see why Teagan would need to know that right at this exact moment, Jack nodded. Obviously Caroline was good with the nonverbal, too, because she blew out a breath of relief.

"I need you to run the plates on a black sedan for me,"

Jack continued with Teagan. He could hear his partner typing away on her keyboard. No doubt arranging for the backup he'd requested. But she could multitask, too, so he rattled off the license plate number to her.

"It's a rental car," Teagan said just moments later. "I'll find out who rented it."

Jack was betting the person who'd done that had used an alias. Well, unless Kingston or the person in the sedan was truly an idiot. That wouldn't make this situation less dangerous, because Jack knew from experience that idiots could kill just as well as smart people. The idiots just didn't tend to get away with it, but that didn't make their victims less dead or instances like this any less lethal.

The seconds seemed to drag before Teagan came back on the line. "Lee Zeller's in the field about twenty miles from you. He's the closest marshal for backup."

Jack kept his speed at a steady pace and considered his options. Zeller wasn't one of them, and he glanced at Caroline to see if she agreed. Judging from the way her forehead creased, she did. Which meant she'd been doing some investigating and had likely hacked her way through the filters in multiple files.

He was getting better at picking up the unspoken stuff.

"Bad choice for backup?" Teagan asked Jack when he didn't respond.

Teagan could read him. She'd been Jack's partner for two years and had read all the files on his father's murder.

Zeller had been involved in an investigation that Jack's father was running at the time he was gunned down. Sex trafficking. Zeller hadn't been a suspect in that case. Heck, there'd been no hints of any wrongdoing on his part, but Jack didn't like the way these particular lines had intersected. Because it would only rattle Caroline even more, he didn't want anyone from his father's investigations playing backup for him.

Well, no one who wasn't family.

That was going to tighten Caroline's forehead, too, and break some rules, but that car behind them certainly wasn't putting her at ease, either. Ditto for Lucille. Both women had turned to watch it again.

"I need to make another call," he told Teagan. "Get me the name on the rental car." Jack hung up and hit the button on his steering wheel.

"Call Kellan," he instructed his phone.

As expected, Caroline whirled back around while shaking her head. Frantically shaking it. There was no need for her to repeat her warning that while she thought she could trust Jack, she didn't feel that way about other cops. Or anyone else with a badge and a police radio who could maybe listen in on their conversation. So, while he waited for the call to his brother to connect, he gave her proof for why she should want Kellan in on this.

Jack sped up.

So did the car behind them.

When he slowed, the sedan followed suit. It let Caroline know that there could be a real threat behind them. Maybe it was Kingston. Maybe hired guns paid for with Kingston's trust fund. It could be someone who wasn't even on their radar, who'd used Kingston as a dupe.

Whatever this was, this situation could get ugly. In fact, the only reason it probably hadn't already was because the driver was waiting until they reached the road leading to Longview Ridge. It was wider and didn't coil around like a rattlesnake. It would be easier to make a move there. Jack was guessing the guy might try to run them off the road or else shoot at them.

Caroline's eyes were already wide, and only grew bigger when she saw how closely the sedan was mirroring their moves. Lucille saw it, too, and she threw her small suitcase on the floor of the truck, no doubt to free up her hands. She drew her gun just as Kellan answered the phone.

"You're on speaker," Jack warned his brother right off. "And I have Caroline and Lucille in the truck with me."

"What happened?" Kellan snapped.

"Kingston Morris, a possible groupie connected to Eric, showed up at the safe house, and now I think he could be following us. And no, you won't find his name in our files. That's because Caroline only told me about him less than a half hour ago. Apparently, Kingston visited Caroline's office while Eric was there, and Kingston made a strong enough impression for her to remember him."

Jack paused to give his brother a second to let that sink in. It sank in quickly.

"She got her memory back," Kellan concluded, and without even taking a breath, he added, "Dad's killer?"

Jack had anticipated that would be the first of his brother's questions. "She claims she doesn't know."

Jack figured the skepticism in his wording was going to piss her off, and it did. But he didn't care. She'd lied to him. And while her lie might not be responsible for the car following them, if he'd known the facts—all of them—he might have been able to pick up Kingston before it even came to this.

Even without having the details spelled out for him, it obviously riled Kellan, too, because he cursed. "Where are you? You need backup?"

"Yes to the backup." Jack gave Kellan his location. "I'm heading to your office, so meet me."

Jack didn't wait for his brother's assurance that he would do just that. No need. Kellan would get there as fast as he could. Maybe it would be fast enough, but Jack didn't like the bad feeling that was slithering its way down his back. That turn with the straighter, wider road was coming up fast.

"You know how I feel involving your brothers in this," Caroline snapped the moment he was off the phone with Kellan. "They could trust fellow cops who are dirty."

"Lesser of two evils," Jack reminded her, and just to prove his point, he slowed down. The sedan kept pace.

She made a sound to indicate she was considering what he'd said, but she didn't argue. Caroline twisted back around to keep watch.

Jack considered just flooring the accelerator and trying to outrace this moron. But that was risky. Curvy roads could lead to accidents, which would in turn make them sitting ducks. Plus, the sedan engine might be souped-up enough that it wouldn't have any trouble catching up with them. Jack wanted to delay the showdown until Kellan was closer.

"Who's Marshal Zeller?" Lucille asked. Her voice was a little shaky. So was she. But she was holding her own and didn't look ready to panic. "Why didn't you want him for backup?"

"Because he could be dirty," Caroline grumbled before Jack could say anything.

As answers went, it was a pretty good one. In her mind, Zeller could indeed be dirty. The jury was still out on that for Jack, but if there'd been any red flags to find, Jack figured he would have found them by now. That was because he'd dug and dug deep. Not just on Zeller but on any-and everyone connected to his father's investigations.

"Zeller headed a sex-trafficking case that popped a little over a year ago," Jack told Lucille. Like the women, he still had his eyes on the sedan. "One that involved some college students. One of those students, Nicola Gunderson, was abducted from a diner in Longview Ridge, and then she turned up dead. That's how my dad got involved. My brother Kellan too, since he was a deputy at the time."

"Oh, yes. I remember." Lucille's voice was a little tight, but Jack knew that wasn't because she had something to hide or even any personal knowledge of the case. However, she did have plenty of knowledge about sex offenses since she'd been a victim of a violent rape fifteen years earlier.

Zeller wasn't the only person Jack had vetted all the way down to ground zero.

Jack hadn't considered Lucille's past a concern, but rather he saw how she responded to it by cultivating her current assets. She'd learned to protect herself and continued her nursing career, and Jack figured that was a bonus skill set when it came to choosing who would be staying with Caroline. Right now, he appreciated that skill set very much, but he hoped he didn't need Lucille to play backup.

"You're taking me to the sheriff's office," Caroline concluded.

Jack couldn't figure out a way to sugarcoat it. "I am."

She sat there, obviously weighing her options as he'd done earlier. She was smart. Smart enough to keep her mouth shut about regaining her memory because she didn't know the snakes from the good guys. And that meant she'd soon figure out that the only choice she had was to go with him to the sheriff's office. That didn't mean she'd like it, though.

Jack had to slow down as he approached the last turn that would take him to town. They were about six miles out now.

Not far.

With Kellan no doubt already en route, it meant he had only a couple more minutes before he could do something about this tail. He wanted to question whoever was behind that wheel. If it was Kingston, he would question him even harder, because maybe he, too, had been at the abandoned hotel the night Jack's father was murdered.

Jack took the turn on the road, and while his attention hadn't strayed from the sedan, he watched it even closer now. Though he soon figured out there was no need for watching, because the driver immediately sped up.

Hell.

Kellan was still nowhere in sight, but Jack got a glimpse of something he sure as heck didn't want to see. The driver's-side window of the sedan lowered. A hand came out. One holding a gun.

"Get down!" Jack shouted to Caroline and Lucille.

Not a second too soon. Because the shot slammed into the truck.

Chapter Four

Caroline ducked down and grabbed on to Lucille to make sure she did the same just as a bullet blasted through the truck's back window. The safety glass shattered, but the pieces that pummeled them had a plastic coating to keep them from being lethal or cutting them to shreds.

The second shot could fall into the lethal category, though.

It slammed into the driver's side of the glass, missing Jack's head by what appeared to be a fraction of an inch.

Fear roared through her, but so did anger. Whoever was doing his—Kingston, maybe—was putting Jack and Lucille in danger, all so he could get to her.

Of course, the flashbacks came. Nightmarish memories of the other attack, the gunfire the night Jack's father had been murdered. Jack was no doubt reliving some bad stuff, as well.

"I can hold the steering wheel so you can return fire," Caroline offered.

With narrowed eyes, he spared her a glance, looking at her as if she'd lost her mind. "You're staying down." And he caught onto her neck to push her lower. "I have no intention of confronting this jerk with Lucille and you in the vehicle. I'll do that later when it's just me and him."

Jack didn't leave any room for argument on that, and he hit the accelerator again just as the shooter sent a third bullet their way. Since Lucille was shaking and mumbling a prayer, Caroline put her arm around the woman to try to comfort her.

Mixed in with the sound of a fourth shot, Caroline heard something else. The howl of a police siren. It gave her a jolt of relief. Then, a wave of more fear. Because this was probably Kellan.

The shots stopped instantly, and behind them was the screech of brakes. When Jack cursed, she risked lifting her head to see what was going on. The shooter had stopped and was turning his car around.

No doubt so he could get away.

Jack pulled to the side of the road, and that was when Caroline looked out of the front of the truck and spotted not one but two cruisers. Two deputies were in one, and they sped past them, heading in pursuit of the gunman. Kellan was driving the second cruiser, and he pulled up next to Jack.

"Is anyone hurt?" Kellan immediately asked, glancing up at the shot-out glass, then his brother. Then, at Caroline. Kellan was probably good at poker, because she couldn't tell what he was thinking other than the obvious concern for his brother and them.

Jack made a quick check of her and Lucille, but his attention didn't stray far from his rearview mirror. Keeping watch for the sedan that had sped away from them.

"We're okay," Jack assured his brother. "I need to get them to the sheriff's office."

Kellan gave a quick nod. "I would have all of you get in the cruiser with me, but the guy might return, and I don't want you out in the open. I'll follow you back and send out another crew of deputies to assist in chasing down that car."

Jack matched his brother's nod and took off. "It'll only take us a couple of minutes to get there," Jack told Lucille and her.

Minutes. Not long before she could be walking into a lion's den. But then, as Jack had said, for her it was the lesser of two evils. She definitely didn't want to hang around, waiting for a gunman.

Those couple of minutes crawled by, and it didn't help that Caroline had broken glass all over her. A reminder of the attack. God, when was this going to end? For over a year she had been fighting for her life, and now she'd apparently brought that fight straight to Jack.

Jack didn't slow down until his truck screeched to a stop in front of the sheriff's office. Kellan must have already called ahead, because another of Jack's brothers, Deputy Owen Slater, was in the open doorway, and he had his gun drawn. As soon as Kellan arrived he took Owen's place, and Owen drove off in the cruiser. No doubt in pursuit of the shooter.

"I called a medic," Kellan said as they all hurried inside. "He'll be here soon." Another of the deputies, Gunnar Pullam, immediately took hold of Lucille's arm. Caroline knew him, and had never gotten any criminal vibes from him, but she still kept her distance.

"Move away from the windows," Jack snapped.

Caroline didn't need a reminder of the danger or another slam of adrenaline, but Jack's words gave her both anyway.

Jack turned to Gunnar. "Do you want to take Lucille to the break room to wait for the medic?" he suggested.

"And after she gets checked out, take her statement," Kellan added.

When Kellan looked at Caroline this time, his face wasn't so poker ready. His mouth was tight, maybe because she hadn't remembered his father's killer. Or perhaps he just thought she hadn't wanted to tell him.

Caroline was certain there was some tightness in her mouth, too. Was she looking into the eyes of a killer? Maybe not. But it was possible that Kellan was covering for one.

With his hand still on her arm, Jack led her across the squad room that was jammed with desks and equipment and took her inside Kellan's office.

"Stay here," he told her and immediately went back out into the squad room, where Kellan waited.

The brothers were only about ten feet away from her, but Jack didn't exactly broadcast what he was saying, keeping his voice barely louder than a whisper. Still, Caroline caught a word here and there. *Three days ago, she said. Dirty cop. You. Yeah, she thinks that.*

The last one caused Kellan to huff and then scowl, but when he glanced over Jack's shoulder at her, the scowl disappeared. The look he gave her riled her to the core. Because it was pity. Kellan thought she was too damaged to think straight. He was dismissing her concerns that a lawman had been the one to help Eric in the attack a year ago.

Jack also glanced back at her, frowned and then mumbled something else to Kellan. She didn't catch a single word of that, but Jack started toward her. Not hurrying, but with every step he took, he kept his eyes on her.

When he reached her, she was about to blast him for spilling all to Kellan, but Jack stopped her with a touch.

He pushed her hair from her face, examining her. Or so she thought until he extracted a blob of the safety glass, then another, from the top of her head.

Dragging in a weary breath, he closed the door, and in the same motion, he turned her to check the back of her hair. "Shake your clothes," he instructed. "Even safety glass can cut if you sit or lean back on it."

Her mouth got tighter, but she shook the dress and glass bits pinged to the tile floor. "You told your brother that I don't trust him," she snapped, "that I think he's a dirty cop involved in his father's murder."

Jack continued to pick off glass bits. "He would have figured it out. He's a lot better at body language than I am."

"You're fine with body language," she grumbled, but Caroline wished she'd kept that to herself.

She whirled around just in time to see him smile that damnable smile, and she wasn't sure if she wanted to throttle him or kiss him. Caroline didn't do either, but it did cause her to freeze.

His next breath wasn't so much one of weariness as it was of relief. The long, lingering look he gave her made her think he was about to touch her again. He didn't. Instead, Jack crammed his hands into the pockets of his jeans.

"If you need to fall apart or cry, go ahead and do it," he offered. "You're shaking," he pointed out before she could insist she didn't intend to do either. She didn't know what she was stewing over more— Jack telling his brother her deep, dark fears or Kellan brushing it off as Jack had done to the glass.

But she was indeed trembling.

Her hands, her mouth. Heck, her legs. She was probably a breath away from both falling apart and crying.

"I nearly got Lucille and you killed," she said, and Caroline cursed her own voice. It was shaking, too.

Jack lifted an eyebrow. "Funny, I thought it was the shooter who nearly killed us."

"The shooter wouldn't have been firing those bullets if it hadn't been for me." She expected him to give her some sugarcoated answer, but she'd obviously forgotten this was Jack.

"That's true." With that hanging in the air, he waited a heartbeat. "And since I'd rather not have any more attempted murders, that means you're going to have to let me help you."

"You mean I'm going to have to trust Kellan," Caroline blurted out. She was feeling a lot less shaky now.

Jack shrugged, took his hand from his pocket so he could tap the badge on his belt. "Every lawman in Texas isn't tainted, and if you dig beneath all the anger, fear and whatever else it is you're feeling, you'll remember that I'm the best shot you've got at keeping us both alive."

He followed that too logical minilecture with a long stare. Jack was obviously waiting for her to come to the only conclusion that she had right now.

"I'm *not* going to trust your brother," she insisted, but left the rest of it unspoken—that she would trust Jack. Again, it was the only choice she had.

He nodded as if they'd just hashed that out with a heated argument. "I'll do whatever it takes to keep you safe." He paused. "Want me to take a bullet for you to prove it?"

Jack didn't wink, but he might as well have, because he was obviously trying to lighten things up. Trying to bring her back down and ease some of the still raw adrenaline. It was working, sort of, since it was something he'd said to her in jest when they'd been lovers. A way of letting her know that he cared that much for her.

"No," she said, drawing out the one-word answer to emphasize it. There was a lot more emotion in her voice than she wanted as she stared at him.

Thinking.

Remembering.

Yes, definitely remembering.

That helped more than his lame attempt at cop humor. His being there helped, too, and despite everything she'd been through—or maybe because of it—Caroline wanted to step right into his arms. Those strong arms with their toned muscles. She wanted to feel the heat, and the comfort that she'd gotten there before. Jack had tugged and pulled at her in a way that no man ever had before.

Or ever would again, she was forced to admit to herself.

Yes, it'd been great sex. The fire between them so hot. The feel of him touching her with those calloused hands. Him, being inside her. She'd felt that, too.

If it'd been just those things, *only those,* she could have pushed it all away. Could have distracted herself with the dark fear that was eating holes in her. But it had been more—way more—and she had to admit that to herself, too.

With those stormy gray eyes locked on hers, he reached up and touched his finger to the center of her forehead. Just a touch, maybe to her scar, the one that Eric had given her when he hit her. Or maybe Jack was trying to ease the tensed muscles there. And despite everything she'd just admitted to herself, Caroline still hadn't been prepared for that touch. For the way his warm breath fell on her. For the look of him.

That face. His eyes. His mouth that had fueled enough fantasies to last her a couple of lifetimes.

"Penny for your thoughts," he drawled. "A dollar for them if you're thinking about sex." The corner of his mouth hitched. Because he knew her thoughts, knew everything she was feeling right now.

Since he was feeling the same thing, Caroline laid her hand on his chest. Over his heart, which she could feel beating to the rhythm of hers.

"Sex won't help," she said, her voice mostly breath.

His slight smile stayed in place. A smile that only he and Mona Lisa could have pulled off. "That depends on the sex."

Jack made her laugh before she could stop herself or remember there was absolutely nothing to laugh about. He hooked his arm around the back of her neck in a casual, easy way, and lowering his head to her, took her laugh with his mouth.

Kissing her.

It was like hot silk sliding through her. Oh, it felt wonderful. That incredible taste. Those clever moves, with seemingly no effort. He made no demands, and yet, also seemed to make the biggest demand of all. Within seconds, he had turned the hot silk to blazing flames.

"It's good to have you back," he whispered against her mouth.

Is it? she wanted to say. She'd brought nothing but trouble with her. But there wasn't time for her question because the door opened, and Kellan stepped in.

Jack moved away from her, but he took his time, which meant Kellan had no trouble seeing Jack's arm around her and their mouths hovering over each other. It didn't make Kellan a happy camper. He scowled at his brother.

"The medic's here to check Caroline," Kellan said, his attention nailed to Jack. "And I just spoke to Kingston on the phone, and he said he'd come in for questioning, to *set some things straight.* He's on his way here right now."

Chapter Five

Jack wanted to curse. Even though he probably should, he didn't regret kissing Caroline. But now he was going to have to listen to Kellan tell him why a kissing regret should be at the top of his list.

And Kellan would be right.

Caroline didn't look so much regretful as she did embarrassed. Nervous, too. That was likely because of the distrust she had for not only Kellan but all the other cops in the building.

"I'll find the medic," she muttered, moving past both Jack and Kellan to hurry away.

Kellan immediately motioned toward Sherry McNeil, one of the deputies at a desk in the squad room. "Keep an eye on her," Kellan said to Sherry, tipping his head in the direction of both Caroline and the ladies' room.

Jack just lifted an eyebrow.

"Caroline lied to you. She waited three days to tell you she'd gotten her memory back," Kellan said, as if that excused the tail he'd just put on her.

"She lied because she doesn't trust me. Not yet."

Kellan made a sound of disagreement. "She looked pretty trusting to me when she was kissing you."

"That was the attraction. It's always been intense between us."

He wouldn't tell his brother that Caroline and he had gone all night their first time together. As if they'd been starved for each other. Hell, they were still starved for each other. If the door had been locked and Kellan hadn't walked in, Jack might have backed Caroline against the wall and taken her then and there.

And she would have let him.

He'd felt that. The way her body had hummed against his. His own body had hummed plenty, too, and Jack knew it wasn't going to be easy to rein in that kind of heat. And he doubted he would be able to count on an interruption to give him the willpower to resist a woman he'd never been able to resist.

"I don't have to tell you this, but I will," Kellan went on a moment later. "Sex could cause you to lose focus."

This was obviously going to be one of the big topics of conversation today. "Lack of sex can do that, too. I haven't been with another woman since Caroline." Jack looked at Kellan then but didn't see even one raised eyebrow. "You don't seem surprised."

"I'm not just a cop, I'm also your big brother. I know you fell hard for her, but she's not the same woman she was a year ago."

"Of course, she's not," Jack snapped. "She was nearly murdered by a serial killer and had amnesia. Hard to come back from that. But Caroline's there. Underneath the tangled mess of memories in her head, she's there."

The sound that Kellan made was still edged with suspicion. "Personally, I like her. There's plenty of toughness beneath that delicate-looking exterior."

Yes, there was, and it was one of the things that had

first attracted Jack to her. But her toughness had some fractures in it now. Thanks to Eric. This latest attack sure wasn't going to help, either.

Jack scrubbed his hand over his face. "I need to figure out how the location of the WITSEC house was breached, and I have to look into those things that Caroline heard the night Dad was killed."

Kellan's jaw tightened. "The police radio transmissions. The mention of this office. The dispatch codes." He glanced around the squad room. "I'll help with that. I trust every person who works for me, but I won't blow off what Caroline told you. That's why I sent Sherry to keep an eye on her. Caroline said the voice on that call to Eric was male, so she should be okay with Sherry watching after her."

Jack sent his brother a silent look of thanks for that.

"The call Caroline heard could have been part of the sick game that Eric was playing," Kellan added after a pause. "Something to throw her off the accomplice who was actually helping him."

That wasn't just possible. It was likely. The trouble would be to convince Caroline of that, and his best shot at doing it was to figure out how Eric could have faked a call like that.

When Jack heard someone clear their throat, he looked to the doorway and saw Tatum Carson, the medic. "Neither of the women has any injuries," Tatum told them, "but if you want me to take them into the hospital for tests, I will."

"No," Lucille and Caroline said in unison. They were behind the medic, and Sherry and Gunnar stood behind them.

Jack looked at both Lucille and Caroline and knew

there'd be no other tests. "Thanks. You can go," he said to Tatum.

With a suit-yourself shrug, the medic gathered his things and headed out.

"Lucille wants to go to her sister's in San Antonio," Gunnar said, stepping up. "I got her statement and her contact info. Her sister doesn't have a car, so Lucille will need a ride. Is it okay for her to go?"

This was touchy jurisdictional territory. The shooting hadn't happened at the WITSEC safe house, which meant technically this was Kellan's case. Jack didn't want to cross any gray lines—when he managed to make an arrest, he needed to have dotted all the i's and crossed all the t's to get a conviction. He also didn't want to step on his brother's toes, so he looked at Kellan, wanting him to respond to Gunnar's question.

"Any chance this shooter will go after Lucille?" Kellan asked Jack.

"Slim to none." Caroline was the target. Jack was certain of that. "But San Antonio PD should be alerted just in case something comes up. That way, they can make sure Lucille is protected."

"She can leave," Kellan said, apparently satisfied with what Jack had just told him. "I can't send Gunnar with her, though, because he's got to testify in court in about an hour. He won't make it back here in time. Sherry, will you drive Lucille and contact SAPD on the way there?"

Sherry nodded, and, as the medic had done, the deputy started to gather her things, too. However, Lucille didn't budge. Instead, she caught onto Caroline's shoulders and looked her straight in the eyes.

"Remember what I taught you," Lucille said.

Caroline nodded. "Open-hand strike to the nose, followed by a hard kick to the groin."

Jack winced, but Lucille smiled, clearly proud of her student. She brushed a kiss on Caroline's cheek, whispered a goodbye and headed out with the deputy.

"Should I take Caroline's statement now?" Gunnar asked.

This was another t-crossing and i-dotting moment. Since Jack had also been on the receiving end of that attack, he couldn't question her. Heck, he shouldn't even be in the room with her during the interview. That meant Caroline was about to be questioned by a male cop whom she maybe didn't trust.

Jack was still mulling over the best way to handle that when he realized the interview and his own mulling were going to have to wait. That was because he saw a now familiar face had stepped into the squad room.

Kingston walked in, and he was wearing the same clothes he'd had on in the security footage. What the footage hadn't captured was the cocky look on his face. It appeared to be a permanent expression.

"Caroline," Kingston purred, his attention going straight to her. "So you're still alive. Too bad that you won't be that way for long."

CAROLINE PULLED BACK her shoulders. Considering Kingston had been friends with a serial killer, she hadn't expected him to look, well, normal, but she also hadn't believed he'd come waltzing into a sheriff's office to dole out what sounded like a threat.

"I'm Kingston Morris," he greeted as if this were a

social call. He thrust out his hand for Jack to shake. "And you're Marshal Slater. Good to meet you."

Jack didn't exchange handshakes, but he gave Kingston a look that could have frozen Hades. He caught onto Kingston, whirled him around and, despite the man's howl of protest, frisked him. No weapon.

"*So you're still alive. Too bad that you won't be that way for long,*" Jack growled, repeating word for word what Kingston had just said. "Along with some other things, you'll want to explain that *now*."

Kingston was wise enough to drop the cocky smile and the protest over the pat down, but he didn't appear as concerned as he should be, considering that Jack looked ready to tear him limb from limb.

"I said that because of the attack." There wasn't much concern in Kingston's voice, either. *Unflappable* was the word that came to Caroline's mind. "Lots of gossip about it, and from what people are saying, someone wanted to kill Caroline and you."

Now Kingston turned to her, their gazes connecting, and Caroline forced herself not to take a step back. Too bad that he spurred the old memories, and she got a burst of the flashbacks before she could stop them. The pain and the fear. She'd thought she was going to die, and the swarm of emotions that had come with that belief hit her now.

Jack must have noticed or else guessed about the flashbacks, because he moved closer to her, his arm brushing against her. It was surprising and unnerving how just a simple touch from him could soothe her. But Caroline would take it. She definitely didn't want to collapse into a puddle from a panic attack when she needed to confront Kingston.

"You tried to kill Jack and me?" Caroline came out and asked, and she made sure she held eye contact with Kingston.

"No, of course not." It sounded more mocking than genuine, but at least the man started to show some concern when Jack turned on a recorder and began to read him his rights.

"You're arresting me?" Kingston demanded several times while he was Mirandized.

"Any reason I shouldn't?" Jack countered after he'd finished. "You were at Caroline's not long before she was attacked."

Jack didn't add more to that explanation, and Caroline thought she knew why. He was giving Kingston a chance to lie by denying it. If so, that would add weight to his arrest.

However, Kingston shrugged. "Yes, I was there," he readily admitted. "I got a text, giving me the address and saying I should go there."

Jack eased up on the glare to give the man a look of skepticism. Caroline felt the same way, and when Kingston obviously picked up on their disbelief, he huffed and took out his phone. After he'd pulled up a message, he handed Jack his phone.

There it was on the screen. No name of the person who'd sent the message, but there was the address of the safe house, along with the message, Want to get a look at the woman who helped kill your friend Eric Lang? You'll find her here.

"I don't know who sent it, and the number is no longer working," Kingston explained. "My guess is he or she used a disposable cell and deactivated it."

"Or else you used such a phone and sent the message to yourself," Jack quickly countered.

Kingston didn't exactly give him an eye roll, but it was close. "There's no reason for me to do that."

Jack didn't waste any time arguing. "Sure there is. You might think a message like that would get you off the hook. It won't. You were in the vicinity of Caroline's house, and you have a motive to murder her."

"A motive?" Kingston challenged. "You mean because of Eric?" He didn't wait for Jack to confirm or deny that. "I wouldn't kill because of him. Yes, I was intrigued by Eric. He was very interesting and charismatic, but I wouldn't have done his bidding. Besides, he's dead."

Jack leveled his gaze on Kingston. "Yet you acted on what you're saying was an anonymous tip to go to the house of a woman you blame for the death of this interesting and charismatic piece of dirt?"

Kingston opened his mouth, then closed it as if rethinking what he'd been about to say. "I don't blame Caroline for Eric's death." He shifted his attention to Kellan. "I believe you're the one who delivered what eventually became the fatal blow."

"I did," Kellan readily admitted. "I just wish I'd been able to put a bullet in him sooner."

If Kingston had a reaction to that, he didn't show it. Instead, he turned back to Caroline. "Someone wants you dead. The attack proves that. And I think the person who sent me that message thought I'd do the job for him or her."

"Do you want to do the job?" Caroline asked, and thankfully she sounded a lot tougher than she felt. More of those flashbacks bolted through her like lightning, and for just a moment she wished she hadn't recovered those parts of her memory.

Again, Kingston took his time answering. "There's no law against admiring a man like Eric. In his own twisted way, he was a genius. And he kept you alive. That's a key point here. Why would I want to go against him on that? If he didn't kill you, then why should I?"

Caroline didn't have to think long to come up with a reason. A sick one. "Because he's dead, and you might want the thrill of murdering me to honor a man who intrigued you."

"No." Kingston looked her straight in the eyes when he said that. "I wouldn't do that, and I'm not responsible for the attack against you. I merely went to your place out of curiosity."

Caroline wasn't sure she believed that, but the problem would be finding the proof. Maybe they'd get that with the rental car. Jack had asked his brother, Texas Ranger Eli Slater, to assist with locating it, though she was concerned that Kingston had covered his tracks there. Strange, though, that he hadn't done the same track-covering at the safe house. But then maybe he hadn't known there'd be security cameras at the back of the property.

"Did you send Eric money the night he took Caroline hostage?" Jack asked Kingston. Obviously, he intended to press the man on more than just the attack. Of course, anything Jack found out about Kingston could give them more fodder to make an arrest.

"I did," Kingston admitted, "but I didn't know what he'd done. It hadn't hit the news yet that Caroline had been taken hostage, and Eric didn't mention it."

Eric hadn't. Caroline had been there for that entire

call, and not once had Eric said anything about why he needed funds.

"How'd you get him the money?" Jack pressed.

"I gathered the cash. Ten grand. It was all my parents had in their safe. I put it in a bag and left it for Eric on the side of the road where he told me to leave it."

Jack gave Kingston another dose of his lawman's glare. "And you didn't think it was a little strange that a person you knew or at least suspected was a serial killer would ask you for money?"

"No. I didn't know or suspect he was a serial killer," Kingston insisted. "That didn't come out until later, until he escaped with Caroline."

Maybe. But Caroline still wasn't buying it.

"Did you get Eric a car that night, too?" Jack continued.

Caroline had to speak up on this. "No. Eric stole it. Or rather, he had me hot-wire it. It was in the driveway of a house not far from the abandoned inn where your father was killed." She paused, stared at Kingston. "But just because you didn't do that doesn't make you an innocent man."

"No, it doesn't," Kellan agreed before Kingston could respond. "I need to take him to the interview room and get his statement." He didn't invite Jack and her to go with him. No doubt because it would be a conflict of interest since Kingston was a suspect in their attack. Still, Caroline wanted to hear what else the man had to say.

"There's an observation room," Jack told her, and they headed out of the office and toward the hall.

However, they hadn't made it far before the front door opened again. This time, it wasn't a suspect who came in but Gemma. In the blink of an eye, the past months melted away, and Caroline felt the warmth of seeing a dear friend. Even though she figured the flashbacks would soon return, she savored the moment when Gemma rushed to her and pulled her into her arms.

"You're okay?" Gemma muttered.

Caroline nodded. It wasn't the total truth, but she hadn't been physically harmed. That was what Gemma needed to know for now.

When Gemma pulled back, Caroline saw tears in her friend's eyes. Not just from the relief of her not being injured but because her memory had returned. Gemma didn't have to say that aloud for Caroline to know that Kellan had told her.

Jack cleared his throat to get their attention. "I'm going to the observation room. Why don't you two talk in Jack's office?"

Only then did Caroline remember that they were too close to the windows. Not a good idea for either one of them. Caroline hooked her arm around Gemma's waist and got her moving.

"How much have you remembered?" Gemma asked.

"Enough." Caroline didn't say more until they were in the office. "I got my memory back three days ago."

Gemma nodded. Then she sighed. Obviously, her friend didn't understand why Caroline had kept it a secret. Heck, Gemma might not even understand after she'd explained. Still, Caroline had to try.

"Eric made a call to someone the night he took me hostage. I heard a police radio in the background. I heard someone say Longview Ridge. The caller used cop words, including dispatch codes. I know, I know," Caroline added before Gemma could try to explain all of that away. "It doesn't mean Kellan's guilty. But he could be unknowingly shielding a killer because he can't see past his friendships or blind loyalty to the badge."

Much to Caroline's surprise, Gemma didn't dismiss that. "So you think it could be one of Kellan's deputies? Or Jack?"

"Not Jack." Caroline should have at least hesitated a split second. "He might have that badge blindness—" or DNA blindness, she silently added, when it came to his brothers "—but Jack doesn't want me dead."

Gemma was one of the best profilers that she'd ever met, and she turned those profiling eyes on Caroline. And she waited as if she knew Caroline was holding something back.

She was.

Of course, Gemma knew about her history with Jack. Knew all about Jack and her being lovers.

"I kissed Jack," Caroline blurted out, cursing herself. She added some more curse words for Jack, too.

"And you think that was a…wise idea?" Gemma asked as if carefully choosing her words.

"No! Of course, it wasn't. It was the worst idea in the history of bad ideas. Someone's trying to kill me. I don't know who to trust, and I feel ready to unravel. The whole time I'm feeling all of that, I'm thinking how can a man like Jack still want me when I'm like this?" Caroline paused, steadied herself and admitted the truth. "But he did want me. As much as I wanted him."

Gemma sighed and took hold of her shoulders. "You can trust him. And you can trust Kellan, though I don't expect you to just take my word for it."

"I'm sorry I can't take your word for it." Caroline scrubbed her hand over her face. "I really am ready to unravel."

"Yes, I can see that. Just be careful not to unravel in Jack's arms."

That sent Caroline's gaze back to Gemma. "You can't believe Jack would want to hurt me."

"No, I don't, but I think he could hurt you here." She tapped her fingers on Caroline's heart. "Hurt himself, too. Caring this much doesn't always help. Just take things as slow as you can. Keep your mind open." Gemma blinked back more tears, then smiled. "And for Pete's sake, quit aiming your suspicious eyes at the man I love."

Gemma's smile didn't last, though, and Caroline could see the concern return to her friend's expression. Caroline figured she was about to get a lecture about staying safe and cooperating with Kellan and Jack, but Gemma stopped when Jack appeared in the office doorway.

"We have a visitor," Jack said, and judging from his tone, it wasn't someone he especially wanted to see.

Caroline moved closer to him so she could peer over his shoulder, and she saw the tall, lean man making his way toward them. Correction—not just a man, but a marshal.

Marshal Lee Zeller.

The very person that Jack hadn't trusted enough to give them backup when the sedan was following them.

"There was no need for you to come," Jack quickly told Zeller.

But Zeller shook his head. "I need to talk to you," he said. "Because I think I might know who's trying to kill Caroline."

Chapter Six

Until Zeller had said that last sentence, Jack had been about to demand that the marshal get the heck out of there. But that stopped him.

Because I think I might know who's trying to kill Caroline.

Jack put on hold his demand for Zeller to leave and gave the man his full attention. He definitely wanted to hear what Zeller had to say, but he'd take every one of the marshal's words with a grain of salt. That was because underneath it all, Jack didn't trust him.

"I'm listening," Caroline prompted when Zeller didn't add anything else. She sounded steady enough. Maybe even a little riled. But Jack knew her nerves were right there at the surface.

Zeller dragged in a heavy breath, put his hands on his hips and stared at Caroline. "I heard about the breach of security at the WITSEC house and about the attack. Are you okay?"

"Obviously not," Jack answered for her. "Someone's trying to kill her, and you just said you might know who that is. Spill it."

When Zeller shifted his attention back to Jack, the man's eyes were slightly narrowed. Probably because he didn't like Jack's prickly attitude. Tough. Jack wasn't going to ease up until he had some answers.

"Well, it's not me who wants her harmed, if that's what you're thinking," Zeller spat out. "I'm here to help, and maybe then you'll start to trust me again. I wear the same badge you do, remember?"

Zeller had likely said that to try to reassure Caroline that she was in safe hands, but considering what she'd overheard with Eric's phone call, Jack figured it had the opposite effect.

"Lily Terrell," Zeller tossed out there, and he let the name hang in the air.

Jack knew who she was, of course. He knew plenty of the names of people connected to his father's investigation, and Lily was one of them. For that matter, so was Zeller. Zeller and his father had been bumping heads over the sex-trafficking case they had both been looking into around the same time his dad was murdered. Jack still had some niggling doubts that those confrontations with Zeller or the investigation itself had led to his father's death, but what was missing was evidence of that.

"You think Lily Terrell is trying to kill me?" Caroline asked, her tone proving that she could sound just as grouchy as Jack.

Zeller sure didn't jump to say yes. "I think someone in her organization could be responsible," he answered, and Jack didn't think it was his imagination that the man had chosen his words carefully.

It'd been a while since Jack had read anything about Lily, but he could still recall plenty of the details. Lily Terrell was a millionaire heiress from San Antonio. Her organization, New Beginnings, ran a counseling center and residential facility for the girls and women rescued from the sex-trafficking ring that Zeller and Jack's father were investigating.

Jack glanced at Caroline. It was clear from her earlier question that she knew who Lily was. Of course, with her hacking skills, she had likely filled in whatever memory gaps she had.

Jack turned back to Zeller. "You have proof that Lily or someone she knows could be linked to what happened to Caroline?"

"No proof," Zeller readily admitted, "but there's something off at New Beginnings. I've been keeping tabs on it."

Jack could see why Zeller would do that. The killer of Nicola Gunderson, one of the girls who'd been trafficked, had never been identified. With all the leads gone cold, Zeller might believe someone at the facility knew something about it.

"A woman has gone missing from New Beginnings," Zeller went on. "I know that doesn't mean she's dead. She could have just left." He shook his head, grumbling some profanity under his breath. "But what if Lily started that place because she was the one behind the sex-trafficking ring? She could have done that to make sure she could squash any incriminating info that could have come out about her."

Jack wasn't surprised, but he saw Caroline's eyes widen. He'd actually played around with that idea. Call him a first-class cynic, but it made him suspicious when someone like Lily made a grand gesture out of the goodness of their heart. Within hours of the sex-trafficking ring being busted, Lily had come forward with her offer to help the girls.

"Tell me about the missing woman," Jack said to Zeller.

Zeller didn't hesitate. "Her name is Skylar Greer. She'd been a runaway when she was lured into sex trafficking. Skylar was eighteen when she was rescued. She went to New Beginnings because she had no other place to go, and she went missing last month."

"Lily reported it?" Jack asked.

Now there was a pause. "No, she said Skylar just left. Like I said, I've been keeping tabs on the place, and I have someone inside I've been paying for info. A handyman named Bennie Darnell. Bennie claims he heard no talk of the girl wanting to go, but he did overhear Skylar talking about finding out who'd murdered Nicola Gunderson."

Now, that was interesting how it'd circled back to his father and his investigation. Well, it was interesting if it was true.

"Skylar had apparently gotten to know Nicola in the short time she was in the sex-trafficking ring," Zeller went on, "and Skylar wanted justice for her." He shifted his attention to Caroline. "Lily ticks some boxes on the profiling scale when it comes to something like this."

Zeller had obviously assumed that Caroline's memory was clear when it came to her profiling skill set. It was, but Jack didn't like that Zeller had seemed to know that. It made him wonder if Zeller had kept tabs on Caroline, as well.

"What boxes?" Caroline asked.

"For one thing, Lily has a record. Her folks paid plenty of money to make the trouble go away, but she had a fondness for drugs when she was a teenager. She wasted away a good chunk of her trust fund and then fell in with some girls who bilked money out of rich old men."

Caroline lifted her shoulder. "A criminal past doesn't

necessarily mean you'll grow up to run your own sex-trafficking ring."

"No, but I have it on good word that Lily's stayed in touch with her criminal friends."

Still, that was a stretch, and Caroline's huff let Jack know they felt the same way about the information Zeller was giving them. It could be pertinent. *Could be.* Or it could be a smoke screen.

"Lily hasn't been arrested since she was a teenager," Jack reminded Zeller. "Everything indicates that she's not only turned her life around but that she also wants to help others."

But Jack was just playing devil's advocate on that, since Lily's life turnaround could indeed be a facade. From what he'd read, Lily was getting lots of charitable donations from her rich friends for New Beginnings, although she'd pumped in some money of her own. That meant a place like that could merely be a sweet tax shelter for her and nothing more.

"Bennie thinks there's something shady going on there," Zeller continued, "and for now I agree with him. I'll keep digging into Skylar's disappearance. Will do the same for Lily, too, and I'll let you know what I find out."

Jack nodded. He wasn't going to refuse information, but he would darn sure consider the source. A source who could want to get attention off himself and place it onto someone else like Lily.

Zeller snorted, his gaze sliding back and forth between them. "And you're not buying anything I'm saying. You have a different angle on who could be responsible for the attack today?" That question snapped out like a bullwhip.

Jack debated how much he would say, but he knew it wouldn't be long before Zeller heard about the man

Kellan had in the interview room. Besides, if Jack was the one to tell Zeller, then he could watch his reaction.

"Kingston Morris showed up at Caroline's WITSEC house shortly before the attack," Jack explained.

Zeller shrugged. If he recognized Kingston's name, he didn't show any signs of it. Of course, he could be faking his reaction, but Jack hoped that it meant Zeller hadn't extended his "keeping tabs" to background checks like the ones Jack and Teagan had made. If Zeller was clean, Jack didn't mind the marshal knowing what they were up to, but the jury was still out on whether or not Zeller was dirty.

"Kingston was one of Eric's admirers," Jack went on a moment later.

Now Zeller's eyes widened and he cursed. "How the hell did he get the address?"

"To be determined. Kellan is questioning him now."

Zeller belted out more profanity. "The marshals should be doing that. A breach of security at a WITSEC house is our jurisdiction."

"Yeah, but the attack happened on Kellan's turf," Jack quickly reminded him. "Three counts of attempted murder trumps a trespassing charge. Plus, Kingston didn't try to break into the house. He just showed up on the security feed and then left."

Of course, Kingston had perhaps left so he'd be in position to fire those shots at Caroline, Lucille and him, but that was only speculation. Maybe Kellan was getting something from Kingston that would qualify as proof so they could arrest the man.

Zeller checked his watch. "I have to leave and help with a prisoner transport," he grumbled. "But I want to know if Kingston gives you anything."

Jack just lifted an eyebrow and waited for Zeller to tell him why he had a need for that kind of information.

"Caroline's attack could be linked to Nicola Gunderson's murder." Zeller ground out the words, clearly not pleased that he was having to explain himself. "Nicola's killer was never caught, and I want to clear the case along with finding Skylar."

Jack wasn't ruling out that all of those events could be connected, but some of the pieces didn't have obvious fits. Kingston, for one. There was nothing to prove he was involved in the sex trafficking. For that matter, Caroline wasn't connected to it, either. Unless, of course, all of this went back to Eric. Maybe Eric had been working with the sex trafficker, and now the person or people behind that wanted to tie up loose ends. If someone thought Caroline was a loose end, that would be motive for the attack.

Zeller checked his watch again and moved as if to leave, but then he stopped and looked at Caroline. "Did you really get your memory back?"

Jack couldn't tell if that was a good guess or if Zeller had heard that from Teagan.

"Some of it," Caroline said.

As answers went, it was a darn good one. Evasive but also probing, because Jack was pretty sure Caroline was studying Zeller to gauge his reaction. However, Zeller didn't give them a chance to study much of anything. He turned away, heading for the door.

"Good," Zeller told her from over his shoulder. "I'll keep you both posted if I find out anything more about Lily."

Caroline and Jack stood there and watched as he left. "What do you think Zeller really wanted?" she asked.

Despite his bone-weary fatigue and frustration, Jack nearly smiled. He'd forgotten just how sharp Caroline could be and how she tended to think like a cop.

Or a criminal.

"I'm not sure," Jack said, "but it felt like a fishing expedition with some mud throwing for good measure. Don't worry. I don't trust him."

The slight sound she made seemed to be approval, but when she dodged his gaze, Jack stepped in front of her, forcing eye contact. Not very smart, considering the last time he'd done that they'd ended up kissing, but he wanted to see what was going on in the depths of her cool green eyes.

Plenty was going on.

Like him, she was tired and a little unsteady. Riled, too. She'd been through so much already and didn't deserve another attempt to murder her. Worse, Jack couldn't guarantee her that there wouldn't be another attack. Which was why he had to take precautions: losing her again wasn't an option.

He hadn't meant for his gaze to stay locked with hers. Also hadn't meant for the regret about the attack and then the heat to creep into his expression. Of course, with Caroline there was always heat, so it was hard not to have it playing into things. Impossible for her not to pick up on it, either.

"I can't kiss you again," she insisted. Then she huffed. "Well, I could, but I'm asking you to back off. I need room to breathe. Time to think."

Jack immediately stepped back, giving her that space and nearly smiling again when it seemed as if she was disappointed that another kiss hadn't happened. But she was right. They definitely needed some thinking time on this. Better yet, this called for some concentration coupled with plenty of detective work.

He scrubbed his hand over his face, dragged in a breath and started laying out some things. "Kellan should have enough probable cause on Kingston to get a look at his financials. That's a start. Also, I can arrange to have Kingston's friends interviewed just to see how deep his obsession with Eric went."

Caroline nodded. "I can help. Not by hacking into Kingston's bank records," she quickly added when he scowled at her. "But I can call the various research assistants that Gemma and I worked with and see if they remember anyone other than Kingston coming in with Eric. It's possible Kingston had some help if he put this attack together."

True, and searching for that might help Caroline keep her mind off the flashbacks and the panic attacks.

"What about Zeller?" she asked. "Is there any chance you can get into his financials?"

"Slim to none, with what I have on him. Which is nothing." Jack paused. "But he's not the only one who can talk to Lily and others at New Beginnings. Maybe Lily can shed some light on why Zeller has her in his sights for a whole boatload of felonies, including coming after you."

"I'd like to hear what she has to say. And no, I don't recall Eric mentioning anything about the sex trafficking, but he did have contact with a lot of bad people. Stupid, gullible people that he could charm into doing what he wanted," she added. "Look at what Kingston was willing to do for him. Maybe there are others who overlap with Lily, Eric and Kingston."

It was one of those angles that had to be checked out,

but it would also be a big time suck. Jack was worried that time wasn't on Caroline's and his side right now. The person who'd attacked her would almost certainly come after her again.

He was about to suggest they go to the observation room to watch the rest of Kingston's interview, but Jack spotted his brother Eli coming in through the front door. Jack also saw Caroline stiffen, and he didn't have to guess why. She didn't have faith in his Texas Ranger brother because in her mind, Eli could also be connected to that phone call Eric had made a year ago.

Eli made a beeline toward them, glancing first at Jack before his attention lingered a moment on Caroline. Eli lifted an eyebrow. "You got your memory back, but you don't know who killed our father."

It wasn't a question. Nor was it especially sympathetic. But then, Eli wasn't known for his soft touch. His recent engagement had given him a sunnier outlook, but it didn't appear that he was going to spread any of that sunshine Caroline's way.

"I'm sorry," she said. "I wish I did know who killed him, because I would tell you. I also wish that I could trust you, but I don't."

Eli kept his attention on Caroline, studying her, before he shrugged. "Understood. But if you remember anything about me, you know I don't do things half-assed. If I'd actually helped Eric, I wouldn't have let a hostage overhear a conversation I'd had with him. A conversation that could have come back to bite me. That's just an FYI," he added in a growl before he turned back to Jack.

What Eli had said was true. He wasn't the sort to leave stones unturned or loose threads untied. Jack just wished his brother had tried to give Caroline a little more reassurance. She was already spooked, and none of them wanted her slipping into a panic mode.

But Caroline didn't panic. She simply nodded in response to Eli. So maybe that was progress. Soon, though, she'd need to trust all the Slater lawmen because they were her best shot at staying alive.

"I found the rental car," Eli threw out there, causing both Jack and Caroline to turn to him. "It was on an old ranch trail less than a mile from where you were attacked. No one was in it, but the CSIs will go through it."

Good. Finally, there was news that Jack wanted to hear. He hadn't expected the shooter to still be with the vehicle, but maybe the person had left fingerprints or trace evidence behind.

"There's a second set of fresh tire tracks on the trail," Eli went on. "Either the shooter had stashed another vehicle there so he could use it to getaway or else someone was waiting there for them."

A partner. Yeah. Jack had considered that, too, though he was hoping the person was working alone.

"Can we get the model of the second vehicle from the tire tracks?" Jack asked.

"CSI will try, but it's the longest of long shots. They said it was a common tread."

Okay, so they likely wouldn't get much from that. Still, there was another angle on this. "Who rented that sedan?" Jack asked.

"Brad Smith," Eli immediately answered.

It was a common enough name, and judging from Caroline's headshake, it didn't ring any bells for her. Jack took out his phone to start a search on the man.

"Smith reserved the rental car online, but he had a valid credit card in that name," Eli went on. "It was one of those deals where Smith used a code the rental company gave him and used it to get the car from a specific spot on the lot."

"In other words, Smith didn't have face-to-face contact with a clerk," Jack concluded.

Eli confirmed that with a nod. "The rental company has security surveillance cameras in the lot where the vehicles are kept, and they've agreed to turn over the feed to us. They're emailing copies here and to the Ranger lab."

Jack was glad the rental car company was cooperating, but he was betting how this would play out. Smith—or whoever the hell he really was—likely knew there'd be cameras and had probably worn a disguise. Heck, a ball cap could have obscured his face. Still, they'd be able to get height and build, which in turn might give them something they could use against Kingston.

Well, it would if Smith matched Kingston's description.

"There's more," Eli said, and this time his tone had a darker edge to it. He made eye contact with Jack. "I had the Ranger lab do a deep run on all the Brad Smiths in the area, and something *interesting* came up."

"I'm listening," Jack grumbled when Eli hesitated.

And even with that prompt, Eli hesitated some more. A muscle jerked hard in his jaw. "Brad Smith was an alias that came up in an investigation a few years ago. Another sex-trafficking ring that wasn't connected to Dad's case. But according to the file notes, Smith was actually an undercover marshal."

Hell. Jack knew how this was about to play out, and he finished what Eli had been about to say. "Brad Smith is Lee Zeller."

Chapter Seven

Finally. That was Caroline's first reaction to what Jack had just said about Lee Zeller being Brad Smith.

That connection between Zeller and the rental car used in the attack brought together some of the pieces of this puzzle. She hadn't been wrong about overhearing Eric talk with someone in law enforcement. Or at least someone pretending to be in that line of work. But there would have been no pretense needed if Eric's conversation had indeed been with Zeller.

Jack turned to her, the questions all over his face, but Caroline didn't have the answers he wanted.

"No, I don't remember Eric ever mentioning Zeller's name," she volunteered. "But he didn't say any specific name during that phone call."

Plus, she'd been injured and drugged. She didn't want to bring that up now, though, because Jack and his brothers already had enough doubts as to what she'd overheard. She didn't want to add to those doubts and cause them to soften their attitudes about Zeller or any of their other fellow lawmen.

Jack made a sound to indicate he was thinking about this. "If Zeller did help Eric, if they were somehow connected to the sex-trafficking ring, then maybe Zeller thought you'd overheard something to incriminate him."

Maybe, and if so, that could be Zeller's motive to eliminate her. Still, there was something that didn't fit. "Why wouldn't Zeller have eliminated me sooner?" Caroline asked. "Or at least tried to do that? He's a marshal and could have easily gotten the location of the WITSEC house."

"Not easily," Jack insisted. "I'd put the location under several more layers of security, and if someone unauthorized had been poking around the files to find the address, the system should have alerted me."

"Still…" She shook her head. "Zeller probably could have managed it. So why wait to kill me?"

"As long as you didn't have your memory, you weren't a threat." Jack answered that so fast that it let her know he'd already reached that possible conclusion.

"But the timing doesn't fit," Caroline argued. "We were attacked only minutes after you learned I'd regained my memory. How would Zeller have…" She stopped when something occurred to her. "Zeller could have known about the computer searches I've done over the past few days. It wouldn't have been easy for him to do that, but if he'd been *keeping tabs* on me, he could have figured it out."

Both Jack and Eli nodded, causing the realization to settle hard in her stomach. Her searches could have been like loading a gun. Then, Zeller had pulled the trigger.

Well, maybe.

A possible motive was still a long way from proof that he'd committed a crime.

"You're sure when your father was investigating the

sex trafficking that nothing incriminating came up about Zeller?" she asked.

Both Eli and Jack gave her flat looks. Of course, they were sure. They'd likely memorized everything about the case, and it had to eat away at both of them. Here it was their job to bring criminals to justice, and they hadn't been able to do that for their own father.

"It was more of a gut feeling," Jack said. "When Nicola's body turned up and my father had to investigate it, Zeller didn't want him involved. Part of me gets that. The sex ring was his case, but Zeller didn't even want to work with my dad. In fact, he tried everything to exclude him."

Caroline had worked with enough law enforcement officers, so she knew it wasn't unusual for one of them to feel that way and go all territorial. But in this case, it could be a red flag if Zeller hadn't wanted Sheriff Buck Slater digging into anything that would incriminate Zeller himself. However, it was just as possible that Jack and his brothers were being hypercritical. A sort of grabbing at straws in the hope that they could bring their father's killer to justice.

"And then there's Zeller's possible connection to the breach of security at your WITSEC house," Jack went on. "That gave me another bad feeling. Someone texted Kingston that address. Maybe Kingston himself, if he managed to hack into Justice Department files, but it could be someone else."

"Someone like Zeller," Caroline finished for him.

Jack nodded. "That's why I'm having Teagan go through the files to see who accessed that address."

"Maybe you don't trust Jack's partner, either?" Eli asked her after a long pause.

"Eric called a man that night," she quickly pointed

out. But then Caroline had to pause, too. "Of course, that doesn't prove Teagan is clean, but I've got enough trouble without putting her under a microscope."

"Good point," Eli grumbled, and then he tipped his head to the computer on Kellan's desk. "You got access to that?" he asked Jack, checking the time. "If so, the surveillance footage from the car rental company should be ready."

"Yeah, I've got access," Jack said as if still in deep thought. *Troubled* thought, Caroline mentally corrected. Even though Jack didn't fully trust Zeller, it still had to be hard for him to think of a fellow marshal trying to murder them.

Caroline went to the computer when Jack did and she stood behind him, watching him work his way through the password and into Kellan's official emails. The file from the car rental company was there. When he clicked on it, Eli came to his side and all three of them focused on the monitor.

"It was an 8:00 a.m. pickup," Eli said, glancing at the notes on his phone.

Good. That would save them from watching hours of the feed. The timing also fit with something else—Zeller would have had plenty of time to get the car and drive out to Longview Ridge. For that matter, though, Kingston would have, too. Or any other suspect.

She watched as Jack fast-forwarded the images, but then he slowed to a normal speed when the figure came into view. A tall man who walked toward the black four-door sedan. And Caroline groaned at the same moment that Jack and Eli cursed.

The man was wearing a baseball cap, and he had on a bulky dark blue windbreaker with the collar turned up high on his neck. He kept his head down, the camera only getting a good shot of the hat and not the man's face. Worse, the build didn't help, either, because it appeared he'd stuffed things in his pants pockets, which could make him look heavier than he actually was.

Jack rewound the feed and went through it frame by frame until he stopped on the image that gave them a partial view of the guy's chin. Between the high collar and the shadow created by the ball cap, it wasn't very clear.

"That could be either Zeller or Kingston since they're about the same height," Jack grumbled under his breath.

Yes. Or someone either of them could have hired to get the car. "What about the handyman Zeller mentioned?" she asked. "Bennie Darnell. Can you pull up an ID on him?"

Jack didn't point out that it was a long shot. Even though it was. He just tapped into the DMV files and accessed the man's photo and the details listed on his driver's license.

This time, all three of them cursed.

Because Bennie, too, had a similar height and weight to Zeller and Kingston. Not only were they not able to rule anyone out, but now they'd added another potential person of interest.

"Bennie has a record," Jack explained as he went through another database. "He was arrested for drug possession and driving under the influence ten years ago. He's been clean ever since."

Obviously, his record hadn't stopped him from getting a job, and Caroline doubted he'd been hired without some kind of background check. Still, it wouldn't hurt to do a deeper run on him. She was about to suggest that when Jack's phone rang, and she saw Zeller's name on the screen.

Eli must have seen it, too, because he muttered something about getting a cup of coffee, and he headed out of the office. Jack answered the call and put it on speaker.

"You wanted to talk to me?" Zeller snapped the moment he was on the line. He sounded annoyed, and Caroline bet his irritation would only increase after this chat.

Jack didn't waste any time responding. "Who knew about your alias, Brad Smith?"

Now there was some hesitation. "Why?" Zeller demanded.

"Because someone using that name rented the car used in the attack against Caroline and me."

She'd been right about the annoyance, but there was also some anger when Zeller belted out a string of profanities. "Someone's trying to set me up."

"Who knew that was your alias?" Jack pressed, speaking right over Zeller's cursing.

"Hell, anybody with access to our computers," Zeller spat out. "Anybody who came in contact with me when I was on an op and using that name."

"Narrow it down," Jack insisted. "Go through your case files and find someone who intersects with Caroline and me."

"Believe me, I will. Because I didn't have anything to do with that car or the attack. What about security cameras at the rental place?" Zeller quickly tacked on.

"I'm looking at it right now, and I can't rule you out."

"No, but you can sure as hell rule me out because I'm not a dirty marshal. Somebody's setting me up," Zeller repeated. "I want a copy of that surveillance feed. While you're getting that to me, I'll go through the files and get back to you." And with that, Zeller ended the call.

Caroline hadn't expected Zeller to just fess up to renting the car and then hiring someone to shoot at them. No. Even if he was as guilty as sin, Zeller wouldn't cop to anything because he'd know there wasn't any concrete evidence against him.

Not yet, anyway.

"I know the Ranger crime lab will try to enhance the security footage," she said, "but I'd like to have a go at it, too. I might be able to match the jawline to Bennie, Kingston or Zeller."

Jack didn't refuse her help, but he did look her straight in the eyes. A look that likely told him that she was exhausted. She also had a dull, throbbing headache. There'd been no time for her to calm down after the shooting. No chance for her to regain her footing. And the kiss hadn't helped with that. Maybe that was why Jack didn't come to her. Instead, he crammed his hands in the pockets of his jeans.

"As soon as Kellan finishes up with Kingston, we should be able to leave for another safe house," he said.

Her first response was relief. She could get some quiet time and try to level out her nerves. But another concern popped up immediately. For her to get to a safe house, she'd have to leave the sheriff's office and go outside, where their attacker could be lying in wait for them. It was a risk. Then again, she couldn't stay here amid all the badges that she wasn't sure she could trust.

So this was the rock and the hard place.

"Where's the safe house?" she asked.

Jack didn't get a chance to answer her, though, because Eli stepped back into the doorway. "You've got a visitor," Eli said, shifting his gaze to both Jack and her.

Instant alarm went through Caroline. Jack seemed to stiffen with attention. He immediately stepped in front of her.

"Who is it?" Jack pressed.

"Lily Terrell," Eli answered. "She says you'll want to see her because she believes she's a suspect in today's attack."

WELL, JACK HADN'T seen this coming. In fact, he'd thought he was going to have to contact Lily to let her know that he had some questions for her. He'd expected an heiress like that to give him some flak. Instead, here she was, walking straight toward Kellan's office.

Jack closed the laptop and checked to make sure there was nothing that a person of interest shouldn't be seeing. There wasn't. Well, nothing other than Caroline. Jack didn't care for the fact that she was going to have to face yet someone else who may have had a part in the attack.

"She's not armed," Eli told Jack.

Jack appreciated that his brother had frisked the woman, but after getting a good look at her, he figured there weren't many places Lily could have hidden a weapon. She was a tall woman, close to six feet, and she was rail thin. The cobalt blue dress she was wearing clung to every inch of her. No chance of her hiding much in the tiny hand-sized purse she was holding.

"Marshal Slater," she greeted, her voice a sultry drawl. It went well with her cool violet eyes and the auburn hair that tumbled over her shoulders.

She flashed him a smile, extending it to Eli and then to Caroline. "Miss Moser," Lily added.

"How do you know me?" Caroline asked, taking the question right out of Jack's mouth.

"I'm familiar with your work on Crime-Track that you did at the university with Gemma Hanson." Lily's answer was quick and unruffled. Actually, *unruffled* was a good description for the woman herself. If she was bothered by being considered a suspect, she didn't show it.

Caroline had indeed worked on that project, and Jack figured that was common knowledge. The media had hashed and rehashed it after one of the research assistants on the project, Eric Lang, had been uncovered as a serial killer.

"It's work you should continue," Lily added to Caroline a moment later. "It could be very beneficial to law enforcement agencies."

Caroline lifted an eyebrow. "I doubt anyone wants to trust a profiler who worked side by side with a serial killer and didn't know it."

Lily made a sound that could have meant anything and turned back to Jack. "The shooting was on the news," she said. "Details were sketchy, but when I heard your name and Caroline's, I thought it best if I came in."

"And why is that?" Jack had no intention of showing his hand until he found out more about this visit.

"Bennie Darnell is a handyman at New Beginnings, and he told me about Marshal Lee Zeller's *interest* in me. When I heard about the attack on the news, I assumed Zeller would be trying to convince you that I was somehow involved. So I came here to clear my name."

Jack exchanged glances with Caroline and saw that she was just as surprised as he was. Zeller had made it seem as if Bennie was his mole, but obviously the handyman still had some loyalty to his employer. In turn, that called into question any info that Bennie had given Zeller, because maybe Bennie was just the sort who liked to tell people whatever it was they wanted to hear.

"Why exactly does Marshal Zeller have an interest in you?" Jack asked. He tried to keep his tone level, more of a request than a demand, since he was still trying to figure out if Lily was playing some kind of game or if she truly was concerned about making sure her name was clean.

"Because of Skylar Greer." She didn't hesitate, and Lily looked him straight in the eyes when she spoke. Then she dragged in a long breath. "Even though he's never come right out and said it, Marshal Zeller seems to believe I had some part in Skylar leaving New Beginnings. I didn't."

Interesting that Lily had used the word "leaving" when Zeller had described it as a disappearance.

"Why did the woman *leave*?" Jack pressed.

Now she dodged his gaze, but only for a few seconds. "I'm not sure. She didn't speak to me about it, but I assume Skylar felt as if there was some other place she wanted to be. Hopefully, a safe place," she softly added.

Yeah, Jack hoped the same thing, and also wished he could know for sure that the woman was actually alive. "You think Skylar could have gotten lured back into sex trafficking?"

Lily didn't jump to deny that, and she glanced at Caroline. "You both know how hard it is to come back from a traumatic situation. Skylar was a troubled young woman and didn't trust easily. I think it would be very easy for her to slip back into her old ways."

Lily's words were right. So was the concerned expression on her face. But something in her voice and body language didn't ring true for Jack. Or maybe he was just projecting because of the sliver of doubt that Zeller had put in his head.

"Skylar didn't trust you?" Caroline came out and asked.

"Sadly, no," Lily answered.

Again, right tone, but it did nothing to ease that bad feeling. He considered a moment how to deal with this and went with the direct approach.

"I want copies of Skylar's records," Jack insisted.

Lily's expression never changed, and she didn't even pause. "I'm afraid I'll have to insist you get a warrant for that. The privacy of the residents is a top priority for me."

It was the exact answer he'd expected from the woman. Maybe stonewalling. Maybe just trying to be ethical. "I'll get the warrant, and then you'll need to come back in here to give me an official statement."

Lily nodded, but some wariness crept into her eyes. "It sounds as if I'll need my lawyer for that."

"That's probably a good idea." Jack didn't especially want to deal with her lawyer, but he liked that his comment had caused her some tension. He wanted Lily out of her comfort zone, since nervous suspects were more likely to make mistakes.

"We'll get into this more after I have the warrant," Jack continued, and he decided to go with a long shot. "Tell me about your relationship with Eric."

Lily's eyes widened, and she fired nervous glances at Caroline, Eli and him. "There was no relationship." Her voice was clipped now. "I knew Eric only because we were in the same social circles."

"You knew him," Jack emphasized.

Lily's mouth tightened for a moment. "Eric and I rarely spoke and only at parties and such."

But the bottom line was that she had indeed known him, and Jack was fairly certain that hadn't come up in the investigation. Of course, there would have been no reason for it to have. Lily hadn't been a suspect, and there'd been no record of Eric ever contacting her. The only reason Jack had asked her about it was because he was toying with the idea that Eric and Zeller might have had some part in the sex trafficking. They could have teamed up to lure Buck to that inn so Zeller could kill him.

That was a long shot.

However, if Eric and Zeller were connected, then maybe Lily was, too. That could explain why Zeller was so hell-bent on pinning something illegal on her. Maybe he wanted her to be put away so she couldn't expose his own crimes.

"What about Kingston Morris?" Jack went on. "You know him, too?"

Lily's slow nod was as uncertain as the rest of her. "Yes. Again, the same circles, and I knew him slightly more than Eric. How is he involved in this?" she asked.

Jack knew it wouldn't be long before word got out, so he decided to tell Lily so he could see her reaction. "Kingston showed up at Caroline's house. Trespassing," he added. "Her address was protected and wasn't easily accessible. Still, Kingston managed to get it, and shortly afterward, Caroline was attacked."

Lily pressed her hand to her chest as if to steady her heart. "You suspect Kingston of trying to kill her?"

"He's being interviewed now," Jack answered, dodging Lily's direct question, and yeah, Kingston was a suspect all right.

"I see." Some of the color drained from Lily's face. She paused, moistened her lips. "Is it because of Grace Wainwright? Is that how Kingston got Caroline's address?"

Jack glanced at Caroline to see if she recognized the name, but she only shook her head.

"Who's Grace Wainwright?" Jack asked.

Lily opened her mouth, then closed it just as fast. Maybe rethinking what she'd been about to say. "Grace was at New Beginnings. She had gotten caught up in sex trafficking," Lily added. "She also had some family problems that prevented her from going home, and she asked if she could stay there while she straightened out her life. However, before that, she was romantically involved with Kingston."

For someone who was hesitant to share much on Skylar, Lily clearly didn't feel the need to hold back with Grace.

Jack stared at Lily. "And why would Grace have known Caroline's address?"

"Because Grace has excellent computer skills and wasn't always ethical about whose information she accessed. She could have hacked into the files, found Caroline's address and given it to Kingston. Or sold it to him."

Jack didn't have trouble latching on to what Lily hadn't said. "Grace accessed information about you?"

Lily's mouth tightened. "She did. Actually, she managed to steal some funds from my bank account. When I caught her, I told her she had to leave New Beginnings. She did, but I've since heard rumors that she's still using her talents for illegal activities."

He was definitely going to have to question Grace

about that. But if she had indeed managed to get into Justice Department files, then she had to be better than just "excellent" when it came to hacking.

Jack made a mental note to contact Grace ASAP, and then he moved on to the next question he had for Lily. "Why is Zeller so hell-bent about coming after you?"

Lily hesitated, and he saw the pulse kick up on her throat. "I suspect it's because he feels guilty." She stopped, huffed. "Look, I'm guessing you're not going to want to hear anything negative about one of your fellow marshals…"

"Trust me, I want to hear it," Jack insisted.

Lily nodded and made a suit-yourself sound. "From what I've gathered from conversations with some of the girls who came to New Beginnings, I believe Zeller knew Nicola Gunderson and that he talked her into helping him bring down the sex-trafficking ring."

Everything inside Jack went still. He definitely hadn't heard Zeller mention knowing the dead girl, and he was pretty sure that should have come out by now. Especially since it was his father who was investigating her murder.

"I'm not surprised Zeller didn't mention any of this to you," Lily went on. "In fact, I suspect he doesn't want anyone to know that he's the reason that Nicola was murdered."

Chapter Eight

Caroline watched as Jack located Grace's number and tried to call the woman. No answer. But maybe she'd call back soon. And perhaps Grace wouldn't try to avoid them simply because she didn't want to be questioned about her possible involvement in the attack.

Of course, if Grace was indeed avoiding them, it likely wasn't because Lily had warned her. Not enough time for that. It had only been a couple of minutes since she'd left the sheriff's office. Plus, why would Lily have volunteered the woman's name if she was just going to go and warn her?

Jack left Grace a message for her to call him and then tried Zeller again. Even though he hadn't put his phone on speaker, Caroline was close enough that she heard the call to Zeller go straight to voice mail.

Unlike Grace, Zeller was someone who could absolutely be avoiding them.

If what Lily had said was true about Zeller coaxing Nicola into helping him, then the marshal should have already spilled that. Not just to Jack's father but to Jack and his siblings. Zeller definitely needed to answer some questions, and with each new bit of information, Caroline was trusting him less and less.

Jack shook his head in frustration over not getting through to Zeller before he fired off a text to someone, and then he looked at her. Whatever he saw on her face caused his frustration to worsen. "You're exhausted," he concluded. "I'm sorry. I should have already gotten you out of here."

"No, you shouldn't have," she argued. "You needed to be here so you can find the person who tried to kill us."

And while things were still unsettled between them, Caroline knew one thing for certain. She didn't want Jack sending her off with anyone else. Especially anyone else with a badge.

Even though touching him was playing with fire, Caroline risked sliding her hand down his arm. A gesture meant to comfort him, along with getting some comfort for herself. Jack was the only person who could soothe her like this.

Now his eyes flashed with a different emotion. Heat layered over the irritation of the stalled investigation, and soon even the worry seemed to fade away. Apparently, she also had a soothing effect on him, and it was effective if she didn't count the whole arousal thing.

Caroline figured that Jack counted it.

Neither of them had time to act on it, though, because of the approaching footsteps. That sound caused them to move apart, and Jack shook his head as if to clear it before he stepped in front of her. Preparing for a threat. But he relaxed some when Kellan appeared in the doorway. Kingston was right behind him.

"Am I done here now?" Kingston asked. He didn't sound smug or cooperative now, which meant Kellan had grilled him hard. Good. Maybe Kellan had also gotten some info they could use.

"No, you're not done," Jack snapped. He shifted his attention to Kellan. "Lily Terrell came in and chatted with us. She'll be back later with her lawyer for an official interview, but for now she had some interesting theories. One that's connected to Kingston."

Kingston groaned. "Did Lily accuse me of something, too?"

"Do you know Grace Wainwright?" Jack went on, ignoring Kingston's question.

Kingston blinked, clearly surprised by the topic. "Of course, I know her. We were once lovers."

Jack didn't pause even a second. "Did she get you Caroline's address?"

"No." Kingston looked ready to gear up with a more detailed, angrier denial, but then he stopped. "Maybe. But if she did, she didn't tell me she was the one who texted it to me."

No, because that would have incriminated her in a felony. Of course, it was possible Grace had given him the address and that he was covering for her. Caroline figured Jack would be digging deep into the woman's background to try to determine that.

Kellan waited until Jack gave him the go-ahead nod before he turned to Kingston. "You can go, *for now*, but don't leave the state. I'll be bringing you back in when I have more info."

That clearly didn't please Kingston, but he didn't waste any time arguing with them. He turned and hurried out.

"Lily thinks Zeller knew Nicola," Jack told his brother when Kingston was out of earshot. "He might have even talked Nicola into helping him break up the sex-trafficking ring."

The muscles tightened in Kellan's face. "I'll make

some calls and see what I can find out." He glanced away and cursed. "We're not getting answers, just a whole bunch of questions."

"Yeah," Jack agreed, the fatigue now back in his voice. "I've already requested authorization to look into Zeller's computer. That might get us something."

It would, unless Zeller had already wiped the hard drive. Or disposed of it. For someone with the right skills, there were plenty of ways to erase data.

"I also need a warrant to get into the records at New Beginnings," Jack added. "I want to have a look at the file of a woman that Zeller says went missing. But I can wait a little while on that. For now, I need to go ahead and get Caroline out of here. You think you can spare a deputy until morning, or should I see if Teagan can help?"

Kellan glanced at Caroline and then out into the bull-pen. "Since Caroline seems to be more comfortable with female officers, why don't you take Raylene. Caroline knows her."

Yes, she did. Deputy Raylene McNeal. Caroline didn't like putting trust in a person simply because of their gender, but in this case it helped her relax a little. Well, relax about who'd be doing bodyguard duty for her, but her nerves went zinging again when she realized they'd be going back outside.

Kellan stepped into the squad room, motioning for Raylene, and a moment later, the sturdy-looking brunette deputy joined him in the doorway, where Kellan, Jack and she had a whispered conversation. Something that Jack said had Kellan frowning and groaning, but Jack persisted and finished whatever point he was making.

When they'd finished talking, Raylene glanced at Caroline in a gesture that was probably meant to reassure her. Surprisingly, it did. Caroline hated that she needed to be babysat like this, but she wasn't stupid. She'd come close to dying too many times to take unnecessary risks by turning down protection.

"Caroline, Raylene and I will go in a cruiser," Jack explained. "Gunnar will follow as backup but will come back here once he's sure it's safe. Raylene will stay with us."

Raylene nodded. "Just let me get the overnight bag I keep in my locker."

While Kellan spoke to Gunnar, Raylene hurried toward the break room. The deputy didn't take long and was back in under a minute. That was still plenty enough time for Caroline's stomach to start churning with the reminder that the person who'd tried to kill them could be waiting outside.

"Move fast," Jack instructed, and he hooked his arm around Caroline's waist to get her moving.

There were two cruisers parked out front. Raylene and Gunnar went out first, each of them hurrying to get behind the wheel of their respective vehicle. Jack had one last look around before he moved with Caroline, and the moment they were inside the cruiser, Raylene took off with Gunnar following right behind her.

Jack continued to keep watch. So did Caroline. She studied each person on Main Street as if they were a would-be gunman, but no one attempted to fire at them. That still didn't make her relax. She kept her eyes on their surroundings, wishing that she had a gun so she could defend herself if it came down to it.

Raylene drove out of town and onto the rural road that snaked through the countryside. There were no pedestrians here to watch, only miles of woods and pastures, and it didn't take Caroline long to realize where they were going. She whirled toward Jack so fast that her neck popped.

"You're taking me to your family's ranch," she blurted out, and was certain her tone and expression let him know she didn't like that.

"Actually, I'm taking you to my place, but as I'm sure you remember, it's on the ranch."

Oh, yes. She remembered all right. It was the wood-and-stone house where she'd spent many nights with Jack. As his lover. And while it might be more comfortable than standing around at the sheriff's office, it wasn't exactly "safe." Not with all the memories the place held. Specifically memories of Jack and her in bed.

"You can't think going there is a good idea," Caroline said.

He shrugged and continued to keep watch. "I have a security system, and the ranch hands will help guard the place."

Again, that didn't make it safe.

"Are all the repairs done?" Raylene asked him, her gaze briefly meeting Jack's in the rearview mirror.

"They are. The damage wasn't that bad."

Caroline didn't need clarification on the repairs or damage because she'd heard about the *incident* that'd happened at his place. Someone who'd been after Jack's brother, Owen, had rammed his car into the porch. She'd heard bits and pieces about it from Lucille and the media reports she'd accessed, but Caroline figured she hadn't gotten the full story. Wasn't sure she wanted it, either. She had enough bad stuff in her head without adding more.

"Considering that an attack happened so recently at

your place, maybe we should take that as some kind of sign not to go there," Caroline grumbled.

"The attack caused me to beef up security," Jack said as if that answered all of her concerns. It didn't. But then Caroline didn't know anywhere they could go where she wouldn't feel the danger looming over her.

Still…

She had to put her argument on hold for a moment when Raylene pulled to a stop in front of Jack's. Despite those repairs and the security upgrade that he'd mentioned, the place looked exactly the same. It definitely wasn't sprawling like the main house just up the road, where Kellan lived and helped run the family ranch. Jack's place only had three bedrooms and two baths, and was as comfortable-looking and laid-back as the owner.

"Wait here a sec," Jack told her.

He got out and ran to the front door. Caroline watched as he unlocked it and then used his phone to disengage the security system. He also went in, likely to search the place, before he came back out. As they'd done at the sheriff's office, they moved fast, and only after Jack had Raylene and her inside did he motion for Gunnar to leave.

While Jack reset the security alarms, Caroline walked into the living room and glanced around. No changes here, either, and that included the two framed photos of Jack and her on the mantel. In one, he had his arm crooked playfully around her, his mouth pressed to her cheek, while she had a huge grin on her face. The other photo was a shot of Kellan and Gemma standing next to Jack and her, all of them smiling. Obviously, they were taken in much happier times.

"You can take the guest room," Jack told Raylene, and he motioned toward the first room off the hall.

With her overnight bag in hand, Raylene headed in that direction, leaving Caroline with Jack.

"I'll take the couch. You can use my room," he added to Caroline, holding her hand to take her there.

She knew the way, every step of it, and every scent was familiar because it was Jack's. By the time she walked into the bedroom suite, her body was humming with that familiarity. With those memories of what had gone on here. None of the bad stuff. Not here. This was all warmth and pleasure.

He'd kept the same quilt, and Caroline knew the feel of it. The soft cotton that had slid against her skin every time she'd been naked in that bed.

"Afraid to be alone with me?" he asked, coming up behind her.

She shook her head. "Fear isn't the right word for it—"

"You told me you loved me," he interrupted. "That morning before Eric took you, you told me that."

No need for him to clarify which morning, but she didn't like his timing in bringing it up now. "I remember." She cleared her throat so it would have some sound, and had to do it again. Great. Her throat was clogged now, and her breathing wasn't faring much better.

Jack moved in front of her, studying her face. He wasn't frowning, but it was close. "You don't feel the same way about me now."

She wanted to groan. Apparently, he wasn't content with just having her surrounded by old memories of them as a couple. He wanted her to relive it with words, too. And it was working. She felt the slow hum of heat circle around her.

"I'm not sure what I feel," Caroline settled for saying, but it required another throat clearing.

Her answer didn't smooth his near frown. But it was partly true. She didn't know about still being in love. She'd had no time to sort out her feelings, but when it came to Jack, she was certain about plenty of other things. She wanted him more than her next heartbeat. More than she wanted to feel strong and whole again.

And that want was quickly turning into a need.

The silence vibrated between them as he stared at her. It ended when Jack cursed. "I considered offering you no-strings-attached sex. Just to burn off this heat so we could possibly think about something else. *Anything* else. But I can't do that."

Silence fell again, this time because he'd stunned her. "You can't have sex?" And she hated the disappointment in her voice.

A flicker of annoyance, and heat, went through his eyes. "I can't give you the no-strings. The sex is going to happen, but not until you know that it won't be just to satisfy some raw animal urges. *Strings*," he repeated, emphasizing it. "I'll want that I-love-you from you again. Maybe not tonight, but I'll want it soon."

Caroline was about to remind him that he'd never given her those words, but Jack snapped her to him and kissed her. It was hard and rough, not just his mouth but the grip he had on her arms. The roughness was something that Caroline quickly realized made it even better. He wasn't going to treat her like glass. The fragile kind of glass that broke with a careless touch.

He was going to break her in a whole different way. And there'd be nothing careless about it.

Cupping the back of her neck, Jack deepened the kiss. The physical part of it, anyway, since the emotional part was already as deep as it could get. Or so Caroline thought. He proved her wrong when he stopped and eased back enough to stare into her eyes.

There it was. The face that could have been created for an ancient god. The pretty ones who could be both ruthless and very, very desirable. His eyes, dark. That rumpled black hair. Oh, and that scent. Leather and male. It seeped into her, mingling with the heat that his kiss had already flamed.

Jack waited a heartbeat, maybe giving her a chance to change her mind, all the while knowing that she wouldn't do that. Caroline knew it, too.

The next kiss was just a brush of his mouth over hers. Slow and sensual with their breaths mingling. And he looked at her again. Gauging her reaction. She was breathing too fast, and her pulse was at a full gallop. Every inch of her was quivering, waiting, and she didn't want the wait to continue for even a second longer.

She didn't have to.

Jack took her mouth again, and there it was. The raw animal urge that went to full flame and beyond when his hand slid underneath her dress and straight into her panties. Caroline made a gasp of pleasure when he plunged his fingers into her. So much pleasure that his touch would have brought her to a fast climax if he hadn't suddenly stopped.

"No. It won't be that easy," he said, his voice as intense as the look he gave her. Jack reached behind her, shut the door and locked it. "It'll never be that easy between us."

It sounded a little like a threat, and he hooked his arm around her, lifting her as if she weighed nothing. Those strong, corded arms closed around her. He kissed her, hard and deep again, while he took her to his bed.

He practically dumped her on the too-soft mattress that swelled up around her.

When he didn't immediately join her, she reached for him, only to realize that his plan was to stay standing so he could strip off her dress.

Which he did.

Jack sent it flying. Then he got on the bed, his knee landing between her legs. As he loomed over her, she could feel his jeans rub against the inside of her thighs. Could hear the rough rhythm of his breath.

He kissed her breasts through her bra. Again, not gently. Both his hands and his mouth were rough as he yanked off her panties and then her bra. He'd said he hadn't wanted easy, whatever that meant, but he apparently wanted fast.

Good.

Because she wanted that, too. Fast meant she didn't have to think about this. For that to happen, she needed him as naked as he'd just gotten her. Caroline went after the buttons on his shirt, but when he took her nipple into his mouth, the heat roared through her. Fingers to toes and every single place in between. She gave up on the shirt and went after his zipper instead.

Jack didn't stop her when she freed him from his jeans and boxers, but he did stop the maddening kisses. Again, their gazes met. And held. Just as he plunged into her.

Caroline made another of those gasps. Pleasure, yes. Definitely that. Mixed with the brief shock of his hard thrust. Then, even more pleasure. So much more.

This was the animal urge part. His eyes held a need of a different kind, though. The pretty, ruthless god planned to claim what he believed to be already his. To possess her. It frightened her a little to think that he could do just that. Frightened her even more that she wanted him to do it.

It didn't take much. A few more of those deep, plundering strokes inside her, and Caroline couldn't have held back the climax even if she'd wanted to. She didn't. But she refused to go falling over that edge alone.

Knowing exactly how to undo him, she lifted her hips, clamping her knees around him and dragging him harder into her. She let the muscles in her body force him into joining her. Her vision blurred, but still she watched him. And he watched her...while they fell together.

Caroline could feel those strings tightening around her, and while Jack gathered her into his arms and kissed her, she prayed for so many things. That this wouldn't be the mistake she was certain it was. Because those strings weren't just about love and broken hearts. They were about priority and focus.

And those strings could get them both killed.

Chapter Nine

Caroline still slept like a rock. Jack now had proof that it was something about her that hadn't changed. Face-down, arms outstretched and butt naked on his bed, she'd slept all night and then through the beep of his morning alarm. Ditto for staying sacked out during his shower and the phone calls he'd gotten and the ones that he'd made.

While Jack would have liked to let her sleep even longer, he had things to do that couldn't wait. So he poured a huge mug of black coffee that he'd brewed strong enough to the point of being bitter. Just the way Caroline liked it. He added a single ice cube to it to cool it down enough for her to drink it fast—which she would do.

When he went back into the bedroom, he had to push aside the punch of attraction he got from seeing her in his bed. The attraction got another punch when he recalled in perfect detail all the things they'd done there.

Oh, man.

He really needed to figure out a way to deal with what he felt for her so he could do everything possible to keep her out of danger. That had to be his mission now because he couldn't lose her again.

She stirred the moment Jack held the mug near her nose, and then he moved it so her flailing hands wouldn't knock into it and spill it. Yawning and groaning at the same time, she lumbered to a sitting position and groped to take the coffee. Jack kept hold of it, too, until he was certain of her grip.

No sips for her. As expected, she downed several long gulps as if it were the cure for all ills, before she looked up as if just realizing he was there. She smiled until her attention landed on his clothes.

"You're dressed," she said, frowning now.

"Been up for a while." Jack eased down on the bed next to her, but not too close. If he touched her, he'd be toast. "You need to slap me. I forgot to use a condom last night."

"Uh." Caroline repeated that sound, pushed her hair from her face. "I'm on the pill. I started it last month to regulate my periods." She added that last part in a barely audible mumble, and continued, "I haven't been with anyone since, well, just since."

Judging from the way her face flushed, that seemed to embarrass her. Ironic, since she was stark naked.

Something his body had noticed, of course.

Actually, what his body wanted to do was get back in that bed with her and go for another round or two. Not going to happen, though. But the comment that embarrassed her pleased him more than it should have. Which was stupid. Because the reason she hadn't been with anyone else was because she'd been hurt and not because of some unremembered commitment to him.

"Zeller still hasn't returned my calls, but Kellan texted me," Jack explained, forcing his mind back where it belonged, and it darn sure shouldn't be on her breasts. "The warrant came through on the missing girl from New Beginnings, and we have the file. Lily Terrell's coming into the sheriff's office with her lawyer in—" he checked his watch "—about an hour."

"An hour," she repeated, and she sounded a little panicked now.

"I'd like to be there to hear what Lily has to say about those files," Jack went on, "and I don't want you here alone. Raylene's already gone home, but Gunnar's her relief, and he's waiting out front in a cruiser to take us in."

That got Caroline scrambling off the bed and into his bathroom. Gulping down coffee and mumbling, she turned on the shower. What she didn't do was shut the door, so he got even more of the drive-Jack-crazy peep show of her naked body behind the clear glass of the shower stall.

"I had your other things brought over from the WIT-SEC house," he called out to her. "They're in a suitcase next to the vanity."

While she showered, Jack gathered up what little willpower he had left and went back into the kitchen to finish his own coffee. He then phoned Teagan. It was his second call to her that morning. The first one had been an hour ago, so maybe she had something on how the location of the WITSEC house had been breached.

"You're not going to like what I'm about to tell you," Teagan said the moment she answered, and that caused Jack to groan.

"What happened?" he snapped, trying to steel himself for what would be bad news.

"All the WITSEC files are intact. None of them have been tampered with." She didn't snap at him, but there was irritation in her voice that let him know he might have preferred that to whatever else she was about to tell him. "I think the breach came from the laptop Caroline was using, the one you had couriered to me. Did you know she has hacking skills?" Teagan tacked on to that without even pausing.

"Yeah. One of her many talents," he grumbled. Along with picking locks, hot-wiring cars and driving him crazy. "There were filters on that laptop," Jack pointed out.

"Caroline got past them, and because her skills are better than ours, it took the geeks all night to find it. Several of the sites she used to do a search on Eric Lang had a tracker on them. Something experimental and beyond my skill set to explain. It's called Geo-Trace. It wouldn't have alerted her, and it was well hidden in the website codes. But the geeks think that's how someone found her."

Jack cursed, not just because he was pissed about the hacking but because this could crush Caroline. This could put her on the fast track to a panic attack and a guilt trip. Hell, she'd want to be offering to take a bullet for him because she would see this as having put him in danger.

"If it works the way the geeks think it does," Teagan explained, "Geo-Trace would have allowed someone to track the computer without getting a warrant. And Caroline wouldn't have known about the risk. Like I said, Geo-Trace is still in the experimental stages. Whoever put it on the sites was probably looking for her."

And had found her.

"See if the geeks can figure out who put Geo-Trace on the sites," he suggested. "Maybe try a reverse hacking maneuver." Ironically, it was something Caroline might be able to do, but he didn't want to go to her with this just yet.

"I'll try, but the Geo-Trace program corrupted itself

when our techs tried to examine it. They got portions of it, but it was as if it had an encoded virus to stop someone from digging into it too much."

A fail-safe. One that would have required some serious computer skills. That still didn't convince him to bring this to Caroline. Even if he caught flak for it later, which he was certain he would.

"Don't mention this to Caroline," he added to Teagan.

Teagan rattled off a string of profanities before she said, "You're not going to question her about it?"

"Not right now. I need to ease her into it so that it doesn't send her into a tailspin."

Teagan groaned. "What part of your body are you thinking with right now?"

"Probably the wrong one," he admitted and ended the call just as Caroline hurried into the room.

She was dressed, mostly, but still adjusting the above-the-knee denim skirt and snug red top. Clothes that hugged curves on Caroline that he wished he couldn't see right now.

Yeah, the wrong part of his body was doing the thinking, and that had to stop. With the breach of the WITSEC location, it wasn't a stretch for someone to figure out that she would have gone with him. That was why he hurried when he got her out of the house and into the cruiser. He had to concentrate on who had attacked them and stop the person from coming after them again.

Jack frowned when he looked up at the sky. The iron gray clouds were already moving on, indicating a storm was on the way. He didn't mind bad weather, but he didn't like the idea of it happening when he was trying to get Caroline back and forth from the sheriff's office.

Gunnar flashed Caroline a grin that he seemed to cut

short when Jack scowled at him. He knew that Gunnar didn't have any romantic interest in Caroline. He was just being friendly, but Jack wanted the deputy in concentration mode, too.

"Did they find the shooter?" Caroline asked.

"No. The CSI team processed the car, and all the prints, fibers and trace they collected were sent to the lab. They might find something," Jack tried to assure her.

Since she'd been a criminal profiler and had dealt with investigations for years, Caroline probably knew that was a long shot. Anything collected from a rental car wouldn't necessarily belong to the last person who'd been inside it. Plus, a would-be killer had likely made sure not to leave any evidence behind.

Caroline shifted in the seat and studied him. "Is something wrong? I mean, something other than the obvious?"

There were two kinds of obvious here. The investigation and the personal. Jack had filled her in on everything about the case except for the likelihood that her laptop had been the reason her location was compromised. He still intended to hold off on asking her about that, which left them with the personal. And yes, there were things about that they also hadn't touched on yet.

Since Gunnar was only a few feet away, Jack reminded himself to keep his voice low. "I'm worried I messed up things last night."

Caroline stared at him, her expression flat. "I'm guessing you're not talking about the sex itself but rather the distraction it caused."

He nodded. Neither of them was going to dispute that the sex had been good. Darn good. Heck, they couldn't even try to pretend that it wouldn't happen again. But in this case, there could be a price to pay.

"You're on fragile ground," he said. "I know that. You're recovering from a nightmare that hasn't ended yet." And now he had to pause and figure out how to sort out the jumble of thoughts and emotions going through his mind. It'd been too long without her, and the need had been too much to overcome. "I'm sorry if this is messing with your head."

Her eyebrow rose, and for a moment he saw the flash of humor. Jack almost expected her to make a joke, something along the lines of it hadn't been her head he'd been messing with. But the humor faded as quickly as it had come.

"I suspect it messed with your head, too," she said. "What I don't want it to do is make you feel that you have to shelter me." But Caroline immediately waved that off. "I'm not talking about protective custody here. I'm not stupid. I need that. I need you."

Jack hated that the needing-him part made him feel a lot better than it should have.

She huffed and moved closer, the side of her arm sliding against his chest as she shifted in the seat. Caroline looked him straight in the eyes. "I want you to treat me the way you did in bed," she whispered. "I didn't feel damaged or broken then. And even if I am both of those things, I don't want you to make me feel as if I am. Understand?"

Oh, yeah. He understood all right. It'd been the heat that had caused him to take her hard and fast. No kid gloves. But the bottom line was that while she was healing, she was indeed still broken, and Jack had no intentions of adding to that. It meant he'd walk a fine line between his feelings for her and his need to protect her. Thankfully, he didn't have to get into the details of how he'd manage that, because Gunnar pulled to a stop in front of the sheriff's office.

Caroline's eyes met his again as if she wanted to delay getting out until he gave her some kind of assurance, but Gunnar remedied that, as well, by hurrying to open the door to the building for them. Clearly, the deputy was standing guard and waiting for them to go inside. On Caroline's huff and Jack's sigh of relief, that was exactly what they did.

As he'd done on their previous visit, Jack didn't linger around. He took Caroline past the noise and chatter in the squad room and into Kellan's office. His brother was there at his desk and working on his laptop. Gunnar peeled off from them and went to his desk.

"Lily's already here," Kellan told them, his eyes still on his laptop. "She's in the interview room with her lawyer." He finally looked up from his computer and his attention landed on Jack. Then on Caroline. "You two look…"

"Think carefully about how to finish that," Jack warned him. He wasn't in the mood for another lecture after he'd already gotten a scolding from Teagan.

"You look slightly more relaxed than you did yesterday," Kellan finished after a pause. "It won't last. Lily's not happy about you getting those warrants, so she came in here ranting."

A surprise, since Lily hadn't reached the ranting stage the day before. But then maybe the woman hadn't thought Jack would actually get the warrant.

"Here's the file on Skylar." Kellan turned his laptop in their direction. "There supposedly isn't a hard copy, only the digital one."

Lily was going to have to wait, because Jack wanted a

look at this before he spoke to her. "Anything about the file jump out at you?" Jack asked Kellan as he pulled up Skylar's record.

But before Kellan could even respond, Jack saw an immediate problem. The file was too short. Two pages. The first was an intake form with basic stuff like name, age and next of kin. The next was a record of places the woman had been sent for job interviews.

"There are no reports from counselors or such," Jack concluded.

Kellan made a sound of agreement. "There's nothing about room assignments, day-to-day chores or any interaction with staff." He shook his head in disgust. "I've asked the computer guys at the Ranger lab to go through the files and see if anything was deleted in the past twenty-four hours. If so, we can look into charging Lily with obstruction of justice."

Was Lily really that stupid as to try to hide info from them? Maybe. People did dumb things all the time.

Caroline reached around Jack and typed something on the keyboard while her gaze skirted over the screen. "The file was modified nine hours ago."

That would have been just before the warrant had been served.

"I can't tell if anything was deleted," Caroline went on, "but the file was created a little over a year ago, and that fits the timing for when the woman would have arrived at New Beginnings." She continued to study the screen. "For only two pages, someone certainly spent a lot of time in this file. Over twenty-five hours."

That was too much for simply logging job interviews and background. Still, it wasn't proof of a crime. "Lily's lawyers could maybe say that the file was just left open and that's why the time doesn't jive with the amount of info that'd been entered."

"I want to talk to some of the other women at New Beginnings," Kellan said. "I'll find out if they've had counseling or anything else since they've been staying there. It might help if I also talk to previous residents and find out why Skylar left."

That was a necessary step, one of those drone-work chores that cops had to do in the hope of finding threads they could tug. It could give them something they could use against Lily, but it would take time.

"Does your warrant cover the computers at New Beginnings?" Caroline asked. "Because if so, I could get you what you need this morning so you wouldn't have to wait for the crime lab."

Kellan shook his head. "It only covers the one file." Then he paused. "But I'll see what I can do about getting another warrant so we can search through any-and everything in the damn building."

He took out his phone and stepped to the side to make the call, but he stopped when the front door opened. Kellan's grunt of irritation caused Jack's attention to zoom in that direction.

Zeller walked into the building.

"If you deal with him, I can get started on that warrant," Kellan said, and when Jack nodded, his brother went out into the bullpen to make the call.

"Don't start giving me grief about why I haven't returned your calls," Zeller griped the moment he stepped into Kellan's office. "I've been tied up on an investigation in Austin."

Jack didn't know about any such investigation, but it'd be easy enough to check. Which probably meant Zeller was telling the truth. Or the partial truth anyway. He could have been working a case and avoiding Jack at the same time.

"Tell me about your relationship with Nicola," Jack said.

Since Lily was waiting, it was best not to waste any time getting that out there. Plus, he liked that Zeller was off guard. Judging from the way the man's eyes widened and then narrowed, he'd been first surprised by the demand and then riled. Good. Because Jack was riled, too, that a fellow marshal could have withheld something like this.

"There was no relationship," Zeller spat out.

"But you knew her," Jack countered. "And don't bother to deny it, because I have a witness." That last part wasn't exactly true. He had the speculations of a person of interest—Lily—but sometimes a half-truth got fast results. In this case, it did just that.

Zeller groaned and glanced up at the ceiling as if hoping for some kind of divine guidance. "I spoke to Nicola, that's all," he finally admitted. "She'd had a friend who'd gotten involved in the sex trade."

Jack didn't feel one ounce of joy over Zeller's confession, since it was coming way too late. "How'd you find that out?"

Zeller took a deep breath first. "Nicola's name came up when I was questioning a group of college students about the sex-trafficking case. A lot of names came up," he quickly added, "and I talked to a lot of people. Nicola, included."

"Her name wasn't in any of your reports," Jack reminded him.

"No, because I didn't get anything from her. I swear I

didn't," Zeller snapped when Jack gave him a hard glare. "My conversation with her lasted less than ten minutes, and I realized her friend didn't have anything to do with my investigation. She was just someone who got lured into turning tricks by her sleazy boyfriend."

Jack mentally went through every word of that, and he was sure that Caroline was doing the same. In the squad room, he saw Kellan finish his call and give Jack a thumbs-up. He hoped that meant his brother had gotten the process started for the warrant for the other computer files at New Beginnings.

Jack turned his attention back to Zeller, who was clearly waiting for him to continue. "So, if your meeting with Nicola was all innocent, as you say, why not mention you'd met her once her body had been discovered?"

"At first I didn't remember talking to her. Not until I saw photos of her body." His breath turned into a long sigh. "And then I started feeling guilty, thinking that maybe something I said spurred her to do something dangerous. Like trying to save other girls like her friend."

Jack latched right onto that. "Was that what Nicola was trying to do?"

"I don't know. That's the truth," Zeller added in a hoarse whisper. "Like I said, I had a short conversation with her, one I barely remember, but I guess it's possible she picked up on something that made her put herself in a situation that turned dangerous."

Yes, it was. But then it was just as likely that Nicola had struck out on her own to try to investigate something she should have left to the badges. Of course, in this case, maybe the *badge* was what had gotten her into trouble if she'd inadvertently mentioned something to Zeller that made him believe she was some kind of threat. Perhaps

Nicola had even known something about his involvement in the sex trafficking.

But if so, Jack had no proof of that.

"Look, I feel like dirt over what happened to her," Zeller went on. "She seemed like a good kid, and she was killed. It doesn't matter that I didn't have anything to do with that. She's still dead."

Either Zeller was telling it the way it was, or else he was darn good at putting on an act. If Zeller was feeling guilty, maybe that was the bad vibe Jack was picking up on and it had nothing to do with being dirty.

This time, it was Jack who took a deep breath. "Just cool your heels for a while. I'll need an official statement from you about Nicola, but for now I have to observe another interview."

"Lily," Zeller quickly supplied. "I heard about the warrant to get the file of the missing woman."

Of course, he had. There wasn't much of a chance of keeping a warrant a secret, and Zeller likely had his ear to the ground to hear anything going on with the investigation. Jack couldn't fault him for that. If their positions had been reversed, he would be doing the same thing.

"I want to be in on Lily's interview," Zeller insisted.

"I'm sure you do, but it's not going to happen." Jack considered telling Zeller that he could watch from the observation room, but Caroline would be in there, and Jack didn't want the marshal near her. "I'll ask Kellan to copy you on the report he writes up after he talks to Lily."

Zeller huffed. "We're on the same side here, Jack. I know you don't believe that." He shot Caroline a nasty glance, no doubt to remind her that she was the reason for the mistrust. But Jack had had his doubts about Zeller before Caroline had voiced any.

"You'll get the report if Kellan agrees," Jack emphasized. "That's the best I can do right now."

Obviously, that wasn't enough in Zeller's opinion. He turned on his heels and stormed out. Jack didn't mind the fit of temper. It was better than the alternative of having Zeller linger around and upset Caroline even more. Jack could practically see the jangled nerves all over her face, but he would need to speak to Zeller again. Would need to make it official that Zeller had neglected to mention the conversation he'd had with a woman who had ended up murdered.

When Kellan tipped his head toward the interview room, Jack and Caroline followed him there. Jack intended to leave Caroline in observation while he conducted the interview with Kellan. But before they could even start, Lily came out, with her lawyer trailing right behind her.

"Are you really trying to get a warrant to get into my computer files?" Lily demanded, and she aimed that at Jack. There was fire in her eyes and raw anger in her voice.

"Yes, Kellan and I are," Jack confirmed. He didn't want Lily including Caroline in on the venom.

Lily made a sound of outrage and batted away her lawyer, who tried to whisper something in her ear. "You have no right!" And this time, she directed her anger solely at Jack. "I'm trying to help women who've been violated."

"If that's all you're doing, then having us look at your files shouldn't be a problem." In contrast, Jack kept his voice calm.

Clearly, it was a problem for Lily, because every muscle in her face tightened in rage. "I'll stop you. So help me, I'll stop you."

"Under the circumstances, my client and I need to re-schedule this interview," the lawyer said.

Jack considered nixing any rescheduling, but he re-thought that. Maybe it would be best to speak to Lily after the warrant had come through and they'd done a computer search. That way, they might have some ammu-nition they could use to get her to confess to any wrong-doings going on at New Beginnings. Of course, it was possible for Lily to successfully fight the warrant. That had been known to happen, but if she managed it, that would make her look as if she were hiding something.

"Tomorrow morning," Jack finally said. "Be back here at nine."

That should give them plenty of time to press for the warrant and start searching through the files. He had no idea how many women were actually in the facility or had been there, but the search might take a while.

And it was something Caroline could help them with.

He'd likely run into some protest from Kellan on that, but Jack understood that Caroline needed to be part of this. She should have a hand in helping eliminate the threat to both of them. Besides, Caroline would get through those files a lot faster than Kellan, he or the techs they could get to work on it.

Lily certainly didn't thank Jack for rescheduling. As Zeller had done, she hightailed it out of there, leaving the anger still vibrating in the air.

"I'd better push on that warrant," Kellan muttered, taking out his phone again. As he'd done with the other call, he stepped into the squad room.

"I'm okay," Caroline told Jack before he could even ask. "Really," she added when he gave her a flat look.

She sighed and pushed her hair from her face. "I just want answers. I want the person who attacked us behind bars."

"That's my top priority," he said, though that was one of those half-truths similar to the one he'd told Zeller.

Finding the person responsible and keeping Caroline safe and sane went hand in hand. But Jack knew that once that happened, it wouldn't be the end of things. Caroline still had to recover from the ordeal that Eric had put her through. She'd need time to deal not only with that but also with her feelings for him. And she did have feelings. No doubts about that. But Jack suspected that was the last thing she wanted to sort out right now.

"Sorry I dragged you in here," Jack told her.

Caroline lifted her shoulder. "You didn't get to do the interview, but we still learned some things. Both Lily and Zeller are scared. Maybe they're that way only because of the damage something like this can do to their reputations, but they're scared."

Oh, yeah. And Jack liked that because it could perhaps cause them to make a mistake. It could also make them dangerous. If one of them had indeed run the sex-trafficking ring and murdered Nicola, then there was nothing they'd hesitate to do to cover their tracks.

Because getting caught could lead to the death penalty.

"If Lily tries to delete or hide computer files, we can arrest her," Jack explained. "Ditto if Zeller tries to cover up the unreported contact he had with Nicola."

Of course, neither of those things would be a direct link to the attack, but it could open a door or two. Right now, Jack would settle for a sliver of an opening.

He was about to suggest that Caroline and he go back to his place to work, but before he could say anything, his phone rang. Jack frowned when Unknown Caller popped up on the screen.

Hell, what now?

He hit the answer button, and while hoping that whatever he was about to hear didn't give them another dose of bad news, he put the call on Speaker. "Marshal Jack Slater," he answered.

Jack didn't care much for the long silence that followed, but he finally heard a woman's voice. "Marshal, you've been trying to get in touch with me. I'm Grace Wainwright. I understand you have some questions for me."

Well, he certainly hadn't expected Kingston's friend, and the former resident of New Beginnings, to return his call. Jack had figured he'd have to track her down.

"Yes, I have questions," he verified. "What can you tell me about an attack that took place yesterday near Longview Ridge?"

Since it was a direct question, he thought maybe she would dodge it. She didn't. "Unfortunately, I know more about it than I should." Grace sighed, and it sounded both heavy and weary. "Marshal Slater, there are some things you need to know about Caroline Moser."

Chapter Ten

Caroline couldn't stop the new round of fear and worry that slammed through her when she heard what Grace Wainwright had just said.

There are some things you need to know about Caroline Moser.

She didn't think she had blank spots left in her memory, but it was possible she did. Also possible that this woman was about to give her news that she wouldn't want to hear. Wouldn't want Jack to hear, either. Still, that didn't stop Caroline from moving closer to the phone so that she wouldn't miss a word.

"Where are you?" Jack asked Grace.

It was one of those square-filler questions that lawmen needed to ask. A face-to-face interview was better than one on the phone, and there was the troubling problem of Grace's safety. If she was involved in this—whatever *this* was—then she could be in danger.

"Sorry, but I'd rather keep my location to myself," Grace answered. She didn't sound angry or resentful. In fact, her voice was surprisingly calm.

"That might not be smart," Jack countered. "I could help you."

"Thanks, but I'll manage. I don't exactly trust lawmen and cops."

Caroline couldn't muster up a nod of agreement when Jack shot her a glance.

"By now, I suspect you've talked to Kingston and Lily?" Grace went on.

Jack paused, obviously considering how much to tell Grace. And when to press her on what she intended to tell him about Caroline. "I have. What do they have to do with Caroline and you?"

Grace made a sound, a sort of hollow laugh. "Everything. Or at least, I think everything. It's all balled up together, you see."

"No, I don't see. Spell it out for me," Jack insisted. "What did you want to tell me about Caroline?"

"That she's part of this. Not the crimes. Not the murders. But she's a part of it."

"All right," Jack huffed. "Keep talking. And I'm especially interested in hearing if you helped your old buddy Kingston get to Caroline."

Definitely no laugh this time. "I didn't. Is that what he told you, that I helped him?"

"Kingston said plenty," Jack settled for saying.

Grace gave another heavy sigh. "Well, I didn't give Kingston any information about anyone. Especially not Caroline. She's in WITSEC, which would have meant me hacking into federal files."

Jack lifted an eyebrow. "You aren't good enough to tap those files?" And this time he was obviously goading Grace, probably hoping to spur her into blurting out more than she intended.

"I'm good at digging out data," Grace answered. "I'm sure you've already heard that, but I wouldn't have done something to bring the feds, or you, coming after me. Especially you. You would have hounded me to the ends of the earth to get back at me for going after your woman."

Your woman. So Grace knew about their relationship. Something like that wouldn't have been hard to access, but what wouldn't have been so easy was getting to the depths of Jack's feelings, which would have indeed caused him to go after Grace and bring her to justice. It meant Grace had been thorough when she'd gotten whatever she had on Jack and her.

"How did you know I was in WITSEC?" Caroline asked, knowing that it was going to earn her a scowl from Jack.

It did.

He obviously had wanted her to stay quiet, maybe because he thought Grace wouldn't spill all if she knew someone else was listening, but Caroline had taken a calculated risk. There was a reason Grace had dug into their relationship. Into their situation. And she'd called Jack. Apparently, the woman had something to say.

"Everything pointed to you being in WITSEC," Grace explained. "When the cops found you in Longview Ridge, Eric was still alive. No way would Marshal Slater have risked Eric getting to you again, and with your head injury, WITSEC is the only thing that made sense."

Maybe. But it was possible that Grace had confirmed that by hacking into Justice Department files. Of course, that only led Caroline to yet more questions. Why would Grace have done that? Why was the woman so interested in her?

"I've been looking into Nicola Gunderson's murder," Grace went on before Caroline could press her for more. "And no, I didn't know her, but her murder grabbed my attention." She paused. "I felt sorry for her, that she died that way."

Caroline looked at Jack to see if he believed that last part, but he only shrugged. It was possible what Grace was saying was true. Nicola's death had gotten the attention of a lot of people. An attractive college student who'd been kidnapped and forced into sex trafficking, only to be murdered. Of course, the media hadn't picked up on Zeller's connection to Nicola.

But did Grace know?

Since that would be giving the woman too much information on their conversation with Zeller, Caroline kept it to herself and waited for Grace to continue. She didn't have to wait long.

"After Nicola's murder and Eric's death, I started researching the investigation," Grace explained. "I believe whoever was running the sex trafficking got Eric to kill Nicola."

Caroline felt that hot tightness in her stomach. "Why do you think that?" she snapped. This time the memories came with a hefty dose of anger. Mercy, were they going to have to add another name to Eric's list of murders?

"Because of info I got from hacking into some files. And no, I won't tell you specifically which ones, because if you do manage to find me, I don't want to be arrested for it."

Caroline could see the debate going on in Jack's eyes. No way could he offer Grace immunity, because hacking was a serious crime. Plus, the woman might not even be telling the truth.

"Does the name Skylar Greer mean anything to you?" Grace asked.

That got every bit of Caroline's attention. Jack's, too,

because his eyes widened, then narrowed. "What about her?" Jack countered, obviously keeping his investigative cards close to the chest.

"She was in the sex-trafficking ring, too, and was rescued," Grace went on after a long pause. "Afterward, Skylar started asking questions and was trying to figure out who'd been running the ring."

Caroline didn't think it was much of a stretch that the woman had done that while living at New Beginnings.

"Do you know where Skylar is?" Jack asked.

"No." Grace didn't hesitate before that answer. "But it's possible she's in hiding. I hope she is, anyway. I hope her questions didn't get her killed."

Caroline hoped the same thing, and it twisted away at her to think of the worst-case scenario here. That Skylar may have been murdered by the same person responsible for taking her into the sex-trafficking ring.

Maybe Lily or Zeller.

Heck, maybe even Kingston. Grace had said this was all balled up together, and Kingston was definitely in the mix.

"Do you know if Skylar saw a counselor or therapist while she was at New Beginnings?" Jack pressed, and Caroline knew why. If she had, then that should have been in the file.

"I'm not sure. Maybe," Grace concluded. "She was eager to turn her life around. Eager to find answers, too, and I think it was that search for the truth that maybe landed her in trouble."

Jack gave an impatient huff. "What did Skylar find in that search and how is all of this connected to Caroline?"

"Again, I'm not sure what she found." Grace hesitated. "But I believe whatever Skylar learned, someone wanted her silenced for it. And that leads me back to Caroline. If Eric did kill Nicola at the request of the person running the sex-trafficking ring, then that person might believe Eric told Caroline about it. Eric had her a long time, and he was cocky. He could have bragged to her about it."

Yes, Eric was cocky, but he'd never mentioned Nicola. Of course, that didn't mean anything. Eric had only talked about his murders in a general kind of way. He'd been far more interested in taunting Caroline for not figuring out sooner that he was a serial killer. The taunts had been like an arrow to her heart because they'd been true.

"Do you have any proof to back up what you're saying?" Jack asked Grace.

"None. It's based on conversations and files that no longer exist. Someone wiped them. Someone who almost certainly wanted to cover up their crimes. I'll leave that to you to figure out."

"Obviously, you wanted to help with that or you wouldn't have returned my call," Jack quickly pointed out.

"No, I returned your call to get you off my back. Also to warn you that I believe this all goes back to Caroline and what the killer thinks Eric might have told her. I don't want to be dragged out into the open so I can be silenced."

That was another arrow strike. Maybe Skylar and Nicola had both been killed to protect a killer's identity. A fatal tying up of loose ends. Both Grace and she also could fall into that category, but there was one major difference between them. Grace obviously knew a lot more about this than Caroline did.

"I want you to back off and not try to contact me again," Grace added, and before Jack could say anything, she ended the call.

Cursing, Jack immediately hit Redial to call Grace back. No answer, and Caroline was betting the woman had used a burner cell, so there was no way to trace it.

"She hacked into the New Beginnings files," Caroline concluded, and she got an instant nod of agreement from Jack.

"That's why I need to talk to her again and find out if something was deleted from Skylar's record." He looked at her. "Any chance you can find Grace?"

"I'll try. I don't know her, not personally, but it's possible we brushed up against each other in cyberspace."

Jack's eyes narrowed a little, enough to let her know that he didn't want that "brushing up" to get her into legal hot water.

"I'll be careful," Caroline assured him.

He studied her a moment, then went to her and brushed a kiss on her cheek. Considering the heat that was always there between them, it seemed almost chaste. Something she hadn't thought possible from Jack. He eased back, their gazes connecting and holding for a long time. Too long. Because she saw more than the fire fueled by the attraction; she saw the worry he had for her.

"I'll be careful," she repeated, and this time Caroline was the one who dropped a kiss on his cheek.

He studied her a moment longer as if he wanted to say more, and then he tore his attention from her. "I'll get you a computer."

Jack went into the bullpen and spoke to Gunnar, and a few moments later, the deputy took a laptop from one of the empty desks and handed it to Jack. Jack was on his way back to Kellan's office when Caroline saw the visitor come in.

Kingston.

She was still feeling raw from everything that had already gone on, but she didn't mind going around again with him. Everything she and Jack learned could put them a step closer to catching their attacker, and Caroline was positive that Kingston knew more than he'd told them.

Jack, however, didn't seem as eager to meet with one of their persons of interest, and it was obvious he didn't trust Kingston, because Jack immediately stepped in between Caroline and him. Then Jack passed her the computer, no doubt to free up his hands. Since she wanted to do the same thing, Caroline put the laptop on Kellan's desk.

"I'm here to sign the statement that I gave to your brother," Kingston said. "Somebody called and told me it was ready."

"I did," Gunnar spoke up. "Give me a sec, and I'll get it for you."

Kingston didn't go to the deputy. He stayed put and cast glances at both Jack and her. "I gotta say that the two of you don't make many friends. I was at the diner across the street and saw Lily when she came out. She didn't seem happy."

"She wasn't," Jack verified. In the same breath he added, "What were you doing at the diner?"

"Waiting on a call that the report was ready. There's a storm moving in, and I thought I'd go ahead and drive out here while the weather was still clear." Kingston got that smug look on his face, as if pleased that he'd had a plausible answer.

Gunnar came to the doorway and handed Kingston the report and a pen. "Look that over and let me know if there are any corrections that need to be made."

Kingston nodded and moved as if to step away, but Jack stopped him. "I just had an interesting conversation with someone you know. Grace Wainwright."

Like Jack, Caroline was watching Kingston's face, and she saw it. The flash of concern. "Grace? What did she want? Where is she?"

The last question seemed to only increase his concern. But Caroline didn't know where that particular emotion of his was aimed. Was he worried about an old friend, or did Kingston think Grace had given them info they could use against him?

"She's fine," Jack answered. "Safe."

Caroline figured that last part was wishful thinking on Jack's part, along with being bait to see more of Kingston's reaction.

"Good," Kingston said, but his expression didn't mesh with the response. "I was worried about her. Grace tends to champion causes that can get her into trouble."

Interesting. And Caroline didn't believe it was her imagination that Kingston had thought carefully about how he was going to say that.

"What causes did Grace recently champion?" Jack asked.

Kingston lifted his shoulder. "I don't have anything specific, but that's just the way Grace is."

Jack stared at him. "Nothing specific, huh? Nothing about the woman missing from New Beginnings?"

"Oh, that." Kingston dismissed it with his tone. "Yes, I suppose it's possible Grace would have poked around with that. She would have likely known the woman since they were at New Beginnings together." He lifted the reports. "I'll just find someplace quiet to go over this."

Jack stepped in front of him before he could leave.

"Does Lily have any reason to harm Caroline or want to silence her?" Jack asked.

Kingston huffed and shook his head. "I don't have any details about the sex-trafficking ring. If Lily had a part in that, I don't have proof."

"Any other reason you can think of?" Jack pressed. "Something that's perhaps connected to Eric Lang?"

Again, Kingston shook his head and turned as if to leave, but then he stopped. "Maybe Lily's still upset about the Crime-Track program that Caroline and Gemma were working on."

Of all the things Caroline had thought Kingston might say, that wasn't one of them. "Crime-Track? Why would Lily be upset about that?"

"Lily tried to invest in it," Kingston calmly said.

Jack immediately looked at her as Caroline said, "I don't remember that." And she didn't. She was sure there hadn't been a single conversation about Lily when it came to Crime-Track. Unless she truly had gaps in her memory and this one had slipped through.

"I don't think she advertised her interest in it," Kingston explained, "but she contacted Gemma. Lily wanted to fund the project, but Gemma turned her down. It might have caused some bad blood between them."

Jack took out his phone and handed it to Caroline so she could call Gemma. She went to the other side of Kellan's office while she did that. Not that the distance would give her much privacy, but at least Kingston wouldn't be able to hear her every word.

Caroline scrolled through the contacts, pressed Gemma's number and said a quick prayer of thanks when Gemma answered on the first ring.

"Is everything okay?" Gemma quickly asked. "Was there another attack?"

"No. We're fine," Caroline assured her, and she felt guilty that she'd caused her friend an obvious moment of terror. Not just because of Jack and her but also because the man Gemma loved could have been in the line of fire.

The breath of relief Gemma took was audible. "Sorry. I'm on edge."

Caroline was right there with her. Too bad things would stay that way until they made an arrest. This phone call might help with that.

"I have a question about Crime-Track," Caroline explained. "Did Lily Terrell ever contact you about it?"

"Yes," Gemma answered after a short pause. "She dropped by my office shortly after the project started, before you started working on it."

So that was why Caroline hadn't recalled anything about this. "You didn't want Lily involved with it?"

"No. Because Lily didn't want to merely be involved. She wanted control of the project."

Control? Caroline tried to think of a logical reason for that. Maybe because Lily believed she could use it to help with stopping things like sex trafficking? But that seemed a stretch since the program was being designed to catch killers.

"It was hard to turn down the funding that Lily offered," Gemma added, "but I wanted the data and reports to be as objective as possible. For that to happen, I thought it best if I handled the process. For all the good that did," she muttered.

Maybe Gemma hadn't meant for her to hear that, but she did. And Caroline couldn't even argue with Gemma on that point or try to make her friend feel better. Because Eric had made dupes out of both of them.

"Was Lily angry when you turned down her funding?" Caroline asked.

"Possibly. I mean, she didn't yell or anything, but she also didn't contact me again. Once when I saw her at a party, she didn't even speak to me."

That sounded like anger to Caroline, but she couldn't see it leading to attempted murder. If it had, Lily would have likely gone after Gemma instead of Jack and her.

"You're staying safe, right?" Caroline pressed, just to make sure.

"Of course." Gemma huffed. "Kellan has one of the reserve deputies guarding me, and the ranch hands are on alert."

"Good. Keep it that way."

"What's this all about?" Gemma demanded. "Was Lily involved in the attack?"

"We're not sure. If she is, you'll be one of the first to know. Take care of yourself, Gemma."

When Caroline finished the call and turned back around to hand Jack his phone, she realized Kingston was gone. "I sent him to the interview room so he could read the report," Jack said. "I figured you didn't want him hanging around here."

"I don't." The guy made her extremely uneasy. Of course, any admirer of Eric would. "Did Kingston tell you anything else about Lily?"

Jack shook his head. "Did you get anything from Gemma?"

Caroline put it in a nutshell. "Lily wanted control of the project, and Gemma refused. I'm not sure if it plays into this, though."

He made a sound of agreement. "Hard to see how it would fit. Well, unless Lily thought she could manipulate the program for some kind of vigilante justice or to launch her own illegal spree. Yeah, I know, it's a long shot," he added.

It was, but… "When Crime-Track first started, it was all about gathering data about murders. The idea was to use that data to try to predict when and where other killings would take place and to combine that with profiles to identify possible suspects. It was meant to become a tool for law enforcement, but maybe someone with unlawful intent would want to stop the project in its tracks."

Jack nodded. "And one way for Lily to do that would be to fund it and then crush it."

Yes, but that seemed like an inefficient way to hide her criminal tracks. Still, it was a possible piece that Jack and she could eventually fit into this puzzle of an investigation.

Before Jack could even put his phone away, it rang, and she saw the muscle flicker in his jaw when he looked at the screen.

"It's Teagan," Jack said, and for a moment Caroline thought he was going to put the call on speaker so she could hear any updates on the case. He didn't. And he stepped away from her when he answered.

Combined with the tight jaw and his sudden secretiveness, this couldn't be good. Nor was the fact that he was practically whispering his fast-clipped responses. She heard him say "What?" Then he followed it with some profanity.

The conversation didn't last long. Less than a minute. But Caroline was certain that Jack had just gotten bad news.

"What's wrong?" she demanded the moment he finished the call.

He took his time answering, which only put her more on edge. "Teagan did a scan of the laptop you used at the WITSEC house, and she found a new tracker called Geo-Trace on one of the sites you accessed. A site about Eric Lang."

She listened carefully to each word, processing it and Jack's dark mood that went along with the explanation. "Geo-Trace," she repeated. "It was still in the experimental stage last I checked."

Jack nodded. "It's apparently operational now, and someone put it on that site."

It didn't take her long to fill in the blanks. "And that someone used my search to track me to the location of the house."

He met her eye to eye. "Yes."

Caroline groaned and pressed her fists against each side of her head. "How could I have been so stupid?"

"You didn't know," he simply said, and it was layered with sympathy. Something she didn't want. Didn't deserve. What she'd done was more than just stupid, though. It had nearly gotten them killed. "God, Jack. I'm so sorry."

"Don't," he warned her, and he went to her, pulling her into his arms. "This isn't your fault. It's the fault of the person who put the tracker on the site."

There was something else in his voice now. Anger. And she didn't think it was directed at her—even though it should have been.

Think, she demanded, fighting her way through the emotions that were flooding her mind. *Think*. Had the Geo-Trace been put on the site specifically to find her?

Possibly.

If so, she didn't have to guess why that'd happened. The person wanted her dead, and it almost certainly went back to the night Eric had taken her hostage. Either someone thought Eric had told her something or that she'd overheard or seen it. Something that her attacker wanted to keep hidden, and the way to do that was to silence her permanently. Jack would just be collateral damage.

"There's more," Jack went on. "I asked the computer guys to do a reverse search to try to find out who put Geo-Trace on the site. And they found the source."

The relief came, but it didn't last. That was because Caroline knew that this wasn't good news.

"Zeller," he said, his voice clipped. "Geo-Trace was loaded on the site from Zeller's office computer."

Chapter Eleven

While Jack slogged his way through the list of calls he had to make, he kept his eye on Caroline. She was at a small table that he'd moved into Kellan's office specifically for her, working on the borrowed laptop. Trying to track down Grace.

He also suspected she was trying to deal with her feelings.

Even though she wasn't talking about it, Caroline was probably still burdened with guilt over the whole Geo-Trace problem. And yeah, she was blaming herself. Jack certainly wasn't. He was putting the blame right where it belonged.

On Zeller.

Well, if Zeller was actually responsible, that is. Jack was trying to sort through his own feelings and questions about that.

It would have been incredibly stupid for a marshal to use his computer to install a tracking device like that. Something that could be traced right back to him. So, unless Zeller had gotten careless, it meant someone had perhaps set him up. And that was a question Jack intended to ask Zeller as soon as he arrived.

Jack checked his watch. One o'clock already. Which

meant Zeller should get to the sheriff's office anytime now. Jack hadn't given the man a heads-up on what the visit was about, but it was possible that Zeller had gotten word about what had been found on his computer. It was hard to keep something like that quiet when others in the office would have known that the techs were running checks.

Still, it didn't matter if Zeller knew or if he'd had time to come up with a story to cover his tracks. A face-to-face meeting would allow Jack to look into his eyes and maybe see if he was telling the truth.

Jack gave Caroline another glance before he went into the squad room to refill his coffee. Kellan was there, doing the same, and he'd no doubt take that fresh cup to the interview room where he'd been working for the past couple hours. His choice, not Jack's. Jack had offered to move Caroline and himself into that room, but Kellan had insisted they stay in his office.

"How's she doing?" Kellan asked, tipping his head to Caroline.

She didn't look up at them. She kept her attention nailed to the laptop screen while her fingers seemingly flew over the keyboard. Next to it was the untouched sandwich that Jack had had delivered for her from the diner. Soon, he'd try to coax her again into eating.

Jack didn't sugarcoat the truth when he answered Kellan. "She's not doing that well. Way too much has happened in the past twenty-four hours, and it's a lot to take on."

Kellan gave a grunt of agreement and sipped his coffee. "Does 'way too much' include you two sleeping together?"

Jack nearly snapped that it was none of Kellan's business, but he knew his brother hadn't meant to pry into his personal life. The bottom line was that sex had complicated things. It had made Jack less objective—though he couldn't remember a time when objectivity had played into his feelings for Caroline.

"It does include that," Jack admitted. He rubbed his forehead, where a dull ache throbbed. "I love her and I want to protect her. If you can figure out a way to stay objective about that, I'd like to hear it."

Maybe because Kellan knew that Jack was dealing with as much emotion as Caroline, he wisely held back any judgment or advice. Kellan just patted his brother on the back and headed toward the interview room. Jack went the other direction. He got Caroline a cup of coffee and brought it to her in the office.

"Thanks," she muttered, not looking up at him, but then she stopped, her fingers still poised over the keyboard.

"Problem?" he asked, knowing there were plenty of them. He just hoped there wasn't something new, since they were already grappling with enough.

"There's no sign of Grace. And the phone she used was indeed a burner." Caroline paused long enough to gulp down some coffee. "I put out feelers through old contacts. *Safe* feelers," she emphasized. "I don't want the wrong person finding her, so I only emailed people I trust."

Good. Because they didn't know who the wrong person was—yet. But it was possible that Grace could become a target if she surfaced.

"I also ran a deeper background check on her," Caroline went on. "Unlike some of the other women who were kidnapped and drugged into the sex-trafficking ring, Grace was lured into it through her drug habit.

From everything I'm hearing, she's clean now, but when she was using, she was out of it. Out of it enough to turn tricks to support her habit."

Jack thought about that a moment. "Any idea who got Grace to start turning tricks?"

She shook her head. "Nothing so far, but I think it's important to find that out. Maybe it was one of our suspects, and if so, we could use Grace to tie Zeller, Lily or Kingston to the rest of what's happening."

He was thinking the same thing. But first, they had to find Grace and convince the woman to trust them. Then he'd have to persuade her to tell all and go into protective custody. No easy feat to do that when it was obvious the woman didn't even want to be found.

Jack slid the plate with the sandwich closer to Caroline's hand, and she glanced at it as if seeing it for the first time. Which was probably true. Caroline tended to get wrapped up when she was doing research.

She frowned but took a bite of the ham-and-Swiss that he knew was her favorite. "There's more," Caroline said, chasing the sandwich with coffee. "I did some checking on Geo-Trace—"

He groaned. "Not a good idea. The Justice Department is all over that. Please tell me you didn't hack into their files."

"I didn't." She was quick to assure him of that. "I went through my own sources, and what I got isn't proof. More of the opinion of others like me."

In other words, hackers. Probably many of them with criminal records. Jack didn't groan again, but that was what he wanted to do.

"Geo-Trace could be a fake," Caroline added after she gave him a couple of seconds to rein in his temper.

Jack went still, letting that sink in. Or rather, trying to let that happen. But he had to shake his head. "But Teagan had heard of it, and it was on the computer."

"There's plenty of talk about it," she verified, "but I'm just not finding the proof that someone has perfected it enough to make it do what it's being designed to do— cull out that kind of info from an IP address."

Jack wasn't a computer idiot, but he also knew this was a conversation that could quickly go over his head. "Put that in layman's terms for me."

She nodded, paused again, this time with her forehead bunching up. "Other than the Geo-Trace that you found on my laptop and Zeller's computer, it doesn't show up anywhere else. That's an electronic red flag because you can bet that someone would have used this program if it were actually available."

Yeah, Jack could see that. Stalkers, thieves and other assorted scum would want their hands on it so they could track the physical location of someone simply because they were using a computer with an internet connection.

"I think the Geo-Trace was just a ruse," Caroline went on. "Something designed to make us think my location had been compromised through the laptop."

If so, that meant someone had set Zeller up.

"Yes," Caroline said as if she'd known exactly what he was thinking.

Since Zeller could arrive any minute, Jack shut the office door so that Caroline and he could have the rest of this conversation without the possibility of Zeller coming in on it.

"It doesn't mean Zeller is innocent, though," she continued. "Maybe I'm wrong about Geo-Trace. It could be that he got his hands on a working program. And even if he didn't, he might be going for some kind of reverse psychology. He might want to make himself look innocent by making us believe someone set him up."

That was something he'd need to give more thought, but Jack could see it from that angle. "Perhaps Zeller or someone else put this fake tracer on your computer and his so it would conceal the fact that the WITSEC file on you had actually been hacked. Geo-Trace would be a way of covering up the hacking."

She stayed quiet a moment, obviously giving that some thought. "It's possible. But it would have taken some serious skills to set all of this in motion."

Jack agreed, and that led him to the next question. "Who's capable of doing something like this?" And one name instantly came to mind. "Grace?"

"Maybe. I don't know how good she is. But I've been in touch with some of my old contacts, and one name keeps coming up. Scotty Milford."

Now, that was a familiar name. "If it's the same guy I'm thinking about, he's a criminal informant."

She nodded. "It's the same guy. He got busted a few years ago for cybercrimes, and he's clean-ish."

"Clean-ish?" Jack scowled. Cursed. "Is that like being a little bit pregnant?"

The color actually rose in Caroline's cheeks. Maybe because she was remembering that he hadn't used a condom the night before. He was still kicking himself over that, but the kicks would have to wait. He made a circling motion with his finger for her to continue.

"My contacts are split as to whether or not Scotty is up to his old tricks again," she explained. "He hasn't gotten caught for anything, but he also hasn't been as chatty online as he normally is. Sometimes, being quiet is a way of not letting others know what you're doing."

That was true in the world of law enforcement, too. "You think he could be involved?" he came out and asked.

"Yes," she said without hesitation.

And that was plenty enough for him. Jack took out his phone so he could get Scotty's contact info.

Caroline stood, picking up the notepad she'd been using. "I already have his number. I got it from one of those contacts, but I should be the one to do this. Scotty would be more likely to talk to me about this than a badge."

He didn't have to think long and hard about that. She was right. So he handed her his phone.

"Any chance that your name and number are in Scotty's contacts?" she asked. "Because I don't want 'Marshal Jack Slater' flashing on the screen."

"I haven't talked to him in a while, and I've gotten a new number since then."

With a nod, she pressed in the number from her notepad, put the call on speaker and waited. After three rings, the call went to voice mail. He saw the brief debate she had with herself about what to do, but she left a message.

"Scotty, this is Caroline Moser," she said. "Call me back at this number ASAP. It's important."

Good. Of course, if Scotty did call, Jack would have to pass his phone to Caroline. He didn't want the man hanging up on them before he even got the chance to question him.

Jack saved the number Caroline had dialed to call the man and put it under Scotty's name. He was still in the process of putting his phone away when there was a knock at the door. As he'd done since this whole ordeal with Caroline started, he moved in front of her and made sure it would be easy for him to reach his weapon before he answered it. The person standing there was exactly who Jack had expected it to be.

Zeller.

And surprise, surprise, he wasn't happy.

Jack had riled Zeller so much in the past twenty-four hours that he was going to owe him a huge apology if it turned out that the marshal was innocent. But Jack had no intentions of believing in that innocence just yet.

There was water dripping off Zeller's hair and running down his face, and that caused Jack to glance out the front windows. The storm had moved in all right, and it was pouring.

"I didn't put anything on Caroline's computer that caused the location of her house to be breached," Zeller spat out, though Jack wasn't sure how he could even talk with his jaw muscles that tight.

"Who told you about that?" Jack immediately asked.

Jack hadn't thought it possible, but the muscles tightened even more. "I have friends at the office, and one of them alerted me that you went behind my back and had my computer checked."

"I did," Jack readily admitted. "And as you obviously know, the techs found something. Care to explain how that tracking program got from your laptop to Caroline's?"

Of course, if Caroline's theory was right, a hacker could have made it look as if Zeller's computer had been used. But no way was Jack going to share that with a man who might want them dead.

Zeller opened his mouth as if ready to shout out an argument, but then he stopped and lowered his shaking head. He stayed that way for several long moments before his attention came back to Jack.

"I didn't do this," Zeller said, his voice weary and hoarse now. "I'm being set up, and the person's doing a damn good job of it. I'm being investigated and people are talking. Even when I'm cleared of the computer charges—and I will be—my reputation will be hurt."

In the beginning, it would be. Jack couldn't see a way around that, but a bruised reputation was a small price to pay for getting away with murder. Heck, Zeller could get away with the computer charges, too, because there might not be enough evidence to pin this on him. A lawyer could argue that plenty of other marshals would have had access to his workplace computer.

"It's either Kingston or Lily who's doing this," Zeller went on. "Kingston maybe because he's carrying out some sick beyond-the-grave orders from Eric." He looked at Caroline. "You know that Eric was capable of doing something like that."

She nodded. "Eric was capable of a lot of things, but he liked to taunt. That's not happening here. The tracer on the site was, well, sneaky. And, yes, Eric could have managed to get someone to do that, but he would have wanted me to know that he'd bested me even after he was dead."

Caroline was right, but Jack could mentally play devil's advocate and see this from a different side. Kingston could have done it as an homage to a twisted SOB that he admired. If so, Kingston might not be in the mindset of gloating and taunting.

And that left Lily.

Jack wasn't sure if Lily had the computer skills, but the woman had enough money to hire someone. Plus, setting up Zeller and having him arrested and convicted would definitely get any heat off her.

"You were getting a warrant on the files at New Beginnings," Zeller continued a moment later. "Lily's stonewalling that, and it could be because she's got plenty to hide."

Jack could feel himself scowling. "How did you know about the warrant request?" he asked Zeller.

But Jack immediately waved that off. If Zeller had heard about the computer tracker being linked back to them, then he could have easily heard about the warrant. In fact, he would have taken that as some possible light at the end of a very dark tunnel if they could use that warrant to find anything to incriminate Lily.

Since Zeller had brought it up, Jack took out his phone and texted Teagan to get an update on the warrant. His partner answered right away.

Lily's lawyers are trying to block the warrant, Teagan messaged. They're claiming some of the files have medical info protected under the law. It might take a while to get it all sorted out.

Hell. They didn't have a while. A delay like this could give Lily a chance to destroy any evidence that might be in those files. Jack consoled himself, though, with the thought that a smart person would have already made sure there was nothing incriminating to find.

"Just let the investigation of your computer play out," Jack told Zeller. "If someone planted the tracer to frame you, that will come to light."

He hoped. While Jack still considered Zeller a suspect, he wanted to get to the truth of what was going on.

Zeller's gaze slashed between Caroline and Jack for several moments before the man cursed and walked away.

He didn't storm out this time, and there was a weariness to his posture as he exited the building. Of course, Jack was cynical enough to think that anything Zeller did right now could be fake. Part of the facade to make them believe he was innocent.

Caroline stepped to Jack's side and watched until Zeller was out of sight. "Do you think his computer skills are good enough to pull off planting a tracker on multiple websites?"

Jack had to shake his head. "I'm not sure."

But it was something he could find out. If he could have gone into his office, he would have been able to talk to his fellow marshals, but no way was he going to leave Caroline. Or take her into what she'd consider a lion's den, since she didn't have a whole lot of trust for lawmen. That meant he'd just have to rely on getting that info from Teagan.

On a heavy sigh, Caroline moved back to the table where she'd been working, but she stopped when Jack's phone rang again. Scotty's name was on the screen. Jack hadn't expected the hacker to actually return Caroline's call, but he was glad Scotty had. He handed his phone to Caroline again so she could answer.

"Scotty," she said after she put the call on speaker, but that was all she managed to get out before the man interrupted her.

"I'm in trouble, Caroline." Scotty's words were rushed together, and he sounded scared out of his mind. "You've got to help me. God, Caroline, I think someone's trying to kill me."

Chapter Twelve

Caroline felt the punch of dread go through her. No. Not another attack.

"Where are you?" she managed to ask Scotty. "What's wrong?"

"Someone broke into my house," he blurted out. "I ran out back, but I don't like the timing because the break-in came shortly after you left me that message. Did you set someone on me?"

"No. Of course not." And Caroline hated that he felt she would have done something like that. "Where are you?" she repeated. "Who broke into your house?"

"I don't know who it was. Some guy dressed all in black and wearing a ski mask. I was in my home office when I saw the person on my security cam. Then I spotted the gun he was carrying, and I got out, jumped in my car and drove off. But I think the person is following me."

Definitely not good, and it caused Caroline's heart to pound even harder. Mercy, was it possible that someone had indeed used her to get to Scotty? She'd checked for trackers on the websites she'd used, but it was possible one of her contacts had said the wrong thing to the wrong person.

"Scotty?" Jack said. "I'm Marshal Jack Slater. I need

you to tell me where you are so I can call someone to help you." He paused, maybe to give Scotty time to react to that, but the only thing Caroline could hear was Scotty mumbling. Or maybe he was praying.

"No cops," Scotty insisted. That came through loud and clear.

Caroline wasn't surprised by that. A lot of hackers, even those who were clean, didn't like the law. Plus, she had her own distrust of cops right now. Not just because of Eric's conversation but also because of Zeller possibly being linked to the attack.

Maybe even linked to this.

Sweet heaven. Was it possible that Zeller had used Scotty to plant that tracker on those sites and had now sent someone to eliminate him? Zeller couldn't be doing it himself because there wouldn't have been nearly enough time for him to get to Scotty in San Antonio.

"It's all over the news that someone tried to kill you, that it happened in Longview Ridge," Scotty went on. "Is that where you are now?"

Caroline certainly didn't jump to answer that. Neither did Jack. And there was a reason for that. It was possible that Scotty wasn't alone, that their would-be killer was in the vehicle with him. Then again, Zeller, Kingston and Lily all knew where she was, so it didn't make the risk any greater to reveal her location to Scotty.

"I'm at the sheriff's office here in Longview Ridge," she finally told him.

"Good, because I'm on my way there now."

Jack didn't curse, but that was what he looked like he wanted to do. "Describe the person and the vehicle that's following you so I can get someone out to help you."

Silence from Scotty, for a long time. "No. Don't send

anyone. I don't want to be gunned down or anything. But tell me what's going on. Why is this happening? And I want to hear the answers from Caroline, not you."

Caroline tried to tamp down the whirlwind of thoughts in her head so she could figure out the right thing to say to him. She also tried to steady her breath and her pulse. This wasn't the time for a panic attack.

"I think someone hacked into either WITSEC files or a Justice Department computer," she explained. "Did you do that?"

More silence, and like Jack, Scotty cursed this time, too. "You know I'm not going to admit to that. I could go to jail." But then Scotty paused. "Is that why someone's after me?"

It wasn't exactly a confession, but it was close enough. "Who hired you to do that?" Caroline pressed.

But that only caused Scotty to curse even more. "I need your help, not your questions. You need to get out here now and meet me."

"That's not going to happen," Jack spoke up. "Where are you?"

Caroline could tell from Jack's rough tone that he wanted that location so he could call in some of his fellow lawmen, but Scotty didn't answer. Not his question, anyway.

"No!" Scotty yelled.

And Caroline heard something else. The squeal of brakes. The sound of a collision. She also heard Scotty groan, and there was no mistaking that he was in pain.

"Scotty?" Caroline practically shouted.

She repeated his name over and over again, begging him to respond, but she only got more of those moans.

The seconds dragged by. Seconds where Scotty could be dying.

"How bad are you hurt?" she pressed. "Tell me where you are, and I can get you some help."

Still, no answer, and she couldn't even hear the moans now. Caroline was about to ask Gunnar to try to trace the call, but he spoke before she could say anything.

"We just got a 911 call about a car accident on the east road, just outside town limits," Gunnar said. "A car hit a light pole."

All of her muscles tightened and twisted. Including the ones in her chest. Caroline had to fight just to drag in a breath. Oh, God. Something bad had happened.

"I'm dispatching an ambulance," Gunnar added, "and I'm on the way there."

Gunnar was already heading for the door when Jack went after him. "It's possible there was an armed suspect in pursuit of the driver. It could be dangerous."

Too dangerous to get an ambulance in there, but the cops would clearly have to respond.

"Help me," Scotty finally groaned out. "I'm dying. Help me."

Caroline figured Jack would give her grief over what she was about to demand, but she was going to do it anyway.

"If Scotty's really dying," she whispered, "I need to try to talk to him. He won't talk to you," she added when Jack opened his mouth. "But he might tell me what he did and who hired him to do it."

Oh, Jack definitely didn't like that, but he couldn't argue her point. This might be their best chance at finding out who had tried to kill them. Of course, there was

also a good chance they could be put in another dangerous situation.

"I need you to go with us," Jack told Kellan when he
came into the bullpen. "I'll explain along the way."

Kellan didn't hesitate. He hurried toward the door,
and the four of them raced out to get into the cruiser.
The rain had slowed to just a drizzle, but Jack figured it
was only a lull. The storm air felt heavy and the clouds
looked ready to burst.

Gunnar took the wheel with Kellan in the front seat,
and Jack and she got in the back. While Jack filled Kellan in, Caroline kept her attention on Scotty.

"Are you still there?" she asked Scotty. She kept a tight
grip on the phone. "How badly are you hurt?"

"Bad," Scotty managed to say through another of
those hoarse groans.

"The ambulance will be right behind us," Kellan let
her know, and she relayed that info to Scotty. Whether
he understood that or not was anyone's guess.

"Scotty, I need you to tell me who hired you to get into
the files," Caroline insisted. "It's important."

Nothing. Not even a groan. And the call disconnected,
causing Caroline's concern to skyrocket. Because someone could be there with Scotty. Someone who wanted to
finish what they'd started.

"Who called in the 911?" she asked Gunnar. She tried
Scotty's number again, but he didn't answer. Caroline
kept trying and silently cursed her now trembling hands.

"Hank Perez," Gunnar answered. "He said he heard a
noise, looked at his window and saw that a little red car
had slammed into a utility pole. His house is on the hill
just above the road, and there are some trees obstructing

the view, but he said he could see the front end of the car bashed in and steam pouring from it."

So Hank hadn't actually witnessed the wreck. "Was there another vehicle, someone following the red car?" Caroline pressed.

"Hank didn't say, but he doesn't have the best eyesight. He's in his mideighties."

Yes, Caroline remembered. During the months before Eric had taken her hostage, she'd seen Hank in town a couple of times. "He uses one of those scooters to get around?"

Gunnar verified that with a nod. Part of her was relieved by that because maybe it meant Hank wouldn't go from his house to the car. She didn't want him getting shot by the person who'd been after Scotty. Of course, that person would be a fool to hang around since he or she would have figured someone would call the cops.

It didn't take them long to get down Main Street and onto the rural road that would lead them to Scotty. Hopefully, before it was too late.

Caroline continued pressing in Scotty's number while she kept watch, and despite the drizzle, she still had no trouble seeing the blue SUV that was coming up the road toward them. Maybe the vehicle that had been chasing Scotty. Gunnar must have thought so, too, because he slowed down a little, and both Jack and Kellan drew their weapons.

When the cruiser passed the SUV, Caroline got a glimpse of the driver inside, and her stomach went to her knees.

"That's Grace Wainwright," Caroline told them at the same moment that Jack's phone rang and Grace's name appeared on the screen.

"Should I go after her?" Gunnar asked.

"No," Jack said, "but call for someone else to do that. I want to question her and find out why she was out here." He answered the call as soon as he'd finished those instructions to Gunnar.

"I didn't do anything to hurt Scotty," Grace volunteered the moment she was on the line. "I was trying to help him, but someone ran him off the road."

"Who?" Jack snapped.

"I don't know." Grace made a sobbing sound. "Is Scotty dead?"

"You tell me," Jack countered.

That only caused the woman to cry even louder. "I didn't see the person who did this to him. But I did see Scotty's car. I drove past because I thought someone was in there with him. Someone trying to kill him. I drove away and called 911."

"There was a second call," Kellan verified in a whisper. He was on the phone with someone, probably dispatch.

"I couldn't help Scotty," Grace went on. "I'm so sorry, but I couldn't help him."

The woman sounded genuine, but Caroline had a ton of questions for her. She was certain Jack did, too, but she didn't get any more info from her because Grace ended the call. Maybe the deputy that Gunnar sent out would be able to intercept her and take her to the sheriff's office. Caroline put that thought on hold, though, when she looked ahead and spotted the red car.

Her breath vanished.

Because the car was practically wrapped around the utility pole. She couldn't imagine Scotty or anyone else surviving that kind of collision.

Gunnar pulled the cruiser to a stop, and he threw open his door. Kellan and Jack did the same.

"Stay here," Jack told her. "Let me check things out before you see him."

He was trying to protect her, to shield her from seeing Scotty. Part of her appreciated that, but if there was any chance Scotty was alive, there might not be much time to talk to him.

But she didn't get a chance to remind Jack of that because of the movement in the ditch.

Caroline caught it from the corner of her eye. Just a glimpse of someone next to the old ranch trail that was across the road from Scotty.

And that someone fired a shot at them.

JACK HAD BEEN so focused on getting to Scotty's car that he hadn't seen the shooter in time.

That was a big mistake.

Because the shot slammed into the back window. Right where Caroline was sitting. There was a bullet-resistant panel over the glass, and it held. The window didn't shatter, but Jack also knew it might not hold up if someone continued to fire straight into it. And that was exactly what happened.

A barrage of bullets came, all blasting into that one area of the window. Jack didn't have time to return fire or even pinpoint the shooter. He scrambled back into the cruiser, catching on to Caroline and pulling her down on the seat. She was already about to hunker down, and she tried to drag him with her.

He couldn't take cover, though, and he didn't close his door. Not with his brother and Gunnar out there. So Jack shifted his position and tried to make sure they were okay. Both Gunnar and Kellan were on the road and were crawling their way back to the cruiser.

Gunnar had also left the door open, and like Jack's, it was on the opposite side from the shooter. It would give Kellan and Gunnar two ways to get back into the vehicle.

Well, maybe.

Jack had to rethink that idea when several of the bullets skittered across the surface of the road. None of the shots hit them, but the gunfire did pin them down. Which was likely what the shooter intended to do, because almost immediately, more bullets blasted into the window before the attacker's aim returned to the area near Kellan and Gunnar. Whoever was pulling the trigger definitely had a target in mind.

And that target was Caroline.

He didn't intend to let this snake shoot her, and that meant he had to do something now to stop it. Jack pushed her down on the floorboard so he could move to the side of the cruiser where so many of those shots were being aimed. Not that he was especially eager to get closer to the bullets, but he needed to get a visual on the shooter. And he got one, all right.

"He's in the ditch," Jack muttered under his breath.

The ditch, he knew, was deep and extended for miles. Worse, there were ranch trails where someone could have—and likely had—hidden a vehicle.

In this case, the trail was littered with trees and thick underbrush. Plenty of places for a gunman to use for escape. Jack didn't want to let things get that far, though. He needed this person, preferably alive, so he could get answers.

Their attacker was low enough, the high banks of the ditch acting as cover, and only the person's head, shoulders and weapon were visible. He was wearing a ski mask. Jack couldn't even be sure the shooter was a male, but whoever it was had to have some backup weapons because he or she wasn't taking time to reload. There were only a few seconds in between each new round of gunfire.

"Scotty," Jack heard Gunnar say, and there was plenty of concern in the deputy's voice.

Jack soon saw why. Scotty's car door creaked open, and the man tumbled out onto the ground. He was alive, thank God. That was the good news. But even from the twenty or so feet of distance between them, Jack could see the blood on his shirt. Scotty was clutching his chest.

"He needs an ambulance," Caroline blurted out, and that was when Jack realized she'd lifted her head up enough to look out his open door and toward Scotty.

Yeah, he did need an ambulance, badly, but unfortunately, that wasn't going to happen as long as there was active gunfire in the area. The EMTs would likely have been able to hear the shots over the police radio, but Kellan had also texted someone, too. He'd requested both backup from the sheriff's office and the ambulance.

The EMTs could stay back until they got the all clear, but whoever was coming for backup would move in to help. Maybe that would happen before the bullets ripped the cruiser apart.

"There's nothing we can do for Scotty right now," Jack told her.

He pushed Caroline right back down on the floor, but he couldn't help but notice her face. There wasn't a drop of color in it, and her breathing was way too fast. Heaven knew what kind of flashbacks this was triggering for her, and it might be too much for her to handle.

She frantically shook her head. "Whoever's doing this wants me. If we make him think I'll come out there, he might leave cover enough for Kellan, Gunnar or you to get off a shot."

So Caroline wasn't near the panic stage after all. That didn't mean she was thinking straight, though. "I'm not going to let you go out there," Jack warned her.

"I agree. I think this person would just gun me down. Maybe he'd do the same to you, too." Her words rushed out with her frantic breaths. "But we have to do something. Maybe I can call out to him to distract him, to make him think I'm coming out? We can't just sit here."

Jack was thinking that sitting there was their safest option. They could wait for backup. Or at least that was what he believed until the direction of the shots changed again. There was a new target for the gunman.

Scotty.

Hell. Jack saw the bullets kick up the dirt around where Scotty had fallen. He couldn't tell if any of the shots had actually hit the man, but it was possible that would happen.

Kellan and Gunnar used the shift in gunfire to barrel into the cruiser. First, his brother. Then, Gunnar, who immediately started the engine. He pulled the cruiser up, blocking Scotty from the gunman's shots.

Good. That was a start. It protected an injured man who didn't appear to be armed. But, of course, the gunman just started firing at the cruiser again. They couldn't just drive away, either, and leave Scotty unprotected.

The bullets continued to blast into the rear window over Caroline's head, but even over the deafening sound, Jack heard something else. A siren. Another cruiser was coming up the road toward them.

And just like that, the gunfire stopped.

Part of Jack was glad that someone was no longer trying to kill Caroline, but he knew what the silence meant. The guy was getting away.

"Do you see him?" Jack asked Gunnar and Kellan. He was hoping they had a better vantage point from the front scene, but both shook their heads.

"The shooter's probably using the ditch to put some distance between him and us," Kellan concluded.

Yeah, Jack figured the same thing. "I'm going out there," he said.

That got a loud, quick "No!" from Caroline.

"The gunman could be moving so he can get a shot at Scotty," Jack reminded her.

That didn't exactly stop the protest he saw in her eyes, but she didn't say "No" this time. Instead, she whispered, "Be careful."

He would, but Jack didn't take the time to reassure her. That was because he needed to get aim on the gunman before he resurfaced and shot Scotty.

Jack got out of the cruiser, and this time he shut his door in case their attacker came out of the ditch with guns blazing. It would be a suicide mission, with three armed lawmen right there and a backup cruiser just seconds away. Still, desperation made people do stupid things.

Hoping to minimize what anyone could label as stupid, Jack used the cruiser for cover, running to the front end of it and keeping down. Keeping watch, too. And it didn't take him long to see what he'd been expecting.

The ski-masked shooter.

The gunman peered out from the ditch, and he'd moved all right. The guy was now a good fifteen yards from the cruiser. He pivoted, taking aim at Scotty. Just as Jack took aim at him.

Jack fired first.

Not just one shot but two, and as much as he wanted answers, he went for the kill instead.

And he got it.

The shots Jack fired took the guy down, and even though he was certain he hadn't missed, he hurried to the ditch to make sure. Keeping his gun aimed and ready, he pulled up next to the ditch and saw the man sprawled in the mud and water that'd been left by the rain.

The guy was dead. Jack was sure of it. But there was someone who was hopefully still alive.

"Get the ambulance in here now!" Jack shouted to Kellan and Gunnar. He started running toward Scotty, and he prayed he wasn't too late to save him.

Chapter Thirteen

Dead.

That was the one word that kept repeating in her head, and Caroline didn't think it would go away anytime soon. Nor would the images of seeing Scotty's car smashed into that utility pole.

She hadn't actually seen his body. Jack was responsible for that. He'd insisted on her staying in the cruiser while the backup and ambulance arrived. Caroline hadn't fought him on that since she'd known in her heart that Scotty was already dead.

So was the gunman.

That didn't ease her frayed nerves, though. She would still hear the sound of all those gunshots and remember the terror she'd felt when Jack stepped outside the cruiser. Yes, she would definitely recall all of that with every detail. And more. She'd have to deal with the worry that this didn't put an end to the danger.

Even though they didn't have an ID yet on the gunman, Caroline figured he'd been hired to kill her. Whoever had done the hiring had likely covered their tracks. Maybe there'd been mistakes made and some evidence or a money trail left behind, but the odds were this would go down as another attempt to get to her.

Caroline drew in slow, deep breaths as Raylene's sister, Deputy Clarie McNeal, pulled the cruiser to a stop in front of Jack's house. Jack had spent most of the drive from the sheriff's office on the phone and keeping watch, but now that they'd arrived at their destination, his focus would be on her.

Or at least it would be once they were inside.

Caroline needed the long breaths not only to try to calm herself but also to try to level out the effects of the adrenaline. If she didn't, Jack would see the panic that was just beneath the surface, and it would make him worry even more than he already did. And there was no mistake about it—he was worried.

It was Clarie who got out first, and ducking against the rain that was coming down hard, she ran to the door, unlocked it and did the security check to make sure no one had gotten inside. Then she motioned for Jack and Caroline, and they hurried in.

"No ID on the gunman yet," Jack told Caroline as he locked the door and reset the alarm. "But we should know something soon. And there is some good news. Lily's turning over the files from New Beginnings."

Wiping the rain from her face, Caroline nodded. That was potentially good. Or at least it would be if Lily hadn't managed to erase any useful information.

Going with that whole attempt to make him not worry, Caroline steeled herself and didn't dodge his gaze when he looked at her. A wary gaze that was examining her for any signs of emotional trauma.

"I'm okay," she assured him.

Judging from the burst of sound that he made, no way was he buying that. Apparently, she wasn't as good at steeling herself as she'd hoped.

"All right," Caroline amended, "maybe I'm not okay exactly, but we're alive and unharmed. That's better than the alternative. Better than Scotty got." It would have been more effective if her voice hadn't cracked on Scotty's name.

Jack glanced at Clarie, who was in the kitchen, and he took Caroline by the arm, leading her to his bedroom. He shut the door, turned to her and started whatever he was about to say.

"You can't blame yourself for any of this," he insisted. He crammed his hands into his pockets, and he probably didn't know that he had blood on his jeans. Not his blood, but Scotty's.

"My guess is that Scotty hacked into WITSEC files," Jack went on, "and the person who hired him to do that sent a killer after him today. We got caught up in it."

She couldn't disagree with any part of that; she had already come to the same conclusion. Scotty hadn't deserved to die, but he'd obviously gotten involved with a very dangerous person. Caroline didn't doubt the danger, either, because that same person was likely after her.

"When the cops go through Scotty's files and his home office, they might find something," Jack added. He was clearly trying to soothe her, but she was beginning to think that he needed just as much of that TLC as she did.

Caroline went closer to him. She didn't touch him, though. Not with the powder keg of emotions already in place. Touching him, even for comfort, would fire up heat of a different kind.

"When I left the sheriff's office to go find Scotty, I knew the risk," she said. "But I thought that if we could get answers, it'd be worth it. It would have been," Caroline amended, and she cursed when her voice cracked again.

Jack cursed, too, because despite her facade, she was right on the edge. He did reach for her, and he likely would have triggered that heat by pulling her into his arms. However, he didn't get a chance to do that because his phone rang.

"Grace," Jack grumbled when he looked at the screen.

Caroline definitely hadn't expected a call from the woman, but maybe this was a good sign. Perhaps Grace would be able to tell them what'd happened.

Jack dropped any trace of the TLC when he jabbed the answer button on his phone, and he put it on speaker. "Why the hell were you on that road just yards from where Scotty crashed?" Jack demanded.

Caroline had no trouble hearing Grace's sobs and broken breaths. "Scotty called me. He's dead, isn't he?"

"Yeah, he's dead," Jack snapped. If there'd been an award for good bedside manner, he would have lost bigtime. There wasn't a trace of sympathy in his voice. "Now I want you to tell me who killed him."

"I honestly don't know," Grace answered through another sob. Caroline didn't think either the words or the crying was fake.

Jack didn't approve of that answer, and he showed that by swearing. "You need to go to the sheriff's office in Longview Ridge. As a minimum, you're a witness to a crime, but I'm betting you know a whole lot more than that."

"I don't!" Grace practically shouted. "And I'm not going to the cops. If a dirty lawman is doing this, I'll end up dead, just like Scotty. Maybe like Skylar and Nicola. Caroline might believe in you, but I don't, and personally, I think she's a fool to trust you."

With that, Grace ended the call.

Jack tried to call the woman back, of course, but neither of them was surprised when Grace didn't answer.

After he shoved his phone back in his pocket, his hands went on his hips, and his gaze fired to hers. Oh, the anger was there. A giant ball of it, and he didn't seem to know where to aim all that dangerous energy.

"Do you really think you're a fool to trust me?" Jack demanded.

He seemed to be throwing some kind of emotional gauntlet, and she thought that maybe he wouldn't be happy with any answer she gave him. So Caroline just stood there. Waiting. And watching the rising storm. Outside, the rain was now battering the windows. There was a crack of lightning. Thunder.

But the storm inside Jack seemed even more intense.

He turned away from her, but the temper had him whirling back around just as fast.

"You're an idiot, you know that?" Jack jabbed his index finger at her. He wasn't shouting or touching her, but it was close. "I love you more than I've ever loved anything or anybody. Hell, I love you more than anyone's probably ever loved before. So believe it when I tell you that you can trust me. I wouldn't let a killer get near you. That includes someone in my own gene pool."

Caroline swallowed the lump in her throat. "You just called me an idiot."

He winced and somehow managed to make that expression look hot. "You noticed that, huh? I was hoping all the I-love-yous would gloss that over." His eyes went dark and serious. The color of storm clouds now. *"Believe it,"* he repeated, his voice a hoarse whisper.

She had no doubts—none—that the words came straight from his heart. "I believe it."

And since there'd been enough words, whispers and shouts, Caroline grabbed on to a handful of his shirt, eased him to her and showed him just how much she loved him right back.

With a kiss.

JACK HEARD HIMSELF say Caroline's name. It was more breath than sound, and he felt those tight muscles relax in his arms and chest. The relief came as his cheek pressed to hers with his mouth against her ear.

Of course, there would have been a whole lot more relief if she'd told him she loved him. But he could wait until she was ready. Believing in him was enough for now.

They stayed that way, standing there, for several long moments. He'd just taken her the night before, but the ache was already there as if he'd gone much too long without her. She was no doubt feeling some of that ache because she shifted, finding his mouth, and her kiss already had that hungry edge to it.

Jack understood the hunger.

He'd failed at being gentle with her before, and he could already feel a repeat of that. This time though, it was Caroline who was in the driver's seat, and it didn't seem as if she had *gentle* in mind.

"Your clothes are coming off," she said like an oath.

He wasn't about to argue with that, but he did have to get his eyes uncrossed when her hand slid down into his jeans and over his erection. He could hardly protest the maneuver since he'd done the same to her, but that bold move made him want their clothes off sooner than he'd planned.

Caroline pressed him face-first against the wall, like

a cop making an arrest. "I can't think when you're kissing me," she said. "Your mouth should be classified as an illegal substance."

Jack got just a flash of male pride, which went to hell in a handbasket when she yanked off his holster. That went on the dresser. Not too long after that, his shirt landed on the floor.

Apparently, no area was off-limits for her, because Caroline's mouth went to the back of his neck, trailing down to his shoulders. Jack had never considered those to be parts of him that he wanted kissed, but it added a heap of fuel to the already blazing heat.

When he started to turn, to take her into his arms, she held him in place, using the lower part of her body and pressing him even harder against the wall. He felt her moving around, maneuvering, and then the touching continued.

While she kept up those long, lingering kisses, she slipped her hands around to his chest. Her fingers were as thorough as her mouth, and she traced each muscle to his stomach.

Then, lower.

She didn't slide her hand into his jeans this time. Instead, Caroline unzipped him, pushing both his jeans and the boxers off his hips, and she was damn clever doing it, too. And slow. Inch by slow inch. Her left hand skimmed over his butt while her right one took care of the front.

"Your body should be illegal, too," Caroline said in a breathy whisper that hit against his shoulder.

No time for male pride this time. Her fist slid the entire length of him. Then, that fist got even tighter. Her mouth—and yes, her tongue—continued on his shoulder, making slow circles and those maddening kisses.

Jack gritted his teeth and swallowed a groan. As good as it felt, and it felt damn good, he didn't want to finish things this way. He was about to tell Caroline that when she lowered his jeans and boxers and then used her foot to push them even farther down so that Jack could step out of them. The moment he did that, she took hold of his waist and spun him around.

Finally!

Or so he thought. But she dodged a kiss, stepping back from him. He could see the heat in her eyes. Hell, he could feel it. The air was firing between them like lightning bolts.

While facing him, she took hold of his hips, and walking backward, she led him to the bed. They stepped over his shirt, and that was when he saw her panties on the floor. He wasn't sure when she'd taken those off, maybe right before all that sanity-robbing touching when she'd had him against the wall.

Caroline reversed their positions when they reached the bed, and pushed him onto the mattress. He landed on his back, and before he could even blink, she landed on him, straddling him.

The scalding kiss she gave him nearly had him forgetting that she still had on her clothes. Minus the panties. Jack got a quick reminder of it, though, when he finally got his hands on her, and he felt the barrier of her top and skirt. Her skirt had shifted up, though, so he could at least get one of his hands on her bare butt as he fumbled around to yank off her top.

But Caroline put an end to that, too. She levered up on her knees, and in the same motion, she took hold of him again. And then dropped so that he was inside her.

Jack didn't swallow the groan that time. Hell, it was

possible his heart had skipped a whole bunch of beats. Pleasure roared through him. Caroline made sure that wasn't a solo thing, either. She shifted, riding him, taking everything he was more than willing to give her.

She found the rhythm. The right one that would wring out every drop of this, and just when she had him right at the brink, Jack reached between her legs to touch her, to give her a little boost to take her to climax with him. Before he could do that, though, she hauled him up to a sitting position so they were face-to-face.

The kiss came. It wasn't filled with hungry greed this time. This was gentle. Soft.

And whispering his name, Caroline wrapped her arms around him and finished them together.

Chapter Fourteen

Caroline didn't bother wondering if having sex with Jack was yet another mistake. It probably was. Loss of focus and all that. But she refused to regret what had happened and figured Jack was on the same page with her. He certainly wasn't doing anything to move her off him in the bed. In fact, he looked pleasured and satisfied.

It wouldn't last, though.

No. Not for her cowboy lawman.

Soon, very soon, he'd start to see the problems that this sort of intimacy would cause for the investigation. That didn't mean Jack didn't love her. He did. But clearly in his mind, this would put a little tarnish on his badge and a whole lot more tarnish on his judgment. It had to be hard to think straight when feelings ran this hot and deep for someone in his protective custody.

Hoping to stop his guilt trip before it started, Caroline lifted her head and kissed Jack right on that incredible mouth of his. Rolling off him, she landed on her back next to him.

"Just remember that I'm the one who started this round," she said.

His breathing was still a little uneven when he turned

on his side and looked at her. "I sure didn't do anything to stop you."

"It wouldn't have worked if you'd tried," Caroline assured him. "And that's all the whining we're allowed over this." She gave him another kiss—a quick, almost chaste one—and she forced herself off the bed. "I'm getting dressed so I can start doing computer checks and calls to look for Grace. Besides, Clarie might be wondering where we got off to."

"Clarie's smart," Jack grumbled. "She'll figure it out."

True, which would make it awkward when Jack and she came out of the bedroom and faced the deputy. Still, it had to be done because Clarie was no doubt working on the case, as well. She might not approve of them rolling around in the sack while she did the job.

Since her clothes were scattered everywhere, it meant traipsing around the room naked while she gathered them. Jack watched, of course, as if entertained by the peep show. But then he huffed, got up and started doing the same thing.

Caroline certainly got some entertainment of her own by seeing his incredible body flex and move, and she reminded herself that they wouldn't get any work done if she kept gawking at him.

"You do know we're going to have to do something, well, drastic, to draw our attacker out in the open?" she threw out there, knowing it would get his mind back where it needed to be.

Of course, he wouldn't like that word *drastic*, and Jack expressed that dislike with a scowl. Then a huff, which actually softened his expression. "Look, I know you're upset about Scotty's death, but—"

That was as far as he got with his protest before his

phone rang. His jeans were still on the floor, so Jack had to rummage around to locate it.

Caroline didn't exactly breathe easier when she saw Kellan's name on the screen. That was because he could be calling with more bad news. She hurried to finish dressing in case Jack and she had to do something right away. Jack answered the call, and he put it on speaker.

"We got an ID on the dead gunman," Kellan said the moment he was on the line. "The name's probably not going to mean anything to you. Amos Treadwell. He's got a record and reputation for being a spine cracker for loan sharks and other lowlifes."

So just a hired gun. That did nothing to make her feel better about any of this, because a paid killer could have done just as much damage as the person who'd hired him, or more.

"Please tell me that you can link Treadwell to one of our suspects," Jack told his brother.

"I wish." Kellan sounded disgusted that he hadn't been able to do that. "But the CSIs did get something when they went through his pockets. Treadwell had other targets, and he'd written down the names on what he called his 'to-do list.'"

Caroline felt a fresh coil of fear slide through her. "What names?" she heard herself ask.

Kellan took his time answering, and that let her know she wasn't going to like what he was about to say. "Scotty, Grace, Jack, you and me."

No, she didn't like it, but it wasn't much of a surprise. At least the first four weren't, but she hadn't expected Kellan to be on that list. Obviously, neither had

Jack, because his now tight jaw muscles went to war with each other.

"Why would Treadwell plan to kill you?" Jack demanded.

She had no trouble hearing the long breath that Kellan took before he answered. "The person who hired Treadwell probably thinks Caroline has spilled all by now and that you spilled it to me." Kellan paused, cursed. "The person could go after Gemma, too."

Or anyone else in Jack's family. That could include his partner, friends. The list could go on and on.

"I've put a reserve deputy on Gemma," Kellan added a moment later, "and I'm heading home right now. Eli and Owen are doing the same."

Caroline filled in the blanks on what Kellan *wasn't* saying. He couldn't keep this level of protection going for long. Eli and Owen had jobs to do along with their families to protect. Their attacker could just wait them out. Maybe wait even long enough until their guards were down and then go after them when they didn't expect it.

Mercy.

They had to do something, now, to put an end to it so they could all get on with their lives. Especially Owen and Eli, since their families included babies who needed protecting.

"I've been mulling over a plan," Caroline said.

As she'd expected, her comment caused some concern followed by anger to flash in Jack's eyes. She figured that if she could see Kellan, he'd have a similar expression. That meant she was going to have to do a hard sell to convince them that what she had in mind could work.

Probably.

But she would keep the word *probably* to herself. They'd have enough doubts without her adding more.

"Both of you know we need to do something to go ahead and draw out this person," Caroline continued. "Our attacker seems to believe that I know something. Something that would incriminate him or her. So why not put it out there that I'm remembering more details of what Eric said when he kidnapped me? I could be bait."

That, of course, didn't go over well. Jack cursed and shook his head. Kellan grumbled some of the same profanity.

"Just let me finish," she said, speaking over them. "Word could get out that I'm going to the Serenity Inn to meet with a therapist or counselor. Someone who can help me use the place to recall those final details that will help us figure out who Eric actually called that night and what he said to him or her."

"The killer won't go for that," Jack concluded, but she knew that he'd said that more out of worry for her than any doubt over the workability of the plan.

"He or she will, if word gets out," Caroline argued. "And we can use Grace to do that."

Jack huffed again. "Grace won't even answer her phone."

"No, but I'm pretty sure she'll read a text. We can ask her to leak that I'll be at the Serenity Inn. Tonight," she added, though Caroline cast an uneasy glance at the window. "If Grace is in on the plan to murder us, then she'll get the info to the right person. To the person who wants us dead. If she's innocent, then she can help us with the leak so we can lure out the killer."

The curtains and blinds were closed, but she could hear the rain battering against the glass. It wouldn't exactly be a good night to go to the old, abandoned hotel, but enduring the weather would be the least of their problems.

No huff from Jack this time, but he gave her a very flat look. "Our attacker could just send another hired thug."

Caroline nodded, knowing that was a strong possibility. The proof of that was the now dead gunman.

"We weren't expecting the other attacks," she explained, "but if we know this one is coming, we can be ready for it. Instead of killing any henchman who shows up, we can take him alive. Maybe shoot him with a tranquilizer gun instead of bullets. After we have him, we can make some kind of deal to get him to talk."

Jack certainly didn't jump on that, either, but she was hoping that once he got over his emotional objection, he would see it could work.

"What makes you think you can trust Grace?" Jack demanded. "What if she shows up and tries to kill you?"

"I'm not sure I can trust her, not completely, but that doesn't matter. If it's Grace who comes to the inn, then you can take her into custody and get her to tell you what she knows about Scotty's death." She paused. "But if she gets out the word, then the real killer or his hired gun might show up. It's worth a try."

Judging from the swear words that poured out of him, Jack didn't agree with her. "I don't want you at the inn," he snapped.

Caroline nodded, knowing he would say that. "I don't especially want to be there, either." Not with all the horrible things that had happened to her. There was the possibility of flashbacks. Heck, there was also the risk of a full-blown panic attack that would pretty much put her out of commission in a fight. "But we can't let this danger and the attacks go on."

"She's right about that," Kellan said before Jack could spout what would have almost certainly been more arguments. "It's dangerous for too many people. I can't protect everyone that this snake might target. He or she is desperate. That's obvious. Maybe because we're getting close to finding out what really happened that night Dad was murdered. A plan like this could be the tipping point to get us that truth."

"Yeah, and it could be the tipping point to getting Caroline shot," Jack fired back. But then he groaned.

Caroline went to him, looked him straight in the eyes. "This could end the danger in just a few hours," she reminded him. Then, she played dirty by adding, "We'd be able to get on with our lives."

Of course, Jack was ready for that to happen. Ready for them to be a couple again. To not have to look over their shoulders to make sure a hired gun didn't have them in his sight.

"Option two," she went on when Jack and Kellan didn't say anything. "I leave Longview Ridge. I disappear. Not through WITSEC or any other way that my location can be hacked or traced. And once I'm gone, none of you will be in danger."

Oh, that brought the storm straight back to Jack's narrowed eyes. "No," he said through clenched teeth. "I'm not losing you again."

Once more, it was exactly the answer she'd expected. Kellan voiced a version of the same by just saying, "You can forget doing that."

Caroline hadn't exactly expected them to agree. Nor did she want to leave Jack. But she'd offered it to give them a choice—which really wasn't a choice at all. So maybe now they'd see that her plan of using Grace was the only way to go.

Jack shook his head again. "What if we have Grace leak that you'll be at the inn first thing in the morning with the therapist? That would give us more time to get everything in place and maybe come up with something better." But almost immediately he waved that off. "It'd give the killer more time, too, and that's something we don't want."

"True." Caroline went even closer, until her body was right against his. "Jack, we need to text Grace and set this all up. We need to do this."

Silence was his reply, but despite it, she could practically hear Jack thinking. Trying to figure out a different way. One that didn't involve her. But other than her walking out of his life, he wouldn't be able to come up with anything that didn't put her in the mix.

Because she was at the center of it.

As long as she drew breath, the killer would come. Caroline just wanted that to happen on their terms and not the killer's.

"Well?" Kellan prompted when the silence dragged on.

Jack hesitated several more seconds before he scrubbed his hand over his face. "Okay. Let's get started."

JACK HAD SO many bad feelings about this, and those feelings came at him like a tornado. He didn't know which one he could latch on to and try to fix, because the whole plan was whirling around in his head and twisting up his insides.

The text had gone out to Grace, and the woman had actually responded right away, saying that she was on board with leaking the information, and that she wanted to help catch the person who'd murdered her friend Scotty. The woman assured them that she'd get the fake news to all three of their main suspects: Lily, Kingston and Zeller. That was good if the leak would actually lure out the killer or his hired gun. That was also good if they could trust Grace, but Jack wasn't sure on either of those counts.

Unlike Caroline.

He wasn't certain how she managed it, but she looked confident and as tough as nails. For the first time since she'd gotten back her memory, he didn't see fear in her eyes. Ironic, since this was the time when fear was plenty warranted. Too many unknowns. Too many things to go wrong. And here she could be within an hour of facing down someone who wanted her dead.

She sat across the dining room table from them, listening while Kellan went over the details. She wasn't nibbling on her bottom lip. Her hands weren't trembling. And she even gave Jack a smile when their gazes met.

Oh, man.

He hated putting Caroline in this position, and it was a potentially dangerous position despite Kellan's and his measures to keep her as safe as possible. One of those precautions was for her to wear a Kevlar vest beneath her clothes. Kellan, Clarie and he would, too, but that wasn't going to protect any of them if the killer or hired guns went with shots to the head. That was why once they arrived at the inn, they'd have to move fast to get Caroline inside.

Kellan's phone dinged with a text message, and he gave Jack a nod. "Gunnar says there's still no activity in or around the inn."

That wasn't a surprise, since the killer likely wouldn't

have had time to get there yet. Unlike Gunnar and Deputy Manuel Garcia. Before Jack had even sent Grace the text, Manuel and Gunnar had gone to the inn to make sure it was vacant. That way, the killer couldn't get a jump on them and maybe set explosives or some other kind of trap.

Gunnar and Manuel had searched through each of the dilapidated rooms and around the grounds to make sure there'd be no surprises. After the two deputies had done that, they'd parked their vehicle on a hidden ranch trail where they could keep watch. They were armed with both tranq guns and their service weapons, with the tranquilizers being their first option so they could take the person alive. It wasn't foolproof—someone could still sneak by them on foot, but at least there would be backup nearby in case something went wrong.

And yes, there was a good chance something would indeed go wrong.

Kellan was right about the killer being desperate, and that increased the risk that the person might do something stupid. Stupid enough to try attacking Caroline with lawmen around. Jack didn't know exactly what the killer might do, but they had to be prepared for any-and everything.

At both Caroline's and Jack's insistence, Kellan would be going to his place with Gemma. No way did Jack want this plan to backfire and have the killer go after someone in his family and hold them hostage. That would give the killer plenty of bargaining power to try to get to Caroline.

"Are we ready to do this?" Caroline asked.

Jack couldn't come up with a reason to delay; they had to hurry this along. He wanted Caroline inside the inn before their attacker had a chance to get there first. Of course, if that did happen, then Gunnar would alert them, and Jack could get Caroline out of harm's way while they dealt with the snake that'd made their lives a living hell.

"Be safe," Kellan said, giving them one last look before he headed outside.

Jack didn't waste any time. He grabbed his equipment bag and got Caroline and Clarie out to the cruiser. The rain had slacked up some, but he'd checked the forecast and knew they could get drizzle on and off all night. He doubted that would keep a killer away, but it would make things uncomfortable for Gunnar and Manuel, who were outside in this weather.

"This is your last chance to change your mind," Jack told Caroline the moment they were in the cruiser.

She immediately shook her head. "You know this is something we have to do."

He wasn't sure of that at all. Yes, he was well aware that the threats couldn't continue. Especially since the dead gunman had been planning on going after Kellan and Grace. The person who'd paid him for that could just turn around and hire someone else to carry through on that to-do list.

Clarie drove, and Jack sat with Caroline in the back seat. Even though it was nearly dark now, he continued to keep watch. They'd also had a couple of the ranch hands patrol the road to make sure no one had pulled off or was lying in wait for them.

More precautions.

And Jack took yet one more. He slid a backup weapon from his equipment bag and handed it to Caroline. If he'd seen any indications that she wasn't comfortable with the gun, he would have rethought his offer. But she took it right away.

"Obviously, it's not a tranq gun," he explained, "but you might need it if someone gets past Gunnar and Manuel."

"Thanks," she said. "By the way, I do know how to use it, and Lucille taught me a lot of self-defense moves."

Hell, he prayed it didn't come down to that, and he forced himself to believe that the best-case scenario would happen. That their attacker would rush to the inn and they could catch him or her.

Even though it was only a few miles, it seemed to take an eternity to get to the inn, and Jack's concerns continued to snowball with each passing second. However, he didn't see or hear anything to make him tell Clarie to turn around and go back to the ranch.

When Clarie reached the inn, she pulled up as close as she could to the wide front porch, and Jack leaned down a little so he could look up at the place. Once it had been a mansion. A showcase for someone who'd had lots and lots of money. When the rich owner had passed away, his heirs had turned it into an inn, a business that had ultimately failed, and they'd let it go when they couldn't pay the taxes. So it had stood abandoned, empty and neglected for years. That was why there was definitely nothing welcoming about it now.

"Talk about creepy," Clarie grumbled.

Yeah, that was the right word for it. Most of the windows had been boarded up, and the ones that hadn't been were just dark holes of jagged, broken glass.

The grounds hadn't fared much better with time and lack of care. Once, there'd been gardens, but now it was an overgrown jumble of trees, underbrush and weeds. Some vines coiled out from that tangle and had snaked their way up the brick-and-stone facade.

Caroline was studying the place, too, but Jack figured

it was more than just creepy for her. It was the place of her own personal nightmares. Where she'd come too darn close to dying over a year ago, when Eric had kidnapped her and brought her here.

After Jack gave Clarie a nod, the three of them got out and hurried up the steps and inside. Nothing was welcoming here, either. Just an empty shell with scarred wood floors and walls with holes and graffiti.

Broken glass was scattered everywhere, and they would hopefully use that to their advantage. When Gunnar and Manuel had gone through the place, they'd kicked up piles of it next to all the doors and the unboarded windows. That way, if an intruder came in, they should be able to hear when he or she stepped on the shards.

Since the killer was supposed to believe that Caroline was there to meet a therapist, Jack and Clarie started setting the scene. He stayed right by Caroline's side while he took out the flashlights. Not for them to carry. No, he would put these in the foyer and the adjoining room so it would seem as if that was where they were.

It wouldn't be.

"This way," Jack said, leading Caroline and Clarie away from the lights.

The plan was to take them to the first room off the hall behind the winding staircase, but Caroline stopped and glanced down.

There was a bloodstain on the foyer floor.

Not fresh, thank God.

Nor was it Caroline's.

It belonged to Gemma, who'd also been attacked here over a year ago. The memory of his father, who had been murdered that night, gave Jack another sucker punch of grief. Even though Gemma had survived the attack, seeing that bloodstain brought it all back, and he was certain it was even worse for Caroline. She'd nearly been killed that night, too.

Jack pushed that all aside and got them moving to the room where they'd wait this out. It wasn't ideal since it did have a window, but at least this one was boarded up. Plus, if things went to hell in a handbasket, they could move into one of the other dozen or so rooms that fed off the hall.

The three of them stood there a moment so their eyes could adjust to the near darkness. Some of the milky light from the foyer made its way here. Just enough to create some spooky shadows and show dust motes floating like little ghosts around the room.

It was no wonder that some folks called the place haunted and only came here when dares, too much alcohol or both played into the mix.

"There's a blanket in the equipment bag," he told Caroline, knowing she wasn't going to use it. She didn't.

Caroline went to the window with Clarie, each taking a side so they could peer out through the cracks in the boards. Jack took up position by the door so he could see not only the hall but the front door.

And the wait began.

Even though Grace had gotten out the "leak" fast, it didn't mean their attacker had managed to get things ready to come to the inn. But that thought had no sooner crossed his mind when his phone dinged with a text message. A message that had Jack cursing under his breath.

"Gunnar spotted someone on the road," Jack relayed to Caroline and Clarie. "The person's on foot and headed our way."

Chapter Fifteen

Caroline forced herself to breathe normally. Well, as normally as she could manage, considering this was possibly the showdown that she'd been preparing herself for.

And the one that she'd feared.

She wasn't immune to the panic that wanted to explode inside her, but she reminded herself that this was necessary. It would be impossible for her to put the past behind her if she was still dealing with it. And she felt in her gut that the attacks were connected to her past.

Specifically, to Eric.

Either someone thought Eric had spilled secrets to her, or else they were just tying up loose ends that they believed Eric had left behind. Lily and Zeller fit with the first theory. Kingston with the second.

"Did Gunnar spot a man or woman?" Caroline asked Jack. Even though she whispered her question, it practically echoed in the empty room.

"He's not sure." Jack whispered, too, but there was an angry edge to his voice. "Gunnar said he only got a glimpse of someone dressed all in black before the person ducked off the road and into some trees."

There were certainly a lot of trees, and they dotted the landscape all the way from the road to what was left of the old gardens surrounding the inn. Someone could use them for cover, but eventually the attacker would have to come out into the open to make it inside.

Well, maybe.

It was possible to get into the house by crawling through the underbrush at the back, but it would still take some maneuvering.

"You want me to move to one of the front rooms so I can try to see this person?" Clarie asked.

Jack stayed quiet a moment, obviously giving her question some thought. "No. Gunnar and Manuel have good positions. They should be able to see if anyone approaches the inn, and if need be, one of them can move closer to get a better shot with the tranq gun."

Caroline knew it was the *should be* that was eating away at Jack. He wanted absolutes when it came to her safety, but that wasn't going to happen. The best they could do right now was to have a good shot at putting an end to this.

"What kind of range is there on the tranq gun they're using?" Clarie asked a moment later.

"They actually have tranq rifles, and the range on those is supposed to be 210 feet. But Gunnar didn't think it was smart to risk a shot that far out. He'll want closer."

Caroline agreed with that. It wouldn't be like firing an automatic or semiautomatic, and if they missed on the first shot, they'd have to manually reload. That could give the person time to get away. However, Kellan had assured them that Gunnar and Manuel were both good marksmen with steady hands. And if they failed, then they'd go for a nonkill shot with their regular weapons.

There was also a possible problem with the tranq itself. It wouldn't have an instant effect, and it could take several minutes to incapacitate the person. Still, the drug should make it a whole lot harder for their visitor to try to kill them. Plus, as soon as Gunnar or Manuel fired the tranq, they'd move in to apprehend.

"Zeller's stupid if he doesn't smell a trap," Jack muttered just loud enough for Caroline to hear.

That, too, wasn't setting well with him. Jack didn't want to think of a fellow lawman being at the center of this, but it was possible. Zeller had the means and opportunity. He had a possible motive, as well, if he was trying to cover up his involvement in the sex-trafficking ring.

But Jack was right that Zeller should be able to smell a trap.

After all, the marshal had personal knowledge of her case and had almost certainly gone over every record of hers that existed. He might know that there were no other memories for her to recover. However, she was hoping he had enough doubts about her, about what she'd possibly remembered, that he would take the risk of coming here.

Of course, it was just as likely that he could have hired someone to do his dirty work, but she didn't want to think about that now. If Zeller was guilty, he would come, and then Jack could arrest him.

Caroline peeked out through the sliver of space in between the boards and tried to get a glimpse of this possible attacker. Nothing. She could definitely see some trees and vines, but not a person. Listening didn't help, either, because the only things she could clearly hear were the patter of the rain and her own heartbeat in her ears.

Jack's phone dinged again, the sound shooting through the room and nearly causing Caroline to gasp. Clearly, she didn't have her emotions under control as much as she wanted.

"It's from Gunnar," Jack said after giving Caroline a quick look. No doubt to make sure she was still okay. Just because she hadn't gasped out loud, it didn't mean Jack hadn't sensed her nerves. "He got another glimpse of the person, and he's pretty sure it's a woman."

Maybe it was Lily, and if so, it meant she hadn't sent a henchman but planned on doing the job herself. Of course, that didn't mean the woman didn't have hired guns in the area.

"Gunnar couldn't tell if the woman was armed," Jack went on, reading the text. She saw him click the button to set his phone to vibrate, probably so the killer wouldn't be alerted by the sound of any other incoming messages. "But she just ducked into some oaks on the east side of the inn."

Caroline wasn't exactly sure which way east was, but she turned her attention back to the window in case the woman came that way. Behind her, she heard the soft clicks of Jack texting.

"I told Gunnar to try to get closer to the woman so he can take her or get a better shot," Jack explained. "But Manuel's staying in place so he has a bird's-eye view of the house and grounds. This person might be a decoy, and I don't want someone else sneaking up on us."

A decoy would definitely be something their attacker would try. He or she had never come at them head-on and likely wouldn't want to do that now. The person was basically a coward, and that played into the mental profile she'd done. So yes, they needed to expect some kind of trickery or deception, and with the sprawling grounds around the inn, this woman could be drawing their attention while someone—maybe another hired gun—slipped closer to them.

She looked over her shoulder and saw Jack move out of the doorway and glance toward both ends of the hall. He must not have seen or heard anything suspicious, because he stepped back in.

Caroline looked outside again, trying to pick through the darkness and the rain. Willing herself to see something.

And she did.

Thanks to a bolt of lightning, Caroline saw the blur of motion next to one of the massive oaks.

"Did you see that?" Clarie immediately asked.

"I did." And Caroline was almost positive that it was a woman. One who was no longer in sight.

"Clarie, switch places with me for a second," Jack told the deputy, and Clarie immediately hurried across the room to take up position by the door as Jack came to the window.

"She's behind the center tree in that cluster," Caroline explained, motioning in the direction where she'd spotted the person. "I didn't get a look at her face, but I think she's wearing a ski mask."

Which would make sense. Not only would it conceal her identity, but it would make her face less likely to stand out in the darkness. Ditto for the black clothes. If it hadn't been for the lightning, Caroline might have missed the figure.

Jack continued to keep watch. Waiting. And Mother Nature cooperated with another lightning flash. It lit up the area by the trees for just a second. Enough for them to see that no one was there. Either the woman had moved or she had stayed behind cover.

Caroline soon got the answer as to which had happened.

Despite the rain and her own ragged breath, Caroline

heard the sound. So did Jack and Clarie. Their heads whipped up in its direction. It had come not from the trees but rather the back of the inn. And it was something they'd been listening for.

The sound of someone stepping on broken glass.

An intruder was inside the house.

JACK SILENTLY CURSED, bracing himself for a fight.

He'd known all along that it would be possible for someone to get in the house without the deputies or anyone else seeing them, but he had hoped that wouldn't happen. Now that it had, he needed to do something about it.

He motioned for Clarie to switch places with him again and for her and Caroline to stay in place at the window. That would accomplish two things. The women could continue to keep watch in case this intruder was a decoy, and Caroline would keep out of the most probable line of fire.

Because Jack was certain the person who'd just stepped on that glass would soon be heading to the lights in the foyer.

Clarie took out her phone to send a text to Gunnar. It was part of the plan they'd worked out while still back at his house. She would let Gunnar know about the problem, and then either Gunnar or Manuel would move in closer to assist. The other would stay back to watch for anyone else.

Jack didn't move. Not yet. He just stood there, waiting for the next sound, and he didn't have to wait long.

More footsteps.

At first, those footsteps crunched over the broken glass, but then that stopped. It didn't mean the intruder had left or had even quit moving. It only meant the glass was no longer in the path to alert Jack.

Dragging in a long breath, Jack tightened his grip on his gun and leaned slightly out the doorway so they could start the next phase of this trap. After all, they'd lured the killer or a henchman here with the news that Caroline was trying to recover all her memories. It was best if he played along with that for now.

"Just take a deep breath, Caroline," he said, trying to make it seem as genuine as possible. "Try to clear your mind and think about what else you heard in that phone call. What did the caller say to Eric?"

With his lines delivered, he motioned for Caroline to jump into this.

"I'm okay." Caroline's shaky voice definitely didn't mesh with the strong woman who was keeping watch out the window. "And I do think I remember. Yes, I can hear the person speaking…"

She purposely let her words trail off. Also as planned.

Jack listened for more of the footsteps. Nothing. But Clarie gave him the thumbs-up to indicate that one of the deputies was moving closer to the house. Since Jack hadn't heard her phone ding with the message, Clarie had likely silenced it.

"Can you tell if it's a man or woman talking to Eric?" Jack asked to keep his therapy conversation going with Caroline.

Again, she mumbled her response, but she strung it out for a few seconds. Hopefully, the intruder would think she was having some kind of revelation and would get there fast to try to silence her. Jack didn't want this dragging on any longer than necessary, and he could stop the person as soon as she came into view.

"There's someone else out there," Caroline whispered.

Even though her voice had been barely loud enough for him to hear, those words roared through his head. "Is it Gunnar?" he mouthed.

"No. Someone else. I think it's the same woman I saw before. She's still out there by the trees."

So that meant it was a henchman in the house, so maybe the fake therapy conversation with Caroline didn't matter. If this thug had orders to kill, then he wouldn't care what they were saying. Wouldn't care if Caroline remembered anything or not, since the plan was for her to be dead soon.

Jack wasn't going to let that plan happen.

Clarie sent another text. Probably to Gunnar again so she could give him a heads-up. No way did they want the deputy walking into an ambush, since the woman by the tree could gun him down. Of course, Gunnar would be looking for exactly that sort of thing.

Jack finally heard another footstep, closer this time, and he considered doing more of the fake conversation with Caroline. He decided against it, though, in case the intruder could use his voice to pinpoint their location in the house.

Another footstep. Then another. The person was coming closer, and Jack knew it wouldn't be long before the person made it to the foyer. It seemed to him that the intruder was making a beeline toward those flashlights.

"The woman outside is moving," Caroline whispered. "And I see Gunnar."

Jack wasn't sure if that was a good thing or not. Certainly Gunnar had gotten Clarie's warning, but the deputy might not have seen the woman.

Or she might have seen him.

Jack considered having Clarie send Gunnar another warning text, but it was too risky with the intruder this close to them. And the person was indeed close. Even though there were no more footsteps, Jack could hear some kind of movement. Maybe he or she was getting his or her own weapon ready to launch the attack.

It felt as if everything went still. As if everyone and everything were holding their breath. Waiting for something to happen.

And it did.

There was a plinking sound. Something metal had dropped to the floor.

At first, Jack wondered if the intruder had let something slip and fall. Maybe his weapon. But he soon realized that it wasn't an accident.

Jack caught the first scent of the tear gas.

Chapter Sixteen

Caroline had had no trouble hearing the sound of something falling on the old wood floor of the inn. But she didn't know what it was and had no idea what had suddenly put that troubled look on Jack's face.

But she soon found out.

"Tear gas," Clarie managed to say at the exact moment the deputy began coughing.

Almost immediately, Caroline felt her eyes, nose and throat start to burn, and if it truly was tear gas, she figured it wouldn't be long before it basically incapacitated them. It wouldn't knock them unconscious, but they wouldn't be able to fight if they couldn't breathe. If they couldn't see.

And it was quickly getting to that point.

"This way," Jack snapped, and he tipped his head toward the hall. He had his left arm crooked and pressed to his face while he continued to grip his weapon in his right hand.

Both Caroline and Clarie rushed away from the window and toward him. When she looked out into the hall, she saw the wisps of the white fog. Yes, definitely tear gas. And as bad as it was right now, they weren't getting the full impact yet. That fog was rolling their way.

But where was the intruder who'd likely set all of this in motion?

She didn't see any signs of anyone, but it was possible the person had put on a gas mask. If so, he or she could come through that fog after them.

Jack's eyes had to be burning like fire—hers certainly were—but his gaze still slashed all around. A few seconds crawled by, and then he motioned for Clarie and her to follow him. The three of them barreled out into the hall with Jack in front of her and Clarie behind.

They ran fast but didn't go far, only a couple of yards, before Jack ducked into one of the other rooms, and he shut the door behind them. Caroline soon saw why he'd chosen this one. There were no boards on the window, something he'd probably learned from Gunnar and Manuel when they'd done their initial search of the place. No boards would mean both easy access for an intruder and escape for them.

Jack hurried to the window and threw it open. "Keep watch," he said, his voice rough and raw.

Caroline knew there was a good possibility that a would-be killer was waiting for them out there. That could have been part of the plan all along. Get them out so they could be gunned down. But the primal part of her brain was screaming for her to escape from the tear gas and get some fresh air.

Jack went out the window first. The moment his feet were on the ground, he glanced around again. He was looking for anyone who might be there to attack, but in the same motion, he took hold of Caroline's arm. He pulled her out with him, pushing her against the side of the inn. Keeping in front of her to protect her.

She dragged in a long, much-needed breath. Then another. And she blinked hard to clear away the remnants of the tear gas. The rain helped, but her eyes were still stinging and she couldn't see clearly.

Clarie climbed out of the window then, landing on her feet right next to Caroline, but they didn't stay put. Maybe because Jack believed the intruder would be coming to that room, to that window.

Keeping close to the wall, they hurried through the weeds and underbrush. It wasn't easy. The ground was soft from the rain, and Caroline's shoes bogged in the mud while the bushes scraped and poked at her. Still, it was better than being in there with the tear gas.

They ran, weaving in and out of the ground clutter until they were at the edge of the porch that stretched all the way across the front of the inn. They dropped down next to what was left of the porch railing. Not far from the cruiser. But to get to it, they'd have to go out into the open.

"Stay down," Jack whispered to her, and he maneuvered Caroline behind one of the overgrown shrubs while he peered around the corner at the porch. "I don't see anyone," he added.

Good. Maybe they'd get a few minutes to regroup and recover. They desperately needed that, and then maybe they could pinpoint the location of the person who'd gone inside.

As her eyes and mind started to clear, Caroline got a horrible thought. What if the person was already gone? It was possible that he or she had already escaped, maybe because they believed the tear-gas ploy had failed. If so, then Jack and she were right back where they started— without any proof as to who wanted her dead.

"I'll text Gunnar and let him know our location," Clarie whispered, taking out her phone.

While she did that, Caroline got as good of a grip as she could manage on the gun that Jack had given her. Even though her hand was weak, she needed to be able to help if it came down to a fight, and everything inside her said that was exactly what was going to happen.

"Gunnar lost sight of the woman by the trees," Clarie relayed when she got a response to her text. "He's going to look for her while he makes his way here to us."

Caroline welcomed the backup, but she knew it would also pose a big problem. They wouldn't be able to fire if they heard or saw something, because they wouldn't want to risk hitting Gunnar. Plus, this meant Manuel was alone and without backup. The deputy wouldn't be a primary target for the attacker, but he was still at risk.

Jack glanced back at her, their gazes connecting for a moment, and she saw the fear on his face. Not fear for himself but for her. Caroline wished she could do something to assure him that it would be okay, but she wasn't certain it would be.

And that cut to the bone.

Once again, Jack was in trouble because of her.

Maybe she should have just gone off on her own, far away from him. But while that would have been the smart thing to do, it would have crushed both their hearts. She didn't want him hurt, or worse, but at least they were together.

"I'm going to get in the cruiser and drive it over here," Jack said. "I'll get as close as I can. Wait here with Caroline," he added to Clarie.

But Caroline was already shaking her head before he even finished. "You can't go out there. If this person had tear gas, you know he'll have a gun. He'll be watching the cruiser."

Jack didn't disagree with any of that. He couldn't. However, the look he gave her let her know that he was going to do it anyway. Maybe because he felt it was the only option they had.

"We can wait for Gunnar," Caroline tried, though it wasn't much of an argument. They could be attacked before the deputy made it to them, and he had his hands full looking for the woman. If they managed to capture her, it could possibly give them as many answers as catching the person who'd used that tear gas on them.

Jack levered himself up, and he gave her one last look. A dozen things passed between them. A silent conversation that Caroline wished she could have said aloud.

She had so many things to say to him.

"Be careful" was the only thing she managed before he moved away.

Keeping low, Jack left the meager cover of the shrubs and started for the cruiser. Like their trek from the window, it wouldn't be easy. He'd have to deal with the soggy ground along with the rocks and tangled underbrush.

Clarie moved in front of her, protecting her as Jack had done, but Caroline kept her eyes on Jack until he disappeared behind what was left of a hedge. She maneuvered herself up so she could try to see him, and that was when she heard the sound behind her.

Caroline pivoted, bringing up her gun.

But it was already too late.

JACK WAS ONLY a few yards away from the cruiser when the front door of the inn opened and the tear-gas canister came shooting out.

Hell. Not again.

He only got a glimpse of the person who'd launched it, someone wearing black clothes and a mask. But whoever it was immediately stepped back, using the darkness and the white cloud of gas to hide behind.

"Caroline," Jack said on an oath. He couldn't see Clarie or her, but he figured this was some kind of ploy to get to her.

And it could work.

Jack had a fast debate with himself about getting into the cruiser so he could use it to get closer to the women and give them some cover. But with the uneven ground and some large landscape rocks, he could get stuck. If that happened, he might be too late to save them.

Cursing, he turned around and started running to get back to them, but the gas stung at his eyes like acid. Plus, even though he'd only gotten a few whiffs of it, he was already finding it hard to breathe. It had to be a lot worse for Caroline and Clarie. They were right there, next to where the canister had gone off, so they were no doubt getting the brunt of it.

With that thought racing through his head, Jack cut through the same shrubs and weeds he'd just trampled through so he could make his way back to them. He seriously doubted that their attacker had simply tossed that canister just to make them more miserable than they already were. No. This was some kind of ploy—Jack could feel that in his gut.

He could hear the women coughing. That was a good sign because it meant they were alive, but their instincts would be to run. To get as far away from the gas as possible. That would take them out into the open where they could be gunned down, and they wouldn't even be able to see their attacker.

Jack tried to keep watch around him. Hard to do, but he kept pressing. Kept moving. And his heart went to his knees when he reached the side of the porch and didn't see either Caroline or Clarie. They'd moved.

But where?

The weather didn't cooperate as he listened for them. The sky unzipped, the rain pounding down on him, making it hard to hear. It would clear the air, but it wouldn't happen nearly fast enough.

Jack kept running, and he finally heard the coughing again. No sounds of a struggle with a would-be killer, thank God, and he needed to make it to them to keep it that way.

He stayed close to the wall of the inn, but that meant checking each window to make sure he wasn't about to be ambushed when he went past it. He didn't see anyone. That was the good news. The bad news was that Caroline and Clarie had likely moved to the back of the building.

From where the intruder had gotten inside.

The person could be there, waiting.

Caroline and Clarie were armed, he reminded himself, and he hung on to that thought while he kept moving.

Now it was the rain that was stinging his eyes, and somehow the tear gas was still making its way to him. There was some gas coming out of the inn, too, which Jack discovered when he hurried past the window where Clarie, Caroline and he had escaped the first canister. Even though he doubted they would go back inside with that tear-gas fog, he made a quick glimpse inside.

No one.

He could no longer hear any coughing or other sounds

of movement, and he hoped that was a good sign. That Clarie and Caroline had managed to find some clear air and a safe place to take cover.

Jack considered texting Clarie to let her know he was nearby, but he decided against that. If they were hiding from an attacker, he didn't want to give away their location. Besides, Clarie knew that Gunnar was also out here, somewhere, so she wouldn't pull the trigger without making sure it wasn't one of them.

He took another step and cursed when he nearly tripped over something. Not something, Jack quickly realized.

Someone.

It was a woman, and she was in a crumpled heap at his feet.

That sent his heart rate into a gallop, and he felt the cold fear ripple over his skin. No. Please. Not Caroline.

Jack dropped to his knees, and he forced himself to rein in his emotions. At least he tried to do that. It was nearly impossible to think of the woman he loved being hurt. Or worse. To think of her dead.

But it wasn't Caroline.

He could see that once he managed to wipe the rain from his eyes so he could get a better look. It was Clarie. And she was breathing. Thank God for that, but she wasn't okay. There was blood on her head and in her hair, and since there was a metal pipe next to her, Jack assumed that was the weapon that'd been used to assault her.

Where was Caroline?

Jack's gaze fired all around, but he didn't see her, and everything inside him was telling him he had to get to her now. Still, he sent a quick text to Gunnar to let the deputy know Clarie's location and that she needed medical help—fast. He hated leaving her there alone, but whoever had done this to her now had Caroline. Jack was sure of that.

Using his forearm to push aside the sopping wet shrubs, Jack hurried toward the back of the inn. He tried to listen for any sounds she might make. But he heard nothing. That certainly didn't tamp down his fears.

When his phone vibrated with a text message, he glanced down at the screen and saw Gunnar's response. I'm on my way to Clarie now.

Good. That would be one less thing on Jack's mind, but he said a quick prayer that Clarie's injuries wouldn't be critical. With an attacker on the loose, it could be a while before they could get an ambulance in here for her.

Jack pushed through another cluster of overgrown shrubs, and he finally saw the edge of the back porch. The pressure clamped around his heart, though, when there was still no sign of Caroline. Hell. Had the person who'd tossed that tear gas managed to get away with her in tow?

He plowed his way through more of the weeds, and running now, he made it to the porch.

And there she was.

Not alone.

Not safe, either.

Caroline was on the porch, and despite the darkness, Jack could see that the color had drained from her face. With good reason. Because there was someone standing behind her.

Someone with a knife to her throat.

"I'm sorry," Caroline said. There was a trickle of blood

running down the side of her head and more blood on her sleeve. "Because of the tear gas, I didn't see him in time."

Jack pushed aside her apology for something that wasn't her fault, and he focused on the "him" who was holding Caroline. Definitely a man. Jack could tell from his size despite most of his body being concealed. The coward was hiding behind Caroline.

Who was it?

Was it just another hired gun who'd been sent to kill them?

Jack couldn't tell, because the guy was wearing a gas mask. Not for long, though. Using his free hand, he peeled off the mask, tossing it onto the porch, and flashed a smile.

"Hello, Jack," Kingston said. "Caroline and I have been waiting for you."

FROM THE MOMENT Kingston had come out of the shadows and clubbed Clarie on the head, Caroline had known it would come down to this. Kingston wanted her dead, but he hadn't killed her when he'd hit her with the metal pipe because he'd first wanted to use her to lure out Jack. Kingston wouldn't have been able to use a dead woman to get himself in a position to murder both Jack and her.

And it had worked.

Jack had a gun, and to the best of her knowledge, Kingston only had a knife now that he'd discarded the pipe, but Jack wouldn't have a clean shot with Kingston using her as a human shield.

"Is Clarie all right?" she asked, hating that her voice shook when she spoke. She didn't want to give Kingston any more satisfaction from this, and hearing the fear in her voice probably added to his sick enjoyment.

But why was he doing this?

Caroline hoped she could learn that before she got out of this dangerous situation. And she would get out. There were so many lives at risk—Jack, Clarie, Caroline herself and the deputies outside. No way was she just going to let this piece of slime kill them. First, though, she'd need to get away from that knife he was holding. It was sharp—she knew that because he'd already cut her arm to prove that—and now he had it against her jugular.

"Clarie's fine," Jack said before he shifted his attention to Kingston. Jack's eyes narrowed, and his expression was hard as steel. "Let me guess. You're doing some favors for your old friend Eric."

"I am," Kingston readily admitted, and yes, he was enjoying this. He wanted them to know what he was doing and why. "Last year, Eric called me right from this inn while he was holding Caroline, and he asked me to tie up any and all loose ends for him. Ta-da! That's what I'm doing."

She didn't recall that conversation because she'd been drugged, but hearing what Kingston had just said caused the anger to roar through her. Caroline had to force herself not to ram Kingston in the gut with her elbow. They needed more info from him. Because Jack and she had their own loose ends to tie up. Yes, they would stop Kingston and arrest him, but when that happened, he might clam up. They had to know if others were involved in this.

"Kingston hired Scotty to hack into WITSEC and find my location," Caroline said. She didn't have proof of that, but considering the circumstances, that was a good guess. "It wasn't very smart of you to show up at my house, though."

"Of course, it was," Kingston immediately argued. "Me being there, it made me look innocent."

It had. Well, in a way. But Kingston had always been one of their top suspects.

"And after you were done with Scotty, you hired thugs to kill him," Jack said.

Jack moved a little to his left, and Caroline felt the pressure of the blade against her throat. "That's a no-no. Stay put, Marshal, or I cut her before I'm ready."

It turned her stomach to hear him say he was going to kill her no matter what. That made it even more important to draw this out. Because Jack wasn't the only lawman out there. Gunnar and Manuel were here, too. Maybe one of them could get into position to take Kingston out.

"Scotty was a loose end," Kingston went on a moment later. "So is Caroline, but she's been a little slippery when it comes to finishing up things. I thought it would be a nice touch to kill her here. Eric would appreciate that."

"Eric was a manipulative sociopath," Caroline spat out. "The only things he enjoyed were using people and killing. He used you, Kingston."

"Maybe because I wanted to be used."

That was almost certainly the truth. He was as twisted as Eric.

"The person who talked to Eric on the phone that night used cop jargon," she threw out there a moment later.

"Yes, a nice touch. That was Eric's idea. He wanted to play with your head, maybe make you think he was talking to Jack."

That gave her another jolt of anger, and she could see that it'd done the same to Jack. It was too late to punish Eric for that, but they sure as heck could make Kingston pay for his part in it.

She had to pause and gather her breath. "Who else did Eric and you use? Zeller or Lily? How about Grace?"

"None of the above." Again, no hesitation, but Caroline wasn't sure it was true.

Apparently, Jack wasn't convinced of it, either. "You're sure one of them didn't help you?"

"Nope. Me and me alone. Well, other than those two incompetent idiots I hired. Amos Treadwell was supposed to shoot you. He failed. Jessa Monroe was the woman who threw the first tear-gas canister. She panicked and tried to run so I killed her."

Caroline didn't like having another dead body added to this, but she was glad Jessa wasn't around to give her boss any help.

"And that's why I'm doing this myself. Oh, but I did get Scotty to set up Zeller," Kingston added. "You know, by planting that tracking device on his computer. All smoke, I assure you, since Scotty had already hacked in and gotten the address."

Caroline figured Scotty had done all of that for money. Lots of it, which Kingston could have gotten his hands on. Scotty probably hadn't figured the hacking would get him killed.

"And Lily?" Jack pressed. Like her, he must have decided to get all they could from Kingston.

"Nothing to do with me, but I had Scotty do some hacking in her files, too, and she was a naughty girl. Very involved in the sex trafficking. Tell you what. You can have those files for free. Just get them from my computer in my home office. I've got her bank records and some personal emails. There should be enough there for you to convict her of multiple crimes."

"Enough to convict her of murder?" Jack snapped.

"No. Not that." He stopped. "Oh, I see. You think Lily might have murdered that woman, Nicola, and your dad. Nope. Lily scared some woman into disappearing, but she didn't kill anyone."

"Skylar's alive?" Caroline managed to say.

"Alive and in hiding. If Lily had gotten to her, I would have heard about it. And it was Eric who did Nicola. Don't know the full story on that, but their paths crossed."

So, Skylar hadn't been murdered after all, and once Lily was behind bars, Skylar would likely surface. It didn't surprise Caroline that Eric had killed Nicola, but there was a huge piece of this that didn't fit.

"Eric didn't kill Jack's father," she said. "I was with Eric when Buck Slater was gunned down."

Caroline couldn't see Kingston's expression, but she could see Jack. His eyes went dark, and she could feel the dangerous edge whipping off him. And she knew why. Kingston was almost certainly smiling.

Because he'd been the one to kill Jack's father.

"Eric needed a distraction," Kingston said. "He wanted gunfire to draw the attention off him so he could get away."

Her knees nearly buckled. The weight was so heavy on her chest that it felt as if someone was crushing her heart in a tight fist. And despite all of that, Caroline knew what she was feeling was a drop in the bucket compared to Jack. He'd just listened to the man responsible for his father's murder dismiss it as a mere distraction.

Caroline tried to give Jack a steadying look. A silent "calm down" because she didn't want the rage overtaking him so that he charged at Kingston. They just needed more time. Time that maybe she could buy them.

"You can't think you'll get away with this," she said to Kingston.

"Depends on what you mean by getting away with it." She felt his shoulder move in what she thought might be a shrug. The arrogant SOB. "With my lawyers, I doubt very seriously that I'll be declared competent or sane enough to stand trial. And my psychiatric records will prove it."

Records that Kingston had likely doctored. Or else Scotty had done that for him. But Jack and she could try to use his confession to prove otherwise. And even if they couldn't, he would still spend the rest of his life locked up in a mental institution. Not exactly justice, but it would have to do.

Caroline finally saw what she'd been looking for. Gunnar. He crept in behind one of the shrubs near Jack. Kingston must have seen him, too, but he didn't react. Probably because Gunnar didn't have any better angle of a shot than Jack did.

"Once Caroline's dead, there'll be no more loose ends," Kingston announced, and the muscles in his arm and hand tightened. He was going to do it.

Kingston was going to kill her.

Caroline was going to make sure that didn't happen. Gathering her breath, she directed her anger and fear to her voice and let out a vicious shout as she rammed her elbow into Kingston. She dropped her weight, getting her neck away from that knife. She felt it cut her again, on the side of her head, but she ignored that and scrambled away from Kingston.

Jack moved in. As fast and as mean as a snake.

Caroline had managed to get only a few feet away before Jack was on the porch. He kicked away the knife.

And tossed his gun aside.

When Kingston lunged at him, Jack went after the man with his fists, and Jack was a lot better at it than Kingston. He rammed his fist into Kingston's face, causing the man's head to flop back. Jack hit him again. And again. His fists pounding Kingston even as the man dropped to his knees on the porch. Jack might have kept it up, but Caroline touched his shoulder.

"Let Gunnar arrest him," she said, trying to keep her voice as calm as possible.

Caroline wasn't sure that would be enough to get Jack to stop.

But it was.

Jack froze, his fist still poised midair and aimed at Kingston's face. Kingston was crying now, his breath coming out in wet, loud sobs. Jack stared at the man several long moments before he stepped back. Caroline was right there to pull Jack into her arms.

Gunnar rushed forward. The deputy hurried onto the porch and cuffed Kingston, hauling the man to his feet. "Jack, I'll take care of this," Gunnar said, sympathy all over his face. "And I'll get the ambulance out here for Caroline and Clarie."

"I'm fine," Caroline assured him, and she thought that might be true. Kingston had cut her, but it wasn't serious. Even if it had been, she probably wouldn't have admitted it. Not now. For now, she needed to hold Jack and get him through this.

"Kingston killed him," Jack muttered. "He killed him. And he tried to do the same to you."

"He failed," she reminded him, and she eased back so he could see her face. Her eyes. She wanted him to know that she was okay.

Jack shook his head like a man coming out of a trance,

and his attention landed on her arm, then the side of her head. Where he no doubt saw blood.

"You need the EMTs," he insisted.

He snatched up his gun, holstering it, before he jumped down off the porch, pulling her down and into his arms. But he didn't stand her on the ground. Jack started carrying her toward the front of the inn.

"I can walk," she said.

However, she didn't fight him on this. It was something Jack needed, and she soon realized she needed it, too. She dropped her head onto his shoulder and let him soothe her in a way that only Jack could. Yes, there were still plenty of things unresolved, but she took these moments of comfort from him.

When they reached the front of the inn, she was thankful to see Clarie up and moving around. Manuel had brought in the other cruiser, and that was where Gunnar headed with Kingston. Clarie was rubbing her head and pacing in front of the other cruiser while she talked to someone on the phone.

"Don't worry, I'll let the EMTs check me out," Clarie immediately told Jack. "I just wanted to fill in Kellan. He'll meet us at the sheriff's office."

Caroline was exhausted, but she knew the night wasn't over, and she wanted to be there when Kellan booked Kingston. Actually, she wanted to be there for Jack and his brothers.

In the distance, Caroline heard the wail of sirens from the ambulance. But she also heard something else.

A shout.

"You bastard," someone yelled.

Jack immediately stood Caroline on the ground so he

could pivot and draw his gun. But he was too late. The shot blasted through the air.

It took a moment for Caroline to fight through the shock and see what had happened. And then she spotted Grace. The woman was on the side of the front porch, a gun gripped in her hand.

A gun she'd just used to fire the shot.

At Kingston.

Grace hadn't missed, either. The shot had gone straight into Kingston's chest.

"You bastard," Grace repeated, the tears streaming down her face. She dropped her gun, and it clattered onto the porch. "That was for Scotty," she said before she lifted her hands in surrender.

Chapter Seventeen

Jack wasn't sure if it was a good sign that he did not feel anything but relief that Kingston was dead. As a lawman, he knew it would be a more fitting punishment for a killer to live out his life in a cage. But because there'd been the possibility of a mental facility rather than a prison, Jack was having a hard time seeing the man's death as a bad thing.

What was bad was that Grace would have to pay for what she had done. She might be spending the rest of her life in prison, and while that did bother him, Jack knew there'd been nothing he could have done to stop it. He hadn't seen Grace in time because he'd been so focused on getting help for Caroline and Clarie. Still, he wished he could have done something.

"Mentally beating yourself up?" Caroline asked.

Jack stopped his pacing so he could look at her. She was still on the treatment table in the ER while a nurse finished up the three stitches she'd needed for her head. Four more stitches had already been put on her arm. Jack knew the nurse, Mary Ann Colley, and knew she was good at her job. She'd even stitched him up a few times.

Caroline's injuries were minor, he reminded himself, but Jack knew there was nothing minor when it came to

Caroline. For the rest of his life, he'd see Kingston cutting her, and that was yet another reason he wasn't sorry the man was dead.

He nodded in response to her question, causing her to frown. Probably because she didn't believe beating himself up was necessary. But it was. He should have done a better job protecting her.

They'd gotten lucky. Not just with Caroline's injuries but with Clarie's, too. The deputy had also needed stitches and had a concussion, but she was going to make a full recovery and would only end up missing a couple days of work.

It could've been a lot worse. And not just with the injuries. Grace could have hit someone else when she'd been aiming at Kingston. Gunnar had been right there, but thankfully Grace's shot had hit only her intended target.

"Are you okay?" Caroline asked. She reached out, caught his hand and gave it a squeeze.

He knew what she was asking. This wasn't about the injuries now, or the aftermath of dealing with the attack. She wanted to know if Kingston's confession was eating a hole in him. In some ways, it was. The grief was right there at the surface. As fresh as it had been a year ago. But there was another side to this particular coin.

"I needed to know the truth," he settled for saying. "It's the start to dealing with this."

Caroline nodded, and he hated when he saw the tears she was blinking back. She quickly swiped one of them away. "Eric claimed a lot of lives," she whispered. "Kingston's included."

Jack huffed. "Now who's doing some mental beating up?" He got right in her face despite the fact that the nurse was there next to him. "I won't let you blame yourself for anything Eric did. And as for Kingston, he had a choice. He didn't have to do anything for Eric. Kingston did it because he wanted to do it. Hell, he took pleasure in it."

No way could she argue with that. Caroline had been there, with Kingston's knife to her throat, when the man had gloated and bragged. He likely would have turned into a killer even without Eric.

"All done," the nurse finally said. She stepped back from Caroline and took her hand to help her off the table. The woman handed Jack a piece of paper. "That's a script for some pain meds in case she needs it. The pharmacy's closed for the night, but if you give them a call, they'll open for you." She patted his arm. "Take good care of her, Jack. Give her lots of TLC."

Mary Ann added a wink, which meant she probably knew that Caroline and he had started up their relationship again. Heck, everybody in town probably knew. Jack frowned at that, not because of folks knowing, but because he wasn't sure exactly what his relationship was with Caroline.

He loved her, yes, and heck, they'd had sex twice since she'd gotten her memory back, but there hadn't been time to talk of the future and such. No time to do anything except try to hunt down a killer. With that done, Jack figured it was time for Caroline and him to have a long talk.

A talk that would apparently have to wait.

Jack realized that when he led Caroline out of the treatment room and spotted his brothers. All three of them. And they weren't alone. They had their fiancées, significant others and kids with them, too. On the surface, it looked to be an impromptu family reunion, but they were all there to try to deal with the grief of losing a father.

His brother Owen stood from one of the seats where he'd been sitting with his fiancée, Laney. She was holding Owen's toddler daughter, Addie, who was sacked out and totally unaware of the storm they'd all just weathered.

Eli stood with his girlfriend, Ashlyn. He was holding Ashlyn's adopted daughter, Cora. Cora was only a few months old and seemed entertained by all the people milling around.

Kellan was there with Gemma, and it was Gemma who came forward first and pulled Caroline into a gentle hug. She, too, was blinking back tears, and Jack figured Gemma was remembering her own nightmarish past with Eric, when he'd tried to kill her.

"I'm all right," Caroline assured her. Jack didn't know how she managed it, but Caroline even added a smile. One that looked surprisingly genuine.

"Caroline stood up to Kingston," Jack told Gemma. It wasn't pride in his voice. Okay, maybe it was a little of that, but it was mostly relief. It would likely make Caroline feel stronger now that she had done that. She hadn't been a victim tonight.

"I heard." Gemma glanced down at his raw knuckles. "And I heard you got in some punches. Good," she added before Jack could say anything. "I wish we could have all punched him a time or two."

So did Jack, because it had indeed helped to take out some of his grief and pain on his father's killer.

When Gemma stepped to the side, the others swarmed in. There were more hugs, more whispered words of comfort. His brothers and he all shared that silent conversation. A pact and a promise that they would get past this and get on with their lives.

Exactly what their father would have wanted them to do.

"Gunnar took Clarie home about ten minutes ago," Kellan explained. "She's fine, but I wanted her to get some rest."

That sounded like a darn good idea to Jack. He wanted the same for Caroline. "I'll need a vehicle." That was because Caroline and he had come to the hospital in an ambulance.

Kellan nodded. "Figured as much. You'll be taking Caroline to your house?" But Kellan waved that off. "Of course, you will be," his brother added at the same moment Caroline said, "Yes."

Jack looked at her to see if she had any doubts about that. Apparently, she didn't, since she brushed a kiss on his mouth. "Yes," she repeated.

Fighting a smile, Kellan took a key from his pocket. "Take my truck. Gemma and I can get home in one of the cruisers."

Jack thanked him and took the key. On the way to his place, he'd call the pharmacy and get those meds for Caroline. She didn't seem to be hurting, but that might not last. He fully intended to give her the meds and that TLC.

"The San Antonio cops have picked up Lily," Kellan continued a moment later. "The CSIs are going through Kingston's office. They've already found some things. Doctored files and such. She'll be charged with multiple felonies."

Jack knew he should probably care a whole lot more about that, and later he would. He wanted the woman punished for anything wrong she'd done. But for now, he had enough issues to deal with. And speaking of dealing, one of his current issues came through the door and into the hospital waiting room.

Zeller.

Hell. Jack hoped this didn't turn into a big blowup. Caroline didn't need that, and he wanted to get her out of there so she could rest. Apparently, his family had the same idea, because they, too, started to file out. All except Kellan. His brother stayed back, maybe because he thought there'd be some trouble between Zeller and him. If it was left up to Jack, there wouldn't be.

Jack went to Zeller and met him eye to eye. "I'm sorry," Jack told him.

Zeller opened his mouth. Clearly, the man had geared up for some kind of argument, but then he groaned softly and shook his head. "Everything was pointing to me. I looked guilty."

"Yeah, because Kingston paid Scotty to set you up." Jack didn't point out that if Kingston hadn't confessed, there might still be a dirty smear on Zeller's reputation. Or at least the questions and gossip.

"How's Grace?" Zeller asked.

Before Jack could answer, Caroline came to his side and slid her arm around his waist. Showing her support, no doubt. Jack appreciated it. Heck, he needed it, but he didn't like that Caroline was going to have to listen to what would likely turn into a chat about the wrap-up of this investigation.

"Grace is in custody," Jack told him. "I'm recommending a psych eval. Her mental state definitely played into what she did tonight."

Ironic, since Kingston had been planning on using that card for his own defense. In Grace's case, though, it might be true. Still, even if she went to prison for the rest of her life, it had been her choice to pull the trigger. That was something Jack needed to remember.

Zeller nodded. "Good, but don't hold it against me if I say I'm glad that Kingston is dead. He tried to set me up. And he nearly succeeded."

Yeah, he had, and Jack figured there were a lot of people who wouldn't be mourning Kingston's death.

When Zeller stepped away to talk to Kellan, Jack knew that was his cue to get Caroline out of there. Unfortunately, the rain hadn't stopped. It was no longer coming down in buckets, but it was still drizzling.

"Wait here," he told her. "I'll bring Kellan's truck up to the door."

She glanced out the glass doors before turning to him and catching on to his hand. "We can walk. The fresh air and rain will feel good."

No, it probably wouldn't. It would just get them wet—again. But Jack really didn't care. The only thing that mattered right now was that Caroline was safe. And that she wanted him.

He had no trouble figuring that out when she leaned in and kissed him. Long and hard. Just the way he liked his kisses from Caroline. Of course, it stirred the heat. Always did, and when she finally eased back, they were both smiling.

And clearly eager to get home.

Jack grabbed a newspaper from a rack by the door, and he used that to cover their heads as they walked out. Not a mad dash but a slow stroll with Caroline's uninjured arm around his waist. They stopped long enough for another kiss. Then, another. By the time Jack finally got them in Kellan's truck, it felt as if they'd just gone through a round of foreplay. Foreplay that continued when Caroline dragged him back to her.

After he got his eyes uncrossed from the intense heat of it, he winked at her. "Are you just trying to get in my pants?"

"I've been in your pants. It's a nice place to be. In fact, I can say that your pants are the only ones I'll ever want to get into again."

Jack had been about to start the truck, but that stopped him so he could look at her. And kiss her again. "That means you'll have to marry me," he said.

She shook her head. "We don't have to be married for that."

He looked at her, making sure she saw that her answer would mean everything to him. *Everything.*

"Marry me," he insisted. "And don't make me repeat that whole outburst about me loving you more than I've ever loved anything or anybody."

"What if I want it repeated? What if I say it to you this time?" Caroline added before he could speak.

The corner of his mouth lifted, and he could have sworn his heart doubled in size. "I think I'd really like to hear that," he said.

She didn't take her eyes off him. "Believe me when I tell you that I love you. More than anybody else. More than anything. More than I ever thought it possible to love someone. Believe me when I tell you I'll marry you and that I'll spend the rest of my life showing you just how much I love you."

Smiling, Jack kissed her, his words whispering over her lips. "I believe you."

* * * * *